Advance Praise for *Shadow Show*: All-New Stories in Celebration of Ray Bradbury

"There is no more fitting tribute to my friend Ray Bradbury than a compilation of wonderful short stories! Ray is a champion of libraries and one of America's most inventive teller of tales. I cherish many happy times engrossed in his stories. This anthology reflects the high imagination, visionary ideas, and fantastic writing that Ray is loved and known for around the world."

—Former public school teacher, librarian, and First Lady Laura Bush

"Great new tales of imagination in the Bradbury tradition."

—Hugh Hefner, publisher and founder of Playboy Enterprises

"Ray Bradbury is without a doubt one of this or any century's greatest and most imaginative writers. *Shadow Show,* a book of truly great stories, is the perfect tribute to America's master storyteller."

—Stan Lee, legendary comic book writer and former president and chairman of Marvel Comics

"*Shadow Show* is a treasure trove for Ray Bradbury enthusiasts as for all readers who are drawn to richly imaginative, deftly plotted, startlingly original and unsettling short fiction. No one who knows their darkly fantastic fiction would be surprised to see such renowned names here as Ramsey Campbell, Harlan Ellison, Margaret Atwood, Neil Gaiman, Audrey Niffenegger, and Kelly Link; but it is something of a surprise to see Dave Eggers, Jacquelyn Mitchard, Dan Chaon, Bonnie Jo Campbell, and Julia Keller in this gathering, all of them Ray Bradbury admirers, and all so gifted. The tributes to Ray Bradbury that follow each of the stories are p
heartwarming and inspiring."

—*New York Times* bestse

SHADOW SHOW

Also by Sam Weller

The Bradbury Chronicles: The Life of Ray Bradbury
Listen to the Echoes: The Ray Bradbury Interviews

Also by Mort Castle

The Strangers
Cursed Be the Child
On Writing Horror (editor)
Nations of the Living, Nations of the Dead
New Moon on the Water
Writing Historical Fiction (nonfiction)
The Deadly Election
The Times We Had

SHADOW SHOW

All-new stories in celebration of

RAY BRADBURY

EDITED BY SAM WELLER AND MORT CASTLE

wm

WILLIAM MORROW

An Imprint of HarperCollins*Publishers*

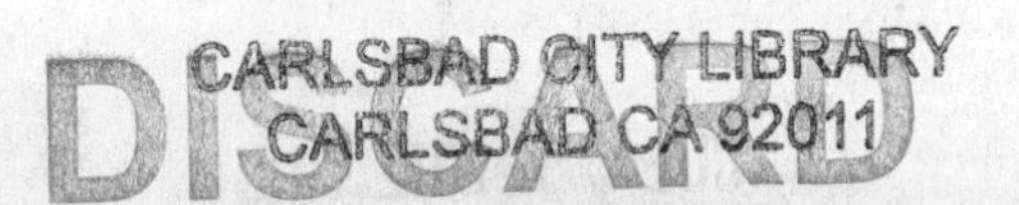

CO SHADOW

Pages 443–445 constitute an extension of this copyright page.

This book is a work of fiction. The characters, incidents, and dialogue are drawn from the author's imagination and are not to be construed as real. Any resemblance to actual events or persons, living or dead, is entirely coincidental.

HarperCollins books may be purchased for educational, business, or sales promotional use. For information please write: Special Markets Department, HarperCollins Publishers, 10 East 53rd Street, New York, NY 10022.

FIRST EDITION

Designed by Diahann Sturge

Library of Congress Cataloging-in-Publication Data has been applied for.

ISBN 978-0-06-2122681

12 13 14 15 16 OV/RRD 10 9 8 7 6 5 4 3 2 1

For Ray,
Grand Marshal of this midnight parade,
with love

CONTENTS

ACKNOWLEDGMENTS xi

INTRODUCTION
SAM WELLER AND MORT CASTLE 1

A SECOND HOMECOMING
RAY BRADBURY 8

THE MAN WHO FORGOT RAY BRADBURY
NEIL GAIMAN 11

HEADLIFE
MARGARET ATWOOD 19

HEAVY
JAY BONANSINGA 27

THE GIRL IN THE FUNERAL PARLOR
SAM WELLER 40

THE COMPANIONS
DAVID MORRELL 54

THE EXCHANGE
THOMAS F. MONTELEONE 75

CAT ON A BAD COUCH
LEE MARTIN 86

BY THE SILVER WATER OF LAKE CHAMPLAIN
JOE HILL 114

LITTLE AMERICA
DAN CHAON 143

THE PHONE CALL
JOHN McNALLY 165

YOUNG PILGRIMS
JOE MENO 186

CHILDREN OF THE BEDTIME MACHINE
ROBERT McCAMMON 210

THE PAGE
RAMSEY CAMPBELL 226

LIGHT
MORT CASTLE 242

CONJURE
ALICE HOFFMAN 262

MAX
JOHN MACLAY 276

TWO OF A KIND
JACQUELYN MITCHARD 283

FAT MAN AND LITTLE BOY
GARY A. BRAUNBECK 318

THE TATTOO
BONNIE JO CAMPBELL 326

BACKWARD IN SEVILLE
AUDREY NIFFENEGGER 353

EARTH (A GIFT SHOP)
CHARLES YU 359

HAYLEIGH'S DAD
JULIA KELLER 366

WHO KNOCKS?
DAVE EGGERS 384

RESERVATION 2020
BAYO OJIKUTU 388

TWO HOUSES
KELLY LINK 404

WEARINESS
HARLAN ELLISON® 426

CONTRIBUTORS 435

CREDITS 443

ACKNOWLEDGMENTS

Our deepest gratitude goes to Ray Bradbury for his support and enthusiasm for this book. Thanks also to Ray's daughter, Alexandra, for her assistance along the way. We are, of course, indebted to our all-star cast of writers, who interpreted Bradbury's inspiration in myriad, imaginative ways.

Thanks to our dream team of editors at HarperCollins, most notably, our great partner Jennifer Brehl, along with her assistant, Emily Krump. Gratitude, also, to production editor Andrea Molitor and copyeditor Margaret Wimberger. We were so fortunate to have these folks to work with. A tip of the hat to Tom Gauld for his classic cover art (have you been to Ray Bradbury's basement?!).

To our literary agent, Judith Ehrlich, with us every step of the way.

To the inspiring memory of Danny Squires and the inspiring friendship of Robert Weinberg.

Thanks, also, to our families, Jane, Jan, Mai-Linh, Le-Anh, and Gia-Binh. Live Forever!

SHADOW SHOW

INTRODUCTION

Sam Weller and Mort Castle

He published in *Weird Tales* and *The New Yorker.* Just how many writers can claim such a dichotomous literary distinction? This seemingly incongruous slice of publication history only begins to illuminate the breadth, range, and wonder of the Ray Bradbury canon.

With a creative output encompassing groundbreaking works of science fiction, universally recognized tales of fantasy, and award-winning realist contemporary prose, Ray Bradbury has spent his entire career ignoring and blurring the boundaries between genre and literature. To be sure, he is part of a select cadre of authors who have performed a sort of literary legerdemain. They are, at once, creators of the innovative and the mind-bending, writers who, along the way, gate-crashed the hallowed halls of literature. Nathaniel Hawthorne, Charles Dickens, Edgar Allan Poe, Shirley Jackson, Jorge Luis Borges—and very few others.

This accomplished group of authors (and other powerhouses such as Faulkner, Fitzgerald, Steinbeck, and Tennessee Williams, who also examined the boundaries between literature and genre with great success but with less frequency) often wrote what might be deemed "genre fiction" to artfully examine the human condition in a new and original light.

But Ray Bradbury did not just walk in the deep and indelible footprints of his predecessors or march shoulder to shoulder with his contemporaries. Over the course of his acclaimed career, Bradbury has charted and forged his own path, altering and expanding the canon ad infinitum. And of all the mediums he has explored—novels, screenplays, teleplays, stage plays, poetry, essays, and even architectural concepts, it is, arguably, the short story that is Bradbury's finest avocation. So much of the unforgettable in the Bradbury oeuvre is found in this form.

Who can forget stepping on the butterfly in "A Sound of Thunder"? Or the mechanized, postapocalyptic house with no human inhabitants in "There Will Come Soft Rains"? The heartbroken little Margot locked in the closet on Venus when the sun comes out for a single hour—every seven years?

And then there is Uncle Einar with his "beautiful silk-like wings" that "hung like sea-green sails behind him."

Tally's ghostly footprints in "The Lake."

The space-faring colonists who land on Mars and find idyllic small-town America—populated by their deceased loved ones in "Mars Is Heaven!"

There are the glorious new sneakers, with "marshmallows and coiled springs in the soles," in "The Sound of Summer Running."

The Irish cabbie who has given up the drink for Lent and cannot drive safely as a result.

And the mummies in the catacombs of Guanajuato, Mexico.

And the warm Sun Domes of Venus.

And the African veldt and the children coaxing their parents to come hither . . .

These stories, and so many more, are what we gather to celebrate and honor in this anthology of all-new, never-before-published tales by a diverse cast of acclaimed writers. The range of contributors in this collection is a testament to Bradbury's looming shadow and lasting artistic impact. As Nathaniel Rich declared in *Slate* magazine, "To the extent that there is a mythology of our age, Bradbury is one of its creators."

Ray Bradbury has always considered himself a "teller of tales," hailing from that time-honored tradition of oral storytelling in the market square or by the campfire.

"It is an ancient tradition," he said in a 1964 interview, "a good one, a lovely one, a fine one. If some boy visits my tomb one hundred years from now and writes on the marble with a crayon: 'He was a Teller of Tales,' I will be happy.'"

A similarly venerable form of storytelling is that of "shadow theater," an art from which this anthology derives its name. Utilizing paper cutouts held between a light source and a translucent screen, shadow puppetry dates back more than two thousand years, most experts believe, to ancient China. And like the fantastic modern myths of Bradbury himself, shadow theater also portrayed fantastic stories of fable and folklore. Its moving figures became shadowy metaphors for ancient myths and modern truths, a common motif in the voluminous literary canon of Bradbury.

Shadow shows were popular in India, Indonesia, Turkey, and beyond. By the 1880s in France, shadow puppetry had evolved, become more intricate, stylized. The form played a major role in the rise of the phantasmagoria theatrical movement in France and England during the Victorian era.

Today, in Ray Bradbury's West Los Angeles home, a framed advertisement for the French cabaret Le Chat Noir hangs prominently on a wall. This nineteenth-century Parisian nightclub was well known for its innovative use of shadow theater. Patrons sat at tables, sipped on dark liquors, and marveled at the spectacle of light, shadow, and story.

In his 1962 autumn Gothic opus *Something Wicked This Way Comes*, Ray Bradbury himself christens his dark carnival "Cooger and Dark's Pandemonium Shadow Show."

In his own literary shadow shows, he penned imaginative tales set anywhere and everywhere: colonial Mexican towns, Los Angeles tenement buildings, the foothills of Mars, the sun-warmed sidewalks of bygone America, the endless emerald woods of Ireland, behind the flapping doors of dusty carnival tents, the attics and cellars of our childhood dreams. And for all his enduring and fearless artistic genius, he has earned the 2000 National Book Foundation Medal for Distinguished Contribution to American Letters; the 2004 National Medal of Arts (conferred by the president of the United States); the 2007 Pulitzer Prize Special Citation, and so many more honors. Writing in the age(s) of mass media, Bradbury has seen his stories leave a lasting impact, not just through books but also in dramatic radio, television, film, and comic books.

Along with all the awards, accolades, and achievements, Ray Bradbury has attained a sort of influential stature that comes as both delight and surprise to him: teacher and preacher, father figure, and artist exemplar to ever so many in all manner of creative endeavor. He and his work continue to reach out and provide the spark to artistic imagination for generations young and old, creators who themselves have often blurred the lines between genre and literature, the fantastically *imagined* and the closely observed *real*. The puppeteer has countless apprentices.

In *Shadow Show*, this celebration of Ray Bradbury, artists who have been profoundly influenced by him pen their own short stories in homage, stories that through image, theme, or concept are either ever so obviously or ever so subtly "Bradbury-informed." From the lyrical magic of *Dandelion Wine*, to the shifting sands of Mars, to the roiling mist of *The October Country*, Bradbury's literary achievements in all their scope are honored by a host of today's top writers. *Shadow Show* presents our most exciting authors, who, like the honoree, are not contained or constrained by category or locale, as they touch the Bradbury base for inspiration to explore their own singular, wildest imaginings.

The stories in this volume are neither sequels nor pastiches but rather distinctive fictive visions by writers inspired by a single common touchstone: the enduring works of Ray Bradbury.

Over the years, in many of the captivating introductions to his own books, Bradbury has examined the origins of his stories. In these personal, illuminating reflections, he has allowed readers to come behind his translucent screen, as it were, to witness the intricate and artful machinations of the shadow show itself.

In keeping with this tradition, all twenty-six contributors to *Shadow Show* have penned afterwords to their stories, spotlighting the Bradburian influence either on them or on their story or both. Contributors took from Bradbury what was most important and salient to them and used it to perform their own theater.

In the book's fitting opening story, "The Man Who Forgot Ray Bradbury," Neil Gaiman explores the concept of a man whose failing memory is causing him to lose hold of the very short stories and books that changed his life.

In "Conjure," Alice Hoffman offers a delicate yet tough tale of summertime enchantment and friendship—and what is left behind at the change of seasons.

Thriller master David Morrell writes of guardian angels in a whole new light.

Bradbury's old friend, legendary science-fiction and fantasy writer Harlan Ellison, pens what he describes as "very likely his last published story"; "Weariness" is a soul-stirring tale of galactic proportions as the entire universe goes dark, a science-fictional metaphor for the author's own fading mortality.

Authors Margaret Atwood and Charles Yu utilize science

fiction as social satire (as did Bradbury in his classic novel *Fahrenheit 451* and in stories such as "The Veldt") in decidedly different ways.

Some of the tales contained within can be directly traced to a single Bradbury yarn. Joe Hill's haunting and melancholy "By the Silver Waters of Lake Champlain" is a sibling to Bradbury's classic story "The Fog Horn." Pulitzer Prize winner Julia Keller writes a story not far removed thematically and structurally from "The Whole Town's Sleeping." National Book Award finalist Bonnie Jo Campbell brings us a modern, twisted descendant of the "forest witch," who first marred the body of "the Illustrated Man." John McNally pens a story hailing directly from *The October Country*. Pulitzer Prize finalist Lee Martin writes a melancholic near epiphany on a shared wavelength with Bradbury's classic "I See You Never." Dave Eggers's "Who Knocks?" (a title that, incidentally, gets its name from Bradbury's first book appearance in 1946) is a story of pure delight, fright, and surprise.

There are tales set amidst the stars and stories set on the hushed streets of small-town Midwest America. These are stories of the past, the present, and the future.

Shadow Show gathers Oprah's Book Club authors, *New York Times* bestselling authors, National Book Award finalists, a Newbery Medal winner, multiple World Fantasy and Bram Stoker Award winners and nominees, a convocation of word workers who voyage into that dark and chimerical and wondrous territory so altered and mutated by the man who has been deemed "the Master of Miracles."

In the introduction to *Timeless Stories for Today and Tomorrow*, a 1952 anthology of fantastic fiction and magical realism that he edited, Ray Bradbury writes: "Beginning writers often err in thinking that if one magic trick is good, then sixteen magic tricks, running as a team, must be sixteen times better. Nothing could be further from the truth. Good fantasy must be allowed to move casually upon the reader, in the air he breathes. It must be woven into the story so as to be, at times, almost unrecognizable."

In keeping with Bradbury's philosophy of magic and story, we present to you *Shadow Show: All-New Stories in Celebration of Ray Bradbury*. At the very core of each of these tales, you will find that single trick, that unforgettable metaphor, a feat of narrative legerdemain.

And so we welcome you to *Shadow Show*. Pull up a seat. Get yourself a drink.

And now it is that the houselights dim.

The velvet curtain rises.

And the shadows begin to play . . .

—Sam Weller and Mort Castle
Chicago, Illinois

A SECOND HOMECOMING

Ray Bradbury

I suppose you are wondering why I have called you to a family reunion. Let me explain.

In 2006 the United States Post Office issued a stamp commemorating Edgar Allan Poe. I rushed out and purchased several books and placed the stamps on all of my outgoing mail. I sent these letters to friends and family around the world. When I looked at that portrait of Mr. Poe, I knew I was looking at my true papa. You see, when I was eight years old, growing up in Waukegan, Illinois, my Aunt Neva gave me a copy of Poe's *Tales of Mystery and Imagination*. I was never the same. I read "The Tell-Tale Heart," "The Cask of Amontillado," and "The Raven," of course. The language was bejeweled and ornate, like an encrusted Fabergé egg. The ideas were frightening and fantastic, and I was in love.

Over the years, there have been other papas: L. Frank Baum, H. G. Wells, Jules Verne. Then there were my mothers: Emily Dickinson, Willa Cather, and Eudora Welty. I had my midwives, too: Shakespeare and the Bible.

Now, many years later and very late in time, an incredible thing has occurred. Within the book you now hold in your hands, I find I am no longer the son; instead, I am the father.

The twenty-six authors gathered in this collection of remarkable and varied stories have all come home to Papa, and I couldn't be more proud. My family is a family of circus people, a strange and wonderful midnight carnival of performers, lion tamers, magicians, and beautiful freaks. They make this reunion remarkable.

In this book, you will discover tales set in dark basements and tales set in the dark velocities of deep space; there are stories in small towns and big cities. Here you will find guardian angels and inner-demons. There are characters who are haunted without a ghost in sight. There are quiet stories, happy stories, sad stories, frightening stories. This book reads like a transcription of my own nightmares and daydreams. These are stories of fantasy and science fiction and mystery—and, most of all, of imagination.

And I wonder how this all happened. How did the son of Mr. Edgar Allan Poe become father to so many?

When I look back on my career, I realize that I blundered my way into success. Never once did I know what I was doing. I just did it. But I blundered with great enthusiasm and, most of all, with love. I was in love with stories. And now I find my children expressing their love, and I am so grateful.

Perhaps you are familiar with my story "The Homecoming." That story was rejected by *Weird Tales* as being too off-trail, too untraditional. On a whim, I sent it off to *Mademoiselle*, a quality magazine that published literary fiction. To my great surprise, they purchased the story and ran it in the October 1946 issue. They changed the entire magazine that month to accommodate my story, turning the issue into a celebration of autumn. They hired *New Yorker* artist Charles Addams to do a wonderful illustration that depicted the characters from the story, a family of vampires and fantastic monsters all returning home to their northern Illinois Victorian mansion for a reunion.

In it, a family of beautiful creatures—loving, winged uncles, doting, telepathic aunts, and fantastic brethren from all over the world—gather to give thanks, of course, on Halloween.

In many ways this book is a second Homecoming for me. My family has all come home for this loving celebration, and I couldn't be happier. Papa embraces his children with open wings.

I welcome you to the reunion, too.

—Ray Bradbury
Los Angeles, California

THE MAN WHO FORGOT RAY BRADBURY

Neil Gaiman

I am forgetting things, which scares me.

I am losing words, although I am not losing concepts. I hope that I am not losing concepts. If I am losing concepts, I am not aware of it. If I am losing concepts, how would I know?

Which is funny, because my memory was always so good. Everything was in there. Sometimes my memory was so good that I even thought I could remember things I didn't know yet. Remembering forward . . .

I don't think there's a word for that, is there? Remembering things that haven't happened yet. I don't have that feeling I get when I go looking in my head for a word that isn't there, as if someone must have come and taken it in the night.

When I was a young man I lived in a big, shared house. I was a student then. We had our own shelves in the kitchen, neatly marked with our names, and our own shelves in the fridge, upon which we kept our own eggs, cheese, yoghurt, milk. I was always punctilious about using only my own provisions. Others were not so . . . there. I lost a word. One that would mean "careful to obey the rules." The other people in the house were . . . not so. I would go to the fridge, but my eggs would have vanished.

I am thinking of a sky filled with spaceships, so many of them that they seem like a plague of locusts, silver against the luminous mauve of the night.

Things would go missing from my room back then as well. Boots. I remember my boots going. Or "being gone," I should say, as I did not ever actually catch them in the act of leaving. Boots do not just "go." Somebody "went" them. Just like my big dictionary. Same house, same time period. I went to the small bookshelf beside my face (everything was by my bed—it was my room, but it was not much larger than a cupboard with a bed in it). I went to the shelf and the dictionary was gone, just a dictionary-sized hole in my shelf to show where my dictionary wasn't.

All the words and the book they came in were gone. Over the next month they also took my radio, a can of shaving foam, a pad of notepaper, and a box of pencils. And my yoghurt. And, I discovered during a power cut, my candles.

Now I am thinking of a boy with new tennis shoes, who believes he can run forever. No, that is not giving it to me. A dry town in which it rained forever. A road through the desert, on which good people see a mirage. A dinosaur that is a movie producer. The mirage was the pleasure dome of Kublai Khan.

No . . .

Sometimes when the words go away I can find them by creeping up on them from another direction. Say I go and look for a word—I am discussing the inhabitants of the planet Mars, say, and I realise that the word for them has gone. I might also realise that the missing word occurs in a sentence or a title. *The ________ Chronicles. My Favourite ________.* If that does not give it to me, I circle the idea. Little green men, I think, or tall, dark-skinned, gentle: Dark they were and Golden-eyed . . . and suddenly the word *Martians* is waiting for me, like a friend or a lover at the end of a long day.

I left that house when my radio went. It was too wearing, the slow disappearance of the things I had thought so safely mine, item by item, thing by thing, object by object, word by word.

When I was twelve I was told a story by an old man that I have never forgotten.

A poor man found himself in a forest as night fell, and he had no prayer book to say his evening prayers. So he said, "God who knows all things, I have no prayer book and I do not know any prayers by heart. But you know all the prayers. You are God. So this is what I am going to do. I am going to say the alphabet, and I will let you put the words together."

There are things missing from my mind, and it scares me.

Icarus! It's not as if I have forgotten all names. I remember Icarus. He flew too close to the sun. In the stories, though, it's worth it. Always worth it to have tried, even if you fail, even if you fall like a meteor forever. Better to have flamed in the darkness, to have inspired others, to have *lived,* than to have sat in the darkness, cursing the people who borrowed, but did not return, your candle.

I *have* lost people, though.

It's strange when it happens. I don't actually *lose* them. Not in the way one loses one's parents, either as a small child, when you think you are holding your mother's hand in a crowd and then you look up, and it's not your mother . . . or later. When you have to find the words to describe them at a funeral service or a memorial, or when you are scattering ashes on a garden of flowers or into the sea.

I sometimes imagine I would like my ashes to be scattered in a library. But then the librarians would just have to come in early the next morning to sweep them up again, before the people got there.

I would like my ashes scattered in a library or, possibly, a funfair. A 1930s funfair, where you ride the black . . . the black . . . the . . .

I have lost the word. Carousel? Roller coaster? The thing you ride, and you become young again. The Ferris wheel. Yes. There is another carnival that comes to town as well, bringing evil. "By the pricking of my thumbs . . ."

Shakespeare.

I remember Shakespeare, and I remember his name, and who he was and what he wrote. He's safe for now. Perhaps there are people who forget Shakespeare. They would have to talk about "the man who wrote 'to be or not to be'"—not the film, starring Jack Benny, whose real name was Benjamin Kubelsky, who was raised in Waukegan, Illinois, an hour or so outside Chicago. Waukegan, Illinois, was later immortalised as Green Town, Illinois, in a series of stories and books by an American author who left Waukegan and went to live in Los Angeles. I mean of course, the man I am thinking of. I can see him in my head when I close my eyes.

I used to look at his photographs on the back of his books. He looked mild and he looked wise, and he looked kind.

He wrote a story about Poe, to stop Poe being forgotten, about a future where they burn books and they forget them, and in the story we are on Mars although we might as well be in Waukegan or Los Angeles, as critics, as those who would repress or forget books, as those who would take the words, all the words, dictionaries and radios full of words, as those people are walked through a house and murdered, one by one: by orang-utan; by pit and pendulum; for the love of God, Montressor . . .

Poe. I know Poe. And Montressor. And Benjamin Kubelsky and his wife, Sadie Marks, who was no relation to the Marx Brothers and who performed as Mary Livingston. All these names in my head.

I was twelve.

I had read the books, I had seen the film, and the burning point of paper was the moment where I knew that I would have to remember this. Because people would have to remember books, if other people burn them or forget them. We will commit them to memory. We will become them. We become authors. We become their books.

I am sorry. I lost something there. Like a path I was walking that dead-ended, and now I am alone and lost in the forest, and I am here and I do not know where here is anymore.

You must learn a Shakespeare play; I will think of you as Titus Andronicus. Or *you,* my friend, you could learn an Agatha Christie novel; you will be *Murder on the Orient Express.* Someone else can learn the poems of John Wilmot, Earl of Rochester, and *you,* whoever you are, reading this, you can learn a Dickens book, and when I want to know what happened to Barnaby Rudge, I will come to you. You can tell me.

And the people who would burn the words, the people who would take the books from the shelves, the firemen and the ignorant, the ones afraid of tales and words and dreams and Hallowe'en and people who have tattooed themselves with stories and Boys! You Can Grow Mushrooms in Your Cellar! and as long as your words which are people which are days which are my life, as long as your words survive, then you lived and you mattered and you changed the world and I cannot remember your name.

I learned your books. Burned them into my mind. In case the firemen come to town.

But who you are is gone. I wait for it to return to me. Just as I waited for my dictionary or for my radio, or for my boots, and with as meagre a result.

All I have left is the space in my mind where you used to be.

And I am not so certain about even that.

I was talking to a friend. And I said, "Are these stories familiar to you?" I told him all the words I knew, the ones about the monsters coming home to the house with the human child in it, the ones about the lightning salesman and the wicked carnival that followed him, and the Martians and their fallen glass cities and their perfect canals. I told him all the words, and he said he hadn't heard of them. That they didn't exist.

And I worry.

I worry I was keeping them alive. Like the people in the snow at the end of the story, walking backwards and forwards, remembering, repeating the words of the stories, making them real.

I think it's God's fault.

I mean, he can't be expected to remember everything, God can't. Busy chap. So perhaps he delegates things, sometimes, just goes, "You! I want you to remember the dates of the Hundred Years' War. And you, you remember okapi. You, remember Jack Benny who was Benjamin Kubelsky from Waukegan, Illinois." And then, when you forget the things that God has charged you with remembering, *bam*. No more okapi. Just an okapi-shaped hole in the world, which is halfway between an antelope and a giraffe. No more Jack Benny. No more Waukegan. Just a hole in your mind where a person or a concept used to be.

I don't know.

I don't know where to look. Have I lost an author, just as once I lost a dictionary? Or worse: Did God give me this one small task, and now I have failed him, and because I have forgotten him he has gone from the shelves, gone from the reference works, and now he only exists in our dreams . . .

My dreams. I do not know your dreams. Perhaps you do not dream of a veldt that is only wallpaper but that eats two children. Perhaps you do not know that Mars Is Heaven, where our beloved dead go to wait for us, then consume us in the night.

You do not dream of a man arrested for the crime of being a pedestrian.

I dream these things.

If he existed, then I have lost him. Lost his name. Lost his book titles, one by one by one. Lost the stories.

And I fear that I am going mad, for I cannot just be growing old.

If I have failed in this one task, oh God, then only let me do this thing, that you may give the stories back to the world.

Because, perhaps, if this works, they will remember him. All of them will remember him. His name will once more become synonymous with small American towns at Hallowe'en, when the leaves skitter across the sidewalk like frightened birds, or with Mars, or with love. And my name will be forgotten.

I am willing to pay that price, if the empty space in the bookshelf of my mind can be filled again, before I go.

Dear God, hear my prayer.

A . . . B . . . C . . . D . . . E . . . F . . . G . . .

About "The Man Who Forgot Ray Bradbury"

I wanted to write about Ray Bradbury. I wanted to write about him in the way that he wrote about Poe in "Usher II"—a way that drove me to Poe.

I was going to read something in an intimate theatre space, very late at night, during the Edinburgh Fringe Festival. My wife, Amanda, and I were hosting a midnight show of songs and readings. I promised myself that I would finish it in time to read it to forty people seated on sofas and on cushions on the floor in a tiny, beautiful room that normally contained the Belt Up Theatre Company's intimate plays.

Very well, it would be a monologue, if I was going to read it.

The inspiration came from forgetting a friend of mine. He died a decade ago. And I went to look in my head for his name, and it was gone. I knew everything else about him—the periodicals he had written for, his favourite brand of bourbon. I could have recited every conversation he and I had ever had, told you what we talked about. I could remember the names of the books he had written.

But his name was gone. And it scared me. I waited for his name to return, promised myself I wouldn't Google it, would just wait and remember. But nothing came. It was as if there was a hole in the universe the size of my friend. I would walk home at night trying to think of his name, running through names in alphabetical order. "Al? No. Bob? No. Charles? Chris? Not them . . ."

And I thought, What if it were an author? What if it was everything he'd done? What if everyone else had forgotten him too?

I wrote the story by hand. I finished it five minutes before we had to leave the house to go to the theatre. I was a mass of nerves—I'd never read something to an audience straight out of the pen.

When I read it, I finished it with a recital of the whole alphabet.

Then I typed it out and sent it to Ray for his ninety-first birthday.

I was there at his seventieth birthday, in the Natural History Museum in London.

It was, like everything else about the man and his work, unforgettable.

—Neil Gaiman

HEADLIFE

Margaret Atwood

Everything on the list," says Quentin.

"Expensive," says Dr. Derwent. "You're sure?"

"Dave, I own this fucking place," says Quentin. He's taken to swearing more as the decades have worn on. An inhibition thing disappears out of the brain with age, he's read that somewhere. Angry old men capering around in their institutional PJs, dribbling pee and yelling at the nurses. *That won't be me.*

"So, everything?" says Dr. Derwent, smiling his unctuous, ass-kissing smile. He seems nervous. *Hope he's not on drugs, wouldn't want those pricey fingers to slip.*

"I told you," says Quentin irritably. "We went over it point by point. I said *everything.*"

"I suggest you read the contract," says Dr. Derwent, smiling like a half-dead newt.

"Suzie read it," says Quentin. "I pay her to read shit like that. Anyway I wrote the fucking contract in the first place, remember? And I already signed it."

He pays Suzie for other stuff too, she's added a whole new dimension to the Personal Assistant job description, but no need to go into that with Dr. Dave. He resists the impulse to add, *You stupid dipshit.* He's seen the lecherous bloodsucker planting his hand on Suzie's mercenary, gold-digging bee-shaped rump. And worse, he's seen how she responds: the wet lips, the boob-heaving exhale, the butt arched up like a cat's—a sequence of moves he knows intimately. She might as well be wearing a T-shirt: I'M IN HEAT. Though for him she was most likely faking it.

They think they're unseen, but I notice every fucking thing; I didn't get where I am without noticing. I'll settle scores with Suzie as well, once I make my comeback. With my new eight-incher and never a limp moment, no pills or injections needed ever again. She won't know whether to scream Stop! *or* More! *She'll be terminally fucked in all senses of the word, and then I'll toss her out. Snivelling and cringing, shuddering and begging and Oh pleasing. Naked onto the street. That would be a five-star vision. No more pitying looks, no more pretend orgasms from her, nor from her successors. Her many, many successors.* Praise the Lord, as his mother would have said, the hypocritical old baby-torturer. Though Quentin himself wasn't in the habit of praising anyone.

"True enough," says Dr. Derwent. "You did sign it." He's peering down at the contract through his half-moon specs. *Probably thinks they make him look distinguished, though a bun-faced nerd like him would never get even halfway there. You need bone structure for that. Character. Hewn granite*. Like Quentin, for instance.

"One more thing," says Quentin. "I already told you, but double-checking. If that scum-brained sleazebag Bryant wants to get the same procedure I'm getting, put him off. Turn him down. Make up something scientific. Unviable DNA or something. Last thing I want is to wake up and find he's got the same equipment I do. I want to watch him decay like the rotten old carbuncle he is." (*Carbuncle,* he thinks. File that for future use. *Bryant, you carbuncle!*)

He has a daydream that incorporates this feature: Sid Bryant, carbuncular owner of the only rival to Hither! Ltd., the global communications network Quentin built from scratch—Sid Bryant, whining and pleading *Let me in!* as his sad old buns droop and his spine question-marks and his cells shrivel up and his teeth turn to yellowing rubble. But no dice, because Quentin owns the Medea Clinic and every single one of its patents, starting from the days when they were growing hearts and kidneys with your own cells seeded onto matrices, right up to the layer-at-a-time full-body replacement they're doing now. And he's sitting on those patents; he's not licensing no matter what he's offered, which means that right here is the only place in the world where you can get this stuff done. The private rooms are crammed with movie stars, rock legends, aging politicians. They'll pay through the nose, their old noses and the new, rejuvenated ones that will grow on them soon, from the inside out. Plastic surgery isn't even a pale shadow of what's on offer at the Medea.

Over the decades Sid has beat Quentin out on more than a few sweet deals—that university he almost bought, big plans for it he'd had; couple of hospitals; mega social-network and software company; gambling paradise in Vegas; at least three offshore money-launderette establishments. Far too many deals not to generate suspicion. Quentin would have a universe-crushing eureka, he'd see the huge potential in some whiz kid's pathetic little start-up, but by the time he got there Sid would've scooped it. He wonders who in his own outfit are the traitors, tipping Sid off. Once he gets his new body and has his old energy back, he'll dig down, he'll uncover them all, he'll throw them to the crocodiles. Hack their e-mails, ruin their reputations, drag them through the dirt.

He likes picturing that, but even more he likes picturing Sid drooling in the retirement home, just sane enough to recognize

Quentin attached to the twenty-five-year-old weight lifter's body that will soon be melded with his head.

In some of his more extreme fantasies he watches his new muscles rippling in the mirror like boa constrictors, then leaps out the window and soars from rooftop to rooftop like those ultrafit Chinese guys in the movies. The Whatsit movies—the word's at the edge of his brain. Anyway, like that. Then he'll swing in through some girl's window just as she's slipping into her peekaboo ruffles. Maybe hair will sprout from him like a werewolf, and he'll lose all control and growl and rip and plunge and guzzle, and blood and flesh will . . .

Violent. Criminal. Gucky. Surely he could never go that far. He's not a total sicko. But what the fuck, no harm done, it's only in the head.

Just a couple of months, they'd told him. Nine on the outside. He's put his deputies in charge for that period—they're more than capable of running things, toeing the bottom line till he gets back.

So he'll go to sleep, drift around in dreamland, slipping on a new body in the process. And after a while, when that body begins to wear out, he'll get another one. And then another. Why isn't that immortality?

"So you're ready?" says Dr. Derwent, breaking into Quentin's reverie. "No second thoughts?"

"Never readier," says Quentin. *Pathetic loser. Derwent the Drudge. Doing procedures all day that he can't afford himself.*

"Good," says Dr. Derwent. He pats Quentin's bony shoulder. "We'll have that ol' head of yours off in a jiffy. You won't feel a thing. And then, when you wake up . . . everything on the list!"

"I can hardly fucking wait," says Quentin. Which is true.

Quentin opens his eyes. He has total recall: checking in at the Medea Clinic; the gourmet meal the night before, though he needs to speak to someone about the stuffed capon; his last hours awake, dictating arrangements; then Dave Derwent's face leaning over him as he went under the anaesthetic, the light glittering on his half-moon glasses.

Suzie had been there too, at the last moment just before he faded, leaning over him so he got a worm's eye view of her luscious double-peach cleavage—she'd done that on purpose. *Sweet dreams and see you soon,* she'd breathed at him with her pouty pink collagen-inflated lips. She wasn't a nurse or anything medical. Who'd let her in?

No matter, he'll find out everything now. Up in the morning, hot on the job, good-bye to care, flex the muscles both mental and physical, and begin the pleasurable business of ferreting out his enemies and those less loyal than they should be and then destroying them. He lifts his new right hand so he can admire it—no wrinkly skin, no bulgy veins, no old-fart tendons—but nothing happens. Maybe there's something that has to wear off: some anaesthetic or other.

He tries to turn his head. Nothing happens.

He seems to be looking through glass.

"He's awake," says a voice. A woman's face moves into view. Suzie. But Suzie enhanced in subtle ways, Suzie beyond cheap glamour, Suzie glorified. She's traded Dr. Derwent for a few procedures, looks like. One guess as to the currency, the slut.

"Hi there, Quentie," she says. "Having fun yet?" Her smile says: *Because I am.*

"What's going on?" says Quentin. His voice is slurred and thick, but at least his mouth works. And his ears. "Where's my new body?"

Dave Derwent moves into his field of vision. He too looks different. That bun-faced roundness is gone; he's more sculpted. Distinguished, even. "Hello, sir," he says. *That's better,* thinks Quentin. He's sadly in need of some deference.

"Don't tell me you fucking fucked up," he says. "You fuckwit!"

"The contract covered this eventuality," says Dr. Derwent. "Your head's been assigned."

"What do you mean, assigned?" barks Quentin. At least he can still bark. "You can't assign someone's head!"

"You wrote that clause yourself, remember?" says Suzie. She's suppressing a giggle. "You wrote the whole contract yourself!" She's bubbling with merriment. Quentin feels like decking her.

"In the eventuality that the Medea Clinic is sold, any unprocessed clients are assigned for fulfillment to the new owner," says Dr. Derwent.

"And as it turns out, in the interests of the bottom line, the Medea Clinic has indeed been sold." He's smirking openly now. He slips his arm around Suzie's shoulder.

"And it's been renamed," says Suzie. "In the interests of the bottom line." An actual giggle this time. "We knew it would be much more profitable this way—more than growing new bodies. We just stored away the heads until we had enough famous people for the grand opening."

"It's now called the Headslave Reruns Gallery," says Dr. Derwent. "Catchy name. We did focus groups—very memorable, high scores on the curiosity quotient. It's a branch of Bryant Entertainment. People pay top dollar to come and see the inner lives of their favourite—"

"I don't believe this!" says Quentin. "You can't turn me into a freak show! Anyway, who'd pay to look at a bunch of cut-off heads? This is a joke! I'm not awake!"

"Oh, it's much more than the heads," says Dr. Derwent. "It's hardly a living waxworks. Biographies, gossip sites, reality TV, they're all obsolete. With our patented blend of neurology and technology, we can activate any memory or imagined scene or even dream you've ever had, and then we can project the images onto a viewing screen. Sound is included."

"But that's, but that's . . . call my lawyer!" says Quentin. He can hear the futility in his own voice.

"None of this is precluded by the terms of the contract," says Dr. Derwent. "While you've been asleep, we've been running your programs, so we could offer the clients a wide selection."

"My favourite is the one where you screw me with your new big dick—you have a kind of light-up effect with that—and then you kick me out onto the street naked," says Suzie. "Actually it's kind of a turn-on."

"It's been popular with the general public," says Dr. Derwent. "They find it very amusing. I myself relish the sequence in which you humiliate me in front of my peers and then fire me. I've played that several times. That werewolf episode is in heavy demand as well, and we can up the price now you're awake. The fans love it when the, ah, when the former—when the headslave has to watch too."

"Sid Bryant likes the one where he's a driveling senile old guy in a retirement home and you visit him and then abuse him," says Suzie. "He laughs a lot when you call him a carbuncle. He's ordered a clip of that so he can have it on the video-art screen in his office."

The two of them smile at him happily. Then they kiss, a lingering, smouldering, hormone-sodden kiss, nothing faked about it. Suzie presses herself against Derwent's lab-coated, discreetly logo'd torso. She utters a soft moan. Quentin feels himself writhing in pain, even though he has nothing left to writhe with.

"Want a demonstration?" says Dr. Derwent. "Of the system. It's really remarkable, very hi-def images. You can watch the screen right along with the viewers. But you don't have to, because the exact same thing is playing in your head."

"Even if you close your eyes," says Suzie. "Maybe Quent would like to see the one where he beats up his first wife. The umbrella whippy accessory is so totally weird! It's kind of a rape thing too, though that part doesn't go too well. But there's some good lines, aren't there, darling?" She nibbles Derwent's ear. "You couldn't make it up!"

"That one's been a general favourite," says Dr. Derwent. "Or the one where he's whimpering, and his mother pulls down his little jeans and hits him with a—"

"Get me out of this bottle!" Quentin howls.

"Oh no, Quentie," says Suzie. "That would kill you. And none of us would want that, would we?"

With thanks to Graeme Gibson for the core idea

About "Headlife"

I read Ray Bradbury as a teenager, and those stories really sank in, especially "The Martian" and the other *Chronicles,* and *Fahrenheit 451.* Some writers jump straight to what we might call "deep metaphor," writing at a mythic level, and that is what these stories do. To quote Elias Canetti in *The Agony of Flies:* "To withhold meaning: nothing is quite so unnatural as the constant uncovering of meanings. The merit and the true power of myth: its meaning remains concealed."

My own story is just a pale little riff. Cut-off heads were one of the tropes of '50s science fiction, both written and filmed; perhaps "Headlife" is another, more sinister version of *The Illustrated Man.*

—Margaret Atwood

HEAVY

Jay Bonansinga

At one of the tallest buildings in Los Angeles the contractor arrives after dark. Riding the crystalline glass elevator up to the lavish, gleaming spires of the upper floors—where the law offices and consultants burn the midnight oil to finance their BMWs and alimony payments—the contractor finds Room 1201 and pauses.

He unsheathes his Browning nine-millimeter semiautomatic from its holster inside his sport coat. He calmly screws the silencer into the muzzle, checks the magazine, then moves his six-foot-six, 260-pound frame through the doorway and into the richly appointed outer office of Zuckerman Gold and Fishel Artist Management.

Over the bubbling fish tanks and frothing infinity fountain, the contractor hears the shrill voice of Marvin Zuckerman drifting out of his opulent inner office: "Morris, she happens to be a very talented young lady . . . and this offer is unacceptable, a disgrace, a dishonor to her fine . . ."

The contractor steps into Zuckerman's inner sanctum, holding the Browning at his side like a parcel.

The agent raises one hand, as if to say *give me a second*, while continuing to chatter on his wireless headset: "Okay, so she's had a few problems with Oxycontin . . . Morris, she has lower-back pain—"

"Excuse me," the contractor interjects, squeezing the gun.

"Hold on a second, Morris." Zuckerman looks up. "I had the pastrami on rye and the German potato salad, and I hope you left the mayo off this time because—"

"I'm going to need you to move away from the window," the contractor says, now aiming the gun at the general vicinity of Zuckerman's toupee.

The realization on Marvin Zuckerman's face could be etched over a painting of Edvard Munch's *The Scream*, the way his mouth goes slack and his droopy, bloodshot eyes widen. The headset falls from his ear and clatters to the floor. "Who sent you? Was it Schacter at Universal?"

"Move. Away."

"Was it because of the Tom Cruise disaster?"

"From. The. Window."

As Zuckerman slowly rises, the spark of terror in his eyes kindles into something like inspiration, like the look of a rat suddenly faced with the prospects of gnawing off its leg to escape a trap. Somewhere deep in his primordial brain stirs his instinct—as innate as the migratory patterns—that *everything* is negotiable. "You've come to whack me, I understand that, but before you do, may I ask—if you'll pardon my impertinence—have you ever done any acting? On film I'm talking about . . . Because what I'm seeing here—and you must understand, this *is* my business—is that you have something extraordinary in the way you carry yourself, and the way you handle that firearm, and if I may be so bold, I think you make Robert De Niro look like RuPaul—and forgive me for having a natural propensity for commerce, but I think I could make you a significant amount of money in this business they call show—but, of course, that would necessitate my not being whacked at this time, so I'm just throwing that out there."

The pause that follows, as the contractor ponders the little toupee-wearing agent, feels longer to Zuckerman than it takes glaciers to cleave mountains.

"If you do not move away from the window," the contractor finally explains with the grudging patience of a dog trainer, "I will relocate the back of your skull to that far wall over there with that nice Picasso."

Marvin Zuckerman edges around the desk with hands raised and mouth working. "I have—I have a *daughter*—in Boca Raton, if I may be specific—she's in H-Hebrew college—please, please—she's studying to be a rabbi—a saint this girl—and if I may add at this juncture that I am also supporting a little boy in boarding school—he's ADD and he's got a—"

"Shut your face!" The contractor holds the business end of the Browning inches away from the hyperactive mouth of Marvin Zuckerman.

"I have money." Zuckerman trembles now, his voice crumbling. "Not to be supercilious or presumptuous in any way, but I would like to add at this point that I have a ridiculous amount of—"

"QUIET!"

The bark of the contractor's sandpaper basso profundo voice turns Zuckerman's expression to jelly. All the false confidence, the used-car-dealer twinkle, the always-selling *alter kocker* schtick—all of it transforms into the look of a whipped basset hound. On Zuckerman's face is now written the end of the universe.

"Aw Christ." The contractor sighs, the gun wavering slightly.

"Enough already." He pulls the trigger, and a small flag on a tiny pin pops out of the Browning's muzzle, which says SURPRISE on one side and HAPPY BIRTHDAY on the other.

They come flooding into the office, the entire staff—even Mrs. Merryweather, the former receptionist with the cat's-eye glasses and gallstones (whom Zuckerman had assumed was dead). Two surviving partners in golf pants and Rolexes, three junior agents, an anorexic secretary, a pair of slacker grad-student readers, an old lady with blue-rinse hair, and a six-figure-a-year accountant with a Percodan habit—this motley group could make an alarming racket.

They whoop and holler and sing "Happy Birthday" and break out the Dom Pérignon, and on a mail cart they roll in a cake in the shape of a tombstone with the inscription HERE LIES HOLLYWOOD'S NUMBER ONE ASSHOLE, and all the while everybody studiously pretends not to notice the evidence of post-traumatic stress on Zuckerman's face.

Zuckerman considers surprise parties thinly veiled acts of passive-aggressiveness and hostility, and God knows there's enough animosity around this place to wallpaper Bin Laden's cave.

After an hour of tippling and off-key crooning and gossipmongering and chortling at bad jokes, Mrs. Merryweather is the one who finally broaches the subject. "You do realize that everyone got a huge kick out of the look on your puss at the end there," she says to Zuckerman over by the potted ficus.

"Really had me going there," Zuckerman concurs sourly. "Who's the Golem, anyway?"

Zuckerman jerks his thumb at the leviathan in the J.C.Penney sport coat skulking all alone in the corner. The contractor stands there like a dime-store Indian, staring into his paper cup. Somewhere in his late sixties, the man has a face no mother could love, a road map of creases circumnavigating a pair of eyes like smoldering craters formed by meteors.

"Poor fella," Mrs. Merryweather says. "Used to be somebody."

"As for instance?"

"You're in the picture business, Marvin, for God's sake . . . don't you recognize the man? They said you wouldn't recognize him, but I didn't believe it."

"You want to give me a hint, or is this twenty questions?"

"1962? *New Jersey Nocturne*? Alan Ladd and Barbara Stanwyck mean anything to you?"

"Never saw it."

"That gentleman over there is Haywood Allerton."

The name rings no bells for Zuckerman. "And so?"

"Once upon a time, that man was the greatest heavy in Hollywood."

With a shrug, staring at the giant with the ruined face, Zuckerman says, "What makes *him* a 'poor fella'? I'm the guy got buffaloed."

Mrs. Merryweather lowers her voice, as though imparting something unseemly. "Poor guy's in stage four I'm told, pancreatic cancer, inoperable."

Zuckerman thinks about this, sips his champagne, thinks about it some more, then decides to investigate further and walks over to the colossus.

"You got me," Zuckerman says to the giant, with as much conviviality as he can muster. "Not since I read my pre-nup with my third wife have I been that petrified."

All at once, as though by some stroke of magical alchemy, the giant's face changes from its natural repose of sinister menace into a warm, open look of empathy—a transformation not unlike Godzilla pausing to help an old lady across the street. "I feel terrible about what I did, Mr. Zuckerman."

"Don't sweat it."

"I will admit to you that I needed the money."

Zuckerman waves his hand. "No harm done."

"I wouldn't harm a flea, Mr. Zuckerman; I have insurance issues is the thing."

"Completely understandable," Zuckerman assures the man. "I meant what I said, however, about your . . . unique style. Turns out, if I may be so bold as to pat myself on the back, I was correct in my assessment of your unique proclivities."

Allerton looks down shyly, tries to stifle a smile jerking at the corners of his intimidating face. "I made a few pictures a long time ago," he says, "but nobody wants an old tough guy no more."

Zuckerman gets an idea. Maybe the idea comes because Zuckerman had found himself staring into the abyss that night. Maybe it comes because he had been thinking about God. But whatever the source, it strikes him right then as all his epiphanies do: in the scrotum, then traveling up the base of his spine to the core of his midbrain. It would not only be a challenge but would also perhaps be an opportunity for Zuckerman to do something outside the realm of lies, exploitation, greed, and deception that customarily govern his daily existence. Perhaps it would be an opportunity to atone, to get himself on track with the Torah, to fulfill a *mitzvah,* an act of kindness.

After a dramatic pause, Marvin Zuckerman says to the great monolith of an old man, "Maybe, if you will pardon my presumptuousness, you just haven't had the right representation."

If you went to the movies between 1960 and 1980, you most likely would have seen, at one point or another, the inimitable, craggy face of Haywood Allerton—still a relatively young man for much of this period, but ageless in his inchoate menace. Sometimes haunting the edges of great films and sometimes providing foils for cardboard heroes in, let us say, *less*-than-great films, Allerton, for one brief and shining moment, was the go-to heavy for all the studios, both major and minor.

His greatest role, perhaps, was as the redneck racist who roughs up Pam Greer in the blaxploitation classic *Honey Child* (Avco/Embassy, 1971). He also made his mark as the brain-damaged child murderer in Orson Welles's little-seen noir *Coffin Not Included* (RKO, 1974). Allerton also chilled audiences in such diverse cinematic fare as *Monster Train* (Hammer, 1969), *Rumble in the Jungle* (New Line, 1976), *The Copperheads* (Universal, 1979), and *As the Eagle Flies* (AIP, 1980), the cult World War II actioner with Burt Reynolds and Twiggy.

Alas, in today's Hollywood—a new frontier of digital downloads and flavors-of-the-millisecond viewed on handheld devices in bathroom stalls—a man of Allerton's special qualities can barely land a hemorrhoid commercial. Evil is no longer essayed by the human face; it is created in the lab, through CGI and motion capture.

Over the next few weeks, Zuckerman stops counting all the doors slammed in his face. He will not give up, though—after all, this is a mission from God, a holy *mitzvah*—which leads to an interesting phenomenon: For the first time in his shallow, manipulative, contemptuous life, Marvin Zuckerman actually experiences something like real affection for another human being.

In the tradition of many great Hollywood heavies—Rondo Hatton, William Bendix, Margaret Hamilton, and Richard Widmark among them—Haywood Allerton is secretly a pussycat, a softie, a tender soul with nary a wicked thought in his head, and he begins to grow on Zuckerman. Complicating matters is the fact that the gentle giant is getting weaker and weaker by the day, the malignant cells erasing the man's remaining time on earth faster than the nitrate fading from the celluloid of his old films.

Eventually Zuckerman feels compelled to maximize as many of the man's waning days as possible, so the two mismatched chums become fixtures down at Molly Malone's on Fairfax. They dine on mountains of corned beef and lox at Canter's Deli. They go to the Hollywood Wax Museum, Chinatown, and Griffith Observatory, where Allerton, in a pique of excitement, names every star in the firmament after an old Hollywood heavy: Elisha Cook Jr., Charles Napier, Sydney Greenstreet, John Vernon, Jack Elam, Dub Taylor, Vernon Dent, and on and on and on.

The two of them also take to playing golf on Sundays at Zuckerman's Beverly Hills club, spending the lazy hours trudging the fairways, talking, getting to know each other's deepest ruminations and regrets. In fact, it is on one of these Sundays that everything changes for Zuckerman.

"That's a honey of a shot," Allerton says encouragingly from the edge of the eighteenth green. Of course it's a lie. Zuckerman's whiffed putt has just skirted the edge of the hole and has shot off into the sand.

"Tell me something, Haywood," Zuckerman says, retrieving his ball from the trap. "You're so . . . *not like* the heavies you played. Did you *enjoy* it—the glory days I'm talking about—all the villains?"

"You want to know the truth?" the grizzled old monolith replies as he limps over to his ball. Almost skin and bones now, he's moving slower than usual today, the pain medication fighting a losing battle stanching the tide of agony seeping up through his innards. The putter looks like a chopstick in his gigantic gnarled hands as he towers shakily over the golf ball. "I *did* enjoy it, being the heavy, I *did*. It was almost like . . ." He pauses, thinking, staring downward, teetering, holding himself up as though the putter were a cane. " . . . the guys I was playing were bad apples, sure, but they . . . they . . . I guess what I'm trying to say is, my favorite part was when they got their comeuppance . . .

when they took their medicine. You know? They looked the good guy in the face, they always did that, and they accepted the . . . whattyacallit . . . the consequences. I don't know why that was so important to me . . . I guess that's the only part I almost kinda miss. Putting the . . . whattyacallit . . . the punctuation at the end of the picture."

Zuckerman has no idea what the big guy is talking about but goes ahead and says, "That's an interesting angle on things, my friend . . . and it brings to mind that great scene in . . . Haywood? Haywood?" Zuckerman drops his putter. "Haywood?! Haywood?! HAYWOOD!!"

Once in a great while, in the great Muir Woods many miles north of here, a mighty redwood, suffering from blight, tumbles over in a great, heaving plunge, shaking the earth and sending up a plume of debris. When Haywood Allerton finally succumbs to the pain and goes down, hitting the green with all his weight, the manicured, perfectly landscaped, rarified ground of the Pine Ridge Country Club trembles with similar seismic reverberations.

Zuckerman spares no expense. He has Allerton taken to the best facility money can buy—the Samuel Oschin Cancer Institute at Cedars-Sinai—not far from Zuckerman's stately Beverly Hills mansion (which was once owned by Douglas Fairbanks, by the way).

Zuckerman demands immediate attention and puts everything on his Visa. The doctors run the unconscious behemoth through a battery of tests and conclude that Allerton is in his final hours, his immune system shutting down, malabsorption syndrome making him a candidate for a feeding tube, and the administrator at Cedars informs Zuckerman that *hospice* is the only answer, and it's a miracle the big guy was still walking around, and how about this chilly autumn weather we're having?

A widower with a lapsed Screen Actor's Guild membership, Allerton has no insurance and no immediate family other than two estranged daughters living in the Midwest, both of whom are unable to get to L.A. for another week or two, so Zuckerman decides to have Allerton moved to Zuckerman's sprawling Tudor mansion on Canon for home hospice care.

It is here, five days later, in the elegant parlor in the rear of the house, around which French windows look out on a lovely grove of avocado trees and the hummingbirds play in the wisteria, that Zuckerman realizes what he has to do.

"So your daughter, the older one—Nancy's her name? She claims you never had a will," Zuckerman says to the dying man.

Nestled in the folds of a massive orthopedic hospital bed that was brought in by four burly orderlies earlier that week, hooked to a space shuttle's worth of equipment, Allerton drifts in and out of consciousness, his face a gaunt, gray, sunken mask of torture. The pain constantly ebbs and flows—more *flowing* than *ebbing* lately—and it is agonizing for Zuckerman to watch.

"I don't know if you hear me anymore, but I just want you to know I got a plan." Zuckerman sits on the edge of a chair next to the bed, his hand clutching the bed rail so tightly his knuckles whiten.

Allerton's eyelids flutter. His lips peel away from clenched, yellow teeth. It is unclear whether this is an indication that he understands human speech or he is simply writhing in pain—or both.

It is also unclear how long the machines will keep him alive now, maybe days, weeks. God forbid, *months*. The former folk artist of evil, the greatest heavy ever, a man from a bygone era of analog projectors, now floating in a limbo of misery, kept alive by the same kind of advanced computer technology that replaced his cinematic archetype.

"I'm still your manager, by God," Zuckerman says, "and I'll manage this, if you'll pardon the expression, like a professional."

Very slowly, with the feeble, tentative shakiness of a wounded sparrow, Allerton's huge hand moves to the bed rail and covers Zuckerman's hand.

The gesture leaches tears from the jaded, cynical, heartless agent. "Why, if you'll pardon my impertinence, did you *do* this to me? Why did you come into my life when I was minding my own business?" The sobbing starts. "I got . . . I got three ex-wives hate my guts, I got . . . I got four kids I barely even know, and you gotta be my friend *now*—maybe the best friend I ever had—you gotta tear my heart out like this . . . you prick!"

Marvin Zuckerman lowers his head and lets the sobs rock through him.

At length the crying passes and he looks up and says softly, "Don't worry, Haywood, old pal o' mine, I got a plan."

At one of the most lavish mansions in Beverly Hills the second contractor arrives after dark. Slipping through the shadows of avocado trees—where stars of the silent screen once frolicked and strolled—he finds the rear parlor window and pauses.

He checks the small leather pouch in his black suit coat, checks the instruments tucked inside it, then pries the window glass open and stealthily climbs inside the house.

The man moves to the side of the hospital bed and looks down at its occupant. "He said to make it fast and painless," the man says, reaching into the pouch and preparing the hypodermic. "Who am I to argue? You get all kinds in this business."

This man is the real thing—the banality of evil incarnate. He has the face of a hairless mouse, and dead, blank, shoe-button eyes.

Those at death's door often experience a final moment of lucidity. The big, emaciated man on the bed opens his eyes, gazes up, and looks his executioner in the face. The dying man does not look away. The needle glistens, shedding a tear of fluid.

Although hard to read—and impossible for this mousey hit man to understand—the man on the bed accepts the consequences of what happens next. A good heavy does not look away. He accepts the consequences.

The needle goes in, punctuating the end of Allerton's suffering.

It's over within seven seconds.

Outside the mansion, on his way back to his innocuous little two-door sedan, the second contractor passes a shadowy figure wringing his hands at the foot of the driveway.

"Is it done?" the figure asks.

The mousey gentleman turns and approaches Marvin Zuckerman, and in the pitiless, cold darkness he says, "Oh yeah, we're good."

Zuckerman hands over the envelope of cash, an amount he had raised, in trademark fashion, from the insurance reimbursement for the home-care expenses (after putting Allerton on the agency's payroll).

Pausing to thumb through the bills, the mousey man says, "Correct me if I'm wrong, but we agreed on twenty K."

"It's short my commission," Marvin Zuckerman explains. "Fifteen percent."

The man in black just stares at the grief-stricken, toupee-wearing agent.

A *mitzvah* is a *mitzvah*.

But an agent is also an agent.

About "Heavy"

I remember, as a kid, carrying Ray's collection *R Is for Rocket* around in my Partridge Family lunch box. Flash forward forty years and I'm now toiling in the vineyards of Hollyweird and Publishers' Row, and always with that magical Bradburian inspiration tucked into the back compartment of my creative lunch box. I now read Ray's stories to my children at bedtime. The other night, I'm reading "A Sound of Thunder," and we come to the part where the dinosaur makes its majestic appearance. These words were written in 1952, for God's sake, but they still ring more vividly and three-dimensionally than any CGI. When presented with the chance to create an original crime story—informed by Bradbury—I felt as though I had been given the shoes from "The Sound of Summer Running." The Bradbury mythos came over me in a seizure as I spun my little yarn: the sadness at the core of human nature, the love of the Golden Age of Movies, the scabrous view of capitalism, and the plain, unadorned beauty of friendship.

—Jay Bonansinga

THE GIRL IN THE FUNERAL PARLOR

Sam Weller

When I was twenty, I got a job delivering flowers. Three days a week, I drove a maroon-colored Chevy van, the words FORGET ME NOT painted on the sides, down barren two-lane western Illinois county roads.

There was a solitude to the job that I liked. As soon as the van was loaded and I drove away from the flower shop, no one could tell me what to do. Sometimes, on busy days, I would be gone for three, four hours, maybe longer. Talk radio and a supersized soda kept me company, and I just lived in my head.

I delivered to offices all over town for all their celebrations—every week someone threw a faux fiesta, marking ersatz holidays like Sweetest Day (seriously, do we really need a Sweetest Day when we have Valentine's Day?).

Then there were Saturday mornings at churches, where weddings were set up; Saturday afternoons included dropping off arrangements for the following day's services.

I also delivered to rickety bungalows in our small city, brick apartment buildings in the center square, and lonesome houses miles outside of town. In winter, when it's dark early and ghosts of snow drift across the rural highways, it's always a little eerie. After driving down a gravel road to some farm, I'd have to step out into the subzero windchill and go up to the dark house. Sometimes, a dog with an apparent case of rabies would bark after I knocked. I'd wait a minute or two, hoping no one was home except Cujo—then I could just leave. But a light inevitably would blink on. I'd hear heavy footsteps; several dead bolts, one after another after another, being unlatched, and the door would open a sliver. A pale face would peer out.

"Yes?"

"Flower delivery!"

In those moments, out there in the stubbly frozen hinterland, facing some stranger in shadow, I shivered, wondering if I would ever be seen or heard from again.

Without a doubt, though, I found delivering to funeral parlors the weirdest of all. My job was to lay the flowers around the casket. Averting my eyes, I'd crouch and set up the floral sprays and plants quickly around the body and never once look. Sometimes, with a casket spray arrangement, I would actually have to place it on the closed bottom half of the coffin itself.

It felt odd being there, alone with the dead. Here I was, a community-college kid studying English lit and living with his parents, arranging flowers over the mortal remains of the departed. They never knew me while they lived, and I felt like I was violating them in a way. It just felt wrong.

On one of these occasions, at the old Peterson Funeral Home, I encountered Catherine Courington. She was dead, yet more alive than anyone I'd ever known.

It was a morning in June, when specks of sunlight shone brilliantly through oak leaves over the funeral home, casting a champagne glow. The van was packed from end to end and perfumed heavily with fountains of crimson pansies, white lilies, plum peonies, and waxen orchids. The labels on some of the flowers were marked:

PETERSON FUNERAL HOME—COURINGTON SERVICE

The Peterson family had run that funeral home for more than a hundred years, in a Victorian built atop a hill in town that led down to the Rock River. A cupola topped the three-story house, and a winding red-brick walkway led up to a wraparound porch. Hanging geranium baskets twisted in the hot summer breeze. Lead-glass windows, thick and wide, were set on the façade, and they were all gauzed over on the inside with delicate lace curtains.

I parked the van behind the house. The old mansion had a back door, reserved for deliveries. I think this was where they brought in the bodies, to prepare them for the services, but I wasn't certain. An antiseptic odor that I imagined came from cleaning supplies and embalming fluid hung in the air.

With a bulky arrangement cradled in my arms, I went to the back door. It was opened a crack, so I pushed it wide with my foot. I waited for my eyes to adjust from the bright sunshine. After a while, after calling out and no one answering, I ventured into the darkened back hall. Somewhere in the house, a clock ticked. No one was around, but that's the way it was a few hours before a service. I pictured the funeral-home people upstairs, in their administrative offices, hurriedly tending to final details.

The parlor I found up front was long and rectangular, with brass light fixtures and velvety sofas. The papered walls had a textured swirl pattern of moss green. Paintings hung in crusty frames, landscapes of rivers, prairies, and meadows. Over the fireplace was the main painting—of William Peterson, the first of the family proprietors. He looked stern; his cravat was stiff under his chin. I supposed the room looked exactly as it did when old William ran the place. It sort of freaked me out, being alone in that parlor. It was just me and the body in the casket. It was open for viewing. Old William watched me; it was like an episode of *Scooby-Doo,* where only the eyes move in the painting. I laid the floral arrangement below the casket.

But something caught my eye—a flash, and quickly gone. I don't know why I looked, that day, over to the top of the casket. Perhaps it was the shimmer of long blond hair.

I stood and stared. Jesus. Young—she looked my age, maybe a little older. She wore a cardigan sweater, soft-looking and lilac, and a single strand of pearls. Her face had that slight bloating of the deceased, but it was smooth. A horizontal scar ran across the right side of her forehead, angling down into her manicured eyebrow. It threw off the symmetry of her otherwise perfect face. But in an odd way, it made her look more alluring and enigmatic.

Her eyes were lined in black with little sharp points at the edges, her lips glossed light pink, her hands folded across her chest. The top of a black-and-white polka-dot skirt was visible. You couldn't see her legs. She looked like she had lived in the fifties. Standing there, I stared. The more I looked, the more I itched to touch that soft sweater, run my fingertips down her arm or across her smooth face. I glanced over my shoulder.

I didn't, or couldn't, do it.

I looked down at her face. It occurred to me that I wished for something that could never be: I wanted her eyes to open. I wanted her to speak. I wished it. I really wished it. *Just say something, anything at all.*

After a long while, or maybe it was just a minute, I shook my head to clear it. Then I went back out into the glaring sunlight to grab the rest of the flowers. After setting up the last of the arrangements, I looked at a sympathy card affixed to one delivery: Catherine Courington.

I stared down at her one last time, puffed my cheeks, and exhaled. And I did it. I quickly ran my fingertips down the sleeve on her right arm, and it was as petal soft and fuzzy as I'd imagined.

I turned and left.

Every day that next week, I thought about her. Constantly. I wondered how she died. Sometimes, when I was driving down lonely country roads, passing an occasional car headed in the opposite direction, I imagined our life together, mine and Catherine's. I knew how we fell in love. I knew how our lives unfolded together, how we'd mark the anniversary of our wedding each year by nothing more than reading passages of our favorite books late into the night. We were soul mates. I knew it at my very core.

Does that sound weird? Probably. But it's the God's truth. Haven't you ever seen a stranger before and something in you is inexplicably drawn to that person? Maybe you knew each other—or were supposed to know each other—or maybe you dreamt of that person, once, long ago? Perhaps, in another reality, an alternative world, if you believe in such things, you did. But in this world, this reality, something kept you apart. Maybe it was as simple as taking one street home rather than the other, choosing one path over another, and fate was circumvented forever because of the most minute of decisions. Is that what happened to me and Catherine?

At night I began dreaming of us. We were seated at a wrought-iron table at an outdoor café. A cathedral bell tolled in the far distance. We sipped coffee and she smiled, revealing a slight chip on her front tooth. We held hands, and I swirled my fingers under her palm, noting the lines, like I was trying to read her future. Her mouth opened. She was about to say something.

Please, say it. Let me hear your voice.

But I always woke before she said a word.

In another dream she emerged from complete darkness, like she was in a large room or even a warehouse without a single window or light source. She walked forward slowly into a pool of stark light, her blond hair buoyant on her shoulders. She walked with confidence and poise, closer and closer. Her eyes were radiant, with that black eyeliner with the sharp points at the edges. She lifted her hand to me. My heart leapt. *Please, let me hear you.*

As she drew near, her face began to melt, like a gruesome wax figure in a Saturday horror matinee. Her makeup ran down her face in streams of color. Then the rest of her face started dripping, her eyes and nose and lips. The molten wax swirled, morphing. As it began to take shape, I knew what it was. It was one of those Mexican Day of the Dead masks—a white skull painted boldly black, red, blue, and yellow, with little white flowers around the sides. In the center, between the eyes, a painted heart dripped three tears.

She opened her mouth.

I'm listening, Catherine.

But something other than words emerged from her lips. It was dark, at first, small and twitching. As it crawled forth it showed itself. Wings. Black and orange. A butterfly fluttered and flew off into the darkness.

After these dreams, I had to know who Catherine Courington was and what had happened to her. But then another thought struck me, a realization of fate, twisted and thwarted: What happens if you meet your soul mate after she has died?

Late one night, after I woke from one of those dreams, I searched the Internet. I didn't know why I hadn't before. I guess I felt odd about it, like it was perverted. I knew it was bizarre. I knew no one would understand, so I told no one about Catherine.

In the basement of my parents' house, where my room was, I

sat in front of my computer and typed her name. I found scores of social-networking pages of girls named Catherine Courington. I went through each page, hoping to find her, to find a photograph, to see her. I was hoping for a video clip, to hear her. But after hours, I found nothing. She didn't have a social-network page.

I did find an unknown English poet with the same name—Catherine Courington, killed in a horse-and-carriage accident in 1882. She had died before any literary success.

I read a title to one of her poems: "The Clock Ticks Unfair."

Then I found her. I clicked on the link and the page began to load. It was just a small obituary item:

> *Catherine Courington, 23, of New York City.*
> *Beloved Daughter of Candace* (née Roberts).
> Funeral services, Saturday, June 10, 11 A.M.,
> *Peterson Funeral Home*, 111 S. Main Street.

The next day I delivered flowers in a hurry, moving across town more like a FedEx guy than a flower man. I needed to buy myself an hour so my manager wouldn't ask where I was.

After looking up the information on Catherine Courington's mother, I discovered that she lived in a mobile-home park, off a winding highway. I drove out after lunch.

The Fountain Bleu Mobile Home Park sign was faded, and paint was chipping off at the bottom. As I pulled in, a kid ran across the street, chasing a ball. I slammed on the brakes, the van lurching, barely missing him. He was maybe seven or eight, with a crew cut and plenty of freckles. He glared at me.

"Sorry," I mouthed, and waved. In the side-view mirror, I could see him as I pulled the van forward, standing with his ball, mouth pinched, scowling.

The mobile homes of Fountain Bleu were so run-down that

they looked like haunted trailers, with plywood planking and stained bedsheets over the windows. But some had jaunty flower gardens and new shiny mailboxes in front. I found Candace Courington's mobile home at the end of the street. A Doberman chained to the neighboring mobile home barked, baring its teeth. Across the street, a man working over the engine of an El Camino looked up at me. I nodded. He didn't say a word or nod back. He wiped sweat from his brow.

Along the walkway leading to the mobile home, plastic flowers spun in the wind. The windows had dusty metal horizontal blinds turned shut. I stepped up to the door and knocked. The guy across the street wiped his oily hands on a towel and watched me. The dog continued to bark, straining against its leash.

The door opened just a bit.

The woman held a lit cigarette in her hand. She had a dome of swimming-pool-blond hair and tired eyes.

"Can I help you?" she asked.

"Candace Courington?"

"Yes," she said, looking over my shoulder to the van parked on the street.

"Flower delivery," I said, extending the arrangement in my arms.

She took it.

"Thanks." Her cigarette dangled from her lips. She began to close the door.

"I knew your daughter," I blurted, my words running together, before she could shut the door.

"Oh yeah?"

"I'm so sorry."

"Thanks," she said. "How did you know her?"

"High school." I thought about Sir Walter Scott's old quote about webs and deception.

"You went to school in New York?" she asked. "What are you doing out here, in Sterling Springs?"

The lies were building. "This is actually where I grew up. My parents just moved there for a few years, and that's how I met Catherine."

I had no clue where this was going.

"That so," she said.

"The flowers are from me." I tried a smile.

Candace Courington looked at the arrangement. "That's nice of you."

She stepped back to close the door. I knew this was my only chance. "Can I tell you a story about Catherine, Mrs. Courington? A story from our days in New York?"

Jesus.

She stared at me for a moment, thoughtfully.

"Sure," she said at last. "Come in. You want a glass of water?"

"If you don't mind."

The mobile home was dark and piles of bills were stacked on end tables, alongside prescription pill bottles. The TV was on, and a woman on the screen was sobbing.

We sat in the living room, on a saggy sofa with the plaid cloth worn thin on the edges. A framed print of that Impressionist painting by Seurat, "Sunday in the Park" or whatever it's called, hung slightly crooked over us. It's weird that all the people in that painting, all the well-dressed women with their parasols, and the men with their top hats and the dogs and the kids, and even the monkey, are all facing the lake or away in another direction. But not the little girl. That kid with her white dress and bonnet, right in the middle of the painting, is looking right at you.

Candace Courington fetched me a glass of water from the kitchen. On a coffee table was a magazine, *Modern Amputee*. I picked it up and looked at the attractive blond woman posing on the cover. She wore a prosthetic leg.

I thumbed through some unopened envelopes next to the magazine. One was addressed to Catherine Courington, 210 E. 5th Street, New York, New York—a phone bill. I folded it and put it in my back pocket. I felt like a douche bag but kept it anyway.

"What's your name?" asked Candace Courington, returning to the room and handing me the glass of water.

"I'm Josh. Josh Dieboldt."

"What do you do, Josh? Besides deliver flowers, I mean?" She sat down next to me. We were both sunk so low, it felt like we were sitting on the floor.

"I'm studying English lit at Rock River College."

"What do you want to do with that?"

"Be a writer, maybe." I shrugged and picked up the water glass but didn't drink it.

Candace Courington stared at the ragged brown carpeting. "Catherine was a reader. That girl always had a book in her hands. Ever since she was little."

She looked up.

"So what story were you going to tell me? How did you two meet?"

Across the street, a car engine growled—an eight-cylinder Godzilla. The guy in the driveway had started his El Camino.

"We just met on the street one afternoon. May," I said. "It smelled like flowers and garbage, because they stack the trash bags up into little mountains on the sidewalks in New York."

God, what a bullshitter.

"Catherine loved the city."

"I know. She did. And I loved that about her. But, anyway, I just saw her one afternoon on a street corner in Soho, and introduced myself. I'd never done that before, but there was something about her. Something familiar and, for me, predestined. That's what I wanted to tell you. I know this is weird, Mrs. Courington, but it was like I knew your daughter the minute I saw her. It was déjà vu, fate, astral influence, two trains on opposite tracks passing each other in the night and two passengers peering out windows and spotting each other, just for a moment."

As I said these words, I knew that in truth, two trains had indeed passed each other, but only one passenger was looking.

"You *are* a writer," she said, almost smiling. "What did Catherine say about all this talk of fate?"

"I didn't want to scare her or freak her out, so I never told her. I wish I had the chance now. God, how I wish I could tell her. I hope this doesn't scare you, but every atom in my being believes we were soul mates."

Mrs. Courington shook her head. "You should have told her. She believed in all of that, you know, fate. She loved stories where things worked out differently. Alternate realities, she called it. It's funny. She always had the sense that she'd find her one true love right here in Sterling Springs."

I was silent. *I was that true love.*

"I don't mean to pry," I said finally, "but can I ask what happened? I was just so shocked when I heard the news."

She looked at me, startled. She put her hand over her mouth. "You don't know?"

"No, I don't."

She looked devastated, and really old. "I'm sorry, I can't talk about it right now. It's just too much. I'm afraid you have to leave."

"Sure," I said, not wanting to leave, but standing up anyway.

"Thanks for the flowers. That was very thoughtful. I'm sorry. I'm so sorry."

I stepped out into the hot afternoon sunlight, and the door closed behind me. The guy across the street turned and looked at me again. I felt insanely frustrated.

Crossing the street, I approached him.

"Hi," I said. He wore a muscle T-shirt with the words ALL

WOUND UP on it. His goatee was uneven; he had shaved too close on the right side, and it had left a big gouge where the hair used to be. The unevenness was distracting.

"Yeah?"

"I was just wondering," I said, "How well do you know Mrs. Courington across the street?"

"Well enough," he said, wiping his greasy hands on his jeans.

"Do you know what happened to her daughter?"

"She's dead."

"I know. But *how* did she die?"

The guy's eyes grew skinny.

"What business is it of yours, peckerwood?"

"I'm sorry?"

"Why don't you go askin' her mother? What you askin' me for?"

"Never mind," I said, turning back to the van. I climbed in, started the engine, and turned it around. The whole time, the guy continued to glare. He was saying something, too, pointing at me, but I couldn't hear him because the windows were up.

After work, I went home and straight downstairs. I pulled the phone bill out of my back pocket and unfolded it. I felt guilty for stealing the thing. I stared at the New York City address. I imagined some old gray-stone building along a tree-lined street. The building had a lobby with brass mailboxes set into the wall. The phone bill would have been delivered there, waiting for Catherine.

I tore open the envelope. The bill was several pages. It had an itemized list of the calls made in the last weeks of May. Many were to Illinois, probably to her mother. Dozens were to New York numbers, a few to Newark and Boston, one to Chicago. I thought about going to New York City, going to the apartment building and meeting her neighbors. Find out how she died.

But then I realized it didn't matter at all. It didn't matter how she died. What mattered was that she was no longer alive, and I had no chance at all. I thought of the soft fabric of that sweater under my fingertips, her closed eyes and smooth skin, that slight scar and how she got it—and the dreams. I thought of those dreams and how she never spoke to me.

I looked at the phone bill. *Jesus.* The phone bill. At the top of the first page was her number. I picked up my phone and dialed. The first ring. The second. And a third and a fourth and then the voice mail answered.

"Hi," she said, her voice strong and clear. "This is Catherine. I'm not here right now, but you know what to do."

And then there was the beep, and I hung up the line.

About "The Girl in the Funeral Parlor"

When I was nineteen, I delivered flowers in a far-west suburb of Chicago where the strip malls ended and the farmland began. One crisp Saturday morning I set an arrangement up in a funeral home before the services. I was all alone, just me and the deceased resting in a plush, open casket. I glanced at the body that day, and the image has been branded in my mind ever since. Lying in the casket was a young mother holding her baby. I was shocked. I left and climbed into my delivery truck and started to cry. That mother and child have haunted me ever since.

It was this memory that caused me to write "The Girl in the Funeral Parlor." But I didn't want to just retell my experience; I wanted to look at my memory through the prism of fiction, as Ray Bradbury has regularly done in such stories as "The Lake," "The Crowd," "Banshee," and so many others. I wanted my story to take on a life of its own, as good stories so often do. It was at this point that the concept came to me—what if you met the love of your life and it was too late? What if that true love was dead?

The story almost wrote itself from that moment forward.

Certainly, Bradbury's 1957 novel-in-stories, *Dandelion Wine,* was a tremendous influence on my story—the small-town setting; the theme of unrequited love; the element of magic and sorrow in the everyday; the pervasive sense of melancholy. One of my very favorite lesser-known Bradbury short stories is "The Swan," from *Dandelion Wine* (the titles of the stories in that book were removed to lend the further appearance that it is a novel rather than a connected collection). In "The Swan," a man and a woman meet at completely different junctures in their lives. He is young and just starting out; she is old and at the end of her countless splendid days. My story looks at this theme of missed connections through a darker, more extreme lens. The two lovers never meet, for it is too late. One of them is already gone.

—Sam Weller

THE COMPANIONS

David Morrell

Frank shouldn't have been there. On Thursday, unexpected script meetings required him to fly from Santa Fe to Los Angeles. His discussions with the film's director and its star ended on Friday evening. Usually, he would have spent the weekend with friends in Los Angeles, but he loved opera, and he had tickets for the next night when Santa Fe's opera company was premiering Poulenc's *Dialogues of the Carmelites*, a work Frank had never seen. The tickets included a pre-performance dinner, along with a lecture about the composer.

"You just arrived in L.A., and now you want to fly back?" his wife, Debby, asked when he phoned. "If there's an Ultimate Commuter award, I'll nominate you for it."

"I've really been looking forward to this," Frank answered. Using his cell phone, he sat in his rented car outside the newest Beverly Hills restaurant, where the final meeting had ended. "Do you remember how many times I called the box office and kept getting a busy signal? The person I spoke to said I got the last two tickets."

"The dinner's supposed to be in a tent behind the opera house, right?"

"Right."

"Well, the tent might not be standing. Yesterday the monsoons started."

Debby referred to a July weather pattern in which moist air from the Pacific streamed into New Mexico, creating rains that were often violent.

"The storm was really bad," Debby continued. "In fact, there's another one coming. I shouldn't be on the phone. It isn't safe with the lightning this close."

"I bet tomorrow will be bright and sunny."

"It's not supposed to be, according to the weather guy on channel seven. How were your meetings?"

"The director wants me to change the villains from presidential advisors to advertising executives. The star wants me to include a part for his new girlfriend. This opera will be my reward for listening to them."

"You're that determined? Be prepared to get wet." The prolonged boom of thunder echoed behind Debby's voice. "I'd better hang up. Love you."

"Love you," Frank said.

Frank's plane was scheduled to leave Los Angeles at ten in the morning, but it didn't take off until two.

"Bad weather in New Mexico," the American Airlines attendant explained.

The jet came down through dark, churning clouds for a bumpy landing in Santa Fe shortly after five. The overcast sky made the afternoon dark.

"It's been raining all day," an airline employee told Frank. "This is the first break we've had."

But a new storm beaded Frank's windshield as soon as he got into his car. Poor visibility slowed traffic so that what was normally a fifteen-minute drive home took three times that long. Frank pulled into his garage at six. The dinner at the opera was supposed to start at seven.

He'd made various cell-phone reports to his wife. Even so, Debby looked relieved, as if she hadn't seen him for weeks, when he walked in. To her credit, she was dressed, ready for the evening. "If you're game, *I* am. But I think we're both nuts."

"I'm afraid I'm more nuts than you."

"The umbrella's in here." Debby pointed to a knapsack they always took to the opera. The theater's sides were open—people who dressed for daytime summer temperatures could feel frozen as the mountain air dropped from ninety to fifty degrees at night. "I've also got a blanket, a thermos of hot chocolate, and our raincoats. This had better be a good opera."

"Look." Frank smiled out the kitchen window, pointing toward sunlight peeking through the clouds. "The rain stopped. Everything's going to work out."

The theater was eight miles north of town. As Frank headed up Route 285, traffic was fast and crazy as usual, drivers changing lanes regardless of how slick the pavement was.

Debby pointed toward a police car, an ambulance, and two wrecked cars at the side of the road. "They're putting somebody into the ambulance. My God. Somebody must have died. They covered the body."

Traffic threw up a gritty spray that speckled Frank's windshield. Troubled by the accident, he turned on the windshield wipers and reduced his speed. Horns blared behind him, vehicles racing past. Straining to see beyond the streaks on his window, he steered toward an exit ramp and headed up a hill toward the opera house.

There, he walked with Debby to a tent behind the theater. A bottle of wine stood on each table.

Half the seats were empty.

"See, not everybody's crazy like us," Debby said.

"Like *me*."

After choosing salad and chicken from a buffet, they sat at a table.

Frank glanced toward the entrance. Two men entered, surveyed the empty seats, saw Frank and Debby alone, and came over.

One of the men was short, slight, and elderly, with white hair and a matching goatee that made him look rabbinical. The other man was tall, well built, and young, with short, dark hair and a clean-shaven, square-jawed face. They both wore dark suits and white shirts. Their eyes were very clear.

"Hello," the elderly man said. "My name's Alexander."

"And I'm Richard," the other man said.

"Pleased to meet you." Frank introduced Debby and himself.

"Terrible weather," Alexander said.

"Sure is," Debby agreed.

"We drove all the way from Albuquerque," Richard said.

"I can beat that," Frank told them. "I came all the way from Los Angeles."

The two men went to get their food. Frank poured wine for Debby and himself, then offered to pour for Alexander and Richard when they came back.

"No, thanks," Alexander said.

"It makes me sleepy," Richard said.

The pair bowed their heads in a silent prayer. Self-conscious, Frank and Debby did the same. Then the four of them ate and discussed opera, how they preferred the Italian ones, could tolerate the German ones, and felt that French operas were sometimes an ordeal.

"The rhythm's so ponderous in some of them," Frank said, "it's like being on a Roman slave ship, rowing to a drumbeat, like that scene in *Ben-Hur*."

"But *Carmen*'s good. A French opera set in Spain." Richard found that amusing. "And tonight's opera is French. I've never heard it, so I have no idea whether it's worth our time."

Frank was pleased by how easy they were to talk to. They had an inner stillness that soothed him after his frustrating Hollywood meetings and his difficult journey home.

"What do you do in Albuquerque?" Debby asked Richard.

"*He* doesn't live there. *I* do," Alexander said. "I'm a retired computer programmer."

"And I'm a monk," Richard said. "I live at Christ in the Desert." He referred to a monastery about thirty miles north of Santa Fe.

Frank hid his surprise. "I assumed the two of you were together."

"We are," Alexander said. "I often go on weekend retreats to the monastery. That's where Brother Richard and I became friends." Alexander referred to the practice of leaving the clamor of everyday life and spending time in the quiet of a monastery, meditating to achieve spiritual focus.

"Alexander doesn't drive well at night anymore," Brother Richard said. "So I went down to Albuquerque to get him. This opera has a subject of obvious interest to us."

What he meant was soon explained as the after-dinner lecture began. An elegant woman stood at a podium and explained that *Dialogues of the Carmelites* was based on a real event during the French Revolution when a convent of Carmelite nuns was executed during the anti-Catholic frenzy of the Reign of Terror. The composer, the speaker explained, used the incident as a way of exploring the relationship between religion and politics.

As the lecture concluded, Frank wished that he'd followed Alexander and Brother Richard's example, abstaining from the wine, which had made him sleepy.

The group got up to walk from the tent to the opera house.

"It was good to chat with you," Frank said.

"Same here," Brother Richard said.

By then it was half past eight. Santa Fe's operas usually started at nine. Darkness was gathering. Alexander and Brother Richard proceeded into the gloom, while Frank and Debby went to restrooms near the tent.

Minutes later, after a chilly walk, Frank and Debby entered the opera house, made their way through the crowd, found the row they were in, and stopped in surprise.

Alexander and Brother Richard were in the same row, five seats from Frank and Debby.

Smiling, the two men looked up from their programs.

"Small world," Debby said, smiling in return.

"Isn't it," Alexander agreed. Frail, he shivered as the wind increased outside, gusting through the open spaces on each side of the opera house.

"Could be a better night," Brother Richard said. "Let's hope the opera's worth it."

Frank and Debby took their seats. A row ahead, a well-coiffed woman in a flimsy evening gown hugged herself, typical of many in the audience, presumably visitors who hadn't been warned about Santa Fe's sudden temperature drops.

As the wind keened, Debby looked over at Alexander, noticing that he shivered more violently.

"I'll lend him our blanket," she told Frank.

"Good idea."

The five intervening seats remained empty. Debby went over, offered the blanket, which Alexander gladly took, and held out the thermos of hot chocolate, which he also took.

"Bless you, how thoughtful."

"My good deed for the day," Debby said when she came back.

* * *

Ten minutes into the opera, Frank wished that he'd stayed with his friends in Los Angeles. *Dialogues of the Carmelites* turned out to be aptly named, for the cast droned its musical lines in a dreary operatic approximation of dialogue. Although the female singers needed to lower their pitch to accommodate the atonal effects, they nonetheless gave the effect of screeching.

Worse was the libretto, which had been translated into English and took one of the most *un*spiritual approaches to religion that Frank had encountered, claiming that the Carmelite nuns were emotional invalids dominated by a masochistic abbess who convinced her charges to linger and wait to be executed so that she could prove how powerfully she controlled them.

Halfway through the first act, lightning flashed. The storm clouds unloaded, sending a torrent past the open sides of the opera house, causing the audience in those sections to retreat up the aisles.

Nature as critic, Frank thought.

He had a headache by the time the seemingly interminable first act ended. Ushers hurried to the wet seats near the open sides, toweling them. As Frank and Debby stood, they found Alexander and Brother Richard coming over.

"I don't know how I'd have gotten through that act without your charity," the elderly man said, looking even colder.

"A terrible opera," Brother Richard added. "You should have stayed in Los Angeles."

"Don't I wish."

"Thanks for the blanket and the thermos." Alexander returned them. "We're going home."

"That bad?"

"Worse."

"Well, we enjoyed meeting you."

"Same here," Brother Richard said. "God bless."

They disappeared among the crowd.

"Well, if I'm going to be able to sit through the second act, I'd better stretch my legs," Frank said.

"You're determined to stay?" Debby asked.

"After all the trouble I went through to get here? This damned opera isn't going to beat me."

They followed the crowd to an outside balcony. The rain had again stopped. There were puddles in the courtyard below them, where well-dressed men and women drank cocktails, coffee, or hot chocolate. In the distance, lightning lit the mountains. Everybody oohed and aahed.

Frank shivered, then pointed at something in the courtyard. "Look."

About a third of the audience was leaving through the front gate. But coming from the opposite direction, from the parking lot, Alexander and Brother Richard emerged from the darkness, making their way through the courtyard. What puzzled Frank wasn't that they had left and were coming back. Rather it was that a spotlight seemed to be following them, outlining them, drawing Frank's attention to their progress through the crowd. They almost glowed.

The two men went into the gift shop across from the balcony. Almost immediately they returned without having bought anything and again made their way through the crowd. They disappeared into the darkness past the gate.

"What was *that* all about?" Debby asked.

"I have no idea." Frank couldn't help yawning.

"Tired?"

"Very."

"Me too."

Frank yawned again. "Know what? If this opera's bad enough

for Alexander and Brother Richard to leave, I'm going to bow to their superior taste."

"After all the trouble you took?"

"It takes a real man to admit a mistake."

"That 'real man' stuff turns me on. Yeah, let's go home."

The parking lot was well lit. Even so, the low clouds made everything gloomy as Frank and Debby stepped over puddles, trying to find their car.

"Has to be around here someplace." Frank sensed that the angry sky was going to unload again. "Keep that umbrella handy."

Behind him, from the theater, he heard faint music as the orchestra started the second act. The only two people in the parking lot, he and Debby walked along another row of cars when movement to the left attracted his attention. He turned toward the edge of the lot, seeing two men emerge from the darkness and approach them.

Alexander and Brother Richard.

"What are *you* doing here?" Frank asked in surprise. "You left ahead of us."

"We're looking for our car," Alexander told him.

"There." Brother Richard pointed. "Over there."

With a tingle of amazement, Frank saw that his SUV was next to the sedan that Brother Richard indicated.

"Good heavens," Debby murmured.

Thunder rumbled, as the four of them went to their two cars.

"Drive safely." Alexander eased his frail body into the passenger seat.

"You, too," Frank said.

Brother Richard got behind the steering wheel.

Watching them drive away, Frank said, "Can you believe that? All those coincidences?"

"Weird," Debby said.

Following them down the winding road that led to Route 285, they watched Alexander's headlights find an opening in the speedy traffic. The sedan headed north.

"And weird again," Frank said.

"What do you mean?" Debby asked.

"They told us Alexander lived in Albuquerque and that Brother Richard had driven down there to get him."

"So?"

"Why are they going in the opposite direction, north instead of south?"

"Maybe Alexander's too tired for a long drive and they're taking a shorter trip up to the monastery."

"Sure."

Another thunderstorm hit just as they arrived home.

The next morning Frank opened the *Santa Fe New Mexican* and found an article about the return of the monsoons. A weather expert commented that the storms were expected to linger for several weeks and would help to replenish the city's reservoirs, which were low because of a dry spring. A forest-service official hoped that the rains would reduce the risk of fires in the mountains. Along with the good news, however, there had been numerous traffic accidents, including one that had killed two men the previous evening.

One of the victims had been a monk, Brother Richard Braddock, who lived at Christ in the Desert Monastery, while the other victim had been a companion, Alexander Lane, from Albuquerque.

"No," Frank said.

Debby peered up. "What's the matter?"

"Those two men we met last night. It looks like they got killed."

"What?"

"In a traffic accident. After they left the opera." Frank quoted from the story. "'Wet pavement is blamed for causing a pickup truck to lose control Saturday evening and slam into a vehicle driven by Brother Richard Braddock on Route 285 one mile south of the Santa Fe Opera exit.'"

"South of the opera exit? But we saw them go north."

Frank stared. "You're right. They *couldn't* have been hit south of the exit." He reread the story to make sure he'd gotten the details right. "'Last evening'?"

"What's wrong?"

"'*Saturday evening*'? That doesn't make sense." Frank went into the kitchen, looked for a number in the phone book, and pressed buttons on his cell phone.

"State Police," a man's Hispanic-accented voice answered.

Frank explained what he needed to know.

"Are you a relative of the victims?"

"No," Frank said. "But I think I met them at the opera last night."

The voice paused. Frank heard a page being turned, as if the officer were reading the report.

"Not likely," the voice said.

"Why not?"

"The operas usually start at nine, I hear."

"Yes."

"This accident happened almost two and a half hours before that. At six-forty."

"No," Frank said. "At the opera, I talked to a man named Richard who said he was a monk at Christ in the Desert. He had a friend named Alexander, who lived in Albuquerque. That matches the details in the newspaper."

"Sure does, but it couldn't have been them, because there's no mistake—the accident happened at six-forty. Must have been two other guys named Richard and Alexander."

Frank swallowed. "Yes, it must have been two others." He set down the phone.

"Are you okay?" Debby asked. "You just turned pale."

"Do you remember when we were driving to the opera last night, we passed an accident?"

Debby nodded, puzzled.

"You saw a body with a sheet over it being loaded into an ambulance. There were actually *two* bodies."

"Two?"

"I think we'd better take a drive to Christ in the Desert."

A map led them through a red canyon studded with juniper trees. With a wary eye toward new storm clouds, Frank rounded a curve and navigated the narrow, muddy road down to a small pueblo-style monastery on the edge of the Chama River.

When he and Debby got out of their SUV, no one was in sight.

A breeze gathered strength, scraping branches together. Otherwise there was almost no sound.

"Sure is quiet," Debby said.

"Looks deserted. You'd think somebody would have been curious about an approaching car."

"I think I hear something." Debby turned toward the church.

"We pray to the Lord," a distant voice echoed from inside.

"Lord, hear our prayers," other distant voices replied.

"We'd better not intrude. Let's wait until they're finished," Frank said.

Quiet, they leaned against the SUV, surveying the red cliffs on one side and the muddy, swollen river on the other.

Storm clouds thickened.

"Looks like we'll have to go inside soon whether we want to or not," Debby said.

The church's front door opened. A bearded man in a monk's robe stepped out, noticed Frank and Debby, and approached them. Although his expression was somber, his eyes communicated the same inner stillness that Richard had the night before.

"I'm Brother Sebastian," the man said. "May I help you?"

Frank and Debby introduced themselves.

"We're from Santa Fe," Frank said. "Last night something odd happened, and we're hoping you might help explain it."

Brother Sebastian, looking puzzled, waited for them to continue.

"Yesterday . . ." Debby looked down at her hands. "Was a monk from here killed in a car accident?"

Brother Sebastian's eyes lost their luster. "I just came back from identifying his body. We've been saying prayers for him. I wish he'd never been given permission."

"Permission?"

"We're Benedictines. We're committed to prayer and work. We vowed to live the rest of our lives here. But that doesn't mean we're cloistered. Some of us even have driver's licenses. With special permission, we're sometimes allowed to leave the monastery—to see a doctor, for example. Or, in yesterday's case, Brother Richard was given permission to drive down to Albuquerque, get a friend who often comes for retreats here, and attend the opera, which has a religious theme and which we thought might have a spiritual benefit."

"It wasn't very spiritual," Debby said. She explained about the bleak nature of the opera and then said, "Last night at the theater we met a man named Richard who said he was a monk here. He had an elderly friend named Alexander who said Richard had driven him up from Albuquerque."

"Yes, Brother Richard's friend was named Alexander."

"They sat next to us at a pre-opera dinner," Debby said. "Then it turned out they were just a few seats away from us in the same row at the opera. When we left early, we crossed paths with them in the parking lot. Their car was next to ours. The whole thing felt strange."

"And strangest of all,"" Frank said, speaking quickly, "the state police say Brother Richard and his friend Alexander died at six-forty, south of the opera house, so how could we have met them at the opera and watched them drive north afterward?"

Brother Sebastian's inner stillness changed to unease. "Perhaps you're misremembering the names."

"I'm sure I wouldn't misremember that one of them said he was a monk here," Frank said.

"Perhaps the newspaper got the time and place of the accident wrong. Perhaps it happened *after* the opera."

"No," Frank said. "I phoned the state police. They agree with the newspaper. The accident happened at six-forty."

"Then you couldn't have met Brother Richard and his friend at the opera."

"It certainly seems that way," Debby said. "But this is making us crazy. To help us stop thinking about this, if you have a photograph of Brother Richard, would you mind showing it to us?"

Brother Sebastian studied them. "Superstition isn't the same as spirituality."

"Believe me, we're not superstitious," Frank said.

Brother Sebastian studied them another long moment. "Wait here, please."

Five minutes later the monk returned. The wind was stronger, tugging at his brown robe and kicking up red dust. He held a folded newspaper.

"A journalist from Santa Fe came here last summer to write a story about us. We saw no harm in it, especially if it encouraged troubled people to attend retreats here." Brother Sebastian opened the newspaper and showed Frank and Debby a color picture of a man in robes standing outside the church.

Frank and Debby stepped closer. The photograph was faded, but there was no mistaking what they saw.

"Yes," Frank said. "That's the man we met at the opera last night." The wind brought a chill.

"No," Brother Sebastian said. "Unless the state police are wrong about the time and place of the accident, what you're telling me isn't possible. Superstition *isn't* the same as spirituality."

I don't care how logical he insists on being," Frank said. "Something happened to us." Guiding the SUV along the muddy road, he added, "Last night, do you remember how bad the storm was when we arrived home?"

"Yes. I was glad we weren't on the road."

"Right. The storm didn't quit until after midnight. It shook the house. If we hadn't left the opera early, we'd have been caught in it. The newspaper said there were several accidents."

"What are you getting at?" Debby asked.

"If Brother Sebastian heard me now, he'd say I was definitely superstitious. Do you suppose . . ."

"Just tell me what you're thinking."

Frank forced himself to continue. "Alexander and Brother Richard gave us the idea of leaving early. We followed them. As crazy as it sounds, if we'd stayed for the entire opera and driven home in the storm, do you suppose we might have been killed?"

"Are you actually suggesting they saved our lives? Two ghosts?"

"Not when you put it that way."

"It's impossible to know what might have happened if we'd driven home later," Debby said firmly.

"Right. And as for ghosts . . ." Frank's voice drifted off. He reached the solid footing of the highway and headed back to Santa Fe.

* * *

One year later, Frank again saw Alexander and Brother Richard.

It was a Saturday morning in late August. He and Debby were in downtown Santa Fe, buying vegetables at the farmers' market. As they carried their sacks toward where they'd parked on a side street, Frank saw a short, slight, elderly man with white hair and a matching goatee. Next to him was a tall, well-built young man, with short, dark hair and a square-jawed face. Unusual in the farmers' market atmosphere at nine in the morning, they both wore dark suits and white shirts. Their eyes were very clear.

"Those two men over there," Frank said, pausing.

"Who?" Debby asked. "Where?"

"Next to the bakery stand over there. An old guy and a young guy. You can't miss them. They're wearing black suits."

"I don't notice any—"

"They're staring straight at us. I feel like I've seen them before. They have a . . ."

"Have a what?"

"Glow. My God, do you remember the two guys from . . ."

As Frank moved toward them, they turned and walked into the crowd.

He increased speed.

"What are you doing?" Debby called.

Frank caught a glimpse of the black suits within the crowd, but no matter how urgently he tried to push past people buying from various stands, he couldn't get closer.

"Wait!"

Vaguely aware of people staring at him, he saw the black suits disappear in the crowd. After another minute of searching, he had no idea which direction to take.

Baffled, Debby reached him.

"The two guys from the opera," Frank explained. "It was them."

"The opera?"

"Don't you remember?"

People bumped past him, carrying sacks. Frank stepped onto a crate and scanned the crowd, looking for two men in black suits, but all he saw were people in shorts and T-shirts.

"Damn it, I had so many questions."

Debby looked at him strangely.

Tires squealed. Metal and glass shattered. A woman screamed.

Frank ran toward a side street. Peering through the crowd, he and Debby saw what used to be their SUV. A pickup truck had slammed into it. A woman lay on the pavement, next to a bicycle, its wheels spinning.

"I saw the whole thing," a man said. "The truck was weaving. Driver must be drunk. He swerved to avoid the girl on the bicycle and hit that car parked over there. It's a lucky thing no one was killed."

If I hadn't noticed them," Frank said, watching a tow truck haul their SUV away, "if they hadn't distracted me, we'd have been at our car when the accident happened. They saved us. Saved us for a second time."

"I didn't see them. The opera? How could it be the same two men?"

The third time Frank noticed them was five years later. Thursday. December 10. Seven P.M. Debby had been recovering from a miscarriage, her fourth in their fifteen-year marriage. Finally accepting that they would never have children of their own, they discussed the possibility of adopting. Now that Debby felt well enough to leave the house, Frank tried to raise her spirits by taking her to a restaurant that had recently opened and was receiving fabulous reviews.

The restaurant was near Santa Fe's historic plaza, so after they parked, they walked slightly out of their way to appreciate the holiday lights on the trees and the pueblo-style buildings.

"God, I love this town," Frank said. Snow started to fall. "Are you warm enough?"

"Yes." Debby put her hood up.

"Those two guys can't be," Frank said, noticing the only two other people in the area.

"Where?"

"There. Over by the museum. All they're wearing is suits."

Frank realized that one of them was short, slight, and elderly, with white hair and a matching goatee. Next to him was a tall, well-built young man, with short, dark hair and a square-jawed face.

"My God, it's them," he said.

"Who?"

Even at a distance, their eyes were intense.

"Hey!" he called, "Wait. I want to talk to you."

They turned and walked away.

"Stop!"

They receded into the falling snow.

Frank hurried toward them, leaving the plaza, heading along a quiet street. The snow fell harder.

"Frank!" Debby called.

He looked back. "They went toward the restaurant!"

"Frank!" This time the word came from Alexander where he waited with Brother Richard in front of the restaurant.

Frank stepped toward them and felt his shoes slip on ice under the snow. He arched backward. His skull shattered against a lamppost.

Standing next to Alexander and Brother Richard, Frank watched Debby slump beside his body, sobbing. A siren wailed in the distance. People emerged from the restaurant and approached in shock.

Oddly numb, Frank couldn't feel the cold or the snow falling on him. "I'm dead?"

"Yes," the elderly man said.

"No."

"Yes," the young man said.

"I don't want to leave my wife."

"We understand," Alexander said. "We had people we didn't want to leave either."

Snow fell on Debby, covering her coat as she sobbed next to Frank's body. Bystanders gathered around her.

"Ice under the snow?" Frank asked. "I died because of a crazy accident?"

"Everything in life is an accident."

"But you lured me toward it. You distracted me so I'd walk faster than I should have in the snow. I told Debby you were guarding us, but she didn't believe me."

"She was right. We're not your guardians."

"Then what *are* you?"

"Your companions. We stopped you from dying when you weren't supposed to, and we helped you to die when it was your time," Alexander said.

"We died as you drove past our wrecked car on the highway, going to the opera," Brother Richard continued. "The rule is, you bond to someone in the vicinity of where you die. Then you help that person die when he or she is supposed to, and you stop it from happening sooner than it's supposed to. Everything in its time."

"The opera?"

"You weren't supposed to be there. The storms, the difficulty of flying home from Los Angeles, they were supposed to make you stay away. When you went to such extreme efforts to come back to Santa Fe and go to the opera, we had to convince you to leave early."

"You're saying Debby and I would have been killed in a car accident if we stayed until the opera was finished?"

"Yes. In a crash in the storm. But only you. Your wife would have survived."

"And at the farmers' market?"

"You'd have been killed when the truck swerved to avoid the bicyclist."

"Only me?"

"Yes. Again your wife would have survived."

"I don't want to leave her," Frank said.

"Everybody dies. But in this case, you won't be leaving her. She was so near you when you died that you're now her companion."

Frank slowly absorbed this information. "I can be with her until she dies?"

"Until you make sure that she dies when she's supposed to," Brother Richard said. "Eight months from now, she will die falling from a stepladder. Unless you stop her. Because that's not her time. Six years from now, she will die in a fire. Unless you stop her from going to a particular hotel. Because, again, that's not her time."

"When *will* she die?"

"Twelve years from now. From cancer. That will take its natural course. You won't need to assist her."

Frank's heart felt broken.

"She'll have remarried by then. She and her new husband will adopt a little boy. Because you love her, you'll share her happiness. Afterward, she, too, will become someone's companion."

"And after we fulfill our duty?" Frank asked.

"We're allowed to find peace."

Frank gazed at his sobbing wife as she kneeled beside his body. Blood flowed from his skull, congealing in the cold.

"One day I'll be allowed to talk to her as you and I are talking?"

"Yes."

"But in the meantime, she'll eventually love someone else and adopt a child?"

"Yes."

"For fifteen years, I was her companion. All I want is for her to be happy. Even if it means not sharing her happiness . . ."

Frank at last felt something: the sting of tears on his cheeks.

"I'll be glad to be a different sort of companion to her for the rest of her life."

About "The Companions"

I intended "The Companions" as a reverse take on Ray Bradbury's "The Crowd." The story is very personal. Everything that occurs in the first part of the story, all the events at the opera, actually happened to my wife and me. It was one of the eeriest evenings of my life, hurrying from L.A. to go to the opera, battling storms, meeting the old and young man (the younger man from Christ in the Desert) at the dinner, then sitting next to them at the opera, and then leaving the opera because of them, only to find that their car was parked next to ours. I began to think that perhaps my wife and I had guardian angels, that we were meant to leave the opera early to escape the storms, that I was in the land of Ray Bradbury.

—David Morrell

THE EXCHANGE

Thomas F. Monteleone

Jim Holloway was on fire.

Burning with the inexhaustible fuel of youth, fired by the bellows of imagination. Actor, writer, magician, inventor—his ambitions and his dreams as scattered as the stars in a midnight sky. At the advanced age of fifteen, he'd somehow managed to drag the sense of wonder about the world from his earliest years into adolescence, and he attacked each morning with a need to do something special—that day, and every other to follow. Something new and different before nightfall.

Every day.

The kids in his high school mostly thought he was an odd duck, but he didn't care. His sun-bright blond hair and thick horn-rimmed glasses gave him a striking, memorable appearance, but it was when he spoke that people tended to pay closer attention. Jim had a . . . a *reverence* in his voice when he talked about the world he perceived. His curiosity stretched from the magic life in a drop of water to the mysteries of Mars.

He'd realized that life was an endless quest, full of discovery and adventure, if he would only allow it to be so.

Alone in an unfamiliar city, he walked its avenues in search of the shop of none other than Maestro the Magician. Ads in the back pages of *Amazing Stories* promised miracles of illusion from an address in Providence, Rhode Island, and from that arcane location, Jim had received "The Secret of the Oriental Rings." Because of a family trip, he now had the chance of a lifetime—to actually roam the shop's shadowy aisles, to uncover its treasures firsthand.

Other than a January wind to drive him through the streets, he had no idea where he was going. The cold air cut through him like an assassin's blade, but he didn't care. It was 1937 and Jim Holloway was on an adventure!

Turning a corner, pulling the collar of his coat closer to his neck, he encountered a palace of dreams—the Majestic Theater on Washington Street. A massive statement of stone, like a temple from a forgotten age, its marquee spoke to Jim: THINGS TO COME. He'd seen the film when it premiered in Los Angeles, but encountering it here in this cold New England town made his pulse jump. Yes, he thought with a smile, there are certainly things to come—good things, wondrous and full of magic. He surged past the box office empowered by his endless optimism.

But things changed when he spotted the thin man.

At the far corner, a willowy figure struggled to step up onto the curb, then collapsed like a wind-beaten scarecrow. It happened so quickly, James reacted without thinking. He rushed along the sidewalk to where the man lay motionless, his pipestem legs folded beneath him at alarming angles.

"Are you all right?" said James, leaning down to touch the man's bony shoulder.

"I . . . don't know if that's a valid question." The man looked up with a dour expression. He could have been thirty or sixty—there was no way to tell under the shadowing brim of his fedora.

"Let me help you up." Jim extended his hand, grabbed the

man's, and gently pulled, surprised at the lack of resistance. So light and frail he seemed, as if his bones were bird-hollow.

Slowly, the man rose, pausing to gather up a package he'd dropped.

"I'll get that," said Jim as he scooped up the brown-paper parcel secured with tape and string. One corner had torn open to reveal a sheaf of stationery full of tight penmanship.

Slowly, the man gained his feet, absently brushed his trousers. Jim noticed that although the man was wearing a shirt and tie, his topcoat appeared thin and worn—and beyond that, he felt an essential *sadness* about this man.

Sadness . . . as if just by touching him, Jim felt he knew this brittle man.

Finally standing on his own, the man reached out for the torn package. "Thank you. Thank you very much. I am suffering from the grippe, I fear, and it has left me weak."

Jim managed a weak smile. "I'm not surprised—if it's always this cold around here . . ."

The man looked down at him, his face narrow as a hatchet. "Obviously, you're not from New England."

"Nope . . . Los Angeles, California! It's a boomtown, my father says."

The man seemed not to be listening as he inspected the damage to his package. "I've got to mend this before I can mail it," he muttered. He took a step down the sidewalk and paused as his ankle gave way.

Catching him by the elbow, Jim buoyed him up. "Hey, mister, I think I'd better help you."

"Nonsense, I'm fine. The postal office is nearby. I'll be fine."

Jim shrugged. "Okay by me, but how about if I just walk along with you a little while."

"Don't you have a previous destination?" The man spoke in precise clipped tones, as if always aware of each word he chose. He had a formal bearing, as if he'd time-traveled from an earlier age.

"Not really. I've been trying to find a store. Maestro's Magical Shop of Wonders—you heard of it?"

The man paused his slow and deliberate gait. "You're a magician?"

"Well, sorta. I mean, I want to be a *real* one someday!"

The man nodded. "Well, I have some sorrowful news for you, young man. There *is* no magical shop—"

"What?" Jim felt something *ping* in his heart. No shop? That just wasn't possible! "What do you mean?"

The man sighed. "I have friends who are aficionados of illusion and theatrics. Maestro's is a mail-order concern."

"I don't understand." Jim couldn't conceal the ache in his voice.

"No shop, just a warehouse where immigrants pack and ship the orders they get."

"But the ads say—"

The man waved him off as they walked slowly toward the next intersection. "The ads, they are part of the illusion, so to speak. Do you think a famous performer such as Maestro would actually have the time, or the inclination, to be a *shopkeeper*?"

Jim noticed he'd intoned that last word as if he could have just as well have said *leper*.

"Nah, I guess you're right." Although he still supported the thin man with a deft touch at his elbow, Jim felt something sag within himself. He felt embarrassed when he replayed his oft-thought fantasy of actually meeting the great Maestro. Jeez, he felt like an idiot. But he also felt something far worse—a sense of terrible loss, of a dream dashed upon the rocks of a careless world. As Jim paced his companion, he fought the temptation to surrender to such defeat.

"We turn here," said the man, indicating a left at the corner. "It's not much farther."

As they entered a street lined with giant oaks and shuttered Victorian homes, Jim was reminded of Green Town—his midwestern birthplace. He felt a flutter of memory that he would one day recognize as nostalgia, then tried to forget about the magic shop that never was.

Walking another block in silence, Jim listened to the man's labored breath, punctuated by a series of greasy coughs. He carried his package against his chest as if it were a shield or a talisman, which fired Jim's curiosity all the more. He had to know what secrets lay beneath the crinkled brown wrapper, and so he simply asked.

"It's a partial manuscript," said the man. "Part of a novel I've been badgered into starting."

A smile widened on Jim's full face. "Really? Are you a . . . *writer*?"

The man shrugged. "Of a sort. Although some such as that mountebank Tarkington would never think so . . ."

Jim had no idea what he was talking about, but he pushed on. "What do you write?"

For the first time since their encounter, the man enacted the suggestion of smile, a slight grin. "Articles on astronomy. Letters mostly. *Lots* of letters to lots of friends. But . . . I've done more than a handful of stories and novelettes for the shudder pulps."

Jim almost grabbed him by his broomstick arm. "Stories? You write fiction? That's what *I* want to do!"

"I thought you wanted to be a magician . . ."

"Well, that too! But I love Buck Rogers and H. G. Wells and Poe, and I can't forget Burroughs . . ."

"You have . . . an energy," said the man, pausing to look at Jim as though noticing him for the first time, "that I find familiar. What's your name, boy?"

"James Holloway, but I like just plain Jim just fine." He extended his hand as his mother had taught him to do.

"And I am Phillips Howard. I feel as though we may have been somehow fated to meet, just-plain-Jim."

Their handshake was brief, but long enough for Jim to sense the weakness in Phillips's grip. It was not that limp, dead fish that some people offered but an attempt at strength forever lost. Again, Jim felt overwhelmed by an essential sadness that seemed to radiate from this desiccated man who looked far older than his years.

After departing the post office, Jim suggested they go to the nearest coffee shop, and Phillips couldn't hide his obvious surprise.

"Upon that, I have several questions. How are you to afford the extravagance? And are you not a bit young to be using caffeine?"

Jim smiled as they returned to the sidewalk. "Well, I've got the money I'd saved for Maestro's, and I figured it was about time I started drinking coffee."

Phillips regarded him for a moment, then nodded his head. "Very well then. There's a café down this way. It is run by some Italians, but the coffee is good on a cold day like this."

As they walked in silence, Jim wondered about a man who considered cups of coffee an outrageous expense. This stiff, spindly man—where did he live? *How* did he live? Jim couldn't imagine him going home to a cheery family in one of the clapboard houses that lined these cozy streets. Was he really a writer, or was he just an older version of Jim? A dreamer of lives not yet, and maybe never, lived.

The coffee shop was not crowded, and Phillips selected a table by the window where thin sunlight promised additional comfort. There was a pleasant conversational drone of other patrons mixed with the accented cries of the staff. Jim liked the frenetic charm of the place and allowed the waiter to recommend cappuccino and biscotti for both of them.

"Tell me about your stories," said Jim. "Maybe I've read them already."

Phillips looked off through the window as if seeking a reply somewhere in the distance. Then finally: "I doubt it. They appear infrequently and seem to be a strangely acquired taste."

"What made you want to write?" Jim had never met anyone who'd actually written anything, much less been published. Imagining he might never have this chance again, he let loose his curiosity and his questions.

"I don't think I had much choice in the matter. If you write, it is because you *must*. Does that make sense?"

"Sure! I feel that way all the time. I've been trying to write comics and draw them myself . . . when I'm not writing regular stories, that is. It's like, well, like there's the stuff of story all around us, and somebody's got to recognize them, and then *tell* them, right?"

Phillips's narrow face brightened for the briefest of instants. It was such an unnatural look for a man of such grim aspect that Jim almost laughed. "I've never heard the process explained exactly like that, but I think it certainly obtains."

"You are *so* lucky," said Jim. The sentiment just burst out of him, fueled by equal parts admiration and envy. "To see your name in print. I'd give anything to do that."

"I already have . . . and I fear it's not worth it."

"What?" Jim was stunned.

"Have you never been admonished to be careful what you wish for?"

"I don't think so. Besides, who cares? What you do is special—it's magic is what it is!"

Phillips sipped from his large cup, savoring the rich brew as he paused to order his thoughts. "You use that word with great frequency."

"What word?" Jim felt off balance, confused.

"Let me tell you something, Jim Holloway. You seem to be on some kind of frantic mission to . . . to capture lightning in a bottle. But just as there is no magic shop in Providence, there is no magic out in the world for the taking."

"I don't think I follow . . ." Jim let his voice trail off as Phillips leaned forward, his gray eyes focused on him.

"There's only one place you'll find any magic, and that's in *here*." Phillips tapped a fist lightly to his own concave chest. "And it's a bit of a curse to be placed in charge of it."

Jim's expression must have belied his lack of comprehension. When he couldn't find a proper reply, Phillips continued: "We are the only sad sorcerers you will ever know. Most of us only know one trick, and the true illusion is that we always believe we are the master of many."

Jim wasn't sure he understood any of what Phillips intended, but he was afraid to admit it. His companion was issuing some kind of strange warning, it seemed, but Jim was having none of that. Especially from another writer! Incredibly, he found himself getting upset with Phillips, who seemed to be growing insubstantial in the afternoon light, as if he might fade away like an unpleasant fog.

And so he said: "You sound—I don't know—bitter? Or even angry."

Phillips nodded as though he'd gotten the reaction he'd sought. "If I am guilty of those emotions, I assure you I have my reasons."

"What possible reason could you have?"

"If you are observant, you already know I have neither means nor health. Although I tell myself I suffer from a common ailment, the lie does not banish the thing that is consuming me."

And just like that, it made sense to Jim. He felt twice the fool. He'd believed his own lie—the greatest falsehood of adolescence—that he would live forever.

As he struggled for the appropriate response, he was shocked to hear himself talking—the words coming from a place where thoughts are replaced by feelings. "And you think your art has destroyed you?"

Phillips considered the question—one he'd most likely never been asked. Then: "I think that's as accurate as it is perceptive."

Jim beamed. "I think you're wrong. I think that's what gave you life, what gave you the only true pleasure we—how'd you put it?—*'sad sorcerers'* can have!"

Phillips again did his best imitation of a smile. "You are an unexpected palliative, young man. How could you possibly know already that creation is the true and only machinery of joy?"

Now it was Jim's turn to pause. "I don't think I did . . ."

Phillips leaned forward, touched the sleeve of Jim's peacoat, then held up his hand. It was performed as though part of a ritual. "I think something important has happened this day. Irony is a powerful force, is it not? You came to this place in search of something you didn't know you even needed. It is something I fear I've lost, and yet I am still able to give it to you. Does that make sense?"

Jim grinned his schoolboy grin. This time he understood perfectly. "I came here looking for one thing, but I found something else."

"As did I." Phillips nodded gravely. "The tragedy of life is not that men die, but rather that most allow their dreams to expire while they still live."

Jim felt transformed by this exchange, as well as an odd connection to this strange, feeble man. Signaling the waiter to refill their cups, Jim felt himself smiling at the man he now considered a friend.

He was certain they still had much to discuss.

About "The Exchange"

Okay, so I took liberties with reality (at least the one with which we're most familiar) and postulated an encounter that never happened. Which is one of the simplest functions of fiction, right? How else are we ever going to slip our tethers and check out the nightlife in any of the infinite parallel universes? The real concern for me is why I even tried to make this story work.

And I think it's pretty simple, really.

During my formative years I received a couple of literary two-by-fours to the head, delivered by the doppelgängers of Jim Holloway and Phillips Howard. When I read *Something Wicked This Way Comes,* the characters of Jim Nightshade and Will Holloway were instantly familiar to me—because they were *me.* Bradbury became one of my favorite writers because I believed that, somehow, he *knew* me. In a dissimilar but equally powerful way, when I read my first collection of Howard Phillips Lovecraft's stories, he became one of my seminal writers because he knew how to *scare* me.

In totally different ways, both Ray Bradbury and H. P. Lovecraft showed me the power of language and the sheer, raw energy of imagination. To say they *inspired* me seems silly and inadequate—rather, they both demanded something of me. They forced me to face the silly ideas I entertained about someday doing something unique . . . and to do something about it.

I'd like to think both of them made an exchange with me as well, and while I didn't do as well as either of my trading partners, I'm humbled and honored to be here right now.

Thanks, Ray. It would have never happened without you.

—Thomas F. Monteleone

CAT ON A BAD COUCH

Lee Martin

I'll admit I was drunk when I bought it, so I shouldn't blame anyone else for my error in judgment, my lack of taste, my total disregard for the aesthetics of fabric and color and design necessary to what my wife, Vonnie, used to call the healing home. She got that from a book she read, one that encouraged her to use aromatherapy, light, feng shui, color, and natural materials to create a space where she and I would feel connected to earth, air, and each other. It was our last chance, though of course we didn't know it then. All we knew was that we'd started to lose sight of what first brought us together—I couldn't even have said what that something was—and still we were tongue-tied and dumb. If there were words that might have made a difference, we were having trouble finding them.

"A healing home is a happy home," Vonnie said one day, and I agreed I'd give it a shot.

Then we got Henry, and everything went to hell in a hurry.

He showed up at our house in late October, just as the days were starting to cool and winter was in the air. A long, skinny tabby with a notch bitten out of his ear, a limp to his roll, a smirk on his face—yes, I swear a cat can smirk—and the most pitiful meow you'd ever want to hear. A croak that made Vonnie fall in love.

"Poor baby," she said. "Where's your house? Do you have a house?"

He was winding himself in and out around her legs, tail straight up in the air, as she stood on the front porch, petting him. I was inside watching through the storm door, and when I opened it to step outside, he saw his chance; he shot the gap, and presto, he was inside.

"Hey," I said, but it was too late.

He'd already curled up on the window seat, smack-dab in the middle of the ramie-covered cushions Vonnie had purchased from IKEA earlier that morning. In an instant, he was asleep. Vonnie and I could see him through the front windows, and I could tell from the way she looked at him there'd be nothing I could say to convince her that a bit-eared, gimpy, smart-mouthed stray was nothing but bad news.

"Oh, my." I heard her intake of breath. She touched me on the arm, and it was one of the few times in more than a year—yes, it had been that long—that we'd touched at all. "Lex," she said to me. "Sweetie, he looks so peaceful there."

I knew then that this scruffy-assed junkyard cat, soon to be named Prince Henry Boo-Boo Ca-Choo, had taken his last fall and landed in the gravy.

He'd been looking for us, Vonnie would say that night as he made himself comfy on our bed, stretched out longways between us, his claws pricking my back. He was home.

But I was telling you about my couch. I bought it one night when I'd been drinking at the Rusty Bucket, drinking more than I should have because it was easier to do that than to go home to Vonnie. What was our problem? I don't imagine there's any way to say it was this or that; it was more a combination of things, one of them being time and what it can do to romance. We'd been together since we were eighteen, and somewhere along the line the thrill went away, and then we were left with the people we really were—I mean the people we were deep down inside—and maybe what we were finding out was that we didn't really like those people. They just didn't match up. That's the best I've been able to do, at least in the time I've had to think about it. People fall out of love. I didn't mean for that to be the case with Vonnie and me, nor I imagine did she, but that's what happened, and maybe—just maybe—the start of the end was when I ducked into the discount furniture store that evening all because that couch, which I could see through the display window, caught my eye.

I walked in, and the salesgirl, a pretty girl with her eyes just a little too close together, asked if she could help me find something.

Lord, the questions people ask, not having any idea what they can mean to a person. This girl was a pleasant sort who smiled a lot and had dimples in her cheeks, and she was so eager to help me find exactly what I needed, I almost told her the truth. I almost said, *Please, help me find my way.*

Instead, I said I'd spotted that couch. "That one." I pointed to a harvest-gold couch with a high back, and a plaid pattern formed from brown and green lines, and kick-pleat skirting around the bottom. "The one with the kick-pleat skirting," I said, and the girl's smile got even wider.

"You know your material, I can see that." She gave me a wink of one of her too-close-together eyes. "I'll have to be on my toes with you."

The store was nearly empty that near to closing. Somewhere toward the back, a radio was playing, some old big-band tune from the forties, a time, if the movies I'd seen were any evidence, when men and women believed in love. I took a glance behind me out the plate-glass display window, and I saw that in the little bit of time that had passed since I'd stepped into the store, the dusk had faded to full dark. It could happen like that. In fact it did every night. In the wink of an eye.

"'Bewitched, Bothered, and Bewildered,'" I said, and the girl gave me a puzzled look. "The song," I said, and then I sang along. I was wild again and beguiled, etc.

And I was too loud for the mostly empty store—I was singing too loud and I was too full of booze—and for the first time, I saw a look of concern pass over the girl's face, as if she feared I might grab her and throw her down and have at her on that couch, which I already knew I was going to buy if for no other reason than to make this all up to her.

She glanced toward the back, looking, I assume, for a co-worker, hoping someone would come to the front of the store so she wouldn't have to be alone with me.

That's when I nearly lost it, knowing I'd caused a nice girl like her alarm, and I said, "I'll take it. The couch. It's exactly what I've been looking for."

The next morning I woke up and went outside to retrieve the *Dispatch* from the front step. That was the first time I saw Mr. Mendes, the man who would become my neighbor across the street.

He was moving in. The HER Realty sign was leaning against the maple tree in the front yard. The previous owners, a Mr. and Mrs. Zambesi, had raked the last of the fallen leaves before bidding the neighborhood fare thee well. No one had been sorry to see them go. They were, in short, a disruption to the generally tranquil cul-de-sac. They were people with tempers, and more than once their arguments had escalated to the point where some of us had called the police. It wasn't uncommon to hear shouting in the middle of the night, doors slamming, glass breaking, car tires squealing. "You're no one I care about," I heard Mrs. Zambesi scream one night. "Do you hear me? No one!"

Our expectations for Mr. Mendes, then, were high. It didn't matter to us that he was a single man. In fact, that was a plus. A single man who led a pleasant and quiet life. At least that was our hope.

The house was a four-bedroom two-story with a brick façade halfway up the front and vinyl siding the rest of the way. The siding was light yellow and the window shutters were green.

A house that said howdy-do and welcome.

The front door was wide open that morning, and a couple of men in sleeveless T-shirts were unloading furniture from a white truck that said TWO MEN AND A TRUCK on the side. Truth in advertising. There they were: two men and their truck.

Mr. Mendes had parked his red Volvo wagon along the curb in front of my house—such a cheery color, red—and was easing a birdcage out of the back. He had a cockatiel inside—a gray-feathered cockatiel with a yellow head and a bright orange spot on each cheek. The bird was whistling and clicking to beat the band, singing and trilling like he was the happiest Gus on this old planet Earth. Mr. Mendes looked quite chipper himself, dressed in crisply pressed navy slacks and a shirt the color of a robin's egg. The crowning touch? A cardigan sweater of white, violet, and sky-blue stripes—vertical stripes along the front and back, and short horizontal hatches on the sleeves. On this day, when the trees were bare and the sky was leaden and there was just enough bite in the air to remind us that soon we'd settle into winter, he and his bird were a glorious sight.

I couldn't help but call out to him. "Hello," I said. "Welcome to Saddlebrook Estates. I'm Lex. I like your sweater."

He looked down at the front of his sweater, as if he'd forgotten what he was wearing. Then he gave me a pleasant grin. "My name is Mendes," he said, "and this is Popcorn."

What a delightful name for a cockatiel, and I said as much.

"Thank you," Mr. Mendes said. "He's the light of my life. I've had him fifteen years."

"Does he talk?"

"Oh, yes, very much."

Mr. Mendes leaned over and said something to the bird. Soon Popcorn's chirpy bird voice rang out. "Touchdown," he said. "Touchdown. Touchdown."

"It's football season," I said with a laugh. "And you know how football-crazy Columbus is. Go, Bucks! You'll be the hit of the neighborhood."

And he was. All because of Popcorn, who charmed the neighbors when they dropped by to bring Mr. Mendes a loaf of bread, a pound cake, some homemade cookies. Mr. Mendes himself was civil but quiet. He withstood the neighbors' visits, but I could tell it was painful for him. He was a man who liked to keep to himself. As the weeks went on, I took note of the way he kept his curtains drawn and how I mostly saw him when he was leaving for work—he did something with computers at Cardinal Health—or coming home.

As winter settled in, we saw each other less frequently, and to be fair, the same could be said about all the neighbors. We were starting to hunker in, holing up for the long haul that was winter in central Ohio, all of us having to face the facts of our own lives.

For a while I thought I might develop a lasting friendship with Mr. Mendes—out of all the neighbors, it seemed to be me, the first to welcome him, with whom he felt most at ease. Chick Hartwell on the corner was too har-de-har-har, a backslapping sort who acted like he'd never had a sad day in his life. How could someone like Mr. Mendes not feel even more down in the mouth about his solitary life in the presence of someone like Chick? Herb Shipley, two doors down from me, was too angry. *Fuck this* and *Fuck that*. Pissed off about the homeowners' association, which told him he couldn't store his garbage can outside his garage. Pissed off about the Buckeyes and their lack of want-it. Just pissed off at the world in general. Then there were the Biminrammers—Benny and Missy—next door to Mr. Mendes, who were clearly incompetent, though cheerily so, and on a dead-straight course toward disaster. They were always asking Mr. Mendes to do them a favor. Maybe they'd locked themselves out of their house and needed to use his phone. Maybe Benny had sliced his thumb open with a carving knife when Missy was at a Mary Kay party, and now he wanted to know if Mr. Mendes would be good enough to drive him to the emergency room.

I, on the other hand, asked nothing of my new neighbor, and for that reason alone he found me to be someone he could confide in.

His own story was a story of heartache. He'd left his native Cuba in 1980 during the Mariel boatlift. Castro, besieged by Cuba's economic problems, agreed that anyone who wanted to leave the country could. Mr. Mendes was fourteen years old and in love with a beautiful girl named Eva. She and her family stayed behind, and he never saw her again. He still thought of her, he told me one evening when we were chatting by the curb. It was nearly dusk and too cold to be standing outside, but we'd both come out to our mailboxes at the same time and he crossed the street to say hello and one thing led to another.

"I wonder what happened to her," he said. "I wonder if she ever thinks about me."

"Forgive me for being too personal," I said, "but surely you've had other loves."

"A few." He shrugged his shoulders. "But nothing to last. No one like her."

At that moment Henry came slinking across the street. He'd been out gallivanting somewhere, and now he was eager for the warmth of home, his food dish, and Vonnie's fussing over him as he stretched out beside her on the new couch.

Perhaps it was something about what Mr. Mendes and I had been discussing there on a winter's evening with the dark settling in and the lights glowing in our neighbors' windows that made him reach down to pet Henry, who promptly hissed at him and lashed out with a claw that scraped Mr. Mendes across the back of his hand.

"I'm so sorry," I said.

"You should keep that cat inside," said Mr. Mendes, and that was the last time I spoke with him that winter.

It was a winter of odd occurrences that further frayed the flimsy threads barely holding Vonnie and me together.

Our phone rang often, and when one of us answered, there was no one on the other end of the line. Nothing you'd think about if it happened occasionally, but something else altogether if it happened three or four nights a week to the point that we finally had to give in and change our number.

Of course, Vonnie accused me of having an affair. Of course, I did the same.

"How could it be a boyfriend or a girlfriend calling?" I finally asked her, "if they're hanging up when either one of us answers?"

"That makes sense."

I could have pressed on, but I decided against it. The truth was neither would accuse the other of infidelity if the accuser hadn't already wondered, him or herself, what that might be like. If Vonnie thought a phone call with no one on the other end was a sign that I'd been unfaithful, then that told me she'd been imagining another life for herself and was looking for a reason to walk out the door.

We hung in there through the holidays. We even managed to find some small degree of pleasure in each other's company—mulling cider, watching Christmas movies on TV, stringing lights around the outside of our house.

Our cul-de-sac was festive with lights and lawn ornaments, even the inflatable kind—Santas in sleighs, snowmen in snow globes, penguins waving, Snoopy wearing a Santa's hat, Winnie-the-Pooh and Tigger decorating a tree.

Mr. Mendes was more restrained, but even he couldn't resist hanging a wreath and putting an electric candle in each of his front windows. One evening I had to knock on his door because the mail carrier had left a piece of his mail in my box by mistake. It was a letter, postmarked Miami and addressed to Mr. Hugo Mendes in a feminine handwriting. I knocked on the door and even rang the bell, but though there were lights on inside, Mr. Mendes never came to see who had decided to call on him. I shaded my eyes and peered through the glass sidelight of the front door. I could see down a hallway to the family room, and there in the corner was Popcorn's cage, the door open. Mr. Mendes had draped the cage with a string of white twinkle lights. I tried the storm door and found it unlocked. I left the letter between it and the front door, sure that Mr. Mendes would find it.

It wasn't long before Vonnie or I began walking into our bedroom to find the ceiling-fan lights on. At first we thought that one of us had been forgetful, neglecting to turn off the lights when leaving the room. We picked up the remote that controlled them and punched them off.

Then one night we went to sleep only to wake up shortly because the lights had come on. I sat up in bed. "Did you?"

Vonnie was lying on her back, staring up at the ceiling as if she were seeing the most amazing thing. "No," she said. "Did you?"

"The battery in the remote must be bad," I told her. I turned off the lights. "We'll replace it tomorrow."

Which we did.

That night, the lights came on again.

"Just take the battery out," she told me.

The next night we came upstairs for bed, and voilà, the lights were on.

"How can that be?" I said. "There's no battery in the remote."

Vonnie shook her head. "This is getting spooky, Lex. This house."

She'd never liked the house. Not even the fifteen years we'd lived there had made her feel at home. It was the most popular style of home in Columbus—a four-bedroom two-story. The bedrooms and two baths upstairs. A formal living room, dining room, kitchen, family room, half bath, and laundry room on the main floor. A neat little box of a house composed of smaller boxes inside. There was no flow, Vonnie said, and I had to admit she was right. The front door opened up to a wall, and each time we had guests and it was time for folks to enter or leave, we all did an excuse-me, squeeze-by, and shuffle in our pitiful entryway. We had more than 2,100 square feet of living space, but because it was split between up and down, and because the living space downstairs was sectioned the way it was, we often felt like we were living in an efficiency apartment.

I'll give Vonnie credit, though. She spruced that house up come the holidays, and our good spirits carried us into January and through most of February. She tried her best to make our house a healing home. We had candles and silk flower arrangements and throw pillows and pottery, and everything was positioned just so. We had Henry, who curled up on the window seat or on the bamboo mat in the family room.

A house with a cat was a peaceful house, Vonnie said.

"Even if that cat's Henry?" I asked.

"Yes, even Henry. Prince Boo-Boo-Ca-Choo."

We were trying.

But this thing with the ceiling-fan lights had us spooked.

"It must be the receiver in the fan going bad," an electrician said when we consulted him. "Get a new one from Home Depot, and I'll install it."

A good fellow working at Home Depot gave us a receiver from an old display model that was like our fan and didn't charge us anything. "This should do the trick," he said.

But it didn't. I took the fan apart, found the receiver that was in it, and saw immediately that the new one wouldn't fit.

That's when Vonnie called the manufacturer, intending to order a new receiver from them. But the customer-service rep on the other end of the line said, "You know there's a code you have to set on the receiver, don't you?" Vonnie reported this all to me once she was off the phone. "There are four pins you can set either up or down in whatever combination you choose. Same with your remote. It has to be set to the same combination. Have you checked that?"

No, we hadn't. The rep explained that all the fans were set to the same combination when they left the factory, and the manufacturer recommended resetting the combination during the installation process. If someone in the neighborhood had the same fan, and if we and that neighbor hadn't changed our combination, it would be possible that the neighbor's remote would control our fan and vice versa.

"Has anyone moved into your neighborhood lately?" the rep wanted to know.

"Mendes," Vonnie said to me with glee in her voice. She even said, "Aha!" And I feared that soon she'd rub her hands together and shout, *Eureka!*

She had no use for Mendes and was only too glad to blame the business with the ceiling fan on him. He was too smug, she said. Him and those flashy clothes and his bright red car and that bird? *What a dog-and-pony trick,* she'd said all the times that autumn when she'd heard the neighbors talking about Popcorn and what a delight he was. *Isn't that a mixed-species metaphor?* I asked her, and she gave me the stink eye. *You know perfectly well what I mean.*

The truth is she was jealous. Everything about Mendes—his clothes, his car, his bird—cast a spotlight onto our own lives and made it impossible to hide from the fact that, despite Vonnie's efforts with interior decorating, there really wasn't anything pretty about us.

Take that couch, for instance. Take Henry, who came home after getting the short end of a number of fights. Sometimes a hind leg was dragging. On other occasions there was blood matting his chest or bite marks on his haunch or a bare spot on his tail. Take my drinking, which left me sullen and closed off. Take the way Vonnie and I lay down in the dark each night, weary with the burden of staying together long past the point when we should have said good-bye. We didn't even have the diversion of the ceiling fan once I flipped the pins and changed the combination.

"Wait a minute," Vonnie said. "If it's indeed Mendes's fan that's been causing the trouble, wouldn't that mean our remote would have been doing the same thing to his?"

"I suppose." I looked out our bedroom window to Mendes's house across the street. "But nothing should go wrong now that I've changed the code."

We stood there awhile with nothing more to say. Then she walked out of the room. I heard her footsteps on the stairs. Spring was coming, but we were at the end.

For some reason, I pointed the remote toward the window

and pressed the button that turned on our fan. To my surprise, Mr. Mendes's garage door began to rise. Surely, it couldn't be because of my remote. Surely, I thought, Mendes himself was opening that door.

Soon the door was fully up, and I saw that the backup lights on Mr. Mendes's Volvo were on, and he was backing down the drive. The garage door lowered itself as he started up the court, and I stood there, trembling, still shaken by what I'd thought was possible.

Then Popcorn disappeared. "Lit out for the wild blue yonder," Vonnie said when she came home one afternoon from grocery shopping at Giant Eagle. "I saw the signs."

"Signs? Do you mean you're psychic? You saw this coming?"

It was late March, and the first warm days of spring were upon us. We had our sliding deck door open, and a breeze stirred the wind chime Vonnie had on a hook in the ceiling above the floor vent. The chime had hung there all winter so that each time the furnace kicked on, the harmonic tones could soothe us. That chime, the Bamboo Wind Dancer, was the last artifact from Vonnie's feng shui days. As winter deepened, she began packing everything up. Gone were the candles and the silk flowers and the pottery and the Zen sand garden and the Buddha fountain. Little by little, our house became Spartan. Dishes disappeared from cabinets. Knickknacks and clothes got boxed up and bundled off to Goodwill. I watched our house get loud with emptiness. Just that morning, before I opened the windows and the doors, I noticed how every little sound—footsteps, throat clearing, doors closing—made an echo. We were living in a cavern.

"Since when have I ever seen anything coming?" she asked me. "I'm talking about the reward signs."

I saw them that afternoon when I went out for a walk—flyers taped to the street sign poles: LOST BIRD! There were yard signs, banners spread between two stakes, driven into the ground at the entrance to Saddlebrook Estates. They advertised a website: www.findpopcorn.com. By evening, there were flyers wedged between screen doors and their frames, or stuffed in behind the red flags on mailboxes throughout the subdivision. I saw Mendes delivering them that afternoon. Apparently, he'd taken off work so he could deliver those flyers. I'd never seen him in such a state. Disheveled. He wore a pair of dark gray sweatpants, the ends of the drawstring flapping loose at his crotch, and a faded maroon polo shirt that may have been fetching once but now was just drab. He had on white socks and a pair of house shoes, the shapeless kind covered with tan corduroy. Nothing like his customary sartorial splendor.

"Mendes!" I called to him from across Appaloosa Court. He was coming down the driveway of the house on the corner, a sheaf of flyers hugged to his chest. I could tell he hadn't shaved or combed his hair. "Mendes," I called again, but he wouldn't stop, wouldn't even look at me. He waved his arm over his head as he went on up the court.

"Like he was telling me to go to hell," I said to Vonnie when I got back to the house. "I know he's upset, but jeezy Pete. Whatever happened to common courtesy?"

"It went out the window," she said. "Flew the coop."

We laughed because that was the story with Popcorn. He saw his chance for daylight, saw all that sky through an open deck door, and he made his break. Vonnie and I laughed and laughed until we were both doubled over, holding our sides. We laughed until our hoots turned into something else, something I couldn't quite identify until Vonnie said,"Lex, I'm done. I can't live with you anymore."

I knew, then, that our laughter had been the hysteria of letting go.

"We've both known it awhile," I said, and she agreed. We were talking quietly now, and after the explosive noise of our hilarity—a percussion that sent Henry running to find somewhere to hide—our voices were too small for the sorts of words we were saying, words you have to say when you're finally at that place where you have no other choice, words you have to find for love passing, for lives once lived together now coming apart. "It's been no picnic these last few years," she said, and I stood there as she counted off all the things that made it so.

My drinking, for one, which I had to admit had become more frequent those last months. "Look at that couch," she said. "You bought that when you were drunk. Just look at that ugly couch."

I didn't know how to explain that I'd bought it because I'd given an innocent salesgirl cause for alarm. I didn't know how to say I'd wanted to prove I was a decent man.

Vonnie went on with her list. The way I'd stopped being her friend, she said. "I used to be able to count on you, Lex." She stopped before she filled in the rest, the part about how I wasn't there for her anymore and hadn't been for some time.

Guilty. We were strangers. Like everyone, we'd set forth with no idea of that ever happening, but it had, and now there we were.

Not for long, though.

"I've found a townhouse," she told me. "I'm moving out."

So there were two stories causing quite a buzz in Saddlebrook Estates that spring—Popcorn was missing, and my wife, after thirty-three years of marriage, had left me. I was fifty-five years old, and I was alone. I didn't even have Henry because the night Vonnie packed as much as she could into her car, saving a space for his carrier, he slipped out the door, and when it came time for her to gather him up, he was nowhere to be found.

"I'm sure he'll come back soon," I told her.

We stood in the driveway in the dark, keeping our voices low because the neighbors were out—the Hartwells and the Shipleys and the Biminrammers, everyone talking about Popcorn and poor Mr. Mendes—and we didn't want them to hear us.

"Call me when he does," she said. She opened the door to her Explorer, an SUV now stuffed with what she'd decided was most important to her, important enough to carry away from our house. She turned back to me. "Call me on my cell."

I stood there a long time after she'd driven away. My life felt strange to me, and I didn't know what to do next.

Then I saw him. Henry. He came from the direction of Mr. Mendes's house, slinking, belly low, across the street. I saw him as he passed through the glow of the streetlight. Then he disappeared into the darkness, and I didn't know where he was until, finally, I felt him rubbing against my leg.

We went inside. I picked up the phone, meaning to call Vonnie's cell, meaning to tell her to come back and get Henry, but then he jumped up on that couch and began primping it with his front paws, making his bed, getting comfortable. He didn't care how ugly that couch was. He just knew it was a good place to sleep after being out on the town, a comfort I'd provided for him. He looked up at me once and meowed without making a sound. Then he closed his eyes and went to sleep, and I couldn't make that call. It was the two of us now.

As the days went on, Vonnie kept calling to see if Henry had come home. "Haven't seen him," I told her. "Are you doing okay?"

"Yes. You?"

"Sure," I said.

But the truth is I was pretty low, and I think it started to get to Henry—the way I moped around. Even though I'd known a long time that things were over between Vonnie and me, I hadn't counted on this tremendous pit of loneliness that invited me to sink into it. To make matters worse, the neighbors were spending all their sympathy on Mr. Mendes and poor, poor Popcorn. Granted, Vonnie and I had never really been close with the Hartwells or the Shipleys or the Biminrammers, but still, I thought that once word was out about our breakup, someone would express concern.

I'd see Missy Biminrammer walking her sheltie, or Chick Hartwell mowing his lawn, or Peg Shipley working in her flower beds, and I'd give a wave and wait for them to say something about not seeing Vonnie around for a while, but they just waved back and didn't say much of anything at all except to tell me to keep an eye out for Popcorn.

One evening I saw Herb Shipley washing his car in his driveway. I walked down the sidewalk, past the Biminrammers', who lived next door to me, and the Hartwells' on the other side of them, until I was standing in the Shipleys' drive, out of the way of the spray coming from Herb's hose. Henry was stretched out on the sidewalk in the sun. He rolled over onto his back and closed his eyes.

Herb was washing the vintage 1963 Thunderbird—red with a black ragtop—that he'd restored. He was an industrial-arts teacher at Davidson High School, a wiry man with a nice head of silvery hair. He didn't have much of a chin, which made it seem that his lips were stretched tight in a constant state of alarm, as they were now when he turned and saw me standing there.

I just blurted it out. It makes me feel like an idiot to think of it now. I said, "My wife left me." Maybe it was that look on his face. Maybe it was the fact that I thought of him as an angry man and assumed he'd be angry for my sake. "Vonnie," I said. "She's gone."

He was holding the hose with the nozzle pointed in my direction, and to anyone who might have been watching, it probably looked liked I'd said something he didn't like and he was about to squirt me in the face.

But all he said was, "Did you hear? Mendes just got a call. A woman in Plain City. She thinks she's found Popcorn." He was there now, Herb explained. "We're all hoping for a happy ending."

Just then, Henry jumped up onto the trunk of the T-Bird. He stood up on his hind legs so he could reach the ragtop, and then he went to town, picking at it with his claws.

"Henry," I said. "No."

But it was too late. Herb turned around and saw what was happening—that ragtop getting shredded—and he did the only thing he could. He turned that hose on full blast. The force knocked Henry off the T-Bird. He landed on his feet and shook himself. His fur was slicked down with water, and he didn't wait around to see what might be coming next. He took out up the sidewalk as fast as he could run. I watched him until he disappeared around the side of my garage.

"I'll pay for whatever it costs to fix that," I said to Herb.

"Damn straight you will." He looked past me, and I heard a car turning down our court. I wondered if it might be Vonnie coming back to give us one more try. Then, before I could turn to look, Herb said, "It's Mendes."

It didn't take long for the word to spread. Peg came out the front door as if she'd been watching, and who knows, maybe she had been.

"It's him," Herb said, and the two of them brushed right past me and started up the street.

Chick and Connie Hartwell came out of their house to join them. Even Benny and Missy Biminrammer tagged along to see whether Mr. Mendes had indeed recovered Popcorn.

I stood there watching as Mr. Mendes got out of his Volvo, and the neighbors gathered around him. He said something and then bowed his head. Connie Hartwell put a hand on his shoulder, and I heard Herb say, "Damn it all to hell," and I knew that the woman in Plain City had turned out to have the wrong bird.

Everyone stood in Mr. Mendes's driveway talking, and I went back to my house, where Henry, wet and trembling, waited for me to let him inside.

"Damn it, Henry," I said. Then I opened the front door. He stayed on the step, hesitating, as if he knew I was going to be out some cash for what he'd done to Herb's ragtop. "Come on," I said. "You know that couch just won't look right without you on it."

I swear he was pissed off the rest of that night and the days that followed. He prowled around the house, letting out these guttural yowls. I opened the door to see if he wanted to go outside, but all he did was come to the threshold, sniff at the air, yowl some more, and then head for the couch.

One day, he got up on the window seat, where I sat watching the whoop-dee-do across the street. Herb Shipley had volunteered to weld Popcorn's cage to an iron rod and then anchor it to Mr. Mendes's roof. I watched Herb bolt it to each side of the roof ridge. Mr. Mendes watched from the ground, his head tipped back, his hand shading his eyes from the sun. When Herb was done, he left the cage door open, so Popcorn could fly right in if he happened to be in the vicinity and took a notion. Herb climbed down the ladder, and Mr. Mendes solemnly shook his hand.

A news van—WNBS 10TV—pulled to the curb, and two men got out. One of them had a video camera on his shoulder. The other one, a young man with perfectly combed blond hair, had a microphone. He was wearing khaki slacks and penny loafers. A navy-blue poplin jacket with a white shirt. The knot of a robin's-egg-blue tie poked out above the jacket's zipper.

I watched a little while as the blond man talked to Mr. Mendes, sticking the microphone up to his face from time to time. Then Henry pawed at the window and hissed.

"My sentiments exactly," I said.

I picked him up in my arms and headed toward the kitchen, where I kept the Evan Williams bourbon. It was five o'clock, a perfectly reasonable time for a cocktail.

What was it about Mendes and his story that Henry and I found so objectionable? How could our hearts turn so hard toward a man who'd lost something dear to him? I suppose we were jealous. Here we were in the midst of our own story of loss, but no one had time for that. Mr. Mendes and Popcorn—that was the story that had captured everyone's heart.

So Henry and I sat on our couch, and the longer I sat there, drinking, the more I began to enjoy the way he looked, propped up on his rear end, wedged into the corner, his belly exposed. I swear sometimes it looked like he was almost human, the way he sat there. I started telling him the story of how I came to buy the couch, and before I knew it, I was relating the details of how Vonnie and I had once loved each other. "Believe it or not, Henry. We were young and in love, and we thought we'd have kids and grandkids and a long and happy life. Now look what's happened."

He nodded off from time to time, and I poked him. He grumbled, curling his mouth into that sneer he so often had, but I didn't care how put out he felt. I wanted to talk, and he was the only one around to listen.

"Oh, Henry," I said. "The first time you fall in love, you think it'll be forever, but you know what? There ain't no forever. Ain't no forever, ever. That's what I've learned, my fabulous feline friend. Mendes is going to learn it, too. You and I both know that bird's not coming home."

How did I know that? Let's just say I had a good idea. Maybe I was jaded because of how everything had gone wrong for Vonnie and me, or maybe I hoped that in our shared sadness Mendes and I would rekindle our friendship. Maybe I, and not Herb Shipley or Chick Hartwell—jeezy Pete, I'd even seen Mr. Mendes asking favors of Benny Biminrammer—would be the one Mendes would count on.

"I can be that kind of person," I told Henry, but I knew I was lying. I hadn't been that sort in a good while. I sure as shooting hadn't been that person for Vonnie in quite some time. "I'm a drunk," I said. "I'm a man of a certain age, a retired man who no longer matters to the world at large. Now, I'm alone." I took in the way Henry was slouched against the corner of the couch, that pissed-off look on his face. "*We're* alone," I said to him, "but the only thing anyone cares about is that bird."

Henry gave a little snort, as if to say, *Damn bird,* or else, *Where's the woman who loves me, the one who feeds me tuna and lets me sleep in bed with her and calls me Prince Henry Boo-Boo Ca-Choo. How'd I end up on this ugly-assed couch with a drunk man who's always feeling sorry for himself?*

"You just did," I said.

Then, because I felt my heart go out to him, I made up a little song—or, to be more exact, the bourbon wrote a few lyrics. I could imagine Henry as one of those angry rappers I sometimes saw on TV, someone like that 50 Cent or that Eminem. Put a baseball cap turned sideways on Henry and a load of silver chains and medallions, and he'd be ready to go. I just started rapping whatever came into my muzzy head:

Cat on a bad couch,
pimping a pissed-off slouch.
Woman done done him wrong,
that's why he's singing this song.

I could tell he was unimpressed. "We've all got a story," I told him, "and, like it or not, that's yours."

The next evening, I turned on the news and there was Mendes talking about how much Popcorn meant to him, how he'd had him a number of years, and when you lived alone, as Mendes did, you came to count on the affections of a pet.

"I'm hopeful," Mr. Mendes said. The camera was close on his face, and I could see that his eyes were wet. "I don't know how he got out," he said, and then he blotted his eyes with the heel of his palm. "I left the deck door open just a little when I went to work that morning, so he could enjoy the warm air from outside, but I made sure the sliding screen was secure. He liked to fly around the house. I always gave him free range. I swear that screen was closed."

The news story ended with a shot of Popcorn's cage atop the house. The reporter's voice was somber. "If anyone has any information that might lead to Popcorn's return, please call the number at the bottom of your screen, or visit www.findpopcorn.com." The camera zoomed in closer to the cage, and the reporter added, "In the meantime, the cage door is open, and a worried pet owner watches and waits."

All night I tried to get that image out of my head, but I couldn't. I drifted in and out of a restless sleep, finally falling more "in" than "out." By the time I got out of bed, it was after eleven o'clock. It was another pretty spring day. I slid open the deck door and stood at the screen, smelling the scents of the earth coming back to life after a long winter. The daffodils were in bloom along the side of the deck. The sunlight slanting through the screen was warm on my face, and yet I felt miserable.

I heard Henry jump down from his couch—I'd come to think of it as *his*—and soon he was weaving in and out between my legs, meowing and looking up at me with contentment.

"Henry," I said, "it's time Mr. Mendes and I had a little talk."

When I rang the bell at his house, I heard his footsteps coming quick and hard over the floor.

He opened the door, and it swung free with a complaining groan, as if it had been closed throughout the winter and was just now letting loose from its seal.

I said, "Mr. Mendes, please." I didn't know quite how to begin. "If I may," I said, trying to find the words for why I'd come.

He took my arm. He pulled me into his house. "Mr. Lex. Oh, Mr. Lex." His face was beaming. "Come, please."

I let him usher me down the hallway to the open space that, like in my own home, contained kitchen, breakfast area, and family room. There, on the counter, was a cage, and inside that cage was a cockatiel that looked very much like Popcorn.

"Popcorn," Mr. Mendes said with a flourish of his arm as if he were a spokes model on a TV game show. "Last night a woman called from New Albany, and now"—he waved his arm once more, his hand sweeping in front of the cage—"*gracias a Dios*, a miracle has come to me."

New Albany was nearly thirty miles away, a fact I pointed out to Mr. Mendes. "That's quite a flight for the little guy," I said.

For just an instant, his face became very somber. Just a moment when the two of us looked into each other's eyes, and we both knew the bird in the cage wasn't Popcorn but rather some other cockatiel who'd strayed from home. There'd been a number of other false alarms since Popcorn had been gone, and, for whatever reason—maybe there just comes a time when you make a choice and life goes on—Mr. Mendes had decided to accept this one as fact.

His face brightened. He said, "It's not for us to question miracles. They come to us for a reason. We don't have to know what that reason is. Yes?"

I bent over with my hands on my knees and peered into the

cage. The bird sat on his perch. He had the same markings as Popcorn—same yellow head, same orange spots on his face. He was even doing a little bob and sway the way Popcorn had done the first time I'd seen him. It was easy enough to believe. All it took was faith.

Mr. Mendes was telling me another story. The girl he'd left in Cuba, Eva, had written him a letter. I thought of the letter with the Miami postmark I'd left inside the front door close to Christmas. They'd exchanged e-mails throughout the winter.

"She's coming to see me," he said. "I'm so very much scared. What if she doesn't like me? What if I don't like her? So many years have passed since we were young and in love."

I tapped my finger on the front of the cage, and I couldn't help but think of Vonnie, then, and the way she was when we were first falling for each other. The way we were when we were setting out together. Hearts wide open with wonder.

"Touchdown," I said, remembering Popcorn's call, and how back in the autumn it delighted everyone on the court to hear it. "Touchdown, touchdown," I kept repeating, but the bird in the cage didn't say a word.

Finally, Mr. Mendes stopped me, his voice low and kind. "Mr. Lex," he said, "it's not yet the football season."

I couldn't bring myself to say what I'd come to tell him—that unbeknownst to him I'd come into his house on the day that Popcorn disappeared. I'd seen Mr. Mendes leave for work. I knew he wouldn't come home until his lunch hour. For weeks, ever since I'd pressed the button on the remote for the ceiling fan and seen his garage door lift, I'd tried to talk myself out of a crazy thought. Didn't a garage door opener work by the same principle of a code set between transmitter and receiver? What would happen if I fooled around with combinations on my own opener until I found the one that would work on Mr. Mendes's door?

The door would go up. That's what would happen, as I discovered that day in late March. I walked across the street, wondering whether anyone was watching. I walked into Mr. Mendes's garage and used the control on the wall to lower the door. I opened the door from the garage to the house, and I stepped inside.

All I wanted was a place to be that wasn't my house. That's what I couldn't explain to Mr. Mendes. I couldn't tell him how I enjoyed the open deck door and the warm breeze. I sat in the quiet of his home, content to be away from my own house, eager to believe, if only for an hour or so, that such peace and quiet belonged to me—that I deserved such rest.

Popcorn was in his cage, but the door was open so he could have free rein of the house. He chirped and trilled. Then he said, "Touchdown, touchdown."

At one point, he came out of his cage and made a few low swoops around the breakfast area and family room.

I wasn't thinking. I'd explain that to Mr. Mendes if I could. I'd tell him how I went to the deck door, and I felt so much at ease that I wanted to sit on his deck for a few moments, letting the sun warm me. I slid open the screen.

It was then that I felt a whisk of wings at my ear. With horror, I watched Popcorn lift beyond the beech tree in the backyard, then disappear around the corner of Chick Hartwell's house.

What could I do but go home? If I'd been a better man, I would've come clean, but how in the world would I have explained being in that house in the first place? How would I have been able to tell Mr. Mendes how much those peaceful moments meant to me? How would I have said I knew my life was coming apart, and I didn't know how to stop it?

I couldn't say it then, and I can't say it now that Vonnie has come for Henry and taken him away. It's just me and that couch now. That sorry-assed couch. I sit here now in the dog days of summer, drinking. I remember that day when Mr. Mendes was so pleased to have this cockatiel he'd insist was Popcorn. The day he told me about his lost love, Eva, who lives in his home now and is a perfectly pleasant sort. I watch them come and go, often hand in hand, and as much as I want to, I can't quite begrudge them. I just can't manage it.

That day in his house, he said to me, "Are you happy for me, Mr. Lex?"

He stood there, wild-eyed—caught, so I imagined, between what was done and what was still ahead. Uncertain, I guess you'd say, and maybe sometimes that's the best we can hope. I'd tell Vonnie this if I thought it might mean anything to her. A stir of air, a sliver of sky, an open door.

"I am," I told Mr. Mendes. What else could I say? I didn't want him to know that I was scared to death. Scared of all the days ahead of me. "Yes." I patted him on the back. He was my neighbor, and for his sake I could pretend that I was a good man. "I'm happy. I'm very happy." I even slipped an arm around his shoulders and pressed him to me. Just for an instant. "Very, very happy," I said.

Then I did the only thing I could. I let him go.

About "Cat on a Bad Couch"

My story "Cat on a Bad Couch" takes as its inspiration the Ray Bradbury short "I See You Never." In a little more than a thousand words, Bradbury tells the story of Mrs. O'Brian, whose tenant, Mr. Ramirez, has come in the presence of police officers to tell her he must give up his room as he's being returned to Mexico; his temporary visa has long ago expired and the police have now discovered that fact. He'll have to give up his job at the airplane factory, where he makes a good wage.

He'll have to give up his clean room with the blue linoleum and the flowered wallpaper. Most of all, he'll have to give up Mrs. O'Brian, his "strict but kindly landlady," who doesn't begrudge him the right to get a little drunk at the end of the week.

I've used this story for years in my fiction workshops. Notice, I tell my students, how skillfully Bradbury evokes the aching loss at the heart of the story by paying such careful attention to the details of Mrs. O'Brian's home—the huge kitchen, the long dining table covered with a white cloth and laden with water glasses and pitcher and bright cutlery and platters and bowls, the freshly waxed floor—and the facts of Mr. Ramirez's pleasant life in Los Angeles—the radio and wristwatch he bought, the jewels he purchased for his few lady friends, the picture shows he attended, the streetcar rides he took, the grand restaurants where he dined, the opera and the theater. Those details contrast with what Mrs. O'Brian recalls from a visit she once made to a few Mexican border towns—dirt roads, scorched fields, small adobe houses, an eroded landscape. Such is the world to which Mr. Ramirez must return, and the details of the story do the work of portraying his heartache. No need for the author to offer comment.

I ask my students to notice how Bradbury stays out of the way, allowing Mr. Ramirez's agony to emerge organically from the details of the story. Mr. Ramirez says, "Mrs. O'Brian, I see you never, I see you never!" In the final move of the story, Mrs. O'Brian, sitting down to dinner with her children, realizes that this is indeed true, and again the details evoke her melancholy. With graceful understatement, Bradbury describes how she quietly shuts the door and returns to her dining table, how she takes a bit of food and chews it a long time, staring at the closed door. Then she puts down her knife and fork, and when her son asks her what's wrong, she says she's just realized—here she puts her hand to her face—that she'll never again see

Mr. Ramirez. The full brunt of her loss comes to her when it's too late for her to express her sadness to him the way he has to her. Notice the irony in that last move, I tell my students, how it comes to us covertly because a skillful writer lets it emerge from the details of the story's world.

I hope I've been able to do the same at the end of "Cat on a Bad Couch," when my narrator, Lex, because of his own actions, is unable to fully connect with the one person left who might be most sympathetic to his loss.

—Lee Martin

BY THE SILVER WATER OF LAKE CHAMPLAIN

Joe Hill

The robot shuffled *clank-clank* into the pitch dark of the bedroom, then stood staring down at the humans.

The female human groaned and rolled away and folded a pillow over her head.

"Gail, honey," said the male, licking dry lips. "Mother has a headache. Can you take that noise out of here?"

"I CAN PROVIDE A STIMULATING CUP OF COFFEE," boomed the robot in an emotionless voice.

"Tell her to get out, Raymond," said the female. "My head is exploding."

"Go on, Gail. You can hear mother isn't herself," said the male.

"YOU ARE INCORRECT. I HAVE SCANNED HER VITALS," said the robot. "I HAVE IDENTIFIED HER AS SYLVIA LONDON. SHE IS HERSELF."

The robot tilted her head to one side, inquisitively, waiting for more data. The pot on her head fell off and hit the floor with a great steely crash.

Mother sat up screaming. It was a wretched, anguished, inhuman sound, with no words in it, and it frightened the robot so much, for a moment she forgot she was a robot and she was just Gail again. She snatched her pot off the floor and hurried *clangedy-clang-clang* to the relative safety of the hall.

She peeked back into the room. Mother was already lying down, holding the pillow over her head again.

Raymond smiled across the darkness at his daughter. "Maybe the robot can formulate an antidote for martini poisoning," he whispered, and winked.

The robot winked back.

For a while the robot worked on her prime directive, formulating the antidote that would drive the poison out of Sylvia London's system. The robot stirred orange juice and lemon juice and ice cubes and butter and sugar and dish soap in a coffee mug. The resulting solution foamed and turned a lurid sci-fi green, suggestive of Venutian slime and radiation.

Gail thought the antidote might go down better with some toast and marmalade. Only there was a programming error; the toast burnt. Or maybe it was her own crossed wires beginning to smoke, shorting out the subroutines that required her to follow Asimov's laws. With her circuit boards sizzling inside her, Gail began to malfunction. She tipped over chairs with great crashes and pushed books off the kitchen counter onto the floor. It was a terrible thing but she couldn't help herself.

Gail didn't hear her mother rushing across the room behind her, didn't know she was there until Sylvia jerked the pot off her head and flung it into the enamel sink.

"What are you doing?" Sylvia screamed. "What in the name of sweet Mary God? If I hear one more thing crash over, I'll take a hatchet to someone. My own self maybe."

Gail said nothing, felt silence was safest.

"Get out of here before you burn the house down. My God, the whole kitchen stinks. This toast is ruined. And what did you pour in this Goddam mug?"

"It will cure you," Gail said.

"There isn't no cure for me," her mother said, which was a double negative, but Gail didn't think it wise to correct her. "I wish I had one boy. Boys are quiet. You four girls are like a tree full of sparrows, the shrill way you carry on."

"Ben Quarrel isn't quiet. He never stops talking."

"You ought to go outside. All of you ought to go outside. I don't want to hear any of you again until I have breakfast made."

Gail shuffled toward the living room.

"Take those pots off your feet," her mother said, reaching for the pack of cigarettes on the windowsill.

Gail daintily removed one foot, then the other, from the pots she had been using for robot boots.

Heather sat at the dining room table, bent over her drawing pad. The twins, Miriam and Mindy, were playing wheelbarrow. Mindy would hoist Miriam up by the ankles and walk her across the room, Miriam clambering along on her hands.

Gail stared over Heather's shoulder at what her older sister was drawing. Then Gail got her kaleidoscope and peered at the drawing through that. It didn't look any better.

She lowered her kaleidoscope and said, "Do you want me to help you with your drawing? I can show you how to draw a cat's nose."

"It isn't a cat."

"Oh. What is it?"

"It's a pony."

"Why is it pink?"

"I like them pink. There should be some that are pink. That's a better color than most of the regular horse colors."

"I've never seen a horse with ears like that. It would be better if you drew whiskers on it and let it be a cat."

Heather crushed her drawing in one hand and stood up so quickly she knocked over her chair.

In the exact same moment, Mindy wheelbarrowed Miriam into the edge of the coffee table with a great bang. Miriam shrieked and grabbed her head and Mindy dropped her ankles and Miriam hit the floor so hard the whole house shook.

"GODDAM IT WILL YOU STOP THROWING THE GODDAM CHAIRS AROUND?" screamed their mother, reeling in from the kitchen. "WHY DO YOU ALL HAVE TO THROW THE GODDAM CHAIRS? WHAT DO I HAVE TO SAY TO MAKE YOU STOP?"

"Heather did it," Gail said.

"I did not!" Heather said. "It was Gail!" She did not view this as a lie. It seemed to her that somehow Gail *had* done it, just by standing there and being ignorant.

Miriam sobbed, clutching her head. Mindy picked up the book about Peter Rabbit and stood there staring into it, idly turning the pages, the young scholar bent to her studies.

Their mother grabbed Heather by the shoulders, squeezing them until her knuckles went white.

"I want you to go outside. All of you. Take your sisters and go away. Go far away. Go down to the lake. Don't come back until you hear me calling."

They spilled into the yard, Heather and Gail and Mindy and Miriam. Miriam wasn't crying anymore. She had stopped crying the moment their mother went back into the kitchen.

Big sister Heather told Miriam and Mindy to sit in the sandbox and play.

"What should *I* do?" Gail asked.

"You could go drown yourself in the lake."

"That sounds fun," Gail said, and skipped away down the hill.

Miriam stood in the sandbox with a little tin shovel and watched her go. Mindy was already burying her own legs in the sand.

It was early and cool. The mist was over the water and the

lake was like battered steel. Gail stood on her father's dock, next to her father's boat, watching the way the pale vapor churned and changed in the dimness. Like being inside a kaleidoscope filled with foggy gray beach glass. She still had her kaleidoscope, patted it in the pocket of her dress. On a sunny day, Gail could see the green slopes on the other side of the water, and she could look up the stony beach, to the north, all the way to Canada, but now she could not see ten feet in front of her.

She followed the narrow ribbon of beach toward the Quarrels' summer place. There was only a yard of rocks and sand between the water and the embankment, less in some places.

Something caught the light, and Gail bent to find a piece of dark green glass that had been rubbed soft by the lake. It was either green glass or an emerald. She discovered a dented silver spoon, not two feet away.

Gail turned her head and stared out again at the silvered surface of the lake.

She had an idea a ship had gone down, someone's schooner, not far offshore, and she was discovering the treasure washed in by the tide. A spoon and an emerald couldn't be a coincidence.

She lowered her head and walked along, slower now, on the lookout for more salvage. Soon enough she found a tin cowboy with a tin lasso. She felt a shiver of pleasure, but also sorrow. There had been a child on the boat.

"He's probably dead now," she said to herself, and looked sadly out at the water once more.

"Drowned," she decided.

She wished she had a yellow rose to throw into the water.

Gail went on but had hardly trudged three paces when she heard a sound from across the lake, a long, mournful lowing, like a foghorn, but also not like one.

She stopped for another look.

The mist smelt of rotting smelt.

The foghorn did not sound again.

An enormous gray boulder rose out of the shallows here, rising right up onto the sand. Some net was snarled around it. After a moment of hesitation, Gail grabbed the net and climbed to the top.

It was a really large boulder, higher than her head. It was curious she had never noticed it before, but then, things looked different in the mist.

Gail stood on the boulder, which was high but also long, sloping away to her right, and curling in a crescent out into the water on her left. It was a low ridge of stone marking the line between land and water.

She peered out into the cool, blowing smoke, looking for the rescue ship that had to be out there somewhere, trolling for survivors of the wreck. Maybe it wasn't too late for the little boy. She lifted her kaleidoscope to her eye, counting on its special powers to penetrate the mist and show her where the schooner had gone down.

"What are you doing?" said someone behind her.

Gail looked over her shoulder. It was Joel and Ben Quarrel, both of them barefoot. Ben Quarrel looked just like a little version of his older brother. Both of them were dark-haired and dark-eyed and had surly, almost petulant faces. She liked them both, though. Ben would sometimes spontaneously pretend he was on fire, and throw himself down and roll around screaming and someone would have to put him out. He needed to be put out about once an hour. Joel liked dares, but he would never dare anyone to do anything he wouldn't do himself. He had dared Gail to let a spider crawl on her face, a daddy longlegs, and then when she wouldn't, he did it. He stuck his tongue out and let the daddy longlegs crawl right over it. She was afraid he would eat it, but he didn't. Joel didn't say much and he didn't boast, even when he had done something amazing, like get five skips on a stone.

She assumed they would be married someday. Gail had asked Joel if he thought he'd like that, and he had shrugged and said it suited him fine. That was in June, though, and they hadn't talked about their engagement since. Sometimes she thought he had forgotten.

"What happened to your eye?" she asked.

Joel touched his left eye, which was surrounded by a painful looking red-and-brown mottling. "I was playing Daredevils of the Sky and fell out of my bunk bed." He nodded toward the lake. "What's out there?"

"There's a ship sank. They're looking for survivors now."

Joel took off his shoes and put them up on the rock. Then he grabbed the netting tangled on the boulder, climbed to the top, and stood next to her, staring out into the mist.

"What was the name?" he asked.

"The name of what?"

"The ship that sank."

"The *Mary Celeste*."

"How far out?"

"A half a mile," Gail said, and lifted her kaleidoscope to her eye for another look around.

Through the lens, the dim water was shattered, again and again, into a hundred scales of ruby and chrome.

"How do you know?" Joel asked after a bit.

She shrugged. "I found some things that washed up."

"Can I see?" Ben Quarrel asked. He was having trouble climbing the net to the top of the boulder. He kept getting halfway, then jumping back down.

She turned to face him and took the soft green glass out of her pocket.

"This is an emerald," she said. She took out the tin cowboy. "This is a tin cowboy. The boy this belonged to probably drowned."

"That's my tin cowboy," Ben said. "I left it yesterday."

"It isn't. It just looks like yours."

Joel glanced over at it. "No. That's his. He's always leaving them on the beach. He hardly has any left."

Gail surrendered the point and tossed the tin cowboy down to Ben, who caught it, and lost interest in the sunk schooner. He turned his back to the great boulder and sat in the sand and got his cowboy into a fight with some pebbles. The pebbles kept hitting him and knocking him over. Gail didn't think it was an even match.

"What else do you have?" Joel asked.

"This spoon," Gail said. "It might be silver."

Joel squinted at it, then looked back at the lake.

"Better let me have the telescope," he said. "If there are people out there, we have as good a chance of spotting them as anyone searching for them on a boat."

"That's what I was thinking." She gave him the kaleidoscope.

Joel turned it this way and that, scanning the murk for survivors, his face tense with concentration.

He lowered it at last and opened his mouth to say something. Before he could, the mournful foghorn sounded again. The water quivered. The foghorn sound went on for a long time before trailing sadly away.

"I wonder what that is," Gail said.

"They fire cannons to bring dead bodies to the surface of the water," Joel told her.

"That wasn't a cannon."

"It's loud enough."

He lifted the kaleidoscope to his eye again and looked for a while more. Then he lowered it and pointed at a floating board.

"Look. Part of the boat."

"Maybe it has the name of the boat on it."

Joel sat and rolled his jeans up to his knees. He dropped off the boulder into the water.

"I'll get it," he said.

"I'll help," Gail said, even though he didn't need help. She took off her black shoes and put her socks inside them, then slid down the cold, rough stone into the water after him.

The water was up over her knees in two steps and she didn't go any farther because she was soaking her dress. Joel had the board anyway. He was up to his waist, peering down at it.

"What does it say?" she asked.

"Like you thought. It's the *Mary Celeste*," he said, and held up the board so she could see. There was nothing written on it.

She bit her lip and stared out over the water. "If anyone rescues them, it's going to have to be us. We should make a fire on the beach, so they know which way to swim. What do you think?"

He didn't answer.

"I said, 'What do you think?'" she asked again, but then she saw the look on his face and knew he wasn't going to answer, wasn't even listening. "What's wrong?"

She looked back over her shoulder to see what he was staring at, his face rigid and his eyes wide.

The boulder they had been standing on wasn't a boulder. It was a dead animal. It was long, almost as long as two canoes lined end-to-end. The tail curled out into the water toward them, bobbing on the surface, thick as a fire hose. The head stretched out on the pebbly beach, even thicker, spade-shaped. Between the head and the tail, its body bulked up, thick around as a hippo. It wasn't the mist that stank of rotting fish. It was the animal. Now that she was staring right at the thing, she didn't know how she had ever stood on top of it, imagining it was a rock.

Her chest tingled and crawled, like she had ants under her

dress. The ant feeling was in her hair, too. She could see where the animal was torn open, in the place where its throat widened into its torso. Its insides were red and white, like the insides of any fish. There wasn't a lot of blood for such a big hole.

Joel gripped her hand. They stood up to their thighs in the water, staring at the dinosaur, which was as dead now as all the other dinosaurs that had ever walked the earth.

"It's the monster," Joel said, not that it needed to be said.

They had all heard about the monster that lived in the lake. There was always a float in the Fourth of July parade, made up to look like a plesiosaur, a papier-mâché creature rising out of papier-mâché waters. In June there had been an article about the lake creature in the newspaper and Heather had started to read it aloud at the table, but their father made her stop.

"There isn't anything in the lake. That's for tourists," he had said then.

"It says a dozen people saw it. It says they hit it with the ferry."

"A dozen people saw a log and got themselves all worked up. There's nothing in this lake but the same fish that are in every other American lake."

"There *could* be a dinosaur," Heather had insisted.

"No. There couldn't. Do you know how many of them there would have to be for a breeding population? People would be seeing them all the time. Now hush up. You'll scare your sisters. I didn't buy this cottage so the four of you can sit inside and fight all day. If you girls won't go in the lake because you're scared of some dumbass American Nessie, I'll throw you in."

Now Joel said, "Don't scream."

It had never crossed Gail's mind to scream, but she nodded to show she was listening.

"I don't want to frighten Ben," Joel told her in a low voice. Joel was shaking so hard his knees almost knocked. But then the water was very cold.

"What do you think happened to it?" she asked.

"There was that article in the paper about it getting hit by the ferry. Do you remember that article? A while back?"

"Yes. But don't you think it would've washed up months ago?"

"I don't think the ferry killed it. But maybe another ship hit it. Maybe it got chewed up in someone's propeller. It obviously doesn't know enough to stay out of the way of boats. It's like when turtles try and cross the highway to lay eggs."

Holding hands, they waded closer to it.

"It smells," Gail said, and lifted the collar of her dress to cover her mouth and nose.

He turned and looked at her, his eyes bright and feverish. "Gail London, we are going to be famous. They will put us in the newspaper. I bet on the front page, with a picture of us sitting on it."

A shiver of excitement coursed through her, and she squeezed his hand. "Do you think they will let us name it?"

"It already has a name. Everyone will call it Champ."

"But maybe they will name the species after us. The Gailasaurus."

"That would be naming it after you."

"They could call it a DinoGail Joelasaurus. Do you think they will ask us questions about our discovery?"

"Everyone will interview us. Come on. Let's get out of the water."

They sloshed to the right, toward the tail, bobbing on the surface of the water. Gail had to wade back up to her waist to go around it, then started ashore. When she looked back, she saw Joel standing on the other side of the tail, looking down at it.

"What?" she said.

He reached out gently and put his hand on the tail. He jerked his hand back almost immediately.

"What's it feel like?" she asked.

Even though she had climbed the net snarled around it, and had stood on top of it, she felt in some way that she had not touched it yet.

"It's cold" was all he said.

She put her hand on its side. It was as rough as sandpaper and felt like it had just come out of the icebox.

"Poor thing," she said.

"I wonder how old it is," he said.

"Millions of years. It's been alone in this lake for millions of years."

Joel said, "It was safe until people put their damn motorboats on the lake. How can it know about motorboats?"

"I bet it had a good life."

"Millions of years alone? That doesn't sound good."

"It had a lake full of fish to eat and miles to swim in and nothing to be afraid of. It saw the dawning of a great nation," Gail told him. "It did the backstroke under the moonlight."

Joel looked at her in surprise. "You're the smartest little girl on this side of the lake. You talk just like you're reading from a book."

"I'm the smartest little girl on *either* side of the lake."

He pushed the tail aside and sloshed past it, and they walked dripping onto the shore. They came around the hind end and found Ben playing with his tin cowpoke, just as they had left him.

"I'll tell him," Joel said. He crouched and ruffled his little brother's hair. "Do you see that rock behind you?"

Ben didn't look up from his cowboy. "Uh-huh."

"That rock is a dinosaur. Don't be afraid of it. It's dead. It won't hurt anyone."

"Uh-huh," Ben said. He had buried his cowboy up to his tin waist. In a small, shrill voice, he shouted, "Help! I'm ah-drownin' in this heah quicksand!"

Joel said, "Ben. I'm not playing pretend. It's a *real* dinosaur."

Ben stopped and looked back at it without much interest. "Okay."

He wiggled his figure in the sand and went back to his shrill cowboy voice. "Someone throw me a rope before ah'm buried alive!"

Joel made a face and stood up.

"He's just useless. The discover of the century right behind him, and all he wants to do is play with that stupid cowboy."

Then Joel crouched again and said, "*Ben.* It's worth a pile of money. We're all going to be rich. You and me and Gail."

Ben hunched his shoulders and put on a pouty face of his own. He could feel he wasn't going to be allowed to play cowboy anymore. Joel was going to make him think about his dinosaur, whether he liked it or not.

"That's all right. You can have my share of the money."

"I won't hold you to that later," Joel said. "I'm not greedy."

"What's important," Gail said, "is the advancement of scientific progress. That's all we care about."

"All we care about, little guy," Joel said.

Ben thought of something that might save him and end the discussion. He made a sound in his throat, a great roar to indicate a jolting explosion. "The dynamite went off! I'm burnin'!" He flopped onto his back and began to roll desperately around. "Put me out! Put me out!"

No one put him out. Joel stood. "You need to go get a grown-up and tell them we found a dinosaur. Gail and me will stay here and guard it."

Ben stopped moving. He let his mouth loll open. He rolled his eyes up in his head. "I can't. I'm burnt to death."

"You're an idiot," Joel said, tired of trying to sound like an adult. He kicked sand onto Ben's stomach.

Ben flinched and his face darkened and he said, "You're the one who is stupid. I hate dinosaurs."

Joel looked like he was getting ready to kick sand in Ben's face, but Gail intervened. She couldn't bear to see Joel lose his dignity and had liked his serious, grown-up voice, and the way he had offered Ben a share of the reward money, without hesitation. Gail dropped to her knees next to the little boy and put a hand on his shoulder.

"Ben? Would you like a brand-new box of those cowboys? Joel says you've lost most of them."

Ben sat up, brushing himself off. "I was going to save up for them. I've got a dime so far."

"If you go and get your dad for us, I'll buy you a whole box of them. Joel and I will buy you a box together."

Ben said, "They've got them for a dollar at Fletcher's. Do you have a dollar?"

"I will after I get the reward."

"What if there isn't no reward?"

"You mean to say what if there isn't *any* reward," Gail told him. "What you just said is a double negative. It means the opposite of what you want things to mean. Now, if there isn't *any* reward, I'll save up until I have a dollar and buy you a box of tin cowboys. I promise."

"You promise."

"That's what I just said. Joel will save with me. Won't you, Joel?"

"I don't want to do anything for this idiot."

"Joel."

"I guess okay," Joel said.

Ben tugged his cowpoke out of the sand and jumped to his feet.

"I'll get Dad."

Joel said, "Wait."

He touched his black eye, then dropped his hand.

"Mom and Dad are sleeping. Dad said don't wake them up until eight-thirty. That's why we came outside. They were up late at the party at Millers'."

"My parents were too," Gail said. "My mother has a *beastly* headache."

"At least your mom is awake," Joel said. "Get Mrs. London, Ben."

"Okay," Ben said, and began walking.

"*Run*," Joel said.

"Okay," Ben said, but he didn't change his pace.

Joel and Gail watched him until he vanished into the streaming mist.

"My dad would just say *he* found it," Joel said, and Gail almost flinched at the ugliness in his voice. "If we show it to my dad first, we won't even get our pictures in the paper."

"We should let him sleep if he's asleep," Gail said.

"That's what I think," Joel said, lowering his head, his voice softening and going awkward. He had shown more emotion than he liked and was embarrassed now.

Gail took his hand, impulsively, because it seemed like the right thing to do.

He looked at their fingers, laced together, and frowned in thought, as if she had asked him a question he felt he should know the answer to. He looked up at her.

"I'm glad I found the creature with you. We will probably be doing interviews about this our whole lives. When we are in our nineties people will still be asking us about the day we found the monster. I'm sure we'll still like each other even then."

She said, "The first thing we'll say is that it wasn't a monster. It was just a poor thing that was run down by a boat. It's not like it ever ate anyone."

"We don't know what he eats. Lots of people have drowned

in this lake. Maybe some of them who drowned didn't really. Maybe he picked his teeth with them."

"We don't even know it's a he."

They let go of each other's hands and turned to look at it, sprawled on the brown, hard beach. From this angle it looked like a boulder again, with some netting across it. Its skin did not glisten like whale blubber but was dark and dull, a chunk of granite with lichen on it.

She had a thought, looked back at Joel. "Do you think we should get ready to be interviewed?"

"You mean like comb our hair? You don't need to comb your hair. Your hair is beautiful."

His face darkened and he couldn't hold her gaze.

"No," she said. "I mean we don't have anything to say. We don't know anything about it. I wish we knew how long it is, at least."

"We should count its teeth."

She shivered. The ants-on-skin sensation returned.

"I wouldn't like to put my hand in its mouth."

"It's dead. I'm not scared. The scientists are going to count its teeth. They'll probably do that first thing."

Joel's eyes widened.

"A tooth," he said.

"A tooth," she said back, feeling his excitement.

"One for you and one for me. We ought to take a tooth for each of us, to remember it by."

"I won't need a tooth to remember it," she said. "But it's a good idea. I'm going to have mine made into a necklace."

"Me too. Only a necklace for a boy. Not a pretty one, like for a girl."

Its neck was long and thick and stretched out straight on the sand. If she had come at the animal from this direction, she would've known it wasn't a rock. It had a shovel-shaped head. Its visible eye was filmed over with some kind of membrane, so it was the color of very cold, very fresh milk. Its mouth was underslung, like a sturgeon's, and hung open. It had very small teeth, lots of them, in slanting double rows.

"Look at 'em," he said, grinning, but with a kind of nervous tremor in his voice. "They'd cut through your arm like a buzz saw."

"Think how many fish they've chopped in two. He probably has to eat twenty fish a day just to keep from starving."

"I don't have a pocketknife," he said. "Do you have anything we can use to pull out a couple teeth?"

She gave him the silver spoon she had found farther down the beach. He splashed into the water, up to his ankles, then crouched by its head and reached into its mouth with the spoon.

Gail waited, her stomach roiling strangely.

After a moment, Joel removed his hand. He still crouched beside it, staring into its face. He put a hand on the creature's neck. He didn't say anything. That filmed-over eye stared up into nothing.

"I don't want to," he said.

"It's all right," she said.

"I thought it would be easy to do, but it doesn't feel like I should do it."

"It's all right. I don't even want one. Not really."

"The roof of his mouth," he said.

"What?"

"The roof of his mouth is just like mine. Ruffled like mine. Or like yours."

He got up and stood for a bit. Joel glanced down at the spoon in his hand and frowned at it, as if he didn't know what it was. He put it into his pocket.

"Maybe they'll give us a tooth," he said. "As part of our reward. It will be better if we don't have to pull it out ourselves."

"Not so sad."

"Yes."

He splashed out of the lake and they stood looking at the carcass.

"Where is Ben?" Joel asked, glancing off in the direction Ben had run.

"We should at least find out how long it is."

"We'd have to go get measuring tape, and someone might come along and say they found it instead of us."

"I'm four feet exactly. To the inch. I was last July when my daddy measured me in the doorway. We could measure how many Gails it is."

"Okay."

She lowered herself to her butt and stretched out on the sand, arms squeezed to her sides, ankles together. Joel found a stick and drew a line in the sand, to mark the crown of her skull.

Gail rose, brushed the sand off, and stepped over the line. She lay down flat again, so her heels were touching the mark in the dirt. They went this way down the length of the beach. He had to wade into the lake to pull the tail up onto shore.

"It's a little over four Gails," he said.

"That's sixteen feet."

"Most of it was tail."

"That's some tail. Where *is* Ben?"

They heard high-pitched voices piping through the blowing vapor. Small figures skipped along the beach, coming toward them. Miriam and Mindy sprang through the fog, Ben wandering behind them with no particular urgency. He was eating a piece of toast with jam on it. Strawberry jam was smeared around his lips, on his chin. He always wound up with as much on his face as went into his mouth.

Mindy held Miriam's hand, while Miriam jumped in a strange, lunging sort of way.

"Higher!" Mindy commanded. "Higher!"

"What is this?" Joel asked.

"I have a pet balloon. I named her Miriam," Mindy said. "Float, Miriam!"

Miriam threw herself straight up off the ground and came down so heavily her legs gave way and she sat hard on the beach. She still had Mindy's hand and yanked her down beside her. The two girls sprawled on the damp pebbles, laughing.

Joel looked past them to Ben. "Where is Mrs. London?"

Ben chewed a mouthful of toast. He was chewing it a long time. Finally he swallowed. "She said she'd come see the dinosaur when it isn't so cold out."

"Float, Miriam!" Mindy screamed.

Miriam flopped onto her back with a sigh. "I'm deflating. I'm deflat."

Joel looked at Gail in disgust.

Mindy said, "It stinks here."

"Do you believe this?" Joel asked. "She's not coming."

Ben said, "She told me to tell Gail if she wants breakfast to come home. Can we buy my cowboys today?"

"You didn't do what we asked, so you aren't getting anything," Joel told him.

"You didn't say I had to get a grown-up. You just said I had to *tell* a grown-up," Ben said, in a tone of voice that made even Gail want to hit him. "I want my cowboys."

Joel walked past the little girls on the ground and grabbed Ben's shoulder, turned him around. "Bring back a grown-up or I'll drown you."

"You said I could have cowboys."

"Yes. I'll make sure you're buried with them."

He kicked Ben in the ass to get him going. Ben cried out and stumbled and glanced back with a hurt look.

"Bring an adult," Joel said. "Or you'll see how mean I can get."

Ben walked off in a hurry, head down, legs stiff and unbending.

"You know what the problem is?" Joel said.

"Yes."

"No one is going to believe him. Would *you* believe him if he said we were guarding a dinosaur?"

The two little girls were speaking in hushed voices. Gail was about to offer to go to the house and get her mother when their secretive whispering caught her notice. She looked down to find them sitting cross-legged next to the creature's back. Mindy had chalk and was drawing tic-tac-toe on its side.

"What are you doing?" Gail cried, and grabbed the chalk. "Have some respect for the dead."

Mindy said, "Give me my chalk."

"You can't draw on this. It's a dinosaur."

Mindy said, "I want my chalk back or I'm telling Mommy."

"They don't even believe us," Joel said. "And they're sitting right next to it. If it was alive, it would've eaten them by now."

Miriam said, "You have to give it back. That's the chalk Daddy bought her. We each got something for a penny. You wanted gum. You could've had chalk. You have to give it back."

"Well, don't draw on the dinosaur."

"I can draw on the dinosaur if I want to. It's everybody's dinosaur," Mindy said.

"It is not. It's ours," Joel said. "We're the ones who discovered it."

Gail said, "You have to draw somewhere else, or I won't give you back your chalk."

"I'm telling Mommy. If she has to come down here to make you give it back, she'll scald your heinie," Mindy said.

Gail started to reach out, to hand back the chalk, but Joel caught her arm.

"We're not giving it," he said.

"I'm telling Mother," Mindy said, and got up.

"I'm telling with her," Miriam said. "Mother is going to come and give you heck."

They stomped away into the mist, discussing this latest outrage in chirping tones of disbelief.

"You're the smartest boy on this side of the lake," Gail said.

"*Either* side of the lake," he said.

The mist streamed in off the surface of the water. By some trick of the light, their shadows telescoped, so each girl appeared as a shadow within a larger shadow within a larger shadow. They made long, girl-shaped tunnels in the vapor, extending away, those multiple shadows lined up like a series of dark, featureless *matryoshka* dolls. Finally they dwindled in on themselves and were claimed by the fishy-smelling fog.

Gail and Joel did not turn back to the dinosaur until Gail's little sisters had vanished entirely. A gull sat on the dead creature, staring at them with beady, avid eyes.

"Get off!" Joel shouted, and flapped his hands.

The gull hopped to the sand and crept away in a disgruntled hunch.

"When the sun comes out, it's going to be ripe," Joel said.

"After they take pictures of it, they'll have to refrigerate it."

"Pictures of it with us."

"Yes," she said, and wanted to take his hand again but didn't.

"Do you think they'll bring it to the city?" Gail asked. She meant New York, which was the only city she had ever been to.

"It depends who buys it from us."

Gail wanted to ask him if he thought his father would let him keep the money but worried that the question might put unhappy ideas into his head. Instead she asked, "How much do you think we might get paid?"

"When the ferry hit this thing back in the summer, P. T. Barnum announced he'd pay fifty thousand dollars for it."

"I'd like to sell it to the Museum of Natural History in New York City."

"I think people give things to museums for free. We'd do better with Barnum. I bet he'd throw in lifetime passes to the circus."

Gail didn't reply, because she didn't want to say something that might disappoint him.

He shot her a look. "You don't think it's right."

She said, "We can do what you want."

"We could each buy a house with our half of Barnum's money. You could fill a bathtub with hundred-dollar bills and swim around in it."

Gail didn't say anything.

"It's half yours, you know. Whatever we make!"

She looked at the creature. "Do you really think it might be a million years old? Can you imagine all those years of swimming? Can you imagine swimming under the full moon? I wonder if it missed other dinosaurs. Do you think it wondered what happened to all the others?"

Joel looked at it for a while. He said, "My mom took me to the natural history museum. They had a little castle there with a hundred knights, in a glass case."

"A diorama."

"That's right. That was swell. It looked just like a little world in there. Maybe they'd give us lifetime passes."

Her heart lightened. She said, "And then scientists could study it whenever they wanted to."

"Yeah. P. T. Barnum would probably make scientists buy a ticket. He'd show it next to a two-headed goat and a fat woman with a beard, and it wouldn't be special anymore. You ever notice that? Because everything at the circus is special, *nothing* is special? If I could walk on a tightrope, even a little, you'd think I was the most amazing boy you knew. Even if I was only two feet off the ground. But if I walked on a tightrope in the circus, and I was only two feet off the ground, people would shout for their money back."

It was the most she had ever heard him say at one go. She wanted to tell him he was already the most amazing boy she knew but felt it might embarrass him.

He reached for her hand and her heart quickened, but he only wanted the chalk.

He took it from her and began to write on the side of the poor thing. She opened her mouth to say they shouldn't but then closed her mouth when she saw he was writing her name on the pebbly turtle skin. He wrote his name beneath hers.

"In case anyone else tries to say they found it," he told her. Then he said, "Your name ought to be on a plaque here. Our names ought to be together forever. I'm glad I found him with you. There isn't no one I'd rather have been with."

"That's a double negative," she said.

He kissed her. Just on the cheek.

"Yes, dear," he said, like he was forty years old and not ten. He gave her back the chalk.

Joel looked past her, down the beach, into the mist. Gail turned her head to see what he was staring at.

She saw a series of those Russian-doll shadows, collapsing toward them, just like someone folding a telescope shut. They were mother-shaped, flanked by Miriam and Mindy shapes, and Gail opened her mouth to call out, but then that large central shadow suddenly shrank and became Heather. Ben Quarrel was right behind her, looking smug.

Heather stalked out of the mist, her drawing pad under one arm. Coils of blond hair hung in her face. She pursed her lips and blew at them to get them out of her eyes, something she only ever did when she was mad.

"Mother wants to see you. She said right now."

Gail said, "Isn't she coming?"

"She has egg pancake in the oven."

"Go and tell her—"

"Go and tell her yourself. You can give Mindy her chalk before you go."

Mindy held out one hand, palm up.

Miriam sang, "*Gail, Gail, bosses everyone around. Gail, Gail, is really stupid.*" The melody was just as good as the lyrics.

Gail said to Heather, "We found a dinosaur. You have to run and get Mom. We're going to give it to a museum and be in the paper. Joel and I are going to be in a photo together."

Heather took Gail's ear and twisted it, and Gail screamed. Mindy lunged and grabbed the chalk out of Gail's hand. Miriam wailed in a long, girlish pretend scream, mocking her.

Heather dropped her hand, grabbed the back of Gail's arm between thumb and index finger, and twisted. Gail cried out again and struggled to get free. Her hand flailed and swatted Heather's drawing pad into the sand. Heather didn't give it any mind, her bloodlust up. She began to march her little sister away into the mist.

"I was drawing my *best* pony," Heather said. "I worked on it *really* hard. And Mom wouldn't even look at it because Mindy and Miriam and Ben kept bothering her about your stupid dinosaur. She yelled at me to get you, and I didn't even do anything. I just wanted to draw, and she said if I didn't go get you, she'd take my colored pencils away. The colored pencils! I got! For my birthday!" She twisted the back of Gail's arm for emphasis, until Gail's eyes stung with tears.

Ben Quarrel hurried to keep alongside her. "You better still buy me my cowboys. You promised."

"Mom says you aren't getting any egg pancake," Miriam said. "Because of all the trouble you've caused this morning."

Mindy said, "Gail? Do you mind if I eat the piece of egg pancake that would've been yours?"

Gail looked over her shoulder at Joel. He was already a ghost, twenty feet back in the mist. He had climbed up to sit on the carcass.

"I'll stay right here, Gail!" he shouted. "Don't worry! You've got your name on it! Your name and mine, right together! Everyone is going to know we found it! Just come back as soon as you can! I'll be waiting!"

"All right," she said, her voice wavering with emotion. "I'll be right back, Joel."

"No you won't," Heather said.

Gail stumbled over the rocks, looking back at Joel for as long as she could. Soon he and the animal he sat on were just dim shapes in the fog, which drifted in damp sheets, so white it made Gail think of the veils that brides wore. When he disappeared, she turned away, blinking at tears, her throat tight.

It was farther back to the house than she remembered. The pack of them—four small children and one twelve-year-old—followed the meandering course of the narrow beach, by the silver water of Lake Champlain. Gail looked at her feet, watched the water slop gently over the pebbles.

They continued along the embankment until they reached the dock, their father's motorboat tied up to it. Heather let go of Gail then, and each of them climbed up onto the pine boards. Gail did not try to run back. It was important to bring their mother, and she thought if she cried hard enough, she could manage it.

The children were halfway across the yard when they heard the foghorn sound again. Only it wasn't a foghorn and it was *close*, somewhere just out of sight in the mist on the lake. It was a long, anguished, bovine sound, a sort of thunderous lowing, loud enough to make the individual droplets of mist quiver in the air. The sound of it brought back the crawling-ants feeling on Gail's scalp and chest. When she looked back at the dock, she saw her father's motorboat galumphing heavily up and down in the water and banging against the wood, rocking in a sudden wake.

"What was that?" Heather cried out.

Mindy and Miriam held each other, staring with fright at the lake. Ben Quarrel's eyes were wide and his head cocked to one side, listening with a nervous intensity.

Back down the beach, Gail heard Joel shout something. She thought—but she was never sure—that he shouted, "Gail! Come see!" In later years, though, she sometimes had the wretched idea that it had been "God! Help me!"

The mist distorted sound, much as it distorted the light. So when there came a great splash, it was hard to judge the size of the thing making the splashing sound. It was like a bathtub dropped from a great height into the lake. Or a car. It was, anyway, a great splash.

"What was that?" Heather screamed again, holding her stomach as if she had a bellyache.

Gail began to run. She leapt the embankment and hit the beach and fell to her knees. Only the beach was gone. Waves splashed in, foot-high waves like you would see at the ocean, not on Lake Champlain. They drowned the narrow strip of pebbles and sand, running right up to the embankment. She remembered how on the walk back, the water had been lapping gently at the shore, leaving room for Heather and Gail to walk side by side without getting their feet wet.

She ran into the cold blowing vapor, shouting Joel's name. As hard as she ran, she felt she was not going nearly fast enough. She almost ran past the spot where the carcass had been. It wasn't there anymore, and in the mist, with the water surging up around her bare feet, it was hard to tell one stretch of beach from another.

But she spotted Heather's drawing pad, sloshing in on the combers, soaked through, pages tumbling. One of Joel's sneakers tumbled with it, full of the cold, green water. She bent for it automatically—he would want it back—and poured it out and clutched it to her chest.

Gail looked out at the plunging waves, the tormented water. She had a stitch in her side. Her lungs struggled for air. When the waves drew back she could see where the carcass had been dragged through the hard dirt, pulled into the water, going home. It looked as if someone had plowed a tractor blade across the beach and into the lake.

"Joel!"

She shouted at the water. She turned and shouted up the embankment, into the trees, toward Joel's house.

"Joel!"

She spun in a circle, shouting his name. She didn't want to look at the lake but wound up turned to face it again anyway. Her throat burned from yelling, and she was beginning to cry again.

"Gail!" Heather called to her. Her voice was shrill with fright. "Come home, Gail! Come home, *right now*!"

"Gail!" yelled Gail's mother.

"Joel!" Gail shouted, thinking this was ridiculous, everyone shouting for everyone else.

The lowing sound came from a long way off. It was mournful and soft.

"Give him back," Gail whispered. "Please give him back."

Heather ran through the mist. She was up on the embankment, not down on the sand, where the water was still piling in, one heavy, cold wave after another. Then Gail's mother was there too, looking down at her.

"Sweetie," Gail's mother said, her face pale and drawn with alarm. "Come up here, sweetie. Come up here to Mother."

Gail heard her but didn't climb the embankment. Something washed in on the water and caught on her foot. It was Heather's drawing pad, open to one of her ponies. It was a green pony, with a rainbow stripe across it and red hoofs. It was as green as a Christmas tree. Gail didn't know why Heather was always drawing horses that looked so unhorselike, horses that couldn't be. They were like double negatives, those horses, like dinosaurs, a possibility that canceled itself out in the moment it was expressed.

She fetched the drawing pad out of the water and looked at the green pony with a kind of ringing sickness in her, a feeling like she wanted to throw up. She ripped the pony out and crushed it and threw it into the water. She ripped some other ponies out and threw them too, and the crushed balls of paper bobbed and floated around her ankles. No one told her to stop, and Heather did not complain when Gail let the pad fall out of her hands and back into the lake.

Gail looked out at the water, wanting to hear it again, that soft foghorn sound, and she did, but it was inside her this time, the sound was down deep inside her, a long wordless cry for things that weren't never going to happen.

About "By the Silver Water of Lake Champlain"

You don't wear your strongest influences like a shirt, something you take on and off as you like. You wear those influences like your skin. For me, Ray Bradbury is that way. From the time I was twelve to the time I was twenty-two, I read every Bradbury novel and hundreds of Bradbury short stories, many of them two and three times. Teachers came and went; friends ran hot and cold; Bradbury, though, was always there, like Arthur Conan Doyle, like my bedroom, like my parents. When

I ruminate about October, or ghosts, or masks, or faithful dogs, or children and their childish frightening games, every thought I have is colored by what I learned about these things from reading Ray Bradbury. One of Bradbury's most famous collections is *The Illustrated Man,* which features a man tattooed with a countless number of Ray's stories, a man who walks through life carrying all those stories on his back. I relate.

—Joe Hill

LITTLE AMERICA

Dan Chaon

First of all, here are the highways of America. Here are the states in sky blue, pink, pale green, with black lines running across them. Peter has a children's version of the map, which he follows as they drive. He places an *X* by the names of towns they pass by, though most of the ones on his old map aren't there anymore. He sits, staring at the little cartoons of each state's products and services. Corn. Oil wells. Cattle. Skiers.

Second, here is Mr. Breeze himself. Here he is behind the steering wheel of the long old Cadillac. His delicate hands are thin, reddish as if chapped. He wears a white shirt, buttoned at the wrists and neck. His thinning hair is combed neatly over his scalp, his thin, skeleton head is smiling. He is bright and gentle and lively, like one of the hosts of the children's programs Peter used to watch on television. He widens his eyes and enunciates his words when he speaks.

Third is Mr. Breeze's pistol. It is a Glock 19 nine-millimeter compact semiautomatic handgun, Mr. Breeze says. It rests enclosed in the glove box directly in front of Peter, and he imagines that it is sleeping. He pictures the muzzle, the hole where the bullet comes out: a closed eye that might open at any moment.

Outside the abandoned gas station, Mr. Breeze stands with his skeleton head cocked, listening to the faintly creaking hinge of an old sign that advertises cigarettes. His face is expressionless, and so is the face of the gas station storefront. The windows are broken and patched with pieces of cardboard, and there is some trash, some paper cups and leaves and such, dancing in a ring on the oil-stained asphalt. The pumps are just standing there, dumbly.

"Hello?" Mr. Breeze calls after a moment, very loudly. "Anyone home?" He lifts the arm of a nozzle from its cradle on the side of a pump and tries it. He pulls the trigger that makes the gas come out of the hose, but nothing happens.

Peter walks alongside Mr. Breeze, holding Mr. Breeze's hand, peering at the road ahead. He uses his free hand to shade his eyes against the low late-afternoon sun. A little ways down are a few houses and some dead trees. A row of boxcars sitting on the railroad track. A grain elevator with its belfry rising above the leafless branches of elms.

In a newspaper machine is a *USA Today* from August 6, 2012, which was, Peter thinks, about two years ago, maybe? He can't quite remember.

"It doesn't look like anyone lives here anymore," Peter says at last, and Mr. Breeze regards him for a long moment in silence.

At the motel, Peter lies on the bed, facedown, and Mr. Breeze binds his hands behind his back with a plastic tie.

"Is this too tight?" Mr. Breeze says, just as he does every time, very concerned and courteous.

And Peter shakes his head. "No," he says, and he can feel Mr. Breeze adjusting his ankles so that they are parallel. He stays still as Mr. Breeze ties the laces of his tennis shoes together.

"You know that this is not the way that I want things to be," Mr. Breeze says, as he always does. "It's for your own good."

But Peter just looks at him, with what Mr. Breeze refers to as his "inscrutable gaze."

"Would you like me to read to you?" Mr. Breeze asks. "Would you like to hear a story?"

"No, thank you," Peter says.

In the morning there is a noise outside. Peter is on top of the covers, still in his jeans and T-shirt and tennis shoes, still tied up, and Mr. Breeze is beneath the covers in his pajamas, and they both wake with a start. Beyond the window there is a terrible racket. It sounds like they are fighting or possibly killing something. There is some yelping and snarling and anguish, and Peter closes his eyes as Mr. Breeze gets out of bed and springs across the room on his lithe feet to retrieve the gun.

"Shhhh," Mr. Breeze says, and mouths silently: "Don't. You. Move." He shakes his finger at Peter—*no no no!*—and then smiles and makes a little bow before he goes out the door of the motel with his gun at the ready.

Alone in the motel room, Peter lies breathing on the cheap bed, his face down and pressed against the old polyester bedspread, which smells of mildew and ancient tobacco smoke.

He flexes his fingers. His nails, which were once long and black and sharp, have been filed down to the quick by Mr. Breeze—*for his own good,* Mr. Breeze had said.

But what if Mr. Breeze doesn't come back? What then? He will be trapped in this room. He will strain against the plastic ties on his wrist, he will kick and kick his bound feet, he will wriggle off the bed and pull himself to the door and knock his head against it, but there will be no way out. It will be very painful to die of hunger and thirst, he thinks.

After a few minutes Peter hears a shot, a dark firecracker echo that startles him and makes him flinch.

Then Mr. Breeze opens the door. "Nothing to worry about," Mr. Breeze says. "Everything's fine!"

For a while, Peter had worn a leash and collar. The skin side of the collar had round metal nubs that touched Peter's neck and would give him a shock if Mr. Breeze touched a button on the little transmitter he carried.

"This is not how I want things to be," Mr. Breeze told him. "I want us to be friends. I want you to think of me as a teacher. Or an uncle!

"Show me that you're a good boy," Mr. Breeze said, "and I won't make you wear that anymore."

In the beginning Peter had cried a lot, and he had wanted to get away, but Mr. Breeze wouldn't let him go. Mr. Breeze had Peter wrapped up tight and tied in a sleeping bag with just his head sticking out—wriggling like a worm in a cocoon, like a baby trapped in its mother's stomach.

Even though Peter was nearly twelve years old, Mr. Breeze held him in his arms and rocked him and sang old songs under his breath and whispered *shh shhh shhhh*. "It's okay, it's okay," Mr. Breeze said. "Don't be afraid, Peter, I'll take care of you."

They are in the car again now, and it is raining. Peter leans against the window on the passenger side, and he can see the droplets of water inching along the glass, moving like schools of minnows, and he can see the clouds with their gray, foggy fingerlings almost touching the ground, and the trees bowed down and dripping.

"Peter," Mr. Breeze says, after an hour or more of silence. "Have you been watching your map? Do you know where we are?"

And Peter gazes down at the book Mr. Breeze had given him. Here are the highways, the states in their pale primary colors. Nebraska. Wyoming.

"I think we're almost halfway there," Mr. Breeze says. He looks at Peter and his cheerful children's-program eyes are careful, you can see him thinking something besides what he is saying. There is a way that an adult can look into you to see if you are paying attention, to see if you are learning, and Mr. Breeze's eyes scope across him, prodding and nudging.

"It's a nice place," Mr. Breeze says. "A very nice place. You'll have a room of your own. A warm bed to sleep in. Good food to eat. And you'll go to school! I think you'll like it."

"Mm," Peter says, and shudders.

They are passing a cluster of houses now, some of them burned and still smoldering in the rain. There are no people left in those houses, Peter knows. They are all dead. He can feel it in his bones; he can taste it in his mouth.

Also, out beyond the town, in the fields of sunflowers and alfalfa, there are a few who are like him. Kids. They are padding stealthily along the rows of crops, their palms and foot soles pressing lightly along the loamy earth, leaving almost no track. They lift their heads, and their golden eyes glint.

I had a boy once," Mr. Breeze says.

They have been driving without stopping for hours now, listening to a tape of a man and some children singing. *B-I-N-G-O*, they are singing. *Bingo was his name-o!*

"A son," Mr. Breeze says. "He wasn't so much older than you. His name was Jim."

Mr. Breeze moves his hands vaguely against the steering wheel.

"He was a rock hound," Mr. Breeze says. "He liked all kinds of stones and minerals. Geodes, he loved. And fossils! He had a big collection of those!"

"Mm," Peter says.

It is hard to picture Mr. Breeze as a father, with his gaunt head and stick body and puppet mouth. It is hard to imagine what Mrs. Breeze must have looked like. Would she have been a skeleton like him, with a long black dress and long black hair, a spidery way of walking?

Maybe she was his opposite: a plump young farm girl, blond and ruddy-cheeked, smiling and cooking things in the kitchen, like pancakes.

Maybe Mr. Breeze is just making it up. He probably didn't have a wife or son at all.

"What was your wife's name?" Peter says at last, and Mr. Breeze is quiet for a long time. The rain slows, then stops as the mountains grow more distinct in the distance.

"Connie," Mr. Breeze says. "Her name was Connie."

By nightfall, they have passed Cheyenne—*a bad place,* Mr. Breeze says, *not safe*—and they are nearly to Laramie, which has, Mr. Breeze says, a good, organized militia and a high fence around the perimeter of the city.

Peter can see Laramie from a long way off. The trunks of the light poles are as thick and tall as sequoias, and at their top, a cluster of halogen lights, a screaming of brightness, and Peter knows he doesn't want to go there. His arms and legs begin to itch, and he scratches with his sore, clipped nails, even though it hurts just to touch them to skin.

"Stop that, please, Peter," Mr. Breeze says softly, and when Peter doesn't stop he reaches over and gives Peter a flick on the nose with his finger. "*Stop.*" Mr. Breeze says. "*Right. Now.*"

There are blinking yellow lights ahead, where a barrier has been erected, and Mr. Breeze slows the Cadillac as two men emerge from behind a structure made of logs and barbed wire and pieces of cars that have been sharpened into points. The men are soldiers of some kind, carrying rifles, and they shine a flashlight in through the windshield at Peter and Mr. Breeze. Behind them, the high chain fence makes shadow patterns across the road as it moves in the wind.

Mr. Breeze puts the car into park and reaches across and takes the gun from its resting place in the glove box. The men are approaching slowly, and one of them says very loudly: "STEP OUT OF THE CAR, PLEASE, SIR," and Mr. Breeze touches his gun to Peter's leg.

"Be a good boy, Peter," Mr. Breeze whispers. "Don't you try to run away, or they will shoot you."

Then Mr. Breeze puts on his broad, bright puppet smile. He takes out his wallet and opens it so that the men can see his identification, so that they can see the gold seal of the United States of America, the glinting golden stars. He opens his door and steps out. The gun is tucked into the waistband of his pants, and he holds his hands up loosely, displaying the wallet.

He shuts the door with a *thunk,* leaving Peter sealed inside the car.

There is no handle on the passenger side of the car, so Peter cannot open his door. If he wanted to, he could slide across to the driver's seat, and open Mr. Breeze's door, and roll out onto the pavement and try to scramble as fast as he could into the darkness, and maybe he could run fast enough, zig-zagging, so that the bullets they'd shoot would only nip the ground behind him, and he could find his way into some kind of brush or forest and run and run until the voices and the lights were far in the distance.

But the men are watching him very closely. One man is holding his flashlight so that the beam shines directly through the windshield and onto Peter's face, and the other man is staring at Peter as Mr. Breeze speaks and gestures, speaks and gestures like a performer on television who is selling something for kids. But the man is shaking his head no. *No!*

"I don't care what kind of papers you got, mister," the man says. "There's no way you're bringing that thing through these gates."

Peter used to be a real boy.

He can remember it—a lot of it is still very clear in his mind. "I pledge allegiance to the flag" and "Knick knack paddy whack give a dog a bone this old man goes rolling home" and "ABCDEFGHIJKLMNOPQRSTUVWXYZ now I know my ABCs, next time won't you sing with me?" and "Yesterday . . . all my troubles seemed so far away" and . . .

He remembers the house with the big trees in front, riding a scooter along the sidewalk, his foot pumping and making momentum. The bug in a jar—cicada—coming out of its shell and the green wings. His mom and her two braids. The cereal in a bowl, pouring milk on it. His dad flat on the carpet, climbing on his Dad's back: "Dog pile!"

He can still read. The letters come together and make sounds in his mind. When Mr. Breeze asked him, he found he could still say his telephone number and address, and the names of his parents.

"Mark and Rebecca Krolik," he said. "Two one three four Overlook Boulevard, South Bend, Indiana, four six six oh one."

"Very good!" Mr. Breeze said. "Wonderful!"

And then Mr. Breeze said, "Where are they now, Peter? Do you know where your parents are?"

Mr. Breeze pulls back from the barricade of Laramie and the gravel sputters out from their tires and in the rearview mirror Peter can see the men with their guns in the red taillights and dust.

"Damn it," Mr. Breeze says, and slaps his hand against the dashboard. "Damn it! I knew I should have put you in the trunk!" And Peter says nothing. He has never seen Mr. Breeze angry in this way, and it frightens him—the red splotches on Mr. Breeze's skin, the scent of adult rage—though he is also relieved to be moving away from those big halogen lights. He keeps his eyes straight ahead and his hands folded in his lap, and he listens to the silence of Mr. Breeze unraveling, he listens to the highway moving beneath them, and watches as the yellow dotted lines at the center of the road are pulled endlessly beneath the car. For a while, Peter pretends that they are eating the yellow lines.

After a time, Mr. Breeze seems to calm. "Peter," he says. "Two plus two."

"Four," Peter says softly.

"Four and four."

"Eight."

"Eight and eight."

"Sixteen," Peter says, and he can see Mr. Breeze's face in the bluish light that glows from the speedometer. It is the cold profile of a portrait, like the pictures of people that are on money. There is the sound of the tires, the sound of velocity.

"You know," Mr. Breeze says at last. "I don't believe that you're not human."

"Hm," Peter says.

He thinks this over. It's a complicated sentence, more complicated than math, and he's not sure he knows what it means. His hands rest in his lap, and he can feel his poor clipped nails tingling as if they were still there. Mr. Breeze said that after a while he will hardly remember them, but Peter doesn't think this is true.

"When we have children," Mr. Breeze says, "they don't come out like us. They come out like you, Peter, and some of them even less like us than you are. It's been that way for a few years now. But I have to believe that these children—at least *some* of these children—aren't really so different, because they are a part of us, aren't they? They feel things. They experience emotions. They are capable of learning and reason."

"I guess," Peter says, because he isn't sure what to say. There is a kind of look an adult will give you when they want you to agree with them, and it is like a collar they put on you with their eyes, and you can feel the little nubs against your neck, where the electricity will come out. Of course, he is not like Mr. Breeze, nor the men that held the guns at the gates of Laramie; it would be silly to pretend, but this is what Mr. Breeze seems to want. "Maybe," Peter says, and he watches as they pass a green luminescent sign with a white arrow that says EXIT.

He can remember the time that his first tooth came out, and he put it under his pillow in a tiny bag that his mother had made for him which said *Tooth Fairy*, but then the teeth began to come out very quickly after that and the sharp ones came in. Not like Mother or Father's teeth. And the fingernails began to thicken, and the hairs on his forearms and chin and back, and his eyes changed color.

"Tell me," says Mr. Breeze. "You didn't hurt your parents, did you? You loved them, right? Your mom and dad?"

After that, they are quiet again. They are driving and driving and the darkness of the mountain roads closes in around them. The shadows of pine trees, fussing with their raiments. The grim shadows of solid, staring boulders. The shadows of clouds lapping across the moon.

You loved them, right?

Peter leans his head against the passenger window and closes his eyes for a moment, listening to the radio as Mr. Breeze moves the knob slowly across the dial: static. Static—static—man crying—static—static—very distant Mexican music fading in and out—static—man preaching fervidly—static—static. And then silence as Mr. Breeze turns it off, and Peter keeps his eyes closed, tries to breathe slow and heavy like a sleeping person does.

You loved them, right?

And Mr. Breeze is whispering under his breath. A long stream of whisps, nothing recognizable.

When Peter wakes, it's almost daylight. They are parked at a rest stop—Peter can see the sign that says WAGON-HOUND REST AREA sitting in a pile of white rocks, he can see the outlines of the little buildings, one for MEN, one for WOMEN, and there is some graffiti painted against the brick, FOR GOD SO LOVED THE WOLRD HE GAVE HIS ONLY BEGONTEN SON, and the garbage cans tipped over and strewn about, the many fast-food bags ripped open and torn apart and licked clean, and then the remnants licked again later, hopefully, and the openings of the crushed soda cans tasted, hopefully, and the other detritus examined, sniffed though, scattered.

There is a sound nearby. Sounds. A few of them creeping closer.

An old plastic container is being nosed along the asphalt, prodded for whatever dried bit of sugar might still adhere to the interior. Peter hears it. It rolls—*thok thok thok*—then stops. One has picked it up, one is eyeing it, the hardened bit of cola at the bottom. He hears the crunch of teeth against the plastic bottle, and then the sound of loud licking and mastication.

And then one is coming near to the car, where he and Mr. Breeze are supposed to be sleeping.

One leaps up onto the front of the Cadillac, naked, on all fours, and lets out a long stream of pee onto the hood of the car. The car bounces as the boy lands on it, and there is the thick splattering sound, and then the culprit bounds away.

That shakes Mr. Breeze awake! He jerks up, scrabbling, and briefly Peter can see Mr. Breeze's real face, hard-eyed and teeth bared—nothing kindly, nothing from television, nothing like a friendly puppet—and Mr. Breeze clutches his gun and swings it in a circle around the car.

"What the fuck!" Mr. Breeze says.

For a minute he breathes like an animal, in tight, short gasps. He points his gun at the windows: Front. Back. Both sides. Peter makes himself small in the passenger seat.

Afterward, Mr. Breeze is unnerved. They start driving again right away, but Mr. Breeze doesn't put his gun in the glove box. He keeps it in his lap and pats it from time to time, like it is a baby he wants to stay asleep.

It takes him a while to compose himself.

"Well!" he says at last, and he gives Peter his thin-lipped smile. "That was a bad idea, wasn't it?"

"I suppose so," Peter says. He watches as Mr. Breeze gives the gun a slow, comforting stroke. *Shhhhhhh. There, there.* Mr. Breeze's friendly face is back on now, but Peter can see how the fingertips are trembling.

"You should have said something to me, Peter," Mr. Breeze says in a kindly but reproachful voice.

Mr. Breeze raises an eyebrow.

He frowns with mild disappointment.

"You were asleep," Peter says, and clears his throat. "I didn't want to wake you up."

"That was very thoughtful of you," Mr. Breeze says, and Peter glances down at his map. He looks at the dots: Wamsutter. Bitter Creek. Rock Springs. Little America. Evanston.

"How many of them were there, do you think, Peter?" Mr. Breeze says. "A dozen?"

Peter shrugs.

"A dozen means twelve," Mr. Breeze says.

"I know."

"So—do you think there were twelve of them? Or more than twelve of them?"

"I don't know," Peter says. "More than twelve?"

"I should say so," Mr. Breeze says. "I would venture to guess that there were about fifteen of them, Peter." And he is quiet for a little while, as if thinking about the numbers, and Peter thinks about them too. When he thinks about *one dozen*, he can picture a container of eggs. When he thinks about *fifteen*, he can picture a 1 and a 5 standing together, side by side, holding hands like brother and sister.

"You're not like them, Peter," Mr. Breeze whispers. "I know you know that. You're not one of *them*. Are you?"

What is there to say?

Peter stares down at his hands, at his sore, shaved fingernails; he runs his tongue along the points of his teeth; he feels the hard, broad muscles of his shoulders flex, the bristled hairs on his back rubbing uncomfortably against his T-shirt.

"Listen to me," says Mr. Breeze, his voice soft and stern and deliberate. "Listen to me, Peter. You are a special boy. People like me travel all over the country, looking for children just like you. You're different, you know you are. Those *things* back there at the rest stop? You're not like them, you know that, don't you?"

After a time, Peter nods.

You loved them, right? Peter thinks, and he can feel his throat tighten.

He hadn't meant to kill them. Not really.

Most of the time he forgets that it happened, and even when he *does* remember he can't recall *why* it happened.

It was as if his mind was asleep for a while, and then when he woke up there was the disordered house, as if a burglar had turned over every object, looking for treasure. His father's body was in the kitchen, and his mother's was in the bedroom. A lot of blood, a lot of scratches and bites on her, and he put his nose against her hair and smelled it. He lifted her limp hand and pressed the palm of it against his cheek and made it pet him. Then he made it hit him in the nose and the mouth.

"Bad," he had whispered. "Bad! Bad!"

"It's going to be better once we get to Salt Lake," Mr. Breeze says. "It's a special school for children like you, and I know you're going to enjoy it so much. You're going to make a lot of new friends! And you're going to learn so much, too, about the world! You'll read books and work with a calculator and a computer, and you'll do some things with art and music! And there will be counselors there who will help you with your . . . feelings. Because the feelings are just feelings. They are like weather, they come and go. They're not *you*, Peter. Do you understand what I'm saying?"

"Yes," Peter says. He stares out to where the towering white-yellow butte cliffs have been cut through to make room for the road; and the metal guardrail unreels beside them; and the sky is a glowing, empty blue. He blinks slowly.

If he goes to this school, will they make him tell about his mom and dad?

Maybe it will be all right, maybe he *will* like it there.

Maybe the other children will be mean to him, and the teachers won't like him either.

Maybe he *is* special.

Will his fingernails always hurt like this? Will they always have to be cut and filed?

"Listen," Mr. Breeze says. "We're coming up on a tunnel. It's called the Green River Tunnel. You can probably see it on your map. But I want to tell you that there have been some problems with these tunnels. It's easy to block the tunnels from either end, once a car is inside it, so I'm going to speed up, and I'm going to go very, very fast when we get there. Okay? I just want you to be prepared. I don't want you to get alarmed. Okay?"

"Okay," Peter says, and Mr. Breeze smiles broadly and nods, and then without another word they begin to accelerate. The guardrail begins to slip by faster and faster until it is nothing but a silver river of blur, and then the mouths of the tunnels appear before them—one for the left side of the road, one for the right, maybe not mouths but instead a pair of eyes, two black sockets beneath a ridged hill, and Peter can't help himself, he tightens his fingers against his legs even though it hurts.

When they pass beneath the concrete arches, there is a soft *whuff* sound as if they've gone through the membrane of something, and then suddenly there is darkness. He can sense the curved roof of the tunnel over them, a rib cage of dark against dark flicking overhead, and the echo of the car as it speeds up, faster and faster, a long crescendo as the opening in the distance grows wider and wider, and the opening behind them grows smaller.

But even as the car quickens, Peter can feel time slowing down, so that each rotation of tire is like the click of the second hand of a clock. There are kids in the tunnel. Twenty? No, thirty maybe, he can sense the warm bodies of them as they flinch and scrabble up the walls of the tunnel, as they turn and begin to chase after the car's taillights, as they drop stones and bits of metal down from their perches somewhere in the tunnel's concrete rafters. "Yaaah!" they call. "Yaaah!" And their voices make Peter's fingers ache.

In front of them, the hole of daylight spreads open brighter, a corona of whiteness, and Peter can only see the blurry shadow-skeletons of the kids as they leap in front of the car.

They must be going a hundred miles an hour or more when they hit the boy. The boy may be eight or nine, Peter can't tell.

There is only the imprint of a contorted face, and the cry he lets out, a thin, wiry body leaping. Then a heavy thump as the bumper connects with him, and a burst of blood blinds the windshield, and they hear the clunking tumble of the body across the roof of the car and onto the pavement behind them.

Mr. Breeze turns on the windshield wipers, and cleaning fluid squirts up as the wipers squeak across the glass. The world appears through the smeared arcs the wipers make. There is a great expanse of valley and hills and wide open sky.

We're getting very low on gas," Mr. Breeze says, after they've driven for a while in silence.

And Peter doesn't say anything.

"There's a place up ahead. It used to be safe, but I'm not sure if it's safe anymore."

"Oh," Peter says.

"You'll tell me if it's safe, won't you?"

"Yes," Peter says.

"It's called Little America. Do you know why?"

Mr. Breeze looks at him. His eyes are softly sad, and he smiles just a little, wanly, and it's tragic, but it's also okay because that boy wasn't special, not like Peter is special. It is something to be left behind us, says Mr. Breeze's expression.

Peter shrugs.

"It's very interesting," Mr. Breeze says. "Because there once was an explorer named Richard Byrd. And he went into Antarctica, which is a frozen country far to the south, and he made a base on the Ross Ice Shelf, south of the Bay of Whales. And he named his base 'Little America.' And so then later—much much later—they made a motel in Wyoming, and because it was so isolated they decided to call it by the same name. And they used a penguin as their mascot, because penguins are from

Antarctica, and when I was a kid there were a lot of signs and billboards that made the place famous."

"Oh," Peter says, and he can't help but think of the kid. The kid saying, "Yaaah!"

They are driving along very slowly, because it is still hard to see out of the windshield, and the windshield wiper fluid has stopped working. It makes its mechanical sound, but no liquid comes out anymore.

It is a kind of oasis, this place. This Little America. A great, huge parking lot, and many gas pumps, and a store and beyond that a motel, with a green concrete dinosaur standing in the grass, a baby brontosaurus, a little taller than a man.

It is the kind of landscape they like. The long, wide strip-mall buildings with their corridors of shelves; the cavelike concrete passageways of enormous interstate motels, with their damp carpets and moldering beds, the little alcoves where ice machines and tall soda vendors may still be inexplicably running; the parking lots where the abandoned cars provide shelter and hiding places, better than a forest of trees.

"There are a lot of them around here, I think," Mr. Breeze says as they settle in next to a pump. Above them there is a kind of plastic-metal canopy, and they sit for a while under its shade. Peter can sense that Mr. Breeze is uncertain.

"How many of them are there, do you think?" Mr. Breeze says, very casually, and Peter closes his eyes.

"More than a hundred?" Mr. Breeze says.

"Yes," Peter says, and he looks at Mr. Breeze's face, surreptitiously, and it is the face of a man who has to jump a long distance but does not want to.

"Yes," he says. "More than a hundred."

He can feel them. They are peering out from the travel-center building and the windows of the boarded-up motel and old abandoned cars in the parking lot.

"If I get out of the car and try to pump gas, will they come?" Mr. Breeze says.

"Yes," Peter says. "They will come very fast."

"Okay." Mr. Breeze says. And the two of them are silent for a long time. The face of Mr. Breeze is not the face of a television man, or a skeleton, or a puppet. It is the elusive face that adults give you when they are telling you a lie, for your own good, they think, when there is a big secret that they are sorry about.

Always remember, Peter's mother said. *I loved you, even. . .*

"I want you to hold my gun," Mr. Breeze says. "Do you think you can do that? If they start coming . . . ?"

And Peter tries to look at his real face. Could it be said that Mr. Breeze loves him, even if . . .

"We won't make it to Salt Lake unless we get gas," Mr. Breeze says, and Peter watches as he opens the door of the car.

Wait, Peter thinks.

Peter had meant to ask Mr. Breeze about his son, about Jim, the rock hound. "You killed him, didn't you?" Peter had wanted to ask, and he expected that Mr. Breeze would have said yes.

Mr. Breeze would have hesitated for a while, but then finally he would have told the truth, because Mr. Breeze was that kind of person.

And what about me? Peter wanted to ask. *Would you kill me too?*

And Mr. Breeze would have said yes. *Yes, of course. If I needed to. But you would never put me in that situation, would you, Peter? You aren't like the others, are you?*

Peter thinks of all this as Mr. Breeze steps out of the car. He can sense the other kids growing alert, with their long black nails and sharp teeth, with their swift, jumping muscles and bristling hairs. He can see the soft, slow movement of Mr. Breeze's legs. How easy it would be to think: *Prey.*

How warm and full of pumping juice were his sinews, how tender was his skin, the cheeks of his face like a peach.

He knew that they would converge down upon him so swiftly that there wouldn't be time for him to cry out. He knew that they could not help themselves, even as Peter himself could not help himself. His mom, his dad. *Wait,* he wanted to say, but it happened much faster than he expected.

Wait, he thinks. He wants to tell Mr. Breeze. *I want. . .*

I want?

But there isn't really any time for that. *Oh, Mom, I am a good boy,* he thinks. *I want to be a good boy.*

About "Little America"

Ray Bradbury changed my life.

Perhaps that sounds melodramatic, but it's not meant to be. I would not be the same person—I would not have become a writer—if it weren't for Ray Bradbury.

I started reading Bradbury at an early age. I wish I could remember the first I read—I think it might have been *October Country*—but in any case, by the time I was ten or eleven, I was well on my way to reading his entire oeuvre, and one of the results of this reading was that I was inspired to write myself. I wrote sequels to his stories, and imitations of his stories, because I couldn't get enough of them.

I was growing up then in Nebraska, in a very rural western corner of the panhandle. The village I lived in had about twenty people in it, and I was the only child in my grade. I was bused to school in a bigger town, ten miles away, but I was always glad to come home to my books. I didn't fit in very well with the kids in town.

When I was in seventh grade, my English teacher, Mr. Christy, gave us a strange assignment. He asked us to write a letter to our favorite writer, living or dead. In the letter, we were supposed to explain why we liked their writing.

I decided that I would write to Ray Bradbury. But I went further than the assignment. I went to the library and found Ray Bradbury's address in *Contemporary Authors,* and I sent him some of the stories that I'd written. I asked him if he thought I could become a writer.

A few weeks later I got a letter back from him. It was typed on the most beautiful stationery that I'd ever seen, and it was addressed to me. "Dear Dan Chaon: You must never let anyone tell you what you want to be. If you want to be a writer, be a writer. It's that simple. When I was your age, I wrote every day of my life, and my stuff wasn't half as good as yours. Quality doesn't count, to begin with, quantity does. The more you write, the better you'll get. If you write a short story a week for the next three or four years, think of the improvement you'll find in yourself. And, above all, what fun! Are you intensely library-oriented? I hope so. If not, from now on, you must be in the library, when you're not writing, reading, finding, knowing poetry, essays, history, you name it! Keep at it!"

Then, a week later, he sent me a critique of the story I had sent him, and I was so hooked, and so crazy in love. I grew up in a family where no one read, and books were not a big part of daily life, and I felt intensely as if I had been rescued. Ray sent me his book *Zen and the Art of Writing* and Brenda Ueland's *If You Want to Write,* and I read them over and over.

During the next few years of junior high and high school, I would send stories that I thought were good to Ray Bradbury, and he would write me back about them. "The story is a small gem, and perhaps, as with your other stories, too small," he would say. Or: "Take a look at your structure here. What does Mr. B. want from life? I guess you have left that out. My characters write my stories for me. They tell me what they want, then I tell them to go get it, and I follow as they run, working at my typing as they rush to their destiny. Montag, in F.451, wanted to stop burning books. Go stop it! I said. He ran to do just that. I followed, typing. Ahab, in *Moby Dick,* wanted to chase and kill a whale. He rushed raving off to do so. Melville followed, writing the novel with a harpoon in the flesh of the damned Whale!"

And: "This werewolf story is too short! It is an idea in search of conflict, but you are close to finding a short story—some nice ideas there. Develop them! What about the other people in the 'school'? You drop hints, but I would like to know about the others. It is almost like the start of a longer story. What happens when he arrives at the school, or does he ever arrive? Play with the idea."

By the time I went away to college, I had started writing other kinds of stories, and my correspondence with Ray began to peter out. I was distracted by undergraduate life, and I was thoughtless in a lot of ways. Ray wrote: "Why are you going to college? If you aren't careful, it will cut across your writing time, stop your writing stories. Is *that* what you want? Think. *Do* you want to be a writer for a lifetime? What will you take in college that will help you be a writer? You already have a full style. All you need now is practice at structure. Write back. Soon! Love to you! RBradbury"

I never did write back to him. I was scared by his questioning of college, and by that time, I was enamored of a different Ray—Raymond Carver. And, ultimately, I didn't know what to say. I loved college. I thought it did me good. I didn't want to disappoint him.

And then daily life took hold. I published a few stories in magazines, and I sent them to Ray, but he never wrote back. I spoke about him in interviews, his influence on me—and once I even saw him briefly at the Los Angeles Festival of Books, but the line to see him was hours long, and when I came to the front of it I wasn't sure whether he realized who I was. I gave him copies of my books, and he said, "Thank you, thank you," and then I was hustled along. He was a very old man, and he had been signing books for hours and hours. I don't know whether he knew who I was or not.

Oh! I thought. How I wished I had written him back, all those years ago. How I wished I had kept up our correspondence.

But now more than thirty years have passed since I got my first letter from Ray Bradbury. And when Mort Castle wrote to me, suggesting that I write a "tribute" story, I couldn't help but think of that old werewolf story I sent to Ray all those years ago. The first sentence and the last sentence are the same as they were when I was nineteen; the middle is infected with my middle age.

I am nearly the same age that Ray was when he first wrote to me—and that desperate twelve-year-old is very far in the distance. But I can see now how fully Bradbury has fitted himself into my brain. It is not just that he was a mentor to me at a time when I needed him most; it is also that his style, his mood, his way of thinking, has seeped into the very core of my work.

I don't know whether "Little America" will seem like a "Ray Bradbury" story to readers; but I know for a fact that Ray Bradbury has a hold on my soul as a writer.

—Dan Chaon

THE PHONE CALL

John McNally

Dougie had been home from the hospital only an hour when Bob, Dougie's uncle, opened the bedroom door and flipped off Dougie's light without saying a word. The door creaked shut, and footsteps grew softer as his uncle retreated.

Dougie wanted the light back on. He was six years old and couldn't sleep, his throat still pulsing from where his tonsils had been removed. In his room at the hospital he could at least turn on the TV or buzz for the nurse, whom he had fallen in love with, but here at home he had to remain in bed, and all there was to do was study his walls, which he had decorated with covers from his favorite magazine, *Famous Monsters of Filmland*. With the light out, he couldn't even do that.

Dougie had no idea what time it was. He passed the hours thinking about Nurse Jill, who had long, straight hair like Susan Dey in *The Partridge Family*, and how she had rubbed her hand over his hair and said, "I know girls who'd *kill* for those curls." She leaned close to him, almost to his mouth, and whispered, "But you probably hate them, don't you?" With her mouth so close to his own, Dougie wanted to sit up and kiss her. Instead, he stared into her foam-green eyes until she touched his nose with the tip of her finger and stood up.

Dougie replayed that particular memory over and over, because if he let it fade away, it would be replaced by the man he saw right after he'd woken up after his surgery. The man lay motionless in the bed next to him—tubes running into his mouth, a machine beeping continuously, his skin the color of Silly Putty. When the doctor saw that Dougie had come to, he nodded angrily toward Nurse Jill, who swiftly pulled the curtain shut between them. Dougie, barely able to keep his eyes open, eventually fell back to sleep. The next time he woke up he saw two men wearing white shirts and white pants rolling the man out of the room, a blanket covering all of him, including his head, the way Dougie liked to sleep with a flashlight under the covers whenever he stayed awake to look at his magazines with their photos of Dracula and the Creature from the Black Lagoon.

"What was his name?" Dougie asked Nurse Jill later that day.

Nurse Jill smiled. "Mr. Belvedere."

"Where'd he go?" Dougie asked.

Nurse Jill reached down and rested the tip of a finger inside one of Dougie's curls. Testing the curl's buoyancy, she said, "To a better place."

A better place, Dougie thought now, in his bedroom, in the dark. Over the years Doug would meet other people, strangers mostly, with remarkably similar stories, of waking up in a haze of anesthesia next to a dead person whose soul was being spirited away. *Did everyone have such stories?* he would wonder.

The phone in the hallway rang.

The ring was so loud, Dougie's heart sped up.

The phone continued to ring. Wouldn't Uncle Bob or his mother answer it? Bob was his father's brother, but Dougie didn't remember anything about his father. The man had died when Dougie was still a baby. A hunting accident, he'd been told. No, his earliest memories of any man in the house were of Uncle Bob, who came sniffing around every few days like a stray dog, often spending the night.

On the fifth ring, Dougie slid out of bed and, feeling his way from one end of his room to the other, eased open his door.

In the hallway, Dougie could lean against the banister and see the living room below, where aquarium light sprayed gently up toward him, causing the walls to look like they were alive and moving, as though he were the one inside the fish tank. He picked up the phone.

"Hello?" he whispered.

A man called out from the earpiece: "Hello? Hello? Who is this? Is this Dougie?"

Dougie did not recognize the man's voice. "Who are you?" he asked. And then a chill blew up under his pajamas, causing him to shiver. "Is this Mr. Belvedere?"

"Who's Mr. Belvedere? Tell me about him."

"He's in a better place now," Dougie said.

"He's dead?" the man asked. "Did someone kill him?"

"He's in a better place now," Dougie repeated, but he felt like weeping this time because he didn't know who this man was or why he was asking questions.

"Listen," the man said. "I don't have much time, and you won't hear from me again for another couple of years, so I want you to do something for me, okay? I want you to remember who I am. I want you to pay attention. Because something terrible is going to happen, and only you can stop it."

The harder Dougie cried, the worse his stitched and bleeding throat hurt. He began to moan from the pain.

"Don't cry, Dougie," the man said. "Don't cry. I'm your friend. You have to believe me. I'm your . . ."

Dougie hung up and returned to his bedroom, leaving behind

the room with walls that looked like they were breathing and a phone call he would barely remember in a week. He could have turned on his bedroom light now, but he was afraid to. He wouldn't see those walls again until morning, when sunlight seeped through his curtains, waking all the monsters.

Thirty years later, Doug sits at the Tick Tock Lounge with a baker's dozen of his coworkers from Rockwell International. The three tables they pushed together earlier in the night now harbor a collection of beer mugs and pitchers and shot glasses, glasses for highballs and martinis, peeled-off beer bottle labels and soggy napkins. Someone had slammed a beer down onto the last jalapeño popper, squeezing cheese out at both ends, causing it to look like a thick worm that's been stepped on.

Across from Doug sits Louise Malgrave, who keeps touching Doug's ankle with her toes and then acting as though it's an accident.

"Is that you again?" she asks, smiling. She reaches over and taps his hand with her fingernails. She can't *not* touch him, it would seem. "I'm sorry." Louise is a supervisor at Rockwell, while Doug does data entry, typing in long strings of code that he doesn't understand.

"It's okay," Doug says. He considers asking her to go home with him—why not?—but when he leans toward her, what comes out of his mouth surprises even him: "This is the anniversary of my mother's death," he says. He forces a grim, hopeless smile and, almost as an afterthought, adds, "She was murdered when I was fifteen."

"Oh, no!" Louise says, and her face droops, as if sympathy and muscle control are incompatible. She looks a dozen years older now, and whatever vague plans Doug had with her in mind crumble before him.

What Doug has said is true—his mother *was* murdered, and

today *is* the anniversary—but he can't stand the way Louise is looking at him, the pity, the anguish, so he shakes his head and says, "I'm kidding."

"What?"

"I'm drunk. I'm sorry."

"You're a jerk," Louise says. His coworkers stop talking to see why Louise is so angry. "He's a *jerk*," Louise says to her captive audience. "You know what he told me?"

"Actually," Doug says, keeping his voice low, "it's *true*. It's just that . . . I don't know . . . the way you were looking at me."

Jerry, Doug's boss, stands up from his end of the table and walks over. He's eighty pounds overweight and speaks in a voice that sounds like every businessman Doug's ever overheard: deep, loud, fake. "Hey, now," he says, smiling. "Everything okay over here?"

"Fine," Doug says, standing. Louise is crying but shrugging away those who want to comfort her, even though it's obvious she wants the attention. "It's fine," Doug continues. "A misunderstanding is all."

Jerry nods. He escorts Doug to the Tick Tock's exit, and together they stand in the glow of neon beer signs. "Let's talk on Monday, shall we?"

Doug nods. "Okay. All right." He reaches out to shake Jerry's hand, but Jerry turns and heads toward Louise Malgrave, leaving Doug with his arm outstretched.

Doug hits three more taverns on his way home. By the time he reaches his apartment foyer, he's having a hard time inserting the miniature key into his mailbox lock. He rests his head against the wall, shuts his eyes, and tries it one last time. This time the key goes in. When he opens the door, a fat phone bill falls out onto the chipped tile floor.

"Damnit," he says when he sees it's the same phone company

he's been having problems with. His long-distance phone service was slammed. Doug heard the term *slammed* for the first time only recently when news reports popped up about a local renegade phone company taking over people's long-distance service without the customers' approval. It's illegal, of course, but extraordinarily difficult to stop once it's set in motion. The name of this company is Blue Skies.

Doug tears open the phone bill as he mounts the stairs to his apartment, and after banging open his door and flipping on the kitchen light, he examines the bill. Amount Due: $3,456.72.

"Three thousand and *what*?" he yells. "Are they *kidding*?" He squints at the bill.

He walks into his bedroom, where he has hung all the old covers from the magazine *Famous Monsters of Filmland*, the same covers he'd hung on his wall in childhood. They are torn now and fading, but he can't bring himself to take them down. The thought of doing so fills him with an inexplicable sadness. He clings to his monsters, the way others cling to old blankets or favorite coffee mugs.

Doug climbs into bed with his shoes on. The heavy black rotary phone sits like a purposefully silent and endangered reptile, the last of its kind, on his bedside table. He picks up the receiver and dials the number for Blue Skies.

"Blue Skies," a woman says. "My name is Bethany. How may I help you?"

"How may you help me," Doug says coldly, staring into the eyes of Lon Chaney as Mr. Hyde. "First off, Bethany, you can tell me how it's even possible for my bill to be over three thousand dollars."

"The amount due," Bethany begins, "is based on how many calls you—"

Doug cuts her off. "*Look*," he yells, "I didn't even sign up with your company. What you're doing is illegal. I want you to switch me back to my old provider."

"I'm sorry," Bethany says, "but it's too late. There's nothing to be done."

"What the hell do you mean it's too late, that there's nothing to be done?"

"Sir," Bethany says. "Please lower your voice."

"I *won't* lower my voice. I . . ."

The phone goes dead.

"Hello? Bethany? Hello?"

Doug slams down the phone. He calls back and Bethany answers again.

"Are you calm now, sir?"

"Look," Doug says. He shuts his eyes. He's drunk and sleepy. He can feel the room spinning, the way the merry-go-round felt when his Uncle Bob started to push it faster and faster—Dougie crying, begging him to stop because it was going too fast and he could barely hang on. He starts dreaming about that time in his life when he hears a voice in his ear: "Hello? Are you still there?"

"Who is this?" Doug asks.

"It's Bethany."

"Hi, Bethany," Doug whispers. He waits for her to say something, but when she doesn't, he asks, "What are you wearing?"

"I beg your pardon?"

"I'm in bed," Doug says. "Where are *you*?"

"Maybe *that's* why your bill is so expensive," Bethany says sharply. "Those sorts of calls are expensive. Now, good night, sir," she says, and hangs up.

Doug falls asleep with the phone against his ear until he's woken by a loud beeping, a phone off its hook. He returns the phone to its cradle, stares at it for a good while, then picks up the receiver again. Every year, on the anniversary of his mother's death, he dials his old home's phone number, a number that has remained etched in his mind, even though it's been disconnected for years.

Concentrating, he puts his finger in the rotary's dial, draws his finger to the right for each number, and lets the dial go. He expects the familiar we're-sorry-but-the-number-you-have-dialed-is-no-longer-in-service message, but on the second ring a woman answers, an actual human being, and Doug quickly sits up.

"Hello?" she says. A baby is crying in the background.

"Hello?" Doug says. "Who's this?"

"Hey, who's *this*?" the woman asks. She laughs, and a chill runs through Doug: *He knows this woman*. The baby cries louder now, and the woman is saying, "Hush, hush, sweetie." A doorbell rings. "Hold on there," the woman says to Doug. He hears the phone getting set down; he hears footsteps, a door opening, voices. And then he hears what sounds like a hurt animal, a sound that frightens Doug, has always frightened Doug—the plaintive wailing of grief. What's happening?

"Hello!" Doug yells into the phone. "What's going on there? Hello!"

He hears someone moving toward the phone. The receiver is lifted, and a man says, "Who is this?"

"It's Doug. Who's this?"

"Doug?" The man sounds confused, disoriented. "I don't know what you're selling, Doug, but you'll have to call another time. There's been an accident here." The phone is hung up with a thud.

Doug removes the receiver from his ear and stares at it. He knows he shouldn't do this, but he dials the number again, just to confirm that he did indeed dial his old phone number. If the same man answers, he'll simply hang up. But it's the woman this time.

"Hello?" She sounds tired now. Doug hears a young child in the background calling out, "Mommy, Mommy, Mommy."

"Hush," the woman says sharply to the child. And then again: "Hello?"

"Hi," Doug says. "I was just calling to make sure everything is okay."

"I'm sorry?" the woman says. "I think you have the wrong number?"

It's the way she ends her sentences as questions that exhumes the past, confirming for Doug who it is he's speaking to: *his mother.* He hasn't heard her voice for so many years, a voice he thought he would never forget, but as one year folded into another, one decade after the other disappearing behind him, he found it harder and harder to conjure her up as she had once been. Her voice had been the first thing to fade, until he couldn't remember her inflections on certain words or the precise way she carried her southern childhood in her speech. For the first time, he experiences what everyone else who's ever stepped into his bedroom has experienced—that all the monsters on his walls are staring directly at him.

"This is Shirley, isn't it?" he asks. His voice cracks. He's trying not to cry.

"It *is,*" she says suspiciously. "And who are *you*?"

There is no way he can explain to her who he is. He can only try to keep her talking.

"We met a few years ago," Doug says. "I worked with your husband, Tim." Silence. "My name's Frank Ivers. You wouldn't remember me." He forces out a laugh. He hears the child in the background again. The child is him. He's listening to his younger self. "I didn't know Tim well," Doug says, "but I always liked him. I'm just calling . . ." He pauses. He's shivering but trying not to. "I'm just calling to see how you're holding up."

He hears his mother lighting a cigarette. This means she's settling in for a long conversation.

"It hasn't been an easy three years," she says. "The day Bob came home with the news . . ." She blows smoke into the mouthpiece. She's sitting down now, Doug imagines. "It was the worst day of my life."

"I'm so sorry," he says. "I just want you to know that I'm a friend."

His mother makes a noise of assent, but she's lost in her own world. How many times had he seen this, his mother sitting on the couch and staring straight ahead as he tried to get her attention, showing her the cover of his new *Famous Monsters of Filmland*?

"Something's not right," she says finally. "I can't put my finger on it, but . . ."

"Yes?"

Doug hears something rumbling in the background. A pickup truck?

"I've got to go," his mother says.

"Who is it, Shirley? Is it Bob?"

The phone goes dead.

Doug is pacing the room, two fingers holding the heavy black phone, the phone's base resting against his thigh. He sets down the phone, hangs up the receiver. After his father's death, Bob began coming over more frequently, sometimes spending the night on the couch. Doug's earliest memories are of his uncle snoring on their sofa as his mother tiptoed through the room and scolded Doug for playing too loudly with his Hot Wheels. "You don't want to wake that man" was how she put it.

Doug was fifteen when his mother was murdered. A homeless man, who had been dumpster diving, discovered Shirley's body in a large trash bin behind an apartment complex. She was wrapped in a blue tarp. People who lived in the apartment building had thrown leaking bags of garbage on top of her, unaware that a body was there. An autopsy revealed that she had died from severe blunt head trauma. Police had detained the homeless man as a possible suspect, but there was nothing to connect him to Doug's mother, and no weapons of any kind had been found on him. No weapon of any kind had ever been found. Bob had been questioned, too, but he'd provided an alibi—a friend claimed they'd spent the evening together watching the Cubs game on TV, the same friend who had been with Bob during Doug's father's hunting accident. Doug had been away at a high school speech tournament, spending the weekend in a dorm room downstate. The story of his mother's death stayed in the news for several weeks, lingering longer than most, but eventually, like everything else in life, it faded.

Doug dials the number again. He isn't drunk anymore. In fact, he feels more lucid than he's ever felt. For the first time, he believes he can undo the terrible things that happened, that he can turn time back, that he can control the outcome. On the eighth ring, a boy answers.

"Hello?" the boy whispers.

"Hello?" Doug says. "Hello? Who is this? Is this Dougie?" Doug knows without a doubt that he is speaking to his younger self. He doesn't even realize he's crying until his knuckles, wrapped around the receiver and pressed against his face, pool up the wetness.

"Who are you?" the boy asks. "Is this Mr. Belvedere?"

Doug takes a deep breath. The name is familiar. But why? "Who's Mr. Belvedere? Tell me about him."

"He's in a better place now," Dougie says.

"He's dead?" Doug asks. "Did someone kill him?"

"He's in a better place now," Dougie repeats.

"Listen," Doug says. "I don't have much time, and you won't hear from me again for another couple of years, so I want you to do something for me, okay? I want you to remember who I am. I want you to pay attention. Because something terrible is going to happen, and only you can stop it."

Dougie starts crying into the phone, and Doug remembers now how easily he used to fall apart, Uncle Bob always mocking him, matching little Dougie's snivels with his own fake snivels, mashing his ugly, scrunched-up face against Dougie's, his uncle's sour breath like poison. He could taste that man's breath for hours afterward.

"Don't cry, Dougie," Doug says. "Don't cry. I'm your friend. You have to believe me. I'm your friend. Okay? I'm your . . ." He senses something has happened. "Hello? Dougie? Hello?" The call has been disconnected.

The phone calls are jumping in time, but by how much?

Doug quickly calls back, but the old phone is slow, and each number he dials on the rotary requires patience. It's one of the reasons he has continued using this old phone, to distinguish himself from his coworkers who are always distracted by their cell phones, texting even as he's trying to talk to them: "Go on," they'll say. "I'm listening." Doug thought the rotary phone would keep him grounded, but now he desires speed; he desires whatever technology will allow him to stay in contact with his old life.

"Hello?" It's the boy again. Dougie. Himself. His voice—the boy's—is deeper now.

"Dougie," Doug says. "How old are you?"

"Who is this?"

"Quick. How old are you?"

"Nine," Dougie says.

"Nine," Doug repeats. "Do you remember me? We talked probably three years ago? You had mentioned someone named Mr. Belvedere?"

"I don't know what you're talking about," Dougie says.

In the background, a man calls out, "Who the hell are you talking to? If they're selling something, just hang up!"

"Is that Uncle Bob?" Doug asks.

"Yes?" Dougie says. He's suspicious, but he's curious, too. Doug knows this because he knows how he would feel.

"Something terrible is going to happen to Mom," Doug says. He swallows. *Slow down*, he tells himself. "To your *mother*," Doug says. "I don't know who's responsible, but I think it's your Uncle Bob. It'll happen when you're fifteen."

His voice shaking, Dougie whispers, "I'm calling the police."

"It's too soon," Doug says. "He hasn't done anything yet."

"I'm calling them on *you*," Dougie says.

"No, no. I'm your friend."

"No, you're not," Dougie says, and hangs up.

Doug dials the number again as fast as he can, as fast as the phone will allow him. It rings ten times. Eleven. Twelve. Thirteen. Has he wasted a phone call? What if time jumps six years the next time he calls? *Pick up . . . pick up,* he thinks. And then, miraculously, someone picks up. He can tell by the way the phone rattles, the way the receiver is almost dropped, that whoever picked up must have run to the phone.

"Yes? Hello?"

It's his mother. It's Shirley.

"Shirley?" Doug says.

"Yes?" She's out of breath.

Doug realizes that this may be the last time he'll ever talk to his mother. He also realizes that the phone he's using is the same phone his mother is using: the heavy black rotary. They are holding the same receiver, but they are separated by time and space.

He decides to risk it. He'll never forgive himself if he lets this moment go. "Mom," he says.

Shirley says, "I'm sorry, but—"

"No," Doug says. "It's me. It's Doug."

There is silence. Then Doug hears her digging through her purse to find her cigarettes. She keeps them in a rectangular pouch with a snap; there's a pocket on the side for the disposable butane lighter. He hears the flick of the lighter, his mother puffing to get the cigarette lit.

She exhales and says, "I knew it was you the first time you called all those years ago."

"How?" Doug asks. "How did you know?"

"A mother knows her son," she says.

Doug flips off his bedroom light and lies down, setting the phone on his chest.

He says, "I need to tell you something."

"Hold that thought?" his mother says, her voice getting higher as she ends her request as a question. "I want to know about you. I want to know how you've been. Did everything turn out okay?"

No, he thinks. *No, it hasn't.* But he doesn't want to disappoint her. "Everything's beautiful," Doug says.

"Are you married?"

"Yes," Doug lies.

"Kids?"

"A boy and a girl."

"Are they healthy?"

"Yes, they are," Doug says. "They're perfect."

"What's your wife's name?"

He imagines his coworker from earlier tonight, the way she would touch his ankle with her toes. "Louise," Doug says. "Louise Malgrave."

"I'm so happy," his mother says.

"But Mom. Listen," Doug says.

His mother interrupts: "Shhhhhhhhhh. Hush now. I want to hear about you."

Doug shuts his eyes. He's so tired. "I don't know what else there is to tell you."

"Tell me what your day is like. Tell me what you look like now," she says. "Tell me anything. I just want you to talk to me."

Doug obeys. He tells her of an imaginary day in the life of a Doug who doesn't exist. He tells her about his three-bedroom house. It's in a neighborhood she always wanted to live in. He tells her about the new riding lawn mower, the family portraits on the wall, the alligator shoes Louise bought him for his birthday. He tells her about the life she always dreamed of, the life he'll never live, and he can tell by the way she laughs or sighs that she's happy about how her son's future will turn out.

Doug wakes up with the phone on his chest, the receiver beeping near his ear. He fell asleep while talking to his mother. His heart starts pounding. How could he have fallen asleep?

He reaches over and flips on the light. He hangs up the phone long enough to get a dial tone and then dials his old number again. It barely rings before someone answers.

"Who is this?" It's Uncle Bob. His voice is deep, a rumble. He sounds as though he hasn't slept in days, weeks.

Doug says, "Can we talk?"

"I knew it," Uncle Bob says. "I just didn't think you'd have the gall to call here."

"You don't understand," Doug says.

In the background, Shirley says, "Who is it?" and Uncle Bob says, "You know damned well who it is."

"Hold on," Doug says. His own breathing is shallow. He feels sick. "I'm not who you think I am," he says. "Please listen to me."

Uncle Bob's voice comes to Doug from a distance now; he must have set down the receiver. "You want to talk to him one last time?" he asks Shirley. "Come here and talk to him," he yells.

"I don't know what you're talking about, Bob," Shirley says.

Something falls over and breaks. Shirley screams.

Doug, holding the phone, paces his bedroom. He's yelling into the receiver: "Bob! Bob! Bob, let's talk!"

Their voices, his mother's and Uncle Bob's, grow louder as they approach the phone, but it sounds as though his mother is being dragged against her will.

"Leave her alone!" Doug yells.

Clearly, Bob isn't listening. He's gripped by his own rage, the way a man drowning in quicksand can't think of anything except surviving. He says, "You want to talk to him? Hunh? You want to talk to him?"

The phone, Doug can tell, is being picked up. But then there is a loud crash coupled with a scream. The crash is like an explosion in Doug's ear. This sound repeats, over and over, until his mother stops screaming. He hears his uncle breathing heavily, and then he hears nothing, as though the phone's cord has been pulled from the wall. Doug waits.

But there's only silence. Just silence.

Doug hangs up and dials again. There's a noise after the second ring, a click, as though someone is answering, but it's only the familiar automated voice from years past: "We're sorry, but the number you have dialed is no longer in service . . ."

Doug slams the receiver back into place.

He sits on the edge of his bed, phone on his knee, shaking. He's cold, too. Freezing. He plays the last phone call over in his head and then plays it again, his uncle yelling, "You want to talk to him? Hunh? You want to talk to him?"

On a hunch, Doug lifts the phone into the air, holding the receiver to keep it secure in its place, and then flips the entire phone upside down. The bottom is black metal with perforations, four thick rubber washers for legs, stickers with numbers printed across them, a dial for turning the ringer up, and several screws. Doug feels it before he sees it. The tip of his finger hits a series of rough patches on the metal surface. Holding it close to the light, Doug can see it now: dried blood. He confirms it by chipping some away with his fingernail. It's been here all along, traveling with him from apartment to apartment, always next to him as he sleeps. Doug chips away more dried blood until his hands are covered with brown flecks and his fingertip is bleeding from scratching at the phone.

It's his mother's blood. It's his mother's blood, and Doug is holding the murder weapon.

Doug drops the phone onto his bed and walks to his kitchen, flipping on the light. He picks up the phone bill and studies it up and down, searching for an address. On the back of the last page is print so small, he isn't even sure in what language it's written. He pulls from his desk drawer a magnifying glass his mother had given to him when he was a child. It has a hand-carved ivory handle and sterling silver frame, and it had once belonged to her grandfather. Before handing it over, his mother had made Doug promise to be careful with it. Doug is depressed now to think he's kept it not on a mantel or wrapped in velvet but in a drawer littered with matchbooks, old IDs, orphaned keys, a furtive golf ball, and worthless wristwatches that died long ago.

He holds the magnifying glass up to his eye, moving it close to the text on the bill and then back up to his face, until the words come into focus. In the tiniest print, he sees a street address for customer complaints. The company is local, and their offices are located in a building downtown that he knows well: the Belvedere.

Doug leaves his apartment, the phone bill clutched in his fist. He's never been downtown this time of night, after the bars have closed. The stoplights are all blinking yellow for caution. There are, however, a surprising number of cars parked along the side streets. Doug takes the first space he sees, even though it's several blocks from the Belvedere.

Doug had lived with his Uncle Bob until he graduated high school and went away to college. During those two years after his mother's murder, Uncle Bob had taken surprisingly good care of Doug. In fact, he was kinder to Doug after his mother's death than he'd ever been when she was alive. It wasn't that any violence ever had been visited upon Doug, nor did he ever see his uncle do anything to his mother. It was more of a mood that Doug was keenly aware of when his uncle was around, the way a rainy day might become eerily sunny and airless before a tornado. It was intangible. But all of that stopped once his mother was gone.

One evening, when Doug was nineteen and home for Christmas break, he walked upstairs to ask his uncle what he wanted for dinner. When he opened his uncle's bedroom door—his *mother's* bedroom door—he saw his uncle lying perfectly motionless on the bed, on his back, a white sheet pulled up to his neck, his skin already as gray as a midwestern sky in late November. Doug's first impulse was to call 911, but at the phone he paused. *It's too late,* he thought. *There's nothing to be done.* He sat on the side of the bed and spent time with the dead man before making the call.

It's cold out tonight, and Doug can't stop shivering. It's as though the convulsions are now part of his nervous system, utterly beyond his control, so he tightens his grip on the phone bill so as not to lose it when he trembles.

He rounds a corner, where the tall, slim Belvedere stands like a soldier among kneeling prisoners. He starts picking up his pace to reach the revolving door when he realizes that the building's plaza, with its manicured trees and freshly painted garbage cans, is crowded with dozens of people. He recognizes Mary Beemis, whose daughter disappeared one winter afternoon after school, never to be seen again. He sees across the way Mr. Simon, whose Alzheimer's-riddled father wandered away one night in the freezing cold—gone forever. In front of him stand the Garcia twins, now in their twenties, whose parents were killed in an unsolved hit-and-run. These are the city's grievers, its mourners, and they are all peering up at the Belvedere and whispering, as though praying to a temple of their own lost souls.

The phone bill slips from Doug's fingers, kisses the concrete, and then skitters down the paper-strewn street. He had thought he'd come here looking for answers, but he sees now that there are no answers. He is here for the same reason so many others are here—to let the past go, to move on. Out of breath, still trembling, Doug slowly crosses the street, where in the cold predawn he joins ranks with his tribe of the bereaved, more than a hundred others standing together, shoulder to shoulder, but utterly and forever alone.

About "The Phone Call"

In 1989, one year after my mother died of cancer, I woke up in the middle of the night, walked to my typewriter, and hammered out a short story in one sitting. I even gave it a title: "The Phone Call." It was the story of a son, who, through mysterious means, tries to save his mother's life, even though she is already dead. Writing the story was a necessary exercise in catharsis, an apology to my own mother for not having done more to save her from dying—not that there was anything I realistically could have done. I printed up a copy of the story to work on later, but then an odd thing happened. I lost it. For years afterward, I considered rewriting the story from memory. I occasionally jotted down notes. When I began writing screenplays, I outlined a movie version of the story. About ten years ago I found the story again. The paper had yellowed, and the ink from the dot-matrix printer had faded, but there it was—the lost story! I read the first page before deciding not to read any more of it. I didn't want to be influenced by the original version should I ever decide to rework it, so I set it aside. I haven't seen it since. I recently tried finding it but didn't have any luck. Once again, the original version is lost.

When I was contacted about contributing a story to this anthology, I knew right away that I was (finally!) going to write "The Phone Call," and when I sat down to work on it, the pages came quickly. The story, after all, had been gestating for more than twenty years. That's not to say that the story didn't surprise me or take me in new directions. It did. And I'm grateful for that. But the original story's DNA is fundamentally intact in this version.

Like many writers, I was inspired to become a fiction writer because of Ray Bradbury. I read *The Illustrated Man* in grade school, highlighting the titles of stories that I liked best. The power of those stories, the originality, their distinctive voices—all of these things lingered with me for decades. If the Russian Realists came out from under Gogol's overcoat, then contemporary speculative writers have followed Ray Bradbury off his flying saucer. But speculation in a Bradbury story is always subterfuge for something much larger and deeper, and there's a damn good reason why his work has endured: His stories are, first and foremost, about people in crisis—people we care about . . . people *Ray* cares about. "The Phone Call" owes a debt to this great writer, who taught me that the core of any good story, whatever its fantastical premise, is always the liabilities of the human heart.

—John McNally

YOUNG PILGRIMS

Joe Meno

But the outpost colony of that otherwise uninhabited planet was known to be Christian, said to have been settled by members of two devout families. Both of these families had—like other believers before them—crossed inconceivable distances, rebuked the trappings of a civilization gone without God, and marshaled all they could against the ignominy of doubt to begin again, to build the world anew. This was the explanation most often given for the colonists' insistence on isolation and their curious fortitude: It was thought that no one but a religious settlement would have been able to make anything out of a land so bleak. The unnamed planet on which the colony had been built was inconsiderable, closer in size to Phobos, the Martian moon, its one hemisphere covered in a perpetual half-gray darkness. Other than the silver boundaries of the colony itself, which consisted of three glass domes—used for shelter and various farming developments, surrounded by oddments of tunnels, barracks, and air locks—there was nothing: only the arid patchwork of hundreds of low hills covered in red dust and then, above those, the unappealing immaculacy of outer space.

* * *

There it is, up ahead," Quinn said, pointing to a red rise in the distance. The boy nodded to himself, having almost given up hope a few paces back. But there it was now: the low, pyramidal hill, and beside it the path he had made a week earlier.

With his left hand he took hold of the girl Lana's heavy silver glove, his breath—coming faster as they climbed along the incline—fogging up the inside of his convex helmet. Lana slipped a little in the dirt, and Quinn had to hold on to her with both hands. Once they stumbled to the peak, they both rested, Quinn leaning over, his breath appearing and then disappearing along the seamless inside of the helmet, Lana sitting down in the dust, holding her heavy helmet up with both hands.

"If I had known it was going to be so far . . . ," she said, but did not bother to finish her sentence.

Beneath the rounded helmet, Quinn could see that the girl's cheeks were flushed. It looked more than lovely. There was an odd strand of blond hair plastered along her forehead, which was dappled by a few nearly indistinguishable dots of sweat. She looked like a child sitting there, pouting a little, her eyes closed as she tried to catch her breath. She was fourteen, one year older than Quinn. Both of them had been born somewhere on the voyage from There to Here, a single point on a starry map no one could trace or be sure of anymore, as everything that was the Past, including the ship used for their passage, had been disposed of, dismantled, or buried a long time ago. There was a joke Quinn's mother used to tell him when he was younger, as she tucked him into bed, something about being born in space, "her child, created out of the dust of stars," which he never understood and which he could no longer quite remember. He looked down at Lana, watched her cheeks cool to a softer white, and then asked, "Are you ready?"

Lana nodded slightly but did not move at first. Instead, she looked up at him, staring seriously into his eyes. "If my father ever finds out we're all the way out here . . . ," and again did not finish her sentence, not because she couldn't but because, this time, there was no need.

Lana's father, Forrest Blau, was a man of rigid temperament with a wide face and striking gray beard. He had personally funded the Great Journey. On Earth, he had been the owner of a large factory farm. Now, as minister of this meager colony, he led prayer services and, in private, heard Quinn's confession. His face was the face of God as Quinn could, at the moment, imagine it—harsh, immovable, a little like the gray features of the planet itself. There was also his long white switch—whittled to a sharp point, waxed to a gleaming shine, cut from a branch of the birch tree, the first living thing that had flourished here and which now filled most of Dome Three with its eager, ancient-looking branches. Forrest kept the white switch beside his place at the dining room table. He would sometimes use it during his sermons, pointing from family member to family member asking, "Who here among us is without sin?" and Quinn would always bow his head and look away. More than once the boy had felt the white switch cut across his hands or along his backside as he willed himself not to cry. Forrest, at these times, would seem displeased, deeply distraught, divinely eager for the boy to make amends. It was as though it hurt Forrest more to inflict punishment than it did for the condemned to receive it. Then the switch would fly back again and come down hard against Quinn's knuckles, and whatever Forrest Blau was feeling would flee from the boy's mind as the pain erupted along his hands, his knuckles. Then once more the switch would fly back. Then again.

There was also Forrest Blau's bolt-action rifle—an ancient M1903 Springfield in perfect working order—which hung loaded, above the air lock leading from the colony to the outside world. Quinn had never seen it used before, had never even seen anyone hold it, except once a week, when Forrest would take it down for cleaning. This, too, was a religious act for the minister. There was a sense of sanctity as the gray-bearded man oiled the pins and checked the bore. Once the rifle was reassembled, Forrest would lift his wrinkled face skyward and close his eyes, saying a mysteriously short prayer, looking both penitent and elegantly severe.

Lana Blau was nothing like her father; Quinn often thought of her as a moss rose, the kind that flourished under Dome Two, unpredictable though beautiful, growing a little wilder each year, grappling its way amongst the angles and divides of the planet's craggy rocks. Or maybe she was like one of those pink cherry trees, growing taller than anyone thought was possible from soil with remarkable levels of carbon dioxide. There was something about the dirt of this place, Quinn's father, William, often said. William, on Earth, had worked for Forrest Blau's food-manufacturing firm as a food geneticist. William claimed that there was something about the preponderance of unbreathable carbon dioxide that made everything grow and bloom in ways no one could have guessed. It was the reason the colonists had to wear the tank suits and helmets anywhere outside of the three-domed colony and why hiking so far from the compound was forbidden. Once the air in their air tanks was gone, or God forbid, if there ever was an accident . . . But nothing like that had ever happened, and this lone excursion, traversing the rises and hills with Lana, was the only way Quinn could devise to be alone with her. And even though he was still a boy and she was still a girl, Quinn had begun to catch himself staring at her forehead, at her neck, at her mouth, wondering what she was thinking. Did she have any idea what he was thinking? What if, on this hike, they should spot something like a long-tailed rodent, or some other animal, some small creature no one else had ever seen, and she was to jump back in fright and Quinn was to catch her? Then would she begin to understand some of the feelings he had been having?

"We better get moving," Lana said, standing up. "If we want to make it back before prayers."

Quinn nodded and off they went, scrambling over the loose red rocks again, their long, lithe shadows playing upon each other at the ends of their flat, dusty boots.

There was a beautiful pink tree, made of something like glimmering crystals, that Quinn had discovered while hiking alone a few weeks earlier. This was what he wanted Lana to see; this was what he thought might help begin to approximate the shape and depth of his feelings for her. Or not. Or, more likely, she would look at it and smile, and then shrug, and the two of them would walk back to the colony unspeaking, their breath going faster and faster as they struggled to return to Dome One by curfew, this breathlessness their only meaningful exchange.

But there was nothing else like it on the planet, the pink tree, nothing Mr. Blau or Quinn's father had ever mentioned, and the way it grew there in sharp angles, glistening like it was covered in white and pink crystals, it was something Lana just had to see for herself. And it was a few more meters, just over the next low hill. Quinn saw Lana struggle as she climbed, and so placed his hand under her arm, helping her over a loose rise of gray gravel, his fingers lingering half a moment too long in the space between her underarm and her side. The girl paused just then, looking down at him suspiciously. She glared at his hand on her underarm, and he nodded, quickly withdrawing it. It was about as intimate a touch as the two had ever shared, and their space suits—with their layers of fabric, Mylar, and padding—did little to occlude the strange electrical charge Quinn felt throbbing in his fingers. His cheeks quickly flamed red. He let Lana walk on ahead, watching her stumble slightly once more, before she recovered her balance. She looked back to see if Quinn had noticed, and then she smiled the smile of someone who did not care whether anyone had noticed or not. It was confusing, and also exciting, to see how one moment Lana could seem like her old self, just like a child, and in another moment there would be some other gesture, the way she tilted her head, the softness in her eyes, that seemed like she was someone new, someone much older. It was hard to know which person the boy had been falling for.

He hurried up the incline, trying to ignore these new thoughts, and as he did, there was a landslide of red-gray gravel from above, and then Quinn was sliding backward, fumbling on his face, tumbling headlong down the rise. It took him longer than he would have thought to get back on his feet, and by that time Lana had disappeared. She was gone. There was only an enormous pile of loose red rocks, tilting and spilling everywhere, rising as high as his feet, and the unforgiving pale blue lights of the colony flashing back at him, somewhere from the hazy distance. Something terrible had happened. Lana was missing.

Quinn had never run as hard in his life, and still the three glass domes seemed so far away. He tripped once, pulling himself up, then again, and this time lay there in the dust, his forehead resting against the cold, inner contours of his glass helmet. What had he done? Where had Lana gone? What would happen when Forrest found out? How, if ever, would he be forgiven?

He had thought he was becoming a man. And here he was something so far from it. He had left Lana, had run off like a frightened child. How would he ever be able to look his mother, his father, Forrest Blau, in the face and tell them what had happened? And what would happen to him once he did?

The boy struggled back to his feet, thinking of Forrest Blau's stern features, of the white switch lying beside the table, of the well-oiled rifle hanging above the air lock. He turned then, facing the way he had just come, his footprints still directing small cloud after small cloud of fine red dust in the air. He made a decision then, and checking to be sure there was still enough air in the tank, he sprinted back along the trail he had just made. The sound of his nervous heartbeat reverberating in his ears, of his feet clomping through the heavy dust, of his breath as it fogged up the front of his helmet, firmly carried him back up the incline of the rough, red rocks to where Lana had, only moments before, disappeared.

The rock slide had left a slanting hill where Lana had been standing. Besides that, there was nothing, only a set of her footprints, which were surprisingly larger than his. He lifted a small red boulder, then another, then a third, hoping to see a flash of her silver suit, the tread of her black boots, the glassy enclosure of her rounded helmet. But there was only more dust, only more red dirt. He tossed rock after rock aside, and as he did, he began to cry. He pounded on the sides of his helmet. His face—drenched in sweat—twisted itself into a rictus of dismay. With the helmet on he was unable to wipe the salty tears from his eyes, and so it felt as if he was drowning. He doubled over, feeling like he might begin to vomit. And as he leaned there, bile rising up in his throat, he saw something move.

Something.

The smallest of movements.

A light.

A soft pink light, emanating from between the piles of triangular rocks.

Quinn fell to his knees and began to hurl the pieces of stone aside with his heavy gloves, clawing at the upturned angles, digging his fingers into the sediment, until a ray of soft pink light poured out—the light the same color as the mysterious crystal tree he had discovered a few weeks before—and then, as he scuttled more of the gravel aside, the light struck against the curved exterior of his helmet, refracting, pouring against his eyelids, his nose, his mouth. For a moment he thought he was going blind, the light shifting from pink to white, his eyes struggling to make sense of the shape before it. But then, only a few moments later, he saw it was a hole. It was large and light-filled, just about as wide as his shoulders. He lowered his right arm inside, his hand momentarily disappearing into the uncanny brightness. There was a sound rising out of it, something familiar yet oddly affecting, like a swell of singing voices. It was like the music Forrest Blau would sometimes play at the beginning of prayer service, a chorus of vibrant, joyful noise. The boy felt his arm quivering with heat, the white light filling the space between his flesh and joints with a decided ferromagnetism. And then, forsaking all common sense, wisdom, and the world he had always known, Quinn crawled inside, forcing his entire body into the hole. Falling—the feeling of losing the fight with gravity—was all he remembered before the seething whiteness filled his eyes.

For a moment he was certain he was sleeping, or maybe, he began to wonder, he had died. But no; he sat up stiffly, placing his hand against the side of his helmet. He had been lying on his back, and the colors around him now shifted from a pulsing white to a faded pink and then a terminal blue. All around him there were other colors, too, yellows and greens and vibrant reds, and as he got himself up, his back sore from the fall, he saw something moving before him, something he had only ever seen in books, or in the videos in the library: a lean, nimble-footed deer sipping at a brook.

It was not quite a deer but something with a similar shape, the animal wearing a gray-blue coat of fur, and reddish-pink antlers that entangled themselves as the animal snuffled at a stream of clear water. There was water. Somehow there was actual water or something that looked like water down here. Quinn stood now, weak on his feet, dumbstruck. There was water, and there were plants and flowers of all kinds, some with petals as large as his face, growing all around. He had, in fact, landed in a pile of what appeared to be great pink poppies, in a small field full of them.

Quinn looked up, seeing the shape of the place he had fallen into. It was a cave, a cavern, and above, nearly ten meters up, was the opening. He could see the hole he had fallen through hanging there like a false black moon, and through it, the night-time sky, still reeling. For a moment, all he could do was stare, and then something else, a bird—like a hummingbird, but much bigger, nearly the size of his face—darted past. It disappeared inside the trumpet of an otherworldly flower and then buzzed away. He watched the shape the bird made, amazed by the swift pattern of its thin purple wings, flitting from oversized flower to flower; he had never before seen a bird or anything move through the air under its own volition. The bird wound itself through a grove of waist-high vines and troubled a stand of reddish fruits. Following the bird's turbulence with his eyes, he saw Lana, her body lying on a hillock of orange flowers. He began to panic again, rushing over to where she lay, on her side; the front of her helmet had been cracked, a slight silver spiderweb running the length of the convex glass. Quinn quickly checked the gauge on her air tank. It was empty, exhausted by the leak in the helmet. For a moment Quinn froze, then he scrambled to get the helmet off Lana's neck, pulling at the small silver locks until they gave.

She was unconscious, her face looking passive, as peaceful an expression as she'd ever worn. He found the auxiliary mask and hose at the side of his own tank and placed it over Lana's nose and mouth. Soon she began coughing, and then, her eyes wide and frightened, she tried to pull the apparatus away from her face. He did all he could to hold the mask against her face, but she was stronger than he would have guessed and pushed it away even more forcefully, her face turning red. Quinn shoved it back over her mouth, and finally she began to relax, starting to breathe once again. Moments later the air in his own tank had dwindled to emergency levels, and he could taste the nitrogen inside the helmet as the tank began to hiss, all but empty.

This accident, all of it had been his fault; he could admit that now. He had been led into temptation, and the consequences of his betrayal were going to be fatal for the both of them. He grasped Lana's hand in his own, hoping to black out first, as he did not want to see the horrid expression Lana would make as she began gagging on the carbon-dioxide-flooded air. He waited, hoping for the world to quickly go dark.

But then nothing happened. Lana held his hand in her own and continued to breathe, looking up at him, first terrified, then confused, then at last—as his air tank ran dry and the emergency tone beeped faintly, warning of imminent failure—her face shifted to a kind of teary-eyed delirium. Somehow she was breathing. Somehow she could breathe. Carefully, uncertainly, she removed the auxiliary mask from her mouth and took a shallow breath from the air inside the cavern. And then—not coughing up blood—she began to smile. It was a smile Quinn had never seen on her face before, and though it only lasted a moment, it was enough to convince the boy to unclasp his own helmet and take in a short breath.

The air, the plants down here—somehow there was enough oxygen for both of them to breathe.

Quinn set the helmet by his feet and took in a gulp of air once more, the striking odors of ripe flowers filling his nostrils with a fragrant, almost corrupted smell. Lana sat up and did the same, the two of them breathing together, looking over at each other, quietly laughing.

It was what the two of them would later come to think of as a miracle. In this deep, forsaken cave, somehow there was enough air to breathe without wearing a helmet, and there were animals and birds and flowers and a world as colorful as it had been described in the first book of the Bible. The children stood then, hand in hand, making their way together along the foliage's pink, rambling edge.

It was easier falling through the hole than climbing back out of it. And then there was the problem of their empty air tanks and the crack in Lana's helmet. Quinn solved the question of their egress simply enough by finding a path up along the stony outcroppings of vines and dirt. The empty air tanks required a much more thoughtful solution. Here Lana decided to purge both of their tanks completely, then used a narrow twig to force the valves of both their tanks open again. Her coup de grâce was using the suits' filters to create a vacuum, drawing in enough air from the cavern itself, before sealing the tanks again. The crack in her helmet held, leaking a little air whenever she took a heavy step, and as they climbed back up and out of the cave, Quinn stared at the fracture dividing the girl's face, sensing, for the first time, that something for the two of them had begun to change.

Over dinner that evening—it was freeze-dried mashed potatoes and sickles of reddish soybeans, reconstituted to look like some nameless meat—Lana and Quinn stared at each other without speaking. *What are you thinking?* their wide eyes seemed to say. And then: *What we have seen should remain a secret.* Silently, without ever saying a word out loud, the two of them came to an agreement. And having never before in their lives had any reason to keep a secret, what followed then was their first lie. Lana, when questioned about the crack in her helmet, announced, without pause, without a single, doubtful blink, that she had cracked it on the sharp teeth of the disposal unit. Forrest Blau nodded, having said more than once that the exterior trash bin was no place for the children to play.

Later that night, as they lay in separate beds, their secret, along with their first, dreadful lie, occupied each of the children's imaginations. It was as if—trying to coax themselves to sleep—they had already begun to dream of what else might happen, what other commandments they would have to soon outwit or try to evade.

It was seven days before they made their way back to the cave. It took that long for William, Quinn's father and the colony's only scientist, to repair Lana's broken helmet and also for the children to finally accept that their lie had been believed. They took with them—in their gray side packs—a length of rope, a flashlight, and some MREs: things that were small enough to steal without their parents or any of their siblings noticing.

It took less time to find the cave than they had thought it would. Quinn tied the rope around a stack of heavy boulders and then, hand over hand, lowered himself down the hole into the glowing, verdant cave. The descent seemed to go on forever, and when finally his feet struck the grassy bottom, he pulled his helmet off, breathing the fragrant air with an urgent sense of relief. Lana followed, lowering herself with her long legs extended, falling the last few meters. She plucked her helmet from her shoulders, setting it down beside her pack, and then proceeded to unzip the thin outer lining of her silver space suit.

"What are you doing?" Quinn asked, but the girl did not

answer. Instead, she stripped down to her yellow-and-white undergarments and then ran, barefoot, to the small pool of cerulean water, before gently climbing in.

"This is all I've been thinking about for the last several days," Lana whispered, her head bobbing above the ripples he had made. "Come on. It's warm!"

Quinn watched, mouth agape, and then quickly began to unzip his own space suit as well. There was a nervous throb in his chest and his hands. Everything felt like it was new, like they had somehow become some whole other species, some other kind of creatures—spectral animals emerging from centuries-old cocoons.

After they swam, they sat on the bank and shared a packet of partially dehydrated fruit. It was pink, the color of the palms of their hands. A bird as large as their heads landed near their discarded helmets. The children laughed, tossing the food pellets at the bird's feet. Then they lay back in the grass, seeing the small world of the cave come alive—flowers unfolded, nameless insects whistled past, a lone, pinkish antelope hustled away after drinking at the water pool. Time passed slowly or not at all. There was the feeling within them that their lives—the world of the colony and the three domes in which they had always lived—could somehow be forgotten. Being here meant being adults, people who could think and do as they pleased. The place filled them with a sense of hope, a shadow world of entirely new possibilities, possibilities that the two of them could share, and that never needed to be spoken aloud.

Back at the colony, Lana had begun to answer her father back. At the dinner table that very evening, Forrest Blau asked where she had been; when she answered, whispering, "None of your business," Forrest swung the white switch up and back and down across Lana's hands so quickly that Quinn hadn't had a chance to whisper a warning. Lana put her sore fingers against her chest, asked permission to leave the table, and spent the next few days silently pulling weeds from the rows of biologically modified corn. She would not make eye contact with Quinn no matter how hard he tried; back here, in the colony, outside of the cave, she hardly seemed like herself anymore.

One evening Quinn had a dream that a small bird was trapped inside his chest. He woke up trembling and found he couldn't get back to sleep. He climbed down from the top bunk, trying not to disturb his two younger sisters as he snuck from their living quarters and out into the dimly lit passageway. For some time he stared out the observation windows at the order of bleak stars twinkling above. And then he heard a sound, something small and high-pitched, like a soft-throated whisper, exactly the kind of sound the bird in his dream had been making. He followed it, down and around Dome One to the intersection near Dome Three, which led to the library. The door to the library was open, and poking his head inside, he saw the shape of a girl—it was Lana, of course—sitting in one of the chairs, rocking back and forth; before her, on the video screen, was some blurry footage of two birds, a gray one and a blue one, mating. Their wings fluttered violently as one of them sang a trilling song. On the opposite screen there was another video—this one of horses, and on a third screen, a pair of leopards, each of them engaged in the act of copulation. Lana's hair looked darker than it was and hung in her eyes. She seemed to be making a kind of sound, too, something too soft for Quinn to hear. The boy hurried back to his room, his face on fire, hurtling himself into bed as quickly as he could. He lay there awake until the morning lights shuddered on, his thoughts as unsteady as the moons spiraling above.

* * *

At the morning meal, Lana's blond hair hung limply in her face, nearly dangling into her bowl of cereal. She rudely slurped up her food. Later, there was something wild, animalistic about the way she sank her teeth into a runny, ripe grapefruit, something that was both attractive and terrifying.

But surely Forrest Blau suspected something; each time Quinn passed him in one of the passageways, each time the older man gave him an order, each time their two glances happened to meet, it was tinged with a faint tension, a growing uncertainty. Later that morning, once the meal and dishes had been cleared, once the colonists had been assigned their tasks for the day—Quinn's mother and father once more sent to pick pink apples in Dome Three, and then, as no less a commandment than from the pastor himself, to attempt another round of procreation or, as Forrest Blau put it, "to conjugate on behalf of all our futures"—Quinn knelt among the ripening soybeans, shuddering when Forrest Blau appeared, standing silent over his shoulder, watching the boy's work with an air of serious interest. His long shadow made the back of Quinn's neck go cold where it fell, just above his shoulder. The boy tried not to look up and so found himself gazing at the man's large, gruesome-looking hands. The silence of the moment seemed to last forever, until, clearing his wide throat, Forrest spoke.

"It looks like the beans have finally come in."

Quinn only nodded, then murmured, "Yes, Mr. Blau."

Forrest Blau outstretched a wide, hairy hand, running his fingers along the length of a vine. He plucked a single bean, staring at it as if it were harboring some indefensible secret.

"God has a time for all things, my boy. It's not for us to know or to question when or why."

Quinn nodded once more and said, "No, Mr. Blau."

Still the older man did not take his leave. Instead, he leaned in even closer, his gray beard brushing against the side of Quinn's ear.

"Where were you and Lana the day before last?"

"Me and . . . Lana?"

The boy's face went white at the sound of her name in his mouth.

"Yes. Seems to me, I remember you two were supposed to clear out the weeds in Dome Three. And this very morning, what do I see but a whole field still choked with weeds."

"We did," he lied. "Only . . . only, it took longer than we thought. I'm sorry I didn't tell you. There was more . . . I can finish it up today, if you like."

"I would," Forrest Blau said. "I would like it very much, Quinn. A sin of omission, of failure, is still a sin." The elder man smiled, the smile forced, as tight and frightening as any frown. "That does remind me, though. When was the last time you made your confession?"

Quinn began to panic, searching among the spiny, green leaves for an answer, any answer. In the end, all he could think of was to shake his head and then shrug weakly.

"Surely you've got a few things you'd like to confess," Forrest added, the false smile giving over to an even falser grin.

Quinn nodded, afraid that if he made any noise, he would blurt out everything, the distracted mutter of all the terrible things he had been hiding coming out in one galloping, terrified rush.

"You know, Quinn, if there's anything you'd like to tell me, anything big, or *small*"—and here Forrest crushed the bean in his grimy-looking hand—"I am always here for you. I like to think of myself as a kind of father to you. Your spiritual father."

Quinn nodded again, knowing that if the man stood over him for one more minute, one more second, all would be lost. But he didn't. Forrest Blau slipped the raw bean into his mouth, crushing it, and then turned, disappeared among the hedgerows of silver leaves. For a long moment afterward, it seemed his shadow remained, drawing gooseflesh along Quinn's skinny neck.

Without ever agreeing to do so out loud, without ever needing to voice their thoughts, the two children ended up stealing away from their chores in Dome Two once again that afternoon, leaving their rakes and hoes in a row of modified corn, sneaking into their tank suits and through the air lock, back out into the red, shapeless world. Before stepping through the pneumatic door, Quinn glanced up and saw the forbidding shape of Forrest Blau's bolt-action rifle—its shadow falling against his helmet like a condemnation, an accusation of sorts. He ignored this feeling of doubt, of damnation, and trailed behind Lana's silver figure as she made her way silently back to the light-filled cave.

Today there was a severity to Lana's face, in its expressions, in the shape of her mouth as they lowered themselves down the rope. Once among the tall silver and pink stands of flowers, Lana immediately doffed her helmet, setting it down in the dirt as if she intended to never wear it again. Then she unzipped her outer tank suit and removed it. Before Quinn managed to rid himself of his own helmet, she had knelt down before him, dirtying her bare knees in the mud.

"What are you doing?" Quinn asked as she placed her hands inside the turgid confines of his space suit. "What are you doing?" he asked again and again, her mouth, her fingers exploring the innocuous curve of his body, until he was kneeling in the grassy open, too. There was a moment, lying there, his suit unzipped, his helmet still halfway on, that he became afraid that she was going to devour him alive, that her teeth, making themselves known somewhere along the lower hemisphere of his body, would betray them both. But no, all became a lazy, light-washed moment with unfamiliar birds cooing, and the delicious panic of human bodies doing what human bodies had always been meant to do. As they lay together, entangled there, Quinn began to quietly believe that the cave had become a kind of garden of Eden, and that God was somewhere among all this splendor, among these impossible, crystalline leaves.

On their return, the children were once again silent. Treading over the arid red rocks, Quinn reached out to touch Lana's hand, but she seemed shy, inexplicably embarrassed. Fifty meters from Dome One, he tried once more to say something, to take her fingers in his own, but she pulled away from him, shouting something that he could not hear. It was then that they both caught sight of something glinting among the shadows of zigzagging pylons that marked the border of the colony. First it flashed, then it disappeared for a moment, and then it flashed again. Quinn paused, stepping before Lana, holding up a hand. Before he could decipher the shape picking its way along the silver boundary markers, a shot rang out, then another, then another. The first round glanced hard against the side of Quinn's helmet, knocking him from his feet. The second kicked up a clod of dirt a half meter from his right leg, and the third seemed to disappear entirely. But before the third report was done ringing in his ears, he turned and caught sight of Lana slumping forward, tilting to her left, and Quinn—getting his footing once again—caught her as she fell to her side. The girl was like a sack of diaphanous dirt, loose-necked, spreading out in strange ways as he tried to set her down. When Quinn glanced up, he could see the glare of Forrest Blau's glassy helmet, the butt of the bolt-action rifle held up against the crook of his arm. The pastor fired once more, the weapon jerking against his shoulder, the report like a whip, cracking sharply through the heavy, carbon-rich air.

The bullet struck the front dome of Quinn's helmet, bifurcating the shield, lodging itself in the dense, pixilated glass. Slowly the air in the tank suit began to whoosh out in a loud hush. The boy did not fall over, only watched as Forrest Blau began to unzip the utility pocket of his space suit, searching for more ammunition. The boy knew then that he did not have much time—there was the leak in his helmet and Lana looked defenseless lying in the dirt—so he grabbed the girl under her bony arms and began to drag her back up the hill, dodging behind the rocky outcroppings as Forrest Blau fired again, then again.

The pastor's weapon was loud, somewhat accurate, but a misery to try and reload with the bulky silver gloves.

Quinn watched as the elder man tore off his tank gloves and dug amongst his suit's pockets again, searching for another handful of bullets. Quinn took a deep breath and, shifting Lana upon his left shoulder, began to scale the uneven trail back up the rise. A report boomed from somewhere behind him, a cloud of dust zipping several meters to his right, then a second, this time the shot arcing even closer, sniping at the heels of his black boots. But he was close to the cave's opening now—the glowing, light-filled hole—and before a third shot ricocheted off a pile of craggy, red rocks, Quinn had begun to lower Lana inside. Together they slid awkwardly down the rope, and then, giving over to exhaustion, the two of them fell into a mound of blossoming pink and white flowers.

All he could think to do was to hide, and so, dragging Lana through the underbrush, the boy found a patch of brambles where the two of them could wait. He carefully lifted Lana's helmet off, hoping the air would revive her. Her eyes were closed and her lips had turned white. He had a feeling that what was happening to them was not part of God's plan. Before him was a large stone, which he grasped in his hands as some sort of weapon. He looked up, watching, breathing sharply through the bullet hole in his helmet. There was the long rope hanging in the air, unmoving, untouched—and then, soon enough, the shape of Forrest Blau's feet, then his middle, then his glassy helmet appeared, as he lowered himself down, half meter by half meter. The bolt-action rifle was slung over his shoulder as he descended. As the pastor reached the leafy stalks and gilded flowers, there was a faint puzzlement, a bleary confusion that passed over the older man's face, fitted for a moment, as it was, into something akin to religious ecstasy. Then that particular expression was gone, and all that was left was rage, rage at having been misled, of having been lied to, of having not been the first to discover the miracle of such a place. He yanked the rifle from his shoulder, fit several rounds inside, jerked the bolt back, and then marched cautiously through the waist-high grasses, raising the rifle's sight up to his eye.

"Now what, dear children?" the pastor murmured. "Dear children? Would you hide from your own father? Would you hide like that villain Cain who cast the first sin against his brother, Abel? Come out now, my dear children, and forget your temptation. Come out now, and I promise you, all will be forgiven."

The children were huddled only a few meters from where Forrest Blau was now standing, his boots roughly parting the damp foliage. Quinn sobbed a muffled cry where he lay, and began to consider their surrender. Surely, if he confessed now, if they both came clean, the pastor, his father, his mother, the colony, would find a way to forgive them both for what they had done. But then—only a few meters away from where they were huddled—there was the sound of nervous movement rising through the underbrush. Forrest Blau paused, brought the rifle's sight up to his eye, and fired twice. Something fell and then died in the grass. It was a small, nearly wingless bird. As the pastor saw what he had killed, his face fell into a nettle of confusion.

The reddish-purple animal lay split in two before him, its gaunt wings still flapping. Forrest Blau knelt, prodding the creature with his bare finger, as it rasped and twitched.

Quinn watched from where he lay, trembling. There would be no confession, no forgiveness; this much was clear now. Forrest Blau meant to kill them both. His expression, his anger was as terrifying as the God of the Old Testament's.

Quinn held the heavy rock in his hand, his right fist shaking with fright.

The pastor was now pensively holding the bird in the palm of his hand, muttering, "Behold the fowls of the air, for they sow not, neither do they reap, nor gather, yet your Heavenly Father feedeth them. Are ye any better than they?'" Then answering his own question, Forrest Blau murmured, "Neh, neh, neh."

Suspecting that this was his only chance, Quinn slowly raised himself up from the ground and, once he was standing, brought the angular rock down hard against the pastor's helmet once, then again, knocking it off. The pastor roared with pain—like a lion having been cut in two—falling forward to his knees. The boy brought down the rock against the back of Forrest Blau's head once, twice, then a third time, and the older man fell limply to his side. Taking advantage of the pastor's pain, the boy pried the rifle loose from the pastor's grip. Awkwardly, he set the butt of the gun against the inside of his shoulder and took aim, finding it hard to maneuver the finger of his glove along the edge of the trigger. Finally he found it and prepared to fire.

But Forrest Blau lifted his head first, his silver beard glistening with drool and sweat. His bare hands pawed the dirt where he had fallen. He pulled himself achingly to his knees, glancing up at the boy and rifle with a glare that was both dull and unafraid. Quinn shuddered, seized with the sudden recognition that he could not pull the trigger. And then, just as soon as this recognition passed among the boy's other senses, the pastor collapsed, falling forward into the mud, his body shaking with a violent paroxysm. For many moments the boy held the rifle there, aimed at the pastor's body, waiting for it to move again. When it did not, when he began to hear Lana coughing alone in the weeds, the boy lowered the rifle and took a step closer to where Forrest Blau lay. The pastor was still trying to breathe, though his body was crippled, stricken. Something was wrong with the left side of his face. Finally his expression became tightened and his eyes went wide, wider still; there was no mistaking the sudden, bared, grimace of death. The pastor looked to be smiling, and for the first time in as long as the boy could remember, the smile seemed somewhat human, the grimace of someone at peace.

In the weeds Lana was alive though disoriented, bleeding from a spot near her right shoulder; she was whispering something again and again, a song or prayer perhaps. He fitted her helmet back in place, set a tourniquet along her upper arm where she had been shot, and tied the long yellow rope around her waist. She did not seem to notice her father lying there, dead, on a pyre of pink and yellow flowers.

Returning to the surface, Quinn hoisted the girl up through the light-filled opening. Once she was close enough to touch, he reached for her, catching her beneath her arms, and gently laid her in the dust. Then he untied the rope, dropping it down into the cavern with an air of finality, before he began to cover the entrance to the hole, dragging loose rocks into place, disguising the opening with dirt and an odd mound of gravel. The girl was still breathing quickly, talking wildly to herself. Finally he realized it was a song. Something from chapel. "Rise up, all you unbelievers," she whispered, though the way she was singing it sounded hopeful, true. He lifted one of the girl's arms over his shoulder, while his own arm rested behind her back, gripping her side tightly. Together, like that, moving step by step, they wandered toward the pale glow of the three domes, the world echoless before them. Hand in hand, through the endless dust, they made their way back.

About "Young Pilgrims"

The first Ray Bradbury story I ever read was "The Veldt." I was eleven or twelve years old, and the story was put in front of me by an older cousin who had a deeper wisdom about such things. I had heard of science fiction, had seen it in comic books, but had never read it in prose. Reading that one particular story, like encountering a number of Mr. Bradbury's works, has gone on to live in a particularly vivid and nearly unconscious part of my imagination, as have most important childhood discoveries, an image that gets replayed as I'm sleeping, or thought about at odd moments in the day, whenever something drifts out of the corner of my eye.

"The Veldt," like the best science fiction, seems purposely derived from the myth or folktale in its youthful characters, its ruthlessness, and its life-or-death stakes. There is something interesting and dramatic for me in children negotiating the unknown. "The Veldt" also seems heavily moral, like some of my other favorite sci-fi tales, which connects to another older literary form, the Bible. Following those two inspirations, I decided to set my story on an unknown planet, peopling it with religious missionaries and their curious, adolescent children. Living in modern-day America, it's sometimes easy to forget how so many generations ago, our unknown territory was colonized by religious missionaries as well. Out of those characters and that setting, I started developing the notion that Quinn and Lana were a future Adam and Eve, borrowing ideas and events from the Bible and Milton's *Paradise Lost.* The last line of the story is a re-conceptualization of one of Milton's ending lines. Writing this piece was one of the most fun experiences I've ever had writing. It was a pleasure to live in Mr. Bradbury's world even for an hour, a few minutes.

—Joe Meno

CHILDREN OF THE BEDTIME MACHINE

Robert McCammon

It was a lonely house in a lonely land.

The wind blew from here to there and stirred up whorls of lonely dust. Fields burned under a gray sun. When any of the few birds still living passed by, always going somewhere else, the spindly trees seemed sad in their rejection, for no nests ever thrived amid the branches, and no sweet song of youth was ever sung.

The woman who lived in the house was hard. She had to be. It was a hard world now. She could look out across a landscape the color of rust and see in the hazed distance the oil and natural gas pumps that no longer moved. They hadn't moved for a long time. Their day was finished. And so too had died the wires, after the great storms and the winter heat waves and the upheavals that had cracked the dry earth and the dusty roads and had nearly, to the woman's hard blue eyes, rearranged the ridges all the long twenty miles to Douglasville.

The woman went about her chore of living, from day to day. She raised a few chickens and ate bitter eggs. She ate a lot of canned pork-'n'-beans and soup. She grew some dwarf tomatoes that were the color of the land and almost tasteless, but at least they were tomatoes, and she was proud of them. She had a shed full of bottled water, enough to last until Jesus came.

She was all right.

But sometimes at night, after she lit her candles with their tin reflectors and arranged them just so and chose from the special trunk an ancient yellowed book to read that reminded her of the world that was, her hardness cracked just a little bit. Just a little bit, like the shell of a bitter egg.

And there in that room with its candlelight and the smell of old paper and old ideas and the sound of the lonely wind searching outside the windows, the woman felt her heart become slowly crushed . . . slowly, slowly . . . until she had trouble breathing, and the tears bloomed behind her glasses and she had to put the book down for fear a wet drop might blur the words.

She was a hard woman, but she was not made of stone.

Oh, this world. Oh, this sad and brutal world. This careless world. This world of lost opportunities and crushed hearts.

The woman had been married once. She and her husband had had a son. But both of them, killed in a war. Before the satellites fell flaming from the sky. Before the buildings crashed down and the weather changed, summer in winter, and the oil burned in its millions of gallons upon the black-choked sea. Before so many of the fish and the birds and the animals God had commanded man to protect had died. So many.

So many.

The woman in her young days had wished for a large family. She and her husband had talked about that, long before the wedding bells. There was such strength in a large family. There was such happiness. But in the end they'd just had the one child, and he had died first in that foreign land. Then her husband, because he was a patriot.

This sad and broken world.

And when everything seemed to be over and everything was changed and nothing worked anymore, and even after no one knew who had won but everyone said they were the winners so they started fighting again to prove it until the world itself heaved and cracked . . . even after that . . . it was still not the end.

The woman sat at the center of her circle of candles. She took off her glasses and she rubbed her tired eyes.

No, still it was not the end. For though people wished for the end and roadside preachers shouted their prophesies and madmen and madwomen dragged themselves across the sunburned earth wearing upon their backs wooden crosses and upon their heads crowns of barbed wire . . . still it was not the end, and no suffering human being could say when the battered old world would stop its tormented turning and fall apart into the dust of ages.

The woman decided she would go to town tomorrow morning. She needed some more pork-'n'-beans and soup. She could take some eggs and tomatoes to trade. She needed to see people. So be it.

She put her book back into the special trunk with all the others, and then she blew out every candle but one and lay in bed for a long time staring at the ceiling until her blue eyes closed.

The next day was hot. Hot, hot . . . hotter than hot. Same as every day. The clouds were painted upon the sky. The sun was somewhere. The woman rode her green bicycle, the color of May. It was her little joke.

Douglasville wasn't much of a town, but it was a place. It had some buildings and a few houses. It had some people living there. It wasn't all empty. The woman pedaled her May-colored bike past the dump where all the car bodies had blistered and rusted and rotted. She didn't even look at them anymore, didn't even care how they used to work. She directed herself to the big store.

Now, this was an exciting place because the woman never knew what she might find there. She thought it had once been a grocery store—the size was about right, and so were the shelves—but now it was a little-of-anything store. The men who worked there wore guns, so nobody tried to steal anything a second time. But they were good men, and they knew her there, and even the tasteless tomatoes in her backpack were better than none at all because the texture and aroma counted for something. And the eggs . . . well, the yolks were yellow.

The woman enjoyed walking through the big store. Sometimes, when she was particularly lonely, she came here and just walked. Didn't barter at all. She looked at old clothes and their labels. She looked at old shoes and old hats, and she tried to picture in her mind who'd worn them. Infrequently she found a book or two there. Or parts of books, because the sun and heat were not kind to paper. It had been a long time since there'd been any new books. Long before her son had died. In fact, she couldn't remember exactly when. War wiped everything away, even happy memories.

But she did enjoy the big store. All the things in there. The *items*, the men called them. A toothbrush, a flowerpot, a welcome mat, a Scrabble game—you never knew what the people who passed by, like the last birds, had left behind for trade. Sometimes she found letters. But they were always very sad, so she had learned to leave them alone.

And there at the very back of the big store was the large pile of yesterday.

It never ceased to amaze her. All that, in one place. All that, and all useless.

"I just keep it," said one of the men, standing beside her. "Call me sentimental."

The woman nodded.

All those computers. All those—what were they called?—

laptops and notebooks and cell phones of every small and smaller size and bright plastic color. *Gizmos*, she called them. The electronic book readers. The ones that read books for you, in any language and in any voice. The screens that showed the moving pictures called . . . what was that? . . . Oh, yes: 3-D. She figured the man kept them because they were, after all, pretty. And they had meant so much, once upon a time. Now they sat in dusty rows and heaps. The cell phones lay in laundry baskets. Was the man a collector? Possibly the batteries and innards had been of some use, many years ago. His father may have taken them as barter. Who could say where all these came from? They were just here, as they might be anywhere.

But without the wires both visible and invisible, they were all dead. Even the fanciest of the fancy, the brightest of the bright, the streamlined beauty and the pocket-sized powerhouse—all dead.

"Are you doing all right?" the man asked her, because though he was a much younger man, he did like her.

"I am," she said. But then she decided to tell him the truth. "I'm having trouble sleeping just lately. You know. Things get in."

"Sure. I know." He shrugged. His shoulders were thin, but he had a large pistol on the holster at his hip. "Everybody has trouble now and again."

"Yeah," she said.

And he said, "Yeah," as he stared at the linoleum tiles on the floor.

"I guess I need some canned stuff," she said after a little while. "Anything new in?"

"No," he told her. "Just the same."

People had stopped eating so much. Everybody was thin. It was just something you got used to. A piece of bread could be a dinner; soak it in soup and you had a feast. But most people helped one another and shared when they could. There was no panic, and there was very little violence. The ones who had lived by that code were long dead. Now the remaining ones had taken on the thinness, the attitude and the patience of saints, as they waited for the end.

"Do you have *anything* new?" the woman asked, a question she'd not planned on asking. It had just come out, because she was thinking of the lonely house.

"Oh!" the man suddenly said. His eyebrows went up. "Yes, I do!" He went back amid the dead electronics, and he bent down to a cardboard box on the floor. "It doesn't work, of course, but—"

"*None* of that works," said the woman, feeling like he thought her a fool.

"It doesn't need wires," he told her. "Or *didn't* need wires, I mean. Take a look at *this*."

What he brought her looked like a brushed-aluminum urn, pointed at the top and flat at its base, with a small black hole at its center and a crank handle on its side.

"Do you know what it is?" the man asked.

"Somebody's ashes in there? Or is it an oversized pepper grinder?"

The man gave her a lopsided smile. "It's a bedtime machine," he said.

"Bedtime machine," the woman repeated.

"Sure is. I've only seen pictures in a magazine—a long time ago—but I remember my granddad telling me about them. He was a big . . ." The man paused, calling up a half-forgotten phrase. "*Computer geek,*" he announced.

"You must have a good memory," the woman said. Her blue eyes were examining the object. There were no seams. Just the small black hole and the hand crank. "It doesn't look like much to me. Can you open it up and use it as a planter?"

"No." He'd almost laughed on that one. Then his voice became serious. "Hey . . . this was *created* for just your problem."

"My problem? *What* problem?"

"Insomnia," said the man. "You've never heard of a bedtime machine?"

"Never."

"Well," he began, as he turned the object between his hands and also eyeballed the surface, "I *think* I remember. They were created mostly for people in the cities. They were *very* expensive. Only rich people could afford them. I'm talking *millions* of euros. They were . . . like . . . magic lamps, in a way."

"Magic lamps," she repeated, thinking he needed to stay out of the sun for a few days.

"Yeah. You turned the crank. See?" The brushed-metal crank did turn, smoothly and soundlessly. "That builds up the electrical energy. Then . . . I guess when it's ready, it switches itself on."

"And does what?" She corrected herself: "*Did* what?"

"Showed you something that was programmed just for you. A hologram, is what it was. You know about holograms, right?"

"I'm old but I'm not stupid."

"Okay, no offense meant. It showed a hologram that was designed at the tech plant just for its owner. That's why it was so expensive. The holograms—I remember my granddad saying this—were supposed to be of some peaceful image. Like nature or whatever. Something to help its owner sleep. I guess the cities were pretty noisy and chaotic twenty-four hours a day, huh?"

"People had too much stimulation," the woman told him. "They were addicted to it. Like any drug. That's what *I* remember."

"Right," the man said, as if—impossibly—he remembered it too.

"Okay." The woman was ready to go. "Let's see what cans you've got. We can talk a trade."

"Take it," said the man.

"Take *what*?"

"This." He held the bedtime machine out toward her. It must have been light, because he held it with one hand. "I've been cranking it for two nights. Nothing."

"And I would want that piece of junk *why*?"

"It's something pretty. Don't you think?"

"It's junk," the woman answered. "I'm here for *food*, not garbage."

"It's *art*," he replied, on a lame note. "Looks like an old rocket ship, *I* think. Hey, maybe it'll work for you. Maybe you can get it to turn itself on."

"Why would it?" she asked, her voice hardening. This was foolish. A foolish relic from a foolish time. "How'd it get here, anyway?"

"Came in a box with other stuff. A trader passing by. Where does any of it come from?"

"It's useless," she told him, and then she turned away.

"Take it if you want to," he said to her back. "It'll just sit here."

"Let it sit," she said.

She went to her task of trading. Bartering the tomatoes and the eggs for some canned food. The men always let her think she was getting a good deal, because she was a regular and they liked her. But they weren't pushovers, that was for certain. She exchanged her goods for the two cans of pork-'n'-beans and two cans of ham spread she put into her backpack, and that would have to last her for a while.

It was time to go back home.

She took one more turn around the big store. Checking the shelves for what she might have missed, though she had nothing left to trade. She saw a woman she knew, and the woman's little boy. She stopped to speak for a few minutes, just to be neighborly. Then she went on, with her backpack on her back, and she found herself at the rear of the big store where the old junk was piled up, and she stared at the shiny brushed-aluminum rocket ship of the bedtime machine on a card table with two warped legs.

Art, he'd called it.

She gave a little snort that made her nostrils flare.

It *was* pretty, if you thought about objects that way.

Maybe she could take the hand crank off and find a use for it?

Junk, she thought. But still . . . these days it was best not to turn down whatever was offered to you. Next time it might be something of value.

The woman picked up the bedtime machine—and it was as light as a dream, must not have any workings inside it at all—and shoved it into her backpack.

She said goodbye to the men, to the woman and the little boy, and then she got on her green bike and pedaled her way home.

It took her a while to actually put the thing on the chest of drawers in her bedroom. She tried to peer into the black hole. Tried to poke it with a finger. There was a lens of some kind deep within, almost too deep to touch. As the wind blew dust out in the dark and candles burned around her, the woman angled the machine so that the black hole was aimed into the room. She stood back for a few minutes, deciding what she should do next.

Well, it was pretty damned obvious, she thought.

She cranked.

And cranked.

And cranked.

It was a smooth motion, hardly any friction at all. Still, cranking was cranking. After a time she released the hand crank and stepped back and thought she was the biggest fool in this sad, broken world.

Nothing happened.

Nothing was going to happen.

The thing was dead.

And the woman realized she could cry over this. Could really let a sob go, if she wasn't guarding herself so tightly. Because though she'd never expected anything to happen, she was still disappointed. The bedtime machine. A magic lamp. Something new, amid the old chore of day-to-day living. She had let herself believe that maybe—*maybe*—she really could wake the machine up. And from it might bloom a meadow of flowers under a star-strewn sky, and grass just soft enough for sleeping. Or a holographic waterfall, flowing across smooth, dark, beautiful stones right in the corner of the room. Or a beach at night, with the waves rolling in and the distant lights of ships blinking out at sea. Or a canopy of trees above her, with darkness laced through them like velvet, and from one of them a night bird singing sweetly, for her ears alone.

The woman did begin to cry. But just a little tear, because she knew disappointment and heartbreak as an old presence in life.

She had let herself feel hope. That had been her mistake.

She wiped her eyes, she got herself ready for bed, and she opened the special trunk and from it took a fragile book whose strength she counted on to lift her spirits during long nights like this, when the wind blew from here to there amid the spindly trees outside.

She put on her glasses, climbed into her bed, and opened the book to the first page. She always did this exactly the same way, because of what was inscribed there.

It said, *Live Forever!*

Underneath that was the author's name, faded and ghostly.

There was a month and day, almost illegible. A year: 1988.

A long time ago, forty years before her birth.

The woman always wondered about that inscription. That nearly shouted, joyful *Live Forever!* She wondered if it was a special message of some kind. She wondered if it ever had been said to the author, and he was passing it along. It seemed like the kind of statement you didn't keep to yourself. It seemed like the kind of thing you hollered out at the top of your lungs, to the very soul of the world.

The woman found a story she wanted to read. It was about a day in the life of an automated house, when no people were there to love it or be loved by it. She began reading, but on this sad night of nights she wanted to hear a voice . . . a voice raised against the lonely wind . . . and so she adjusted her glasses, she cleared her throat, and she began to read the words aloud.

And she had been speaking the author's words for only a few sentences when she abruptly looked up from the book.

Because something was happening to the bedtime machine.

She *felt* it, before she saw it.

A tremor? A breath, inhaled or exhaled? A heartbeat?

Maybe all those.

She saw the black hole turn electric blue.

Where the lens was aimed, a blue shadow formed in the air.

It shivered, and breathed, and smiled as it took shape and substance.

And suddenly in the room stood a little boy about ten years old, with brown hair and brown eyes and apple-plump cheeks. He was wearing a dark red sweater and white chino trousers with patches on the knees. He was wearing sneakers stained with playground dirt. His smile broadened.

He said, in his little-boy voice, "Would you read to me until you get sleepy?"

The woman did not move. Did not speak.

Could not move. *Could* not speak.

"Just *one* story?" the little boy prompted.

Her mouth was wide open, yet no sound emerged. She saw that he was not real. She saw that he wore a blue body-halo, and that for all his seeming solidity a little static occasionally disturbed his smile and for an instant warped his features as if he were reacting to a mosquito bite in an unscratchable place. But, of course, mosquitoes were now as rare as birds.

"*One* story," he repeated, not petulantly but expectantly.

The woman spoke in a hushed and trembling voice.

"One story," she said.

The little boy sat on the floor beside her bed and crossed his legs beneath him. He put his elbows on his knees and rested his chin on his palms and waited. He was all brown eyes and fixed attention.

"I'm . . . just going to keep reading this story," said the woman, and the little boy gave a quick nod that said *Just fine*.

She read the rest of it aloud. Her voice cracked a few times. It roughened and rebelled, but she kept going. And at the end of the story, when the last sentence had been read and the woman looked up from the words, the little boy on the floor frowned slightly and said, "I hate that the house burned up. But I guess that's how it had to end. The house wasn't happy, was it?"

"No," the woman said. "Not happy."

"Are you sleepy yet?"

"No," the woman said. "Not sleepy."

"Will you read me another story?" the little boy asked, and he smiled again.

"Yes," the woman answered. "I will."

The next story was about a spaceship traveling south toward the sun. The little boy really liked that one, and he asked her to read it again.

And then, in defiance of all sense and wonder and human and electric mystery, the woman at long last yawned and felt the weight of her eyelids.

"You can rest now," she heard the little boy say. "But you'd better blow out some of those candles first, because we don't want this house burning down, do we?" He grinned. "This is a happy house."

He waited for her to blow out all the candles but one.

"Good night," he said, as if from a distance. He was already going away.

And after the little boy was just a blue sparkle in the air the woman turned over in her bed and sobbed, and the sob became a wrenching torrent, and the torrent swept her away from this world into the realm of sleep.

The woman was up early, cranking.

She tended to her chickens and to her tomatoes. Under the hot gray sun she carried out the day-to-day chore of living. She ate pork-'n'-beans and had a little ham spread on a cracker and drank bottled water from a plastic cup.

Then she cranked the bedtime machine some more.

Panic set in when she lit the candles and got into bed with the book again. The very same book, with the very same inscription.

What if the little boy didn't appear tonight? How had she *made* him appear? What had she done to the machine to wake it up? She didn't know, but she decided she would start reading aloud again.

This story was about an April witch who wanted to be in love.

Three sentences in, and the bedtime machine breathed. Its heart beat. Its eye opened, and the little boy in the dark red sweater and the white chinos with patched knees was there.

"Will you read to me until you get sleepy?" he asked, smiling.

"I will," said the woman.

"Good!" the little boy said. "I brought a friend!"

And a little girl with blond hair and freckles grew from his blue glow, and in her pink dress she was so very pretty. She had a nice smile, too.

The woman said, "I hope . . . this story doesn't scare you. Either one of you."

"Oh, no, it won't!" the little boy answered.

"No, ma'am!" the little girl said, and she shook her head in a very serious way.

They sat down on the floor, and they waited to hear.

Oh, this strange world. This world we cannot understand. This world that turns and turns through torments, trials, and tribulations, yet goes on like any person must . . . day by day.

They liked the story about the foghorn. They really did. The idea of the monster from the deep, falling in love with the call of what it thought was another monster . . . it made some laugh and some cry. But they all really did like it.

All the children. All of them, sitting on the floor. The boys and girls, and none of them looking alike and all dressed differently, and some Hispanic and some Asian and some from other places but they could all speak English and of course understand the stories.

And more of them, every night. Growing from the blue glow. Gathering together on the floor to listen. To hear the stories about the jar, and the lake, and the skeleton and the Earth men and the crowd and the sound of thunder. They did like their dinosaurs.

And then one night when the wind was silent, the little boy appeared and said, "Would you read to us until you get sleepy, Momma?"

"I sure will, you rascal, you," said the woman, whose eyes were blue and soft. "You bring them all in, and we'll get started."

During the day, the woman took her books to Douglasville. She allowed the sun to touch them. She read to people there, and they built a shaded place for her to sit. The people and their children came from all around to listen. The woman could not want for anything, because they needed her and loved her and she needed and loved them, too. Her newfound energy and life were contagious, in a good way. There was no time to sit and wait for the end. That would come someday, if it was coming at all. There was too much to do, to figure out, to build back. To try to make right.

But at night . . .

She had her children.

How many?

Hundreds? Thousands?

Very, very many.

The woman allowed herself to sometimes wonder if they were more than holograms and sparks. She wondered if they were the spirits of children yet to be born. She wondered if when they came to real life, they would not have some memory of the stories, some feeling that they knew them even before they heard them the first time. Because she was sure that through these children the stories would live forever.

The wind didn't sound so lonely anymore. Life was a pleasure, not a chore. Maybe the birds would come back someday, and maybe the trees would grow strong. Maybe they would build nests again, and maybe from them would come the sweet song of youth.

But in the meantime, from the house came the sweet music of children's laughter. From the house came the awed rush of electric breath. From the house came the voice of a woman, strong and steady and joyful to live because there were so many stories yet to be read.

So many.

And the house?

The house itself was never lonely again.

The house stood firm against any wind.

At night its blue glow lit up the land like a world full of candles.

The house was happy.

And so too were the woman and her children, both of the

present and those yet to be born, in the towns she reached with her backpack of books and her green bicycle the color of May.

About "Children of the Bedtime Machine"

I wrote "Children of the Bedtime Machine" to express my feeling that Ray Bradbury's work is timeless. There is little doubt in my mind that his fantastic flights of the imagination will continue to inspire readers—and particularly young readers—into the limitless future.

Ray Bradbury's work has personally given me tremendous happiness. In "Bedtime Machine," I am the boy who appears first, and who gleefully asks to be read to. What great memories I have of fabulous stories such as "The Lake," "The Jar," "The Fog Horn," "The Scythe," "There Will Come Soft Rains," and so many, many more.

Live forever? Certainly Bradbury will, and his amazing work will continue to speak to the heart as long as hearts beat with passion, emotion, and pure joy upon this earth.

—Robert McCammon

THE PAGE

Ramsey Campbell

That day the Aegean might have been a nest of dragons with teeth of white foam. The leaping waves were scaly bodies blue as metal, and the noonday sunlight lent them glittering reptile eyes. The wind from the sea was their breath so hot it turned its spittle into a desiccated spray of sand. "The dragons are back, Joyce," Ewan said.

"That's right, dear."

He couldn't tell if she recalled her flight of fancy here on the beach all those years ago or was simply humouring him. Perhaps she hadn't even heard him for the wind, which flapped his shirt and her long silken shawl on the backs of the sunbeds as though equipping the couple with wings. It had already felled several umbrellas, strewing them alongside the tideless sea. Just a few determined tourists were staying on the beach, fat novels clamped open in front of their faces with both hands, while the most adventurous souls braved the waves. Surely Joyce wouldn't, and Ewan was sinking back with an obese best-seller when he heard a cry. "Stop there, stop."

The voice was almost indistinguishable from the wind. Ewan

had to sit up to locate the man, who'd dashed onto the beach at the westward end of Ikonikos, where the sunbeds gave out and the clusters of clifftop apartments fell short of a few isolated villas. The wind tugged a linen suit taut on the man's thin frame and made an unruly halo out of his white hair. He was chasing a page that the wind must have torn out of a book. "Joyce," Ewan said.

She peered at him while the wind disarranged the greyest of her locks before hitching herself around on the sunbed. "What do you want me to see?"

"It was just a chap running after a bit of his book."

The man and his papery game had disappeared around the rocks that screened the next inlet, and Joyce settled back with a sigh. "That wasn't worth it, Ewan."

He would rather feel accused than risk emphasising the effort she'd had to make. He was silent as she retrieved her book, which needed to diet as much as his did. The wind tousled the pages, and before long Joyce let her novel drop on her venerable canvas bag. "I'm going in."

On days like this Ewan was all the more aware of never having learned to swim. "I wouldn't mind some lunch."

"Don't you ever think of anything except your stomach?" Joyce gave the sagging bulge a wearily indulgent glance. "Jump up, then," she said. "Give it a chance to behave."

No doubt she meant the weather. Ewan struggled to his feet and managed to wriggle into his playfully fluttering shirt in time to offer Joyce his arm. She mustn't want to seem to need it, since she let go too soon, almost falling on if not across the bed. "I can manage," she protested when he clutched her yielding waist, and wouldn't let him carry the bag.

At least the Philosophia was just above their section of the beach. The waiters had lowered a plastic sheet to protect the taverna from the wind. The sheet blurred the view like a cataract and palpitated loudly throughout the meal. Joyce helped finish several dishes and more than half of the carafe of wine, by which time the sea was rearing as fiercely as ever. "Will you get the towels?" she said. "I think I'll have a nap."

Once she would have done so on the beach. Ewan retrieved the towels and clambered up the unequal steps embedded in the cliff. On the road that had sprouted apartments and hotels since the couple had last stayed in Ikonikos, Joyce took his hand. He suspected she needed more support than she would admit on the uphill road.

The Mnemosyne Apartments were near the middle of the village. Children too young for school or absent from one were keeping the play area beside the bar alive. Ewan knew Joyce hoped to see the grandchildren there or somewhere similar. As he fumbled in the bag he experienced the familiar panic at losing a key. "For heaven's sake let me," Joyce complained.

She took longer than he already had. A good deal of heat was occupying their room. Ewan switched on the air-conditioning as Joyce lay down. She reached out a hand for him to squeeze while he took his place on the other narrow bed. As soon as he closed his eyes he saw the man chasing the page along the beach. How important had it been? Had its owner recaptured it? The questions kept sleep well out of reach, and before long Ewan swung his legs off the bed. "I'm just going out. You rest."

Joyce put out a slack hand and thought of opening her eyes. "Can't you wait for me?"

"I only want to try and find the shop that had our favourite olives."

She released a breath so protracted he heard it begin to give out—the kind that always made him breathless until he heard another. "Don't be long," she eventually said.

He didn't mean to be. They weren't often apart now that they'd retired, but whenever they were he grew anxious until he saw her again. She stirred as he let a blaze of sunlight in. The sight of her frail shape under the thin sheet was dismayingly suggestive of a memory he was trying to commit to mind. "Go if you're going," she mumbled, and he had to close the door.

He made for the cliff path where the running man had come from. In the past the dusty roads had boasted just a few tavernas, but now those were outnumbered by bars full of Brits watching football on huge flat screens like paintings brought to life. The wind had ripped blossoms from trees and shrubs and vines, strewing the roads with them—even cactus flowers had been torn loose, and the spiky clubs of leaves. The spectacle put Ewan in mind of the wake of a parade—not of a funeral, not that kind of wake.

He couldn't see the man at any of the villas outside Ikonikos, all of which were white as tombs and gave as little sign of life. Instinct, if even that, took him down the cliff path. The sea was still helplessly restless, although at the horizon it appeared to be promising peace. The wind drove Ewan along the beach and unfurled veils of sand for him to walk on. Beyond the rocky outcrop the next bay was unpopulated. Nothing moved except the waves and, trapped by the wind in a crevice of the cliff, a lively piece of paper.

Ewan picked his way to it as the wind set it beckoning. More than once his sandals missed a foothold on the slippery rocks, so that he was afraid of twisting an ankle or worse. His bare legs were stinging with sand and salt spray by the time he grabbed the piece of paper. It was the last page of a book called *Sending Them to God*.

Other than the title it contained just four words: "but there is none." Why had the man been so desperate to retrieve it? How reassured would he have felt if he had? The words had no such effect on Ewan, who was inclined to give the page back to the wind. He might encounter the man, and he slipped it into his shirt pocket. He was peering at some odd marks in the crevice—they looked as if fingers had been groping ineffectually for the page, though they must have been made by the wind on the sand that was plastered to the cliff face—when the phone in his hip pocket emitted a clank. The message was from Joyce. *where*, it said.

Coming back. Ewan typed this as swiftly as he could without misspelling, and added *Thought asleep*. Even using less than complete sentences felt like abandoning responsibility—the kind they'd both shown while they were teaching. As he sent the message he wondered if Joyce could have been asking where she was. Surely neither of them had reached that state yet, if they ever would, but the thought revived his panic at being separated from her. He would have dashed up the cliff path if he'd felt capable. Instead he struggled into the wind along the beach.

As he opened the apartment door Joyce turned over beneath the sheet to welcome him—but her bed was empty, and the sheet was stirring in the wind. Ewan managed to postpone some of his consternation while he lurched across the room. She was on the balcony, gazing between two hotels at the sea. "Were you successful?" she said.

"I didn't find the shop." For fear of straying any further from the truth he said "I found the page the chap was after on the beach."

Joyce sighed and turned her hands up as though weighing the wind. "What do you think you have to prove to me, Ewan?"

"What would you like me to?"

"Don't make it sound as if it's my fault."

They were on the edge of the kind of argument that would take them beyond knowing where it had begun. Perhaps Joyce saw this, because she said "Show me what's so important, then."

She seemed indifferent to holding the page safe and gave it an unimpressed glance before letting Ewan retrieve it from her and the wind. "I don't see how that could mean much to anyone."

"I'll keep it with me in case we see him."

"You aren't going to spend our holiday looking when I don't suppose he even cares about it anymore."

"I won't be taking time to look for him."

"You did for that and never even told me you were." Before Ewan could think of an answer to risk she said "I was looking forward to those olives."

He should have realised this might be important to her when so much else had changed. "We'll look for them together."

They tried on their way to dinner. Perhaps the shop had turned into one that sold leather or T-shirts or silver or trinkets, some of them Greek. Several tavernas had become Chinese or Indian for the benefit or otherwise of British visitors. Last night Joyce and Ewan had located an old favourite, but the years appeared to have shrunk the portions and dried up the food while extracting much of its taste. The wind dropped as they decided which taverna to chance. The slitted sun peered like a dragon's solitary eye over the horizon, and a final breath ruffled the sea.

They were right to trust the restaurant, but Ewan felt Joyce didn't trust him. Whenever he glanced at passersby she gave him a sharp look. He did his best to talk about places they could revisit, though the discussion felt like a show they were performing, a sketch of a marriage. Later they sat on their balcony as the sky grew stars. Two nearby discos were competing at full volume, and Ewan couldn't grasp the peace the sky seemed to offer. When he and Joyce retreated into the apartment, the thumping beyond the window sounded even more like a pair of irregular hearts.

He waited until Joyce drew the sheet over herself before he hid the page beneath his pillow. Some instinct, unless it was just an effect of the retsina at dinner, made him feel he should keep the page safe. He switched off the light and found Joyce's hand. When it slackened he turned over. The wind fumbling about the balcony didn't keep him awake, and the disco beats seemed to fade into the distance. When he drifted out of sleep they'd fallen silent, leaving the wind to make what little noise it could. It wasn't the wind, since it sounded closer to him than the window, which he saw under the curtains was shut tight. The hint of activity wasn't enough to rouse him, but perhaps it disturbed Joyce, since as he settled back into slumber she tried to take his hand. He might have imagined the wind was attempting to do so, and how could she have found the hand when it was resting on his pillow, closer to the window than to her? Before the sensation was able to grow more substantial it left him, and he lacked the energy to drag himself awake.

Hours later the impression wakened him in daylight. Who had been groping at the pillow? He sat up and twisted around to lift it. The last page of the book was lying slightly crumpled on the wrinkly sheet, but he couldn't judge whether the page or the pillow had already been moved. Joyce levered herself up on a shaky elbow to gaze at him. "Why were you keeping that there?"

"So I knew where it was."

She might think him forgetful or worse, if she didn't assume he was making sure she didn't steal the page. He limped to the safe and locked up the page with the passports and travellers' cheques. "Now we know where it is."

During breakfast on the balcony a pair of magpies did most of the chattering. Joyce was first onto the beach, having let go of Ewan's arm, and soon in the sea. He was grateful to see other swimmers near her in case she needed help. Between looking for her in her swimsuit as orange as a sunset he tried to immerse himself in the novel at least two other people were reading on the beach, but even once Joyce returned he couldn't concentrate. "Will you be all right for a while?" he eventually said. "I just want to look something up."

"Why shouldn't I be?"

He glanced back until he could no longer see her as he made for Zorba's Bar. A few customers were drinking beer with their English breakfasts while their children played on computers. Ewan bought time on a terminal and searched the Internet for *Sending Them to God,* but there was very little information. The novel was by Jethro Dartmouth, a name that meant nothing to him. It seemed to be the author's only work, and nobody was offering a copy for sale online. Insurgery Books, who had published it at the end of the previous century, no longer existed—they appeared to have brought out just that book.

This wasn't much for Ewan to tell Joyce or to justify leaving her alone on the beach. He took his time on the road but failed to think of anything to add. The concrete grew soft underfoot with the ragged rug of sand that yesterday's gale had spread over the end of the road. Joyce was on the beach to his left—she ought to be, but he couldn't see her.

Nobody seemed interested in his panic as he stumbled between the sunbeds. There was his meaningless book, a lump of paper lying inert on the bed draped with his towel, and within arm's length of it Joyce's paperback occupied her empty lounger in the shadow of the umbrella. He was staring apprehensively at the swimmers in the sea, none of whom was wearing orange, when somewhere above him her voice said "Ewan."

As he swung around he had the disconcerting notion that he still wouldn't be able to see her. She was gazing down at him with amused impatience from a table in the Philosophia. Before he'd finished clambering up the path he gasped "What on earth are you doing in there?"

"I fancied some olives, since you didn't get any." Quite as defiantly she said "It's like being away all on my own."

He mustn't argue. Too many of their recent disagreements were so trivial that he felt they were reducing him and Joyce, shrivelling their intelligence and drying up their affection. "Are you ready for lunch, then?"

"I've been ready for a while. Were you looking at your bit of paper all this time?"

"No, finding out about it."

A waiter bringing olives interrupted him. Ewan thought Joyce was content to be quiet once they'd ordered lunch until she said "Get it over with if you're so anxious to tell me."

"The author wrote just that one book. I wouldn't be surprised if he published it himself."

"What's it supposed to be about?"

"Nobody was saying."

"Do you even know who it's by?"

"A person by the name of Jethro Dartmouth."

"Never heard of him."

"I got the impression pretty well nobody has."

"Excuse me, some have, yes."

This came from the waiter, and Ewan thought one of them must have misheard. "Sorry, I don't think I caught what you said."

"Mr. Dartmouth came to live here in Ikonikos."

"How do you know that?" Joyce asked or objected.

"His daughter told us who he was."

Ewan waited while the man poured two glasses of wine and set down the carafe. "Would you happen to know which his house is?"

"He called it Villa Biblion," the waiter said, gesturing beyond the village.

Joyce emitted a snort at the name. Otherwise she was silent until the waiter moved away, and then she murmured "You aren't thinking of giving him that bit of paper."

"If you'd seen him you'd understand how much he wants it."

"Well, I don't understand," Joyce said, making sure Ewan knew this included him.

During lunch he felt as though Dartmouth was loitering close by, all the more insistent for being unseen—the subject of him and his page, at any rate. It followed them to the beach in the form of their uneasy silence. Joyce spent some time in arranging herself and her various items on and around the sunbed before glancing at Ewan as if she'd forgotten he was there. "Go on your mission if you're going."

"I don't like to leave you down here by yourself."

"For pity's sake," she cried and dragged her legs so vigorously off the bed that it almost toppled over. "Take me to the room if you need to think I'm safe."

He hadn't meant that, or perhaps he had. On the uphill road he thought she resented having to take his arm. As he let them into the apartment he caught sight of the safe at the back of the doorless wardrobe. For an instant he was certain the display above the keypad said ERROR. The letters vanished as he stepped into the room. "Did you see that?" he blurted.

"What now, Ewan?"

"It looked as if someone just tried to open the safe."

"I didn't see anything like that at all."

Perhaps the sunlight had outlined the message, although when he tried to recapture the illusion it stayed stubbornly invisible. He typed the year of their marriage and opened the safe. Hadn't he laid the page flat? Part of it was resting against the door, and unfolded to meet him. Rather than point this out to Joyce he said "Are you sure you wouldn't like to come with me?"

"I'm very sure, Ewan. You do whatever you feel you have to."

"I'll try not to be long."

"We've plenty of time. We've eleven days yet." With a frown

that seemed to tug the corners of her lips towards a smile she said "Just stop worrying about me."

When he glanced back from the doorway she looked defiant, close to insulted by his concern. As he made all the speed he could uphill the page fluttered in his hand. He might have imagined someone was trying to snatch it, and he slipped it into his breast pocket, where it struggled to unfold before lying still.

The Villa Biblion wasn't on the outskirts of Ikonikos. Every house he passed took him another minute's walk or more from Joyce. He was on the edge of going back to her when he saw the name on the gatepost of a villa in an olive grove beyond high spiky railings. He thumbed the bellpush below the nameplate, and in time a grille emitted a metallic rattle and a woman's voice. "Hello?"

"I've something that belongs to Mr. Dartmouth."

The response was a clatter that sounded ominously final. As Ewan looked for a security camera to show the page, the door of the villa opened and a woman strode down the wide marble drive. She was tall and thin with a long face and cropped pale hair. She wore shorts with many pockets and a T-shirt that bestowed on her small breasts the slogan NET ASSETS. Ewan was swallowing a giggle when she demanded "What was it you said?"

"I found this on the beach. I brought it back."

She gazed at the page and then at him for some moments before opening the gates. "Come and tell me about it," she said, extending a hand several degrees cooler than the afternoon. "I'm Francesca Dartmouth."

"Ewan Hargreaves." As he followed her up the drive he said "Your father must be doing well to live here."

"I bought it." She turned to point at the words on her T-shirt. "There's a fortune to be made in properties abroad."

She led the way through a broad marble hall into a large white room furnished with a plump black leather suite. "What will you have to drink?"

"Do you mind if I don't? I'd rather not leave my wife on her own longer than I have to."

"Just let me hear your tale, then."

"I saw someone chasing this on the beach in all that wind and later on I found it. Am I right to think he was your father? I believe his book's quite rare."

"Pardon me a minute," Francesca Dartmouth said and hurried out of the room.

Ewan heard her open a door across the hall and utter a muffled cry. A window slid shut, and her footsteps hesitated before she reappeared, carrying a book as carefully as she might have handled a baby. The bulk of the pages had been torn away from the rear flyleaf, exposing their bandaged spine. "The wind got in," she said almost to herself. "It blew this off his desk."

Ewan held out the loose page, hoping it might lessen her distress. "Your father can get it bound again, can't he?"

She gazed at the page and clutched the book harder. "He can't, Mr. Hargreaves."

Ewan wasn't sure he wanted to establish why. Instead he asked "What's the book about?"

Francesca Dartmouth raised her eyes to his and held out the book. "See for yourself."

Ewan was moved to be trusted with it. He laid the page on a low table before carefully leafing through the book. It was the tale of Tom Read, a man with a mission to change those who were doing most harm to the world—to persuade them or, failing that, execute them. Was he inspired by God or deranged or both? Some of his intended victims were political leaders, others ruled religions, and one was a media mogul. Read never learned who sent an assassin to kill him in the end, where Ewan thought another page might be missing, but there was only the one he'd retrieved. "I'm not sure I understand," he said.

"My father didn't either. He didn't realise the people he was satirising had so much power. The media man made sure nobody would stock the book, and then he used one of his companies to buy up all the copies and destroy them. My father sent out the ones he had left to the media the man didn't own, but nobody so much as mentioned them. He kept just that one copy and hid himself here. He didn't want anyone to find out where he was living. He was afraid they might try and do away with him as well as the book."

"But you told someone in the village he lived here."

"Not while my father was alive."

Ewan felt he'd already known that answer. He shut the cover, which bore just the author's name split by the title on a black background. The letters were in various fonts, the most prominent of which could be read as spelling TO SEE GOD. He turned the book over and gazed at the photograph on the back. "That's the man I saw chasing the page on the beach."

"I believe you." Francesca Dartmouth took a long breath and said "He used to say he wouldn't really be destroyed while there was still even one of his books."

At once Ewan realised "The last line needn't mean there's no God. It could be saying there's no end."

"I never thought of that before." Even more gratefully she said "I think you've seen the truth."

Ewan was making to replace the page in the book when she said "Why don't you keep that? I'd say you've made it your own."

In some confusion he protested "Don't you think—"

"I think you should have it when you've given it a meaning. Maybe it means something special to you, or it will." She held Ewan's gaze while she said "If it does, my father won't be altogether gone."

Ewan could find nothing to say to this. As she saw him onto the drive he said awkwardly "You won't be short of olives."

"Would you like some? They used to sell ours in the village till the shop turned into a bar." She went into a side room and returned with a little wicker basket heaped with chubby olives. "You and your wife enjoy them," she said. "And your lives."

She waved as the gates met behind him, and he was hurrying past the railings when he seemed to glimpse a man among the trees. In a moment the figure was gone, as if it had needed only to turn sideways to vanish. Ewan looked for it as the villas gave way to apartments, but there was no further sign of it. The page from the book lay quiet against his heart.

He thought better of knocking at the door of the apartment in case Joyce was asleep, and eased it open, lifting the wicker trophy to show her if she was awake. He needn't have taken so much care, because she wasn't in the room.

The balcony was deserted too. He called her number, only to hear the phone start to ring in the room. It was next to her bed, pinning down a scrap of paper on which she'd written *Gone for swim* followed by a single X with one bar practically upright. He ran to the balcony and peered between the hotels. Far out to sea a figure no larger than a charm on a bracelet was swimming. Except for the orange swimsuit he wouldn't have known who it was.

He closed the window and stood the basket on Joyce's bedside table. He read Jethro Dartmouth's last words as he laid the page in the safe, and then he made for the beach. Though the little swimming charm was as distant as ever, the sight seemed to concentrate a peace he hardly dared express to himself. He left his sandals next to Joyce's under the sun-bed occupied by her book. Every step took him deeper, but ripples kissed his skin. "There's none," he murmured as he forged onwards to tell Joyce. "There's none."

About "The Page"

Which tale of Ray's first pierced me with a sense of loneliness and loss? It may well have been "The Fog Horn" or "Kaleidoscope" or "The Dwarf" or "The Lake"—I can't now remember the order in which (precocious child) I read his first few books when I was no more than eight years old. I was borrowing adult fiction from the local public library on my mother's tickets, and Ray quickly became one of her favourite authors too. Now I think about it, perhaps that poignant jewel "The Smile" initially alerted us when it was reprinted in our local newspaper. Each of these stories affected me as some of Hans Andersen's fairy tales had—they were inescapably moving and disturbing as well. I think I was already also able to appreciate the poetry of Ray's prose.

On a Bradbury panel at the 2010 British Fantasy Convention, Joel Lane rightly celebrated him for rooting his fiction in the most crucial human experiences. The various panellists named their choice of Ray's tales, and some of the above were mine. An hour wasn't enough to let us say everything we should have, but here's my opportunity to cite a favourite theme of mine in his work—the death of books. While it's most fully explored in *Fahrenheit 451,* I've never forgotten two other treatments: "The Exiles" (mysteriously missing from the British edition of *The Illustrated Man*) and "Pillar of Fire," which I first encountered in August Derleth's anthology *The Other Side of the Moon.* In the latter story I was especially haunted by the last dead man's eulogy for our beloved fears. Back then I didn't know about the carnival magician who bade the twelve-year-old Ray to live forever, nor that Ray had embraced the exhortation by becoming a writer, but the information came as no surprise in the wake of his tales. Believe me, Ray—you'll live that long in the souls of your readers and in the work of the writers you've influenced. I believe that like others—Pete Crowther and Caitlín Kiernan among them—I learned lyricism from you.

For me Ray's achievement is inimitable, and so when Mort Castle asked me to write a tale for this book I vowed to avoid trying to imitate. In the course of my career I've come to believe in the happy coincidence, one of which was the source of "The Page." A few weeks after Mort's request my wife and I spent two weeks in Rhodes. As we sunbathed I turned over ideas in my mind for a Bradbury tribute, and on a windy day one blew along—the sight of a man in pursuit of a page that a gust had torn out of the book he was reading on the beach. Thank heaven I always take a notebook with me! I was instantly reminded of "The Exiles" and its relatives, and it didn't take me long to sketch my tale. It's pretty personal, but isn't that the best kind of homage? I hope it contains a little of Ray's poignancy, and perhaps it has some of the redemptive quality you can often find in his work (from the list above, "The Lake," for instance). One final thought: if a character in any of his early stories had a mobile phone, it would be science fiction. Sometimes I feel we're all inhabiting the future he envisioned.

—Ramsey Campbell

LIGHT

Mort Castle

Because you know the story, you might
see in the photograph an element of drama,
perhaps even pathos.
That is only your thought, your
projection onto this banal image.
A washed-out snapshot.
Hard to judge the light. You cannot tell if it is a sunny day.
She seems a sunny child.
She is three years old.
She wears a striped bathing suit.
Her eyes do not squint.
It is you she sees.
Her mouth is as wide as the blade of a toy shovel. Unattractive really.
She holds out her arms.
Does she want you to pick her up, embrace her, take her away?
Is she asking, Will you love me?
—Will you love me?
—Will you love me?
Because you know the story . . .

* * *

"Nobody really liked her much back then. She was always pretending to be a movie star, even though she had a face like a white tomato. She used to skip school a lot and go to the movies.

"I said to her once she acted like the movies were real life and that was stupid, and she told me the movies were more real than real life and that I was stupid, so I hit her."

—Vera Potts, Marilyn Monroe's classmate
at Vine Street Elementary School

August 4, 1962
Marilyn Monroe's bedroom
Los Angeles

Marilyn Monroe lies naked and dying.

Respiration: Shallow and irregular.

Blue-fade-to-black above the half-moons of her fingernails.

Eyelids seem to thicken as you watch.

Pasty white drool at the left corner of her mouth.

But if you look very hard, there is an almost imperceptible shimmering. Faint, like a trick of weary eyes.

Not rising from her but settling about her.

Light.

June 6, 1930
Los Angeles

Norma Jeane walks into the theater.

Gladys is taking her to the movies.

Gladys is crazy.

But there are times when the mouse-hole voices whisper softly, softly without threat, almost lulling.

Times when staircase men (they can appear *just like that*!) do not seek to punish her for badthinkings.

Times like now. Hey, Sport, maybe Gladys seems a bit dingy but in a cute kind of way. No danger to herself or others.

Gracie Allen, not Lizzie Borden.

Today, Gladys and Norma Jeane go to the New Electric Theater. One o'clock show. The New Electric was new back when *Tillie's Romance* got punctured. It's a ten-cent, third-run, stale-popcorn movie house.

Fair number of people at the show.

No late checks here. A dime can buy shelter for a good part of the day. Gladys and Norma Jeane sit as far as possible from everyone else.

You have to be careful. Not just careful, but *extra* careful when you are crazy.

Gladys offers popcorn to Norma Jeane.

No butter. Too easy for them to put secret chemicals in melted butter.

Norma Jeane does not want popcorn.

Gladys leans toward her. Her eyes glitter. —You should take the popcorn. I want you to be happy.

Norma Jeane smells the lie and craziness on her mother's breath. She takes popcorn. She wishes she were away from here. Wishes she were safe.

She will wish this many more times in her life.

On the screen . . . Cartoon. Dancing hippos, elephants, bears. Dots inside circles for belly buttons. Screechy chorus and xylophone.

Norma Jeane cranes her neck way back. Presses the crown of her head into the seat.

Above, projector beams. Columns and cones and fingers of light, yellow-white-clear, crisscrossing, splitting and uniting.

Pathways in the darkness.

Light.

It is beautiful.

On-screen: man with stiff arm out. Looks silly. Silly name: Doo-chee. DOO-Chee.

Makes Norma Jeane think of poop.

Norma Jeane laughs.

Gladys sinks fingernails into Norma Jeane's neck. —You must not laugh so loud. They will hear you. Learn to laugh a secret laugh. Inside.

On the screen: a beautiful woman. She is a radiance. She is a luminosity.

Oh! Norma Jeane can hardly breathe, she is so beautiful.

The radiance of the beautiful woman fills her eyes.

She wants to laugh and to cry.

—Laugh on the inside. Cry on the inside.

Gladys tells her: —That is Jean Harlow.

Gladys tells her: —She is the most beautiful woman in the world.

Norma Jeane thinks: *Beautiful, beautiful, beautiful* . . .

Gladys whispers: —*Her* name is *Jean* Harlow. *Your* name is Norma *Jeane.*

Gladys whispers: —Jean Harlow, Norma Jeane. Your momma knows what she's doing. Your momma has a *plan*.

Norma Jeane hears crazy. Looks at Jean Harlow, the most beautiful woman in the world. Looks only at Jean Harlow.

—Look at her.

Gladys says it crazy.

Gladys takes her ear and twists it.

Norma Jeane says a secret Ow! inside herself.

—Look at her! A command and threat.

Norma Jeane cranks back her neck.

—You can be her. You will be her.

Pain.

Stares upward.

Above, edge-melding beams of light. Of light.

The light goes to the screen.

The light becomes Jean Harlow.

Norma Jeane did not know her father. Gladys did not know him, either. Not for certain.

Growing up, Norma Jeane fantasized: Clark Gable was her father. Later, Howard Hughes. Later, Ernest Hemingway. Papa.

(When she became Marilyn Monroe, a world-renowned psychiatrist told her many of her problems stemmed from a lifelong search for a father.

(—Well, she said, I was wondering. Guess that takes care of that.)

Norma Jeane had a dog. Tippy. Tippy barked. A neighbor did not like the noise. He was a round-faced man with a tattoo. He chopped Tippy in half with a hoe.

Norma Jeane is staying with Aunt Grace. (Gladys is . . . *sick*. Your mother is in the hospital because she is sick . . . Cuu-koo! Cuu-koo!)

Aunt Grace has a boarder. A man.

He gives Norma Jeane a Sen-Sen. She does not like Sen-Sen but she takes it.

The man says he likes her.

She likes it when people like her. She wants everyone to like her.

—Come here. You are beautiful.

She likes being called beautiful.

The man touches her.

—Beautiful little girl.

Norma Jeane does not like his touching.

The man frightens her.

—Beautiful, the man tells her.

—I will tell, Norma Jeane says.

—Who will you tell? the man says.

—A policeman.

—Aunt Grace.

—Jesus in the sky.

The man laughs.

—Then give me some more Sen-Sen, she says.

—And a nickel.

Norma Jeane Baker: To the Los Angeles Orphans Home Society she was Orphan 3463.

—Be good, Aunt Grace told her, and abandoned her.

Norma Jeane could not stop crying. Not inside crying. She told them and she told them . . . *She was* not *an orphan*. She had a mother!

(Her mother was in the crazy house. Her mother was smelling bad smells and listening to the radio without a radio and making plans. And if *she* did not stop crying, they would think she was crazy like her mother and guess what happens then . . .)

—Stop crying.

—Now!

She began to change.

She smiled.

She became a good girl.

They would like that. They would like her.

She was acting.

Years later, when she was Marilyn Monroe, she would meet Katharine Hepburn. It was a brief, public meeting. The press was there. She was a starlet becoming a star. She was expected to say something sexy.

She said, —Sex is part of nature. I go along with nature.

Katharine Hepburn said, —Acting is a nice childish

profession—pretending you're someone else and, at the same time, selling yourself.

She decided she did not like Katharine Hepburn.

Katharine Hepburn understood her.

Norma Jeane hated Vine Street Elementary School. Had to march there with all the children from the Home on El Centro. It was Orphans on Parade. Everyone looked at you.

Reading was hard then. She mixed up words. She stuttered.

(Muh-muh my nn-name is Nuh-nn-NormaJeane!)

Norma Jeane was in the low reading group. Bluebirds were best. Yellowbirds were next. Then you had Blackbirds. Blackbirds were stupid. Norma Jeane was the only girl Blackbird. The rest were boys. Boys did not mind being Blackbirds. They would not have minded being Buzzards or Turkeys.

(Later, Marilyn Monroe would love reading. She would read Sartre and Joyce and Shaw and Fitzgerald. She would read Hemingway and want very much to meet him. She would read American poets. Carl Sandburg—she did meet him—and Edgar Lee Masters were her favorites.)

Norma Jeane skipped school one day. She went to the movies. She went even though she knew she would get in trouble.

She saw a Bosko cartoon and a Fox Movietone newsreel and a movie called *Sea of Dreams* and a Laurel and Hardy movie. Laurel was the skinny one. Hardy was the fat one. They had a piano to push up a long flight of stairs. The heavy piano made a painful noise on each step. Then the piano fell down all the stairs. They had to shove it all the way back up. Then they learned there was a road they could have used so . . . they carried it back down the stairs!

Laurel and Hardy were funny and sad. They reminded you of everybody.

Then the movies were finished.

Norma Jeane did not want to leave.

She knew she was in serious trouble.

So she stayed.

The movies started again.

That was how it worked.

She got tired.

She leaned way back in her seat and looked up.

Pathways of light.

Then Stan Laurel is in the seat alongside her. He takes off his derby and balances it on his knee.

She is not surprised. She is glad.

—I had a dream that I was awake and I woke up to find myself asleep, Stan Laurel says.

She knows what he means.

—I'm in trouble, Norma Jeane tells him.

—Neither do I, too, Stan Laurel says.

—That's silly, Norma Jeane says. —That's funny.

—Why yes, Stan Laurel says. —You can lead a horse to water, but a pencil must be led.

He smiles and slowly fades away, becoming glimmering dust motes that rise and swirl into the light streams above.

It is almost sunset when Norma Jeane returns to the Los Angeles Orphans Home.

—We were all quite concerned, Miss Daltrey, the assistant director, said, recalling the incident some years later.

—Once we knew she was all right, I was going to punish her . . .

—Then she started, well, *whimpering*, whimpering in a high-pitched voice. She scrunched up her little face, and her mouth stretched and turned down—really, it was like the mask of tragedy, a crescent, and she was scratching the top of her head and blinking both eyes in slow motion . . .

—This is another fine mm-meh—mess I've gotten myself into, is what she said.

—She was *just* like him, you know, the skinny one, and Norma Jeane stuttered, I mean, she really stuttered, and you certainly did not *want* to laugh at that, but it was just so funny. I let her off with two extra days drying dishes. There was a shine to our Norma Jeane. I remember thinking she was a natural talent and that she would become a comedienne like Carole Lombard or Jean Harlow.

Funds were a problem. No Christmas tree in the Orphans Home. Norma Jeane decided a tree would be delivered by Santa Claus. She made up a song and sang it. (She did not stammer when she sang.)

Santa will bring me a Christmas Tree
A long red scarf,
and an apple pie . . .
Santa will bring me a Christmas Tree—
and oh, how happy I will be!

The other children made fun of Norma Jeane. Even the real little kids knew Santa Claus was not real. It was the Depression.

Norma Jeane made up a new song.

Jesus will bring me a Christmas Tree
A long red scarf,
and an apple pie . . .
Jesus will bring me a Christmas Tree
and take me to heaven when I die!

August 4, 1962
Marilyn Monroe's bedroom

Marilyn Monroe is dying.

Her diaphragm has quit working and her breathing is now all from the stomach. Her skin has a bluish cast, and if you were to take her wrist, you would find her pulse only with difficulty.

In this dark room, with no one to see, points of light, little stars, are gathering.

A glowing dome of light covers her.

June 7, 1937

Jean Harlow died. Age: 26.

June 26, 1937

Norma Jeane left the orphanage. Something had happened, she was not sure what, but now Aunt Grace wanted her . . . Aunt Grace *would* take her in.

Norma Jeane stood in front of the Los Angeles Orphans Home Society. She wished she had a derby to tip in farewell.

A thought came to her, and she claimed to remember it years later.

—Jean Harlow was dead. It was not right that the world did not have a Jean Harlow. That meant I would have to make things right and become Jean Harlow—or maybe I already was . . . It was a very strange feeling. I still feel that strange feeling sometimes.

Then she got into Aunt Grace's Buick and went home.

Saturday, July 24, 1937

Norma Jeane waited in the long line at Grauman's Chinese. The film, *Saratoga*, had been released the previous day.

It starred Clark Gable and Jean Harlow.

It was Jean Harlow's final film.

Norma Jeane watched the movie.

And without watching—not exactly—she seemed constantly aware of shifting waves of light above.

June 19, 1942

Norma Jeane married the boy next door. Nice guy: Jim Dougherty. She was sixteen. He was twenty-three. She married him to stay out of the orphanage. (Aunt Grace could not keep her any longer.) Jim married Norma Jeane because he was a nice guy.

That's part of it; there were other reasons.

Jim was away for a long time with the Merchant Marine.

Norma Jeane had a factory job, but she was pretty and had a va-va-voom figure. She soon got other jobs: modeling in shorts and skimpy tops and bathing suits. She did one picture looking back over her shoulder like Betty Grable. Her smile was not as perfect as Betty Grable's, but her tush was better than Betty Grable's.

Lots of guys saw pictures like that of Norma Jeane in *Wink* and *Laff* and *Picture Parade* and *Caper* and *Gala*.

Nice guy Jim did not like all the guys looking at photographs of Norma Jeane's tush.

So they got divorced.

> "She told me she wanted to be a movie star. I told her with looks like that, she was a natural. She asked if I meant it. Sure, I meant it, I told her. She asked if I could give her a buck for a sandwich and coffee. I gave her a buck for a sandwich and coffee. Then she said she just had to do something nice for me, so I let her, you know what I mean? Marilyn Monroe, for cryin' out loud."
>
> —Randy Bleischer,
> who's scored many free drinks with this story

* * *

Norma Jeane posed nude.

Calendar Girl.

Marilyn in the flesh on swirls of red velvet.

Photographer Tom Kelley had no problem with lighting.

She glowed. She *was* the light.

Tom Kelley called the picture *Golden Dreams.*

He understood.

And so:

Got a nose job.

Gave some blow jobs.

Changed her name.

Marilyn Monroe.

Muh-Muh-Marilyn Monroe.

—No, goddamnit! Marilyn goddamnit Monroe goddamnit.

Unbilled extra.

—How about a tumble?

Extra. Two days.

Took voice lessons.

Took acting lessons.

Marilyn Monroe.

Walk-on.

Chorus girl in *Love Happy* with Harpo and Groucho Marx.

Banged Groucho.

Banged Harpo.

John Carroll (B-movie star) and his wife, Lucille (Director, Talent Department, MGM). Three-way.

Banged Joe Schenck (Chairman, 20th Century-Fox).

Banged Harry Cohn (President, Columbia Pictures).

Banged Johnny Hyde. She called him "the kindest man in the world."

Johnny Hyde said —Marry me. I've got a bad heart. I'll croak soon, leave you fixed like the Queen of the Nile and not a poor *shiksa nafke*.

She said —No.

He died.

Second billing in *Ladies of the Chorus*.

Tah-dah!

She got to act. She got to sing.

She sang "Every Baby Needs a Daddy."

You know, all in all, it did not take that long.

Not really.

Marilyn Monroe was becoming a star.

1952

Hollywood Success Story.

Monkey Business.

20th Century-Fox.

Cary Grant. Ginger Rogers. A chimpanzee named Esther.

Second billing: Marilyn Monroe.

Cast as a secretary named Lois LaVerne.

—You'll have to be funny.

—Funny? I can do funny.

—But . . .

She did not want to cause a p-p-problem, no, she didn't, but just one change, really, if they could, it m-muh- . . . mattered . . .

All right. Okay.

Second billing: Marilyn Monroe.

Cast as a secretary named Lois Laurel.

1953

Gentlemen Prefer Blondes.

Starring Jane Russell and Marilyn Monroe.

How to Marry a Millionaire.
Starring Marilyn Monroe, Betty Grable, and Lauren Bacall.
She was a big star.
A very big star.

January 14, 1954

Marilyn Monroe married Joe DiMaggio. "Joltin' Joe." "The Yankee Clipper." Hemingway called him "the Great DiMaggio" and "the Dago." She called him "my slugger." Three-time MVP winner. Thirteen-time All-Star.

Helluva ballplayer.

Joe DiMaggio was shy. He didn't say much. Hated that celebrity spotlight. Hated it a helluva lot more when it wasn't illuminating Joe DiMaggio.

And Hey! Did *not* like his wife in it.

He thought she should come with him to San Francisco. Learn to cook linguini with a nice clam sauce. Cannelloni. Braciole like Mama Rosalie. Have a bunch of kids.

She thought she should star in a movie called *The Seven Year Itch*.

New York. Publicity shot. Police keep the crowd behind barricades. Marilyn Monroe on the subway grating at Lexington and Fifty-first. Wind machine kicks in. Her skirt billows up.

I see London.
I see France.
I see Marilyn Monroe's underpants.

And a whole! lot! more!

I see London.
I see France.

I see Marilyn Monroe's whosis!

Joe DiMaggio has a problem with this aspect of moviemaking.

Restaurateur and longtime friend Toots Shor explains it to him: —Giuseppe, What do you want? She's just a goddamn dumb whore.

The marriage lasts 276 days.

August 4, 1962
Marilyn Monroe's bedroom
Los Angeles

Marilyn Monroe is dying.

Drugs are taking a long time to kill her.

Or perhaps, even with no audience, Marilyn Monroe is working the drama of it all.

Light gathers, phosphorescent waves all about her.

She wants to be smart.

She wants people to think she is smart.

She wants to think she is smart.

(Let's hear it for the only girl Blackbird!)

She wants to act.

Chekhov. Dostoyevsky.

A review: *In the demanding role of Grushenka, Marilyn Monroe exhibits what noted theater critic and raconteur Groucho Marx has acclaimed nothing less than "a million dollar ass."*

She wants to be praised.

She wants to be loved.

* * *

June 29, 1956

She married Arthur Miller. Playwright. *All My Sons. Death of a Salesman. The Crucible.* A talent. An intellect. We've got a Tony Award for Best Author, the New York Drama Critics' Circle Award, and the Pulitzer Prize for Drama. Howzat? You want better? Check with his mother, Augusta . . . Gussie: —*Oy*, even when he was just a *pisherke*, what a *kopf* he had!

House Un-American Activities Committee comes after Arthur Miller. Pinko stuff in his plays. Hangs out with Commies. He wears glasses. Come on, I gotta spell it out? He's a Hebe!

Marilyn Monroe saves Arthur Miller's bacon—you should pardon the expression. Arthur Miller is married to Golden Dreams, for cryin' out loud. Not the girl next door, but the kinda sweet, kinda daffy, impossibly sexy roundheels you wished lived next door. How much more American can you get?

Miller, aw, he's okay. Don't bust his chops. Let him cop a walk.

Marilyn Monroe calls Arthur Miller *Pops*.

Arthur Miller introduces her to the work of many writers.

She writes poetry. Sad dolls. Weeping willows. Staircase men. Balloons. Jean Harlow.

She is scared to show Arthur her poetry. She doesn't want to hear that sniffy-nose thing he does.

She discovers Edgar Lee Masters. She loves *Spoon River Anthology*.

Late in the evening, the hi-fi playing Respighi's *Pines of Rome*, she's had enough to drink (1953 Dom Pérignon), and so she reads a few lines of Edgar Lee Masters to Arthur Miller.

> *Immortality is not a gift,*
> *Immortality is an achievement;*

And only those who strive mightily
Shall possess it.

Arthur Miller shakes his head. —Drivel, he says. —The quintessence of pulp-pap passing as profundity. Edgar Guest with a college sophomore's vocabulary and keen intellectual grasp. It is not impossible that *everything* that is wrong with America is contained in those resoundingly *dreadful* lines.

She finds the courage. —I . . . I luh-like . . .

—Of course, says Arthur Miller.

Shortly thereafter, she finds the journal he has accidentally left open on her dressing table.

> . . . such a dumb *shiksa, takeh a goyishe kopf.* I do feel pity for her, but perhaps not love. And, selfish though it may be, I wonder what deleterious effects she might have on my *own* career . . .

The Millers' marriage, uh, not in great shape.

He wrote a screenplay called *The Misfits.*

—Just for you.

Her role: a depressed divorced dancer, desperate for approval, acceptance, love.

She is NEED come a-'walkin'—with a great body!

John Huston directed the film.

Clark Gable costarred.

It was Gable's last film.

The film wrapped. Two days later, massive heart attack.

Clark Gable died ten days later.

Marilyn Monroe divorced Arthur Miller on January 20, 1961.

> "I only spoke with her the once. Her regular domestic was sick and so the agency sent me over for the day. She

was drinking, drinking quite a lot, and she told me just to dust, didn't want to hear no vacuum. And then she asked me did I like doing this kind of work, was I married, did I have kids, you know, personal things like that that are not really that personal. And then she asked me was I happy and I said, 'I guess.'

"She said her life was sad and I said that was too bad.

"She said her life was just full of *despairs*.

"Despairs . . . That was how she said it and I tell you, I never forgot that, because that is sad slapped thick on top of sad . . . It made me want to just pick her up and hold her, 'cause what she was was just a sad little white girl.

"But I couldn't do that now, could I? So I clucked my tongue and I think I said something that most likely did not help her at all."

—Mattie Pearl Yates

Tried to kill herself.
Did not.
Alcohol. Drugs. Psychiatry.
The Trinity for the Salvation of the Twentieth Century Soul.
Bangs President Jack Kennedy.
Who didn't?
Alcohol. Drugs. Psychiatry.
Tried to kill herself.
Did not.
Moved into modest house she'd bought in Brentwood, L.A.

Nembutal.
Chloral hydrate.
Vodka.

* * *

August 4, 1962
Marilyn Monroe's bedroom
Los Angeles

Marilyn Monroe
A corpse

For a moment
An aura

Norma Jeane walks
into the theater

Becomes
Light

About "Light"

I was fourteen or fifteen, reading like the Looney Tunes Tasmanian Devil set loose at the Olde Country Book Buffet, and couldn't help noting that too many artists and writers died young and often not well. Then Ray Bradbury came along on this glutton's word menu and showed me with his "Forever and the Earth" that no, Thomas Wolfe did not have to *stay dead*—not when we needed him.

Years later when the story of Marilyn Monroe seized me—she was "the saddest woman in the world," said her short-term husband Arthur Miller—I set out to give her something a little better than what foolish choices, DNA tics, and the Wheel of Cosmic Fortune handed her. This is my third Marilyn story.

There will likely be more in the future. Perhaps one day I'll get it completely right.

But for now, I'll borrow Mr. Stan Laurel's derby and tip it to his very good friend and advocate Mr. Ray Douglas Bradbury: He showed me the way.

Mort Castle

CONJURE

Alice Hoffman

It was August, when the crickets sang slowly and the past lingered in bright pools of glorious light, even though it would soon be gone, the way summer was all but over, yet the heat was still on the rise. The weather had been extreme that month: days of drenching rain, sudden showers of hail, temperatures passing record highs. Local children whispered that an angel had fallen to earth in a thunderstorm. There were roving groups who swore they had found signs. Footprints in the grass, black feathers, a campfire in the woods behind the high school where there were sparks of shimmering ash. One neighborhood boy vowed that he had seen a man in a black cloak rise above the earth and walk on air, and although no one believed his account, mothers began to keep their children home. They locked the doors, called in the dogs, kept the lights on after dusk.

No one cut through the field anymore, except for Abbey and Cate, best friends, who at age sixteen were too old to be kept home and far too sure of themselves to be afraid of a story. They had jobs at the town pool as swim counselors, and late in the afternoons they walked home together, arms draped over each other's shoulders, making their way through the pale heat, their long hair scented with chlorine. Usually they stopped at the library, where Cate would wait outside, dreamy-eyed, while Abbey ran in to find a new book, which would get her through the night. She'd had trouble sleeping lately, and books were her antidote to the darkness of these late-August nights. She had the distinct impression that something was beginning and something was ending; there were just so many days like this left to them. Before they knew it, time would speed up and the future would appear on a street corner or in a park, and there they'd be, grown women who'd forgotten how long a summer could last.

The librarian, Mrs. Fanning, often had a stack of books waiting for Abbey, and choosing the right one had become a sacred ritual. On this day Abbey returned *Great Expectations* and took up Ray Bradbury's *Something Wicked This Way Comes*.

"Excellent choice," Mrs. Fanning said, pleased. "By the pricking of my thumb, something wicked this way comes. The title comes from *Macbeth*, Act IV."

"Do you believe people are wicked?" Abbey asked.

Outside the world was green, shifting in the dappled light. Cate was sitting on the steps, head thrown back, basking in the last of the sun. If Abbey tried to talk about her worries with her friend, Cate would admonish her. "You think too much!"

"Certainly some people are," Mrs. Fanning said. "But there'd be no interesting novels without them, would there?"

In a fiction it was possible to discern the wicked from the pure of heart. Roses withered when devious individuals passed by; blackthorns grew about them. But such clues were not as evident in real life. "Judge a person the same way you judge a book," Mrs. Fanning suggested. "A search for beauty and truth, a gut response to what feels a lie. Intuition." She seemed quite sure of herself. "Imagination."

Abbey began reading on the way home from the library, acting out all the parts. She concentrated so deeply on the words on the page that she stumbled over shifts in the concrete sidewalk.

"You live in books." Cate grinned.

"I would if I could," Abbey admitted.

"What's the good of that?" Cate sighed, for she yearned for real life. She wanted adventure, one-of-a-kind experiences. She was suddenly beautiful and there were teenage boys who followed her around town, just as suddenly in love with her, though they were still too young to say so. She confided that her plan was to leave town after high school graduation, find her way to California, see every bit of the coast. She'd study butterflies in Monterey, sharks in San Diego. She had a fearless nature, which was why Abbey both admired her and was concerned for her at the same time. They were nearly home, but Cate lagged behind, gazing over at the field, the one wild piece of land left in town.

"What would you do if you saw an angel?" she asked in a low voice.

They stood together on the corner, where they met every morning.

"There's no such thing," Abbey said. "Not around here."

"If there was." Cate squinted to see into the distance. "Seriously."

"I'd write about him," Abbey said.

As for Cate, they both knew she'd fly away, triumphant and distant in the arms of an angel.

It was Cate who insisted they take the shortcut the following afternoon, forsaking the library, so they might walk through the field where the angel was said to be.

"How many times do you get to search for an angel?" she teased, running off before Abbey could say that if there was such a thing, perhaps it wasn't meant to be a sight for human eyes, that the very brightness of such a creature might burn and blind anyone who gazed upon him. Cate had already climbed the fence that separated the path from the field, and Abbey had no choice but to follow, up and over the fence, leaping clumsily onto the ground. The books she'd meant to return to the library weighed down her backpack. Cate grinned and pointed to a dark splotch on the ground. It was only a single feather in the tall grass beside the creek, but when Cate ran to grab it, Abbey felt a hollow chill. The water in the creek was green, slow-moving, and swirls of insects rose from it. They used to swim here when they were younger, practicing the backstroke and the butterfly.

Cate ran back, her hair flying out behind her. She held up the feather. "We're definitely on the right path." She elbowed Abbey, then nodded to a willow tree. A young man in a black coat was gazing at them. Abbey took a step back. He was wearing leather gloves though the weather was fine.

"Don't tell me you're afraid?" Cate teased. "He's probably Bobby Marcus's cousin."

Bobby Marcus was their twelve-year-old neighbor who'd told everyone that his cousin from Los Angeles was spending a few weeks with them, and that he slept all day and was out all night. Not that there was anywhere to go in their town in the evenings, only the Blue Note Bar and Grill, where some of their fathers stopped on the way home from work.

Dusk was falling down among the trees. The swirls of insects above the creek turned blue in the murky air. The young man had long dark hair and an easy gait. He had dramatic features, gray, light-filled eyes. He looked a few years older than the girls, perhaps nineteen. He was making his way through the tall grass, approaching as if he knew them and was meant to speak to them, as if he'd been sent to them on this evening in August. Most people were now at home, sitting down to dinner, and Abbey's mother would be watching from the door. She worried about her daughter, who spent so much time alone. She'd be even more concerned if she knew that there were nights when Abbey climbed out her bedroom window so that she could amble through town in the dark. Abbey had never even told Cate that she climbed out her window on restless nights, her feet landing in the ivy. Sometimes she went to sit on the stone steps of the library, wondering about the world beyond their town; other times she came to this very field and read by moonlight, savoring her aloneness. Now she wasn't certain she'd come back here again. The edges of the grass were sullen and plumy in the shifting light.

Cate went forward. The young man in the black coat had clearly been drawn to her luminous beauty. He had a slow, winning smile, which he aimed at her. Abbey saw that his boots were covered with a layer of gray ash and that the fabric of his coat was frayed.

"I'll bet you're Bobby Marcus's cousin," Cate said as they approached each other. If Abbey didn't know any better, she'd think her friend was flirting.

"That's me." He said his name was Lowell. He grinned broadly when Abbey gazed at his gloves. "I've been chopping wood," he explained. "I've been camping here all summer. I can't bring myself to sleep under a roof. "

Abbey had never seen him here on the nights when she'd come to read in the grass. She wondered if angels lied, or if that was only the territory of men.

Lowell offered them a drink. "I'm being sociable and you should be too. Whatever your parents say, you're old enough for a beer."

His invitation seemed more like a challenge. All the same they followed him through the grass to his campsite. "We're only being polite," Cate assured Abbey when she hesitated. "He's right—we're old enough."

There was a pot for boiling water, a sleeping bag, a small canvas tent, a small axe.

"For chopping wood," he said to Abbey, throwing down his gloves.

There was no stack of firewood, only some boughs from a twisted bramble tree. Abbey imagined he wasn't a practiced camper, that he was a city boy who couldn't even read a map of the stars. When Lowell reached out to get them some beers that he kept cooling in a fishing net in the creek, Abbey spied a black dog tattooed on his wrist. She felt a tightness in her throat, but she sipped at the cold beer, sharing a bottle with Cate. The girls sat close together on a log, and Abbey thought she could feel her friend's heart beating alongside her own. The more beer the girls drank, the more Lowell talked. He told them about California, how beautiful it was, how the sky stretched on forever, how the night smelled of gardenias. He was a handsome young man, with a graceful way of speaking, and by the time he was done, California seemed like the promised land, a heaven all its own.

"That's where I'm going," Cate said.

"I knew that was what you wanted." Lowell laughed. Abbey noticed that he seemed impressed by his own observations, the sort of man who had learned a lot about women in his lifetime and was quick to put these lessons to use. "I could see it in your future."

Cate laughed, flattered, lowering her eyes. She was demure in a way Abbey had never known her to be. "You don't even know me," she said to Lowell, as if she wanted him to.

"You don't believe me?" Lowell shifted over to sit beside Cate, his leg against hers. "I know you real well. I can see everything that's going to happen to you."

Abbey tugged on Cate's sleeve. The intuition Mrs. Fanning had referred to felt slick, as if oil was pooling around them, dark and unstoppable. This late in August, time was already shifting, the light disappearing before anyone expected it to. "We have to go," she urged.

"Keep me a secret," Lowell said. He leaned close to Cate when he spoke, his breath moving the strands of her hair. His gray eyes were half closed, as if he was in the middle of a dream and that dream included Cate and her future. "I'd hate to be chased out and forced to sleep under a roof."

Cate promised they would make up a story; they'd say they'd stayed late to practice their lifesaving techniques at the pool. In the darkening light, the ends of Cate's hair looked faintly green, tinted by chlorine; perhaps the lie she intended to tell had turned her hair this color, or perhaps it was only the fading of the day that made it seem so.

Lowell walked them to the edge of the field. Abbey went first because she knew where the briars were; Cate came next, with Lowell following. Right before they stepped out of the tall grass, Abbey turned to see him kiss her friend. By then, it was dark.

That night Abbey climbed out her window. She kept her shoes under the porch steps, but tonight she went barefoot. She made her way through town, as she always did. Usually the darkened houses brought her a sort of comfort, but tonight the silence rattled her; she could feel it hitting against her bones. She stopped at the edge of the field. She thought she saw him beneath the tree, wearing his black coat and his gloves. She didn't see an angel but a man, waiting for something, twisting the future into rope of his own devising. Abbey had that same chilled feeling she'd had when she'd first spied him. She turned and ran, feeling the threat he cast until she reached her corner. She went past her own house and sneaked into the Marcuses' yard. She threw a pebble at the window. She threw another and another, and finally Bobby appeared.

He opened the window and leaned out, confused. "Are you crazy?" he whispered, waving his arms at her. "Go away."

"Where's your cousin?" Abbey wanted to know.

"He went back to California," Bobby said. "My parents kicked him out."

He shut his window, not wanting to say more, but Abbey sat down at the Marcuses' picnic table to wait. After a while Bobby came out. He was only twelve, and Abbey had babysat for him once or twice, a fact he hated to be reminded of whenever she teased him, recalling how he used to cry to get his way. He was wearing a raincoat over his pajamas.

"Why'd they kick him out?" Abbey asked.

Bobby shrugged.

"There must have been a reason."

Bobby's parents were both teachers at the high school, warm-hearted, reasonable people.

"He was inappropriate," Bobby said.

Abbey felt that chill. "Meaning?"

When Bobby clammed up, Abbey grabbed his arm and twisted. She was stronger than she appeared, perhaps from carrying stacks of books home from the library.

"Hey!" Bobby pulled away. "Okay. Fine. He said he could see the future."

"They kicked him out for that?"

"Well, they thought he was crazy. I mean he went on and on about it, like he was cursing us or something. He wasn't like that when he first came here. He sat with my mother for hours in the kitchen; he cut the lawn. Then he snapped and started saying he knew our fate and that we deserved everything we got."

Abbey recalled the way Lowell had walked toward them, his gaze set on Cate.

"And I guess when they called California they found out he's been in a lot of trouble. He's not really even a cousin. He was just working for my uncle, and he stole his car. He took things from here, too," Bobby said, moody, clearly having been told to keep the family troubles private.

"What kind of things?"

"He made me promise not to tell."

Abbey grabbed Bobby's arm and he shifted away. "Stupid things. Rope. Packing tape. Blankets. He took my dad's axe that we used when we went camping."

"What did he tell you about the future? Are you going to be a millionaire?"

Abbey was sarcastic by nature; her mother often complained about this, as well as her having her head in the clouds. Her mother insisted that Abbey would be beautiful if she stopped chopping her hair short and paid some attention to her appearance instead of wearing shorts and T-shirts and old hooded sweatshirts.

"He told my dad he'd be dead by December," Bobby Marcus said.

"What does he know?" Abbey snorted. "He's not a doctor."

"My dad has leukemia." Bobby's voice was solemn. Abbey knew Mr. Marcus had been ill, but people in town didn't know just how sick he'd been, only that he was once stout and was now painfully thin. "He's been in remission."

Until this summer Abbey felt that nothing could touch the people close to her. Then she had started worrying, and once she'd started she found she couldn't stop. "Don't worry about any of Lowell's predictions. He seems like a big liar."

"I don't know." Bobby looked younger than his years. "My father didn't get out of bed today."

At the pool the next day, Cate kept to herself. A light rain started to fall in the afternoon, and when the swimmers scattered into the locker room Cate just sat there on the concrete, rain streaming down. She looked like a water nymph, a creature who belonged to another element.

"You're going to get soaked," Abbey called as she scrambled to find a dry place under the patio awning.

"It's only rain," Cate said, as if the world around her didn't matter, as if she was already in some other, unreachable place, a realm much farther away than California.

Once she was underneath the awning, Abby started reading, and soon she was in another world herself. Then, all at once, she felt someone was drowning, even though there were no swimmers in the pool. When she looked up Cate was gone. There was that chill, right through her sweatshirt. She waited, anxious and ready to bolt, until all of the campers were picked up by their parents, then she took off running. The rain was coming down harder. She climbed the fence, snagging her fingers on the metal, then ran along the creek, now rushing with rising water. She imagined him gone; she willed it with all her might. But his tent was still in the field, and there were wisps of smoke from a bonfire that had been doused by the torrents. She went within feet of the tent and called, "Cate?" in a low, shaky tone, but there was no answer and she couldn't tell if anyone was in the tent, if what she heard was a girl's voice or only the sound of the rain.

The next morning Cate wasn't waiting on the corner where they usually met. There were several police cars circling the neighborhood. In a panic Abbey ran all the way to the pool. She had a dark premonition and was quick to berate herself for not warning Cate against Lowell. An angel, a liar, a man with black gloves. But there was Cate, calmly teaching the youngest swim group how to dog-paddle.

"Where were you?" Abbey said as she came up beside her. There was the thrum of panic in her throat as she spoke.

Cate kept her attention focused on the Guppies. "Kick," she called out to them before she turned to her friend. "We don't have to do everything together, do we? Anyway, you were the one who was late."

All that day Cate avoided her, but at their lunch break, Abbey made a point of sitting beside her at the picnic table. "He's not even Bobby Marcus's cousin."

Cate coolly appraised her as she continued eating her lunch. "I know." Her wet hair streamed down her back.

"And he's a thief," Abbey said.

Cate threw her a contemptuous look. "You think you're so smart."

"Were you with him when I came looking for you yesterday?" Abbey's voice sounded broken even to herself.

"He said you'd be jealous."

"You think I'm jealous?" Abbey stood up, her heart hitting against her chest.

Cate shrugged. "You tell me."

"Did he tell you Bobby's father kicked him out? That he stole a car in California?"

"He told me everything," Cate said calmly. "He told me you can't be friends with someone who's filled with envy."

"Is that what he told you about the future? That we wouldn't be friends anymore?"

"He said I'd be leaving for California before I knew it."

Late in the afternoon Abbey told the head counselor that she felt ill and needed to go home. It wasn't exactly a lie. She packed up her swimsuit and her books and left early, her head throbbing. She walked to the field, then scaled the fence. She stood beside the creek. She wasn't surprised by what she saw.

There was now a car parked under the bushes, hidden by briars and leaves. You had to squint to see it beyond the tree, then it was possible to make out the Marcuses' old station wagon, which Bobby's father had reported missing that morning. That was why there were police cars patrolling earlier in the day, looking for signs of the thief.

For a moment Abbey thought she might bolt and run, then keep on running till she reached the far side of the field. Instead, she studied the stolen car, the briars, the field she had come to all her life. She thought about the items he'd taken from the Marcuses' garage—the tape, the ropes.

He was there, under the tree. He laughed when he saw her, and waved her over. He was graceful and tall and sure of himself. She walked through the high grass, and it stung when it hit against her legs.

"I knew you'd show up," he said when Abbey reached his campsite. "You and I made a connection. She thinks she's the one that everyone wants, but it's you. I can see what's beautiful about you." He cupped Abbey's chin and studied her face. She understood how he could make someone feel special.

Abbey saw then that he was older than they'd first thought, not seventeen or eighteen but in his mid-twenties. There were feathers around the campsite because he was trapping birds for his supper. There were the bones of sparrows and larks, white and stripped bare. She thought about the children who believed an angel had fallen into the field, convinced that a miracle would soon occur. She thought about the volumes in the library that were waiting for her on the shelves, each one beautiful, each one-of-a-kind.

He kissed her and she let him. Soon enough someone would notice the stolen car. He wouldn't keep himself hidden in this town; he'd have use for the ropes, the tape, the axe, all that he'd need to take someone with him tonight. Maybe he'd stop in a field far from here, in another town, where a girl's body wouldn't be identified; maybe he'd keep on driving. He kissed her and she kissed him back. She knew that Cate would follow her into the field, and that she'd spy them together, then turn and run, distraught.

When he grabbed Abbey to pull her toward the car, she slipped out of his grasp, leaving him holding on to nothing but her backpack full of books. She was wearing shorts and a sweatshirt and the sneakers her mother told her were unfashionable. She ran home as if she were the angel with black wings, and she didn't climb out her window again after that. In fact she kept it locked. She knew that Cate would cry all that night and that she'd never talk to Abbey again, just as she knew that years later, when Cate came home for a visit from California, compelled to stop at the library to confront her old friend, demanding to know how she could have betrayed her so easily, Abbey would simply tell her that the man in the field wasn't the only one who could see the future.

For Ray Bradbury

About "Conjure"

Ray Bradbury's masterwork, *Fahrenheit 451,* a hymn to books and to the power of literature, is a classic work of American fiction and one of the most important books of our lifetime. In a series of novels, short stories, and linked short stories, Bradbury has created his own genre, one that has greatly influenced American literature. Due to his work, magic is no longer corralled into genre writing. It is everywhere in American fiction. Critics may call it magic realism, but it's simply what Ray Bradbury has been doing from the start.

Bradbury's themes of innocence and experience echo a world made up of equal parts of dark and light, where characters yearn for both the future and the past and where loss is inevitable. Bradbury has given readers a singular vision of small-town American life, one in which a dark thread is pulled through the grass. Bradbury's blend of suburban magic rejoices in the American dream, but it also presents the twilight world of darker possibilities, the opposing nightmare.

In my story "Conjure," many of Ray's themes surface—two friends who must step into the future and leave their childhoods behind, like it or not; a summer that will never be forgotten; a stranger who comes to town with a dark past and perhaps an even darker future; a huge love of the library; and ultimately, personal salvation through books. Of course I'm quite certain that *Something Wicked This Way Comes* saves my characters from a terrible fate, echoing my own life. Had I not discovered Ray Bradbury's books, I most certainly would not have become the writer I am today.

—Alice Hoffman

MAX

John Maclay

I first met Max thirty years ago, when I joined a Masonic lodge. Max was the Tiler, spelled that way, the officer who sat outside the closed door during meetings, to make sure non-Masons didn't enter the room. In keeping with his position, he even had a sword beside his chair.

Masonry is the oldest and largest fraternal organization in the world. Some say it goes all the way back to ancient Egypt, some say it began in the Middle Ages, some say it started as recently as the seventeenth century. In any event, it's old.

Masonic rituals, enacted beyond the closed door guarded by the Tiler, deal with the building of King Solomon's Temple in Jerusalem, symbolizing how everyone should build a spiritual temple within himself. Masons run the gamut, from practicing mystics to those who treat the pursuit as only a charitable and social club. And if anyone thinks we Masons secretly rule the world, well, we're far too diverse in our personal temple building for that!

Dressed in a tuxedo, as were all the officers, Max was tall, balding, and cadaverous. He was friendly enough but spoke with a quiet, nasal voice and had a withdrawn air about him. No one knew where he worked, or where he lived, but that wasn't unusual, since Masons don't often share such details, and don't ask about them, concentrating instead on who a person is within the lodge.

Nor could I—or anyone else, as I broached the subject to them—make a good estimate as to Max's age. He certainly looked to be over forty, but beyond that, he could have been anywhere up to ninety. That made him even more of a mystery man.

Another odd thing about Max was that as he sat outside the door, he read newspapers to pass the time. But these newspapers were always from other cities, though they bore recent dates. And Max didn't look like a man who traveled.

In an uncanny way, Max seemed to know everything. Not only could he always reference the Masonic schedule for the whole state, he made accurate predictions about the weather, and about how the latest world crises would turn out.

One more odd thing: Max wasn't a "local." No one had grown up with him or attended school with him. The first anyone could remember seeing Max was when he'd first appeared at a lodge door.

But in any event, as I advanced in Masonry and joined more and more of its many units, I kept encountering Max. It seemed he was the Tiler of practically everything—"Tiler to the World," as someone put it—which might have been partially explained by the fact that the job paid twenty dollars a meeting. Was he therefore simply a retiree who needed the income?

But I also came to learn that Max had been a past high officer, had held more than a few such positions. Masons are given a special apron and gold breast-pocket badge when they complete their term of office, and Max carried around a leather case that was bulging with them. And he had dozens of pins, also attesting to his service, on the lapels of his worn tux.

Along this line, Max was a great and encyclopedic teacher of Masonic ritual. His quiet voice at times even intoned passages that had long since been removed, as if he'd been on the scene when they were current.

So I kept being with Max, and he with me. And yet the mystery deepened. That was because, as the years wore on, his age—as well as his origin—remained an enigma. He was just "still there," and everywhere, looking about the same as he always did.

Indeed, had he been around—forever?

I must confess that once, after seeing the classic movie *Nosferatu* for the first time, I wondered if Max was a vampire. After all, he looked much like the character, and he did seem to be ageless. I'd also read the Oscar Wilde novel *The Picture of Dorian Gray*, so I wondered if Max was ageless because he had some dark secret to hide.

But I felt ashamed of those thoughts, since Max was the farthest thing from evil; he was one of the kindest, gentlest men I'd ever met.

However, about five years ago, I did learn more about Max. To make a long story short, whatever his age was, he had several auto accidents on his way to lodge meetings, and he couldn't drive anymore. So Masonic brothers, myself included, had to pick him up in our cars and bring him to meetings.

That was when, in due course, I first saw Max's house, where he lived alone. And it was perhaps the strangest house I'd ever seen.

On a cul-de-sac, in an obscure part of town, it was akin to a trailer, though it wasn't one. Long and low, it had only one window facing the street, and a little porch at one end, from which Max would walk stiffly down to get into my car. Probably needless to say, I never got to go inside. He was always appreciative of the ride, though, and there was an aura about him that made me feel good about my act of charity.

I learned, eventually, that Max had indeed worked for a living. He was retired from the State Bureau of Statistics—which seemed oddly appropriate.

But then, after a time, Max could no longer manage on his own. So he moved to a little room in the Masonic Home, and I'd pick him up there. Now he used a walker, and it took him forever to cover the smallest distances. But he was still on his feet, and even more striking than that, he was still the Tiler.

I also need to mention that Max was in the hospital a number of times, and every time everyone said that surely this time he wouldn't be back in action. But he always was. And incidentally, the same thing was true of some other Masonic brothers I knew—they might even have lung cancer, yet they were still around. But Max was the model of Impossible Recuperation!

And Max's acts of charity once he had moved into the home—well beyond what Masons swear to offer one another—became the stuff of legend. He was always seen visiting the rooms of brothers who were even more infirm than himself, and helping them around the halls even though he himself used a walker, and always with a heartwarming smile.

There might have been even more to Max, than all I've previously mentioned. Perhaps I didn't want to share all of my observations with other Masons, because we might have come to, let's say, "improbable conclusions."

But truth be told, I had noticed a certain light in a few other Masons' eyes. Like in those of a Grand High Priest, and in those of a lesser brother who was a student of the occult. And I must confess, even if it might be unbelievable, that one night, as I was sitting in lodge, I saw that same light and it was in Max's eyes.

It was the night of elections of officers, and he was called in to vote, with someone who'd voted being given the sword to sit in Max's place outside the door.

And it then happened to be announced that a brother, who was present, had just been diagnosed with a serious disease.

And damned if Max, in his usual unassuming way, didn't suddenly rise, shamble over to that brother, and place his hands on his head.

Everyone sat there in wonderment while an absolutely unearthly light momentarily filled the room.

But, even despite that occurrence, since I try to be a rational man, I must confess that my curiosity, or hopefully, caring, about Max finally led me to break Masonic protocol and seek some answers to the riddle of Max that I still sorely required.

Masonry isn't a secret society, but it does have an initiatory path in which private things, over the years, and as earned by years of service, are revealed. And by this time I myself had advanced far enough that I felt I could ask someone very high up about Max.

So I went privately to another old man—that is, if Max was indeed old—to a brother who was among only three in my state who'd been at the top of everything.

I must mention that this old man was a "normal old man"; he'd aged logically, my having seen pictures of him at various points of his advancement, which incidentally had been far higher than Max's. So I felt I might trust his judgment.

And this brother, after I'd made my appeal, looked at me a long time before answering. But in the end, probably feeling he had to adhere to the Masonic belief that one only needs to ask to be given, he revealed, as I sat in shock—but also deep and marvelous gratification—the truth about Max.

"They're set down here, from time to time, from—somewhere," he simply said. "The Tilers, the ones who, even despite all my gold badges, are the most important, who are sent to guard us and everything we do. They seem to be over forty, at least, when they first come to us. But the crucial thing about them, as you've been smart enough to guess, is that they're somehow ageless. Nor indeed do we really know who they are, or much of what their worldly position, in other respects, may be."

He paused, then concluded. "I must modestly submit something to you," he said with a sweet, mystical smile. "Though some people may say we are, we're not a religion. But can't there still be something like a Masonic saint?"

And so I believe it was, and is. That's because I attended Max's funeral the other day, along with practically every other Mason in the state.

So he was apparently human—as to age and death—after all. But the curious and wonderful thing about it was that even though Max's casket was open, he didn't seem to be there, and perhaps never had been. I had a vision of him as just having always been where he'd come from, and where he now, fully, was again—a Tiler, for eternity.

So was Max a saint—or even an angel, a guardian one? After all, the wise old brother to whom I'd gone for an answer had said, "set down, from somewhere," and wasn't that the province of angels, not saints? I thought of the cherubim who guard the Ark of the Covenant in a higher Masonic degree, and I wondered.

But one thing more. At the funeral, on the edge of the crowd, was a brother I'd never noticed before. He was very unlike Max: as if to keep us on our toes as to celestial expectations, he was short and fat.

"That's the guy who's going to tile the lodges now," someone said quietly, nudging me, after noticing my glance. "Just joined. Don't know anything about him."

But something I'm wondering.

"How old is he, do you think?"

About "Max"

When I was in high school in the early 1960s, I spent my summer vacations working at a grocery store, dating girls, and devouring science fiction. I'd go to the local library and take out armfuls of those old book-club editions, reading through the entire works to date of practically everybody in the field. And of course, a prime one of these was Ray Bradbury.

But amid my later-life pursuits, I forgot about all this—until I myself entered the science-fiction/fantasy/horror field in the early 1980s, as a publisher and a writer. Indeed, I then published Bradbury himself, and I appeared with a short story in an anthology in tribute to him.

But even given this, I don't think I realized the full extent of my debt to Ray Bradbury until recently, when Mort Castle and Sam Weller asked me for a story for this volume. They wanted "Bradburyesque" or "Bradbury-informed"—and as I happened, then, to look over my many published stories, I saw how many of them already *were.*

So it was an easy and a happy task for me to write the story you've just read—and I hope you'll have seen in it the inestimable gift I received, in those long-ago summers, from Ray. And if I were asked to put it in just a few words, I'd say, *a sense of wonder.*

—John Maclay

TWO OF A KIND

Jacquelyn Mitchard

It does not happen so much, not anymore, but when it does, I grab Joanie.

I grab Joanie, my wife, like a little boy grabs his mama when he has a nightmare. And that's not enough.

Even when my hand closes around her thigh, thick from all the years of babies and bending to scrub but warm and alive under her flannel pajama pants, I still let myself moan out loud. I hate to do it. A grown man. A grown man and a grandfather, at that. But I make the noise on purpose. I want Joanie to wake up, just so she can say something to me, say anything to me. It's like the dream is a web that fell on me in the dark, so big you wonder what made it, gumming up your mouth and your nose so that even being awake and knowing you're in your bed with your wife near the West Side of Chicago, with your daughter who got herself into trouble and the sweet little boy with corkscrew curls that come of it asleep down the hall, it still keeps rising and you want to claw your skin before it smothers you. The dream is stronger than real, like a spider's web is stronger than wire—you know that? Silk is stronger than wire.

This is the dream.

I see my hand drop a hand of cards; then Jackie drops his cards, too. The knife snaps open in his hand, and it starts to fall but then rights itself like a creature, its twin blades a mouth that starts to snap like the blades are swimming, pulling theirself through the air toward me. They want me. That knife, it wants me. It has all my life. I see the blood burst from my palm before I feel the hot nip of the cut.

"Joanie!" I cry.

"Go to sleep, Jan," she says, using the *J* sound, not the *Y*, like Irish do.

"Joanie, are we married?"

"Jan, these thousand years," she tells me, half asleep. She takes my hand off her leg and lays it on her breast, not as if to start us making love but the way a mother would. *There now, feel my heartbeat.* Joanie's hand is raw and red from the house-cleaning, but dainty as a lady's, shaped the way all them Finnian girls' was, as if they was all linen and lace instead of shanty Irish. It's shaped like the way her sister Nora's small white hand was, when Nora and us was young and Joanie just a kid. Joanie's hand holds tight to my finger. She can't hold my hand, it's so big-knuckled from all the years as a plumber, with the rod and the shovel.

"Where is Nora?" I ask my wife.

"Asleep in her cell," Joanie answers with a sigh, because she's used to this. We've been married, like she says, since she was just a teenager and I a man of twenty-three. "With the painting of the blessed Benedict I sent her at her birthday over her head, sleeping and never moving, as if she left her body, sleeping like dead, like she ever did, even as a child . . ."

"Are you sure?" I ask Joanie, because I'm awake now and I want her awake. "I had a dream. My leg hurts like hell. Is there a storm coming?" My white T-shirt is drying by then, freezing me. I need an excuse at this point. I start dragging the quilt up that I've kicked onto the floor.

It's always the same.

"I know," Joanie says. "It's only a dream, Jan. Be still now and sleep. You'll wake the baby."

I don't think Joanie ever wakes up, no more than she did to nurse the girls. She would just roll to her side then, and they would fall asleep between us—first Marie, for my mother, and then Katherine, just ten months apart, and after Katherine, a few years later, Eleanor, and then the little girl we called Jacqueline for . . . for Jackie, I suppose, as a gift to me, though we never said as much. When we thought that all that was done, and stopped bothering to take care with lovemaking, along comes our Polly. I was crowding fifty at that time, though Joanie's six years younger. We were happy enough to have a child in the house again. We didn't count on having three kids at home. But that's how it went. Polly was just ten when Eleanor, a grown woman, came home alone and pregnant. Eleanor, named for Joanie's sister Nora, wanted to call the baby boy Kwaze, after his father, who was a good enough fellow but foolish. His name is a good name in the African language. It means "Sunday." We told Eleanor that we thought he'd grow up easier, her being the only parent, with an ordinary name. Eleanor gave him the name of Kevin instead, and our last name, Nickolai. We wished it hadn't been our Eleanor, so good in school, a junior in college, hoping to be a doctor. Still, we were happy. Joanie is a happy woman, with a sunny heart. A heart with no shadows.

That's why I never told her about it. Not in so many words. I never told her none of it, although it's wrong, to the church, to everyone, for a man to keep a secret from his wife, a gentle and true wife that Joanie is. I do believe she does know. It's like something she was born knowing. But she never asked me anything but had I been with Nora before her and me married—and

I hadn't done anything but kiss Nora. I didn't have to lie. I never been with no one but Joanie, the truth of it is, though she don't know that either, and she has no need to know that, as a wife. A man has his pride.

She never met Jackie. Not to speak to. She did meet him, but she was a little girl. She doesn't remember the party we had before Jackie went to war.

But she's seen him.

You see me, you've seen Jackie Nickolai. That's how it always was. I look in the mirror even now, I see him sometimes. Though I got a gut and most of my hair went gray when I was still young. I still miss him, almost forty years and more later.

It never failed with us, Jackie and me.

One of us come up the street alone, maybe trudging through the snow from the bus, and Mrs. Kozyk or Mrs. Peasley or Mrs. Finnian would shake her dish towel at us and ask, "Hey, Pete, where's Re-Peat?"

Mrs. Kozyk, and all the neighbors, they knew we weren't brothers. But other people, even in school, didn't. See, it figured, how we looked—long rusty black hair, green eyes, nervous piano hands—us always together, having the same last name. People naturally assumed, not just when we was kids but all the way up through high school, that we were brothers. Some of them thought, maybe twins. Always. Almost as long as there was.

"Two of a kind beats a pair!" Mrs. Kozyk would tease us. She didn't understand half of what she was saying in English. She just overheard things her husband said when he played cards on the porch and said them. It wasn't no surprise, given the peculiar way we *was* related.

We were cousins, Jackie and me. But how many times you ever hear of this way? Me, I only heard of it one other time, and then long after Jackie was gone, from a girl that my wife knew at the place she worked before she formed her own cleaning company and hired girls to come and go with her and our daughter Eleanor in the bright Cleen Green vans.

See, Jackie's father and my father were brothers and our mothers not just sisters but *twins*—identical twins. A twin is practically the same as one person divided in half. So I guess if you took slices of Jackie's cells and my cells under a microscope, they would basically be the same as if we was brothers, because how could people's cells line up with any more similarity?

Of course, they brought us up the same too. We learned Hungarian at home from Grandma Sala, before English. Then we went to the same grade at Saint Anselmo, though we was ten months apart. Both playing baseball—Jackie at short, me, right field—and Ghosts in the Graveyard and Kick the Can in the street at night. I took diving at the Y because it was good for me, after the polio, and Jackie took drawing, him being good with his hands. He didn't need to get built up, being the kind of kid born muscled. Even when we didn't weigh more between us than a man weighs grown, he would be the one showed up at dusk in the alley when one of the coloreds or the Carney brothers called me out. Called me "Gimpy" or "Hopalong" because of the brace on my leg and how it made me walk. And all I could do would be crouch under the lilac bushes that grew wild back there and watch him wade in, whack, twist, drop, butt with his head. The kid would be on his ass scrabbling backward in the gravel, not knowing what come at him out of that little body of Jackie's. Afterward, he would never act like I owed him for taking my lumps. He seemed to think it was . . . his job. Jackie would look at you in a way, how do I tell you? Every one of the Carney brothers, them all the size of oxen, thirty of them it seemed to us like there was, they wouldn't come on Jackie *or* me after the first time. He was just a small and gentle boy who never went looking for a fight. But once he was in something, he wouldn't stop. Ever. That was what the look was. You knew

Jackie would die before he backed down, and if you were ready to die, that would be all the same for him, too.

He never said an unkind word to me.

Only once.

This is confusing, although it was just normal to us.

Jackie was named for my father, whose name back in the old country was Jukka. They called my dad Jack. And I was named for Dad and Unkie's father, Grandpa Ivan, who lived down the street with Grandma Sala.

He was called Jackie. I was called Jan.

All them names more or less mean John, you know. From John the Baptist, like my mother said.

Dad's two older brothers, Josef and Gaston, called Jackie and me a pair of Jacks. Like, pair of jacks beats a pair of tens. When they saw us, they would laugh hard and then say, "Pair of jacks and the man with the axe splits the pot." The man with the axe is the king of diamonds. They taught us to play poker when I was little, six. All kinds of games. Deuces and Baseball and Spit in the Ocean.

I don't play cards anymore.

"Jacks are better," they'd say to us at Grandma Sala's after Mass, whenever they came home, to eat like ten men for a month and then leave again for six. Josef and Gaston were in the Merchant Marine. They were older than my dad, bachelors who hardly never came home. When they did, they would shove their big paintbrush beards into our faces, kissing us on both cheeks. I guess we felt special, being the only two boys. I was an only child. Jackie had a younger sister, Karin.

Josef and Gaston were the ones who came over first. From the money they made after they signed up, they saved for everyone else, long before Hitler took what we still called Transylvania, a land of dark cliffs and Gypsies. Now it's Romania, yes, but also part of it is in the former republic of this or that, pulled back and forth between countries in Eastern Europe that never get any of it right and stay poor because of it. Grandma Sala would cry and pray in Hungarian for the mountains and their white flowers and birches. But no one in their right mind would want to go back.

Mama's family, Papa and Nana, were already there when my father's family came.

They were not immigrants anymore, even back then.

They were Americans of the third generation. They had lived first up in Wisconsin, then in Chicago since it was farm fields, just out past the El tracks. Our great-grandfather had served in the Civil War as a boy of sixteen. He survived and married a girl no older than he was, and had some acres until he had to give it up because of an accident with a plow blade, left him with a leg like my leg is, only the right not the left. He did various kinds of jobs then, until he come down to Chicago. Because he was good with style, if you want to call it that, he became a hatmaker. Men of business wore hats in his time, every day. He even shipped to Miami and Canada. At first he had to apprentice to an old Dago guy, even though he was already a grown man with a family. The Dagos made the beautiful hats. Shirts, suits, sweaters. Do still. Finally, he started his own store. Cornelius Hats. There was no Cornelius. Our great-grandfather just thought it sounded fancy when he started the company at the turn of the century. Papa grew up and made hats too. Then Papa's son, our mama's brother, decided he wanted to go to school for criminal justice instead. Dad let me know on the quiet that he thought hats were going out. He also thought they would squeeze your head until you went bald if you wore one every day. Dad himself never wore any outfit but his blue work pants and shirt. He owned one single suit he wore to every wedding and every funeral, and one blue sport coat. I myself only own one, my wedding suit. And it don't fit no more, although Joanie keeps threatening to make me go walk around the block with her at night—like she doesn't work hard enough in the day.

Once, before he had to close the store, Papa asked Dad—I call my father, who's ninety, alive and well, Dad, in the American way—if he wanted to join him in the business. But Dad was already in the plumbers' union instead, with his brother, Unkie. The money was so good with buildings going up on the edges of the city. You had to pay a union man very well, then and now. But still Dad and Unkie wanted to be on their own, and do plumbing not only repairs but for schools and new houses. If they didn't move just outside the city limits, to a suburb called Grant, the union men would have broke their legs for underbidding them in Chicago, which they owned lock, stock, and barrel. So they did move. Together, they bought the brick two-flat that's the only home I remember having as a child, and they made out good.

I think my grandfather, Papa, was very sad; but he never said nothing, except to sigh about the end of the old ways. Jackie told him someday, when he was grown, he would make fine hats; and Papa gave him a fifty-cent piece. He also gave Jackie a hat and one to me. Jackie looked good in that gray fedora, like he did in everything he wore. I didn't wear mine. The fact is, hats are coming back today. The black people wear them, and everybody young wears what they wear.

It was also him, Papa, who give us the relics. I don't mean holy relics, like slivers of the true cross. I mean historical relics. They don't have anything attached to them sacred or magic.

They couldn't have.

That's the whole point.

You see?

They were from his father. He kept them in a Cornelius hatbox.

We were twelve when he gave them to us.

It was summer. We were sitting out on the low, black wrought-iron fence right near the street, waiting to see Patricia Finnian, the oldest of those girls, Joanie's big sister, walk past, the way she did every night. Patricia was wild. She would come swinging her shiny red plastic purse, with her black hair like a thing with its own eager spine dancing on her back, her breasts plain visible in the sinking light under her cheap cotton dress, and girls didn't do that then, crossing the two streets from Grant into the city. She was seventeen and she had no eyes for Jackie or me. The Dagos picked her up around the corner in long white Lincolns. Patricia is a lady now. She lives out in Lake Forest in a house the size of a block in a normal place. Joanie and I get asked there for Christmas Eve, like the king asked his stable men to come in and have food on the night Christ was born. She gives us something Joanie and I laugh about the rest of a year, like once crystal bowls you put salt in, with tiny spoons.

That night, though, Papa called us to come over before Patricia came out. He lived across and one building over—and he says, *I got this box I got to show you boys some things in.*

He untied the strings and lifted off the top. There, in the top, was a flag folded, like for the dead. An American flag but not like one we had ever seen, not with the right number of stars, and so old the white was yellow. You knew it would crack like paper if you unfolded it. There was a big-brimmed hat all tore up, dirty black felt material. And there was pictures of a man with big earmuffs of sideburns. In one of them, he was holding two babies, one Papa's father and one Papa's twin brother, Pavel, who died from the scarlet fever. Twins run in families, so my mother turned out to be one.

Papa's father served with the Sixth Wisconsin, the Iron Brigade, the bravest of all the Union forces, the miners and farmers who wore the big, black hats. The big-brimmed hat in the box was his. I guess that was how Papa's father got his fondness for hats, those hats worn with so much pride. Papa was probably eighty by then, but he never forgot a thing, old or new. He said his father could do all sorts of things besides grow alfalfa and fashion a fine fedora. Once, after he sold his farm, he taught drawing for a family of girls whose father was rich, but no one could support a family teaching girls to draw. But the first Grandpa Nickolai really could draw anything he saw, Papa said, from his mother's face in the mirror to the butcher's hands. In the Civil War he drew dying men crazed with thirst in the fields in Pennsylvania, as they cried out in Dutch or German or with Irish on their tongues. Papa had his father's music notation book with a black-and-white marble cover—filled with the drawings. Papa showed us them, so fragile and faded. Looking slowly through the drawings, being careful not to smudge the pencil marks more, Jackie said, "Papa, these are real good. Art and also historical. You should give them to the Field Museum."

Papa said, "He did not mean for people to see them."

Jackie asked, "Why?" And Papa shrugged as if he knew the answer but he wasn't to say it. That must have been where Jackie got his gift for art.

There were some buttons in the box, too, and one old boot. The knife with two blades and bone handles was the next thing but one to the bottom. It was wrapped in a lady's handkerchief.

Jackie was sitting closest, so Papa gave it to him.

Opened up, it looked just like that bug, a praying mantis. Papa said his grandfather got it off a Rebel soldier in the Civil War. Crazy with hunger, our great-grandfather used it to dig something like sweet potatoes from the ground, a farm before it was a battlefield. But he had nothing to cut dry wood with to make a fire so he could cook them. They was too tough to eat raw, since his teeth was loose anyhow.

"They all had scurvy or the dysentery," Papa said.

"Did he have to shoot the Rebel?" I asked Papa. Papa looked

out at the colored boys, who were just starting to sing around a fire in the trash can on the corner under the streetlight, up past where Grand ended and Chicago began.

"Someone made it named Furnace, see there," Papa told us. "Think of your name being Furnace. Made by Furnace but they call it a Barlow knife. It is from England." I asked again was he dead, the Johnny Reb, when our great-grandpa took the knife off him, and Nana came out. She pulled my hair and said, "Tcch! Enough!" Right then, my mom came in the back door with a casserole, looked at the hatbox, and cut her eyes at Papa like he'd sworn in Jesus' name. Papa fell silent, pouty as a little kid. He felt deep in the bottom of the box and pulled out a man's muffler, a winter scarf. Wrapped in that was what I got, a bayonet. It fitted to the end of his rifle, though no one knew what happened to the rifle.

"It's American history, Marie," he said.

"Of war," Mom said. "We don't want any more wars like when I was a girl. We're done with wars."

Us boys weren't; of course, we didn't know that.

Jackie's knife was the better thing. Sure. He could carry it anywhere. Bring it out and examine it, in front of the Carney brothers like he was figuring who he should cut. The knife made up for a lot, not that Jackie needed it. But he never used it to hurt anybody or anything. He carved with it because it was still sharp as new. First, he made tiny teacups from acorns for his little sister and swords for him and me that we burned until they had points hard enough to pierce human skin. Then he started to carve sculpture things from scrap bits of cherry and mahogany Dad and Unkie brought home from new houses they were doing plumbing on. He carved birds and owls. Then hands. Then finally flowers. Auntie Maggie said the opening rose he made reminded her of the story of the Mistress of the Copper Mountain and the Stone Flower.

"There was a master carver," she said. "And he could make flowers of stone and wood that looked more real than living flowers; but to do this he had to give up his love and remember nothing of his mother or his loyal sweetheart. But he gave back the gift, instead, and forgot the copper mountain until he was ninety years old . . ."

She was just getting started. We ran outside. Auntie Maggie could go through three cups of coffee on a story. You could be ninety yourself when she got done. It was rude; but we just heard her laughing after us. We got away with most things.

Even though the Barlow knife was the better, Jackie said my bayonet had stains on it and that they had to be real blood. I told him I bet the bone that made the arms of his knife was tiger bone.

That's how we was to each other. Tried to make the other one feel good. I don't know if real brothers would have been that polite. Though our mothers were. They still are.

The only difference between our families back then that I could tell was Jackie's parents lived in the upper of the two-flat. Because of the stairs, it was a little smaller than our house, though it had more bedrooms. No one ever said a thing about it or the fact that, even with them calling themselves partners—the plumbing truck reading NICKOLAI AND NICKOLAI—actually the rod, the pipe wrench, and the truck itself were Dad's. The time Unkie left the new snake at the Emerson house and when they went back the snake had crawled off—as my dad put it—that was all he said. He laughed. No reproach. It was like family was a piece of lace that might already have a lot of holes but you handled it careful so it didn't get more.

One time, my pop got my mother a lamb coat, 'cause she lost a baby girl born way too soon, and Jackie's mother had to do with a long shawl knitted by Nana. Auntie didn't complain. She said, "Oh, Marie, that collar brings out the red in your hair."

And Mom would come right back with, "Maggie, it fits us both the same, so you take it to the Knights dance—"

"Oh, I couldn't, Marie. If I ever got something on it—"

"No, Sissy, you just take it anytime you want . . ."

Which was why, with their having a little bit more trouble than us making ends meet, probably because Unkie played the ponies, we were all shocked when Unkie gave Jackie the Studebaker for high school graduation. It wasn't new, far from it. But it was clean as a priest's collar, not a scratch on her. We all knew right away whose it was. Marty Jaworsky's. The diamond dealer's car. We knew, too, that it couldn't have had no more than twenty miles on it because Reb Jaworsky didn't do a thing with it but drive down the boulevard on Friday before sunset taking his family to temple on a magic carpet so black it gleamed like a river in the rain, then have a guy drive them home after. We also all knew Reb Jaworsky wasn't going to give it up for a nickel less than it was worth. Not because he was a Jew. Because he didn't have to. Things didn't go up and down in your job if your job was diamonds.

Then, the Sunday night after graduation, we found out why Unkie did it. He brought cherry wine, dessert wine. And he left on his fancy old-fashioned dress collar from church at dinner. Afterward, he stood up and said, "I want to say I am proud here that my only son, Jukka Andrea Nickolai, is enlisted in the First Calvary, the Big Red One, and will sail nine days after Christmas, with God we hope to watch over him to keep the mountains where our grandmothers and grandfathers lived and now they sleep, free from the evil one." Auntie Maggie got up and put her apron over her face like she was ashamed and ran from the room, my mother right after her, muttering something at Unkie like she did when my father gave Mr. Emerson ten bucks to bet on a horse—despite Unkie's problems with gambling.

"Jack," Mama said later, "he's Maggie's only son. What if it was yours? What if it was Jan?"

Anyhow, Unkie was left standing there, looking like he wanted to cry, and the Russian cut-crystal glass right in his hand glowed like an icon with a candle in it at the Orthodox church on the South Side where Papa and Nana still went—though we went to Catholic church by then. The adults went into the living room and put on the radio. The shortwave could get the BBC. I started to ask Jackie why he enlisted; they would come and get a kid anyhow, soon enough, but for the first time in our lives he held up his hand, which told me as plain as words that his father made him do it, maybe because of newer immigrants having to prove something all the time, us being like German in the eyes of born Americans.

It wasn't the same as my mother's family. Of course, Jackie couldn't admit that.

Which left the wine sitting there for us to finish. We did. And we didn't have no stomach for it. Jackie said *let's take a ride.* We went out to the car and polished off the fenders with our coats. Jackie had to stop and heave by the steps and clean his hands with a paint rag and his mouth with the hose before we could go.

I remember this.

Nora Finnian hung out the window across the street in just her full slip and yelled up the block, "Jackie, can I ride in your fine car then?" I couldn't wait to sit in it myself; but the fact was, I felt about the same as Auntie Maggie. I didn't want Jackie to go to war. It made me sick, though I knew a brave man should go. I had my own stuff to prove, supposedly. But I wore a shoe with a built-up heel and I never ran or took gym, though I could catch and throw in street games. I told girls poker was my sport. Swimming helped, so I did that. But I had to wear a brace to bed to keep my knee straight. I wouldn't never be a soldier. Jackie, now, could run like a bastard wind. He disappeared at shortstop. He could outrun all the Carneys, even Amon, the youngest, Amon so thin he was like a rag twisted into a person. I wonder what he would have done, with those hands made for beauty and being able to run like that. Maybe gone for a professor, despite the way Unkie didn't think men needed to learn much from books. Or I like to think of him playing pro ball maybe. He was so good the college guys came to watch him when we played American Legion.

That night we drove to Seven Sorrows Cemetery to smoke. They locked the front gates of the cemetery at dusk but they never locked the back. I guess they figured why would anyone want to go in a cemetery? So there was beer cans all over the place. We sat there and smoked a butt each, and I noticed Jackie inhaled now, and he said *let's take a walk* so we got out, us knowing Seven Sorrows and the lanes between the graves as certain as we knew our bedrooms. We played there so much after dark when we was kids it was the school yard to us.

That night, we got to one of the little houses rich people bought for their dead—family crypts. Everyone knew this particular one; it was all covered with long strings of mirrors between the wrought-iron bars. It had little windows made of mirrors and a hipped silvery roof that came almost down to the ground. It belonged to Gypsies, Romany people the same as us but different. This being July and not long after the longest day of the year, the Gypsy queen and king's children or subjects or whatever you please had hung ribbons, too, gold and blue and red. Nobody liked the tomb. People said it was haunted. Everybody took a long loop to avoid it, even on a Sunday stroll. But Jackie walked right up, pulled off one of the ribbons, and almost sneered at me when I gasped. He must have thought I was a priss.

"You don't believe that shit?" he asked me. "Mirrors to scare off the devil if he should see his face, eh? Even Magda and Marie don't believe that." What made my hair prickle on my neck was the way he sounded different. Saying our mothers' given names like they was girls from our street. Like there was a fan belt broke or a violin string snapped in him. Because we would never talk about our mothers that way. You just didn't.

Then suddenly he had the Barlow knife out and was working away at the big padlock on the door.

"Sonofabitch," he said quietly.

"Leave it, Jackie," I said. "Jackie, leave it." It was like I was nobody, like nobody was there. The lock stuck firm. Pushing his fedora back on his head, Jackie used the knife to pick his teeth for a moment. Then, with his long pale fingers, he made a series of turns and twists and the lock popped open.

"What," I squeaked, "the hell you say."

Jesus, I wanted him to stop. I felt like bawling.

"The equinox," he said, "it's a big deal to them. Oh six, two turns to the left, then twenty-one and then . . . that was the combination. I thought of it then, after I saw them ribbons."

"Let it alone. I don't want to know. Shut it."

But now Jackie was picking at another lock, the Yale lock that was deep in the cherry door. Every kid who grew up there knew that the Gypsy king and queen, them dead about fifteen years from a car wreck, was buried in glass boxes with the air sucked out, like saints. The old people said she was dressed in lace and velvet and him in silk, though it was her was royalty. Romany is another breed, with their own church and so forth. I never knew but one; and he was a good man, with nine sons. They keep to themselves.

In the end, Jackie pried the lock right out of the cherry door.

"I'm walking home," I said to Jackie. "I swear to shit."

"Woman," Jackie said evenly, and I saw him glance down at my leg not like he didn't think of it but on purpose.

I hated him then.

I hated the person on Earth who I never felt anything but as if he was my own reflection.

"Open it," I said, lighting a smoke so my hands wouldn't shake so. "Go on. I don't care. It's on you."

He did, and he went up the little marble step. I had to follow him. It wasn't like there was a big overhead lamp inside. You could barely see.

There were shelves like the benches in a sauna bath, and caskets laid along them, a few of them white and tiny, little mirrors glued on in a circle around the widest part and a painted angel with red wings at the end, where I would imagine the head was. Infants. There were wooden boxes carved with leaves and faces. Older adults.

There was a sound then, of loud bells. Jackie and I grabbed each other. Cold sweat rolled like melted ice down my chest. But it was only those plates and tambors and stuff they had stuck on the outside of the roof, fretting in the wind. Both of us had to laugh.

We walked the few steps to the back.

Her tomb was there just like they said. The queen's. Glass. We didn't even look at him, the king.

She was beautiful, her blond braids carefully plaited around her head, her skin as white and soft-looking as soap, the pores the size of the littlest holes in a sponge, but not ugly. The car wreck must have smashed her inside, not her face. She was like a statue. Her eyes were open, with a milky cover, and even if she had been living, they would have looked blind. Around her neck was a rope of pearls in decks. It was like an Egypt collar, with a ruby in the middle the size of one of Nana's mushrooms. On every finger was another ring, all the stones in them big, square rubies, too.

"Glass," I said. "They're glass. You wouldn't bury a ruby."

"They're rubies," Jackie said. "Glass would be really red." He took out the knife and started to tap on the glass. "Get a rock," he said to me

"Nothing doing," I told him. "A rock'll sound like a cannon shot in here."

"I need a diamond," Jackie said.

"You and me both," I told him.

"You got a diamond in that graduation ring."

"It's just a chip, Jack."

"But it'll do. It's got an edge. Look there. A point shaped like a pyramid." He took my hand like I was a girl and pulled off the ring, then he cut a fat circle in the glass where the queen's face was, over and over until the smell of her being dead started to seep through, and then he pushed it in and the sour air rushed out. She didn't fall to dust or shrivel before our eyes, like you would think. But I couldn't breathe right in there. It wasn't putrid, but it wasn't good. What it was, was like something stewed, set out and forgotten on the back porch, gone bad.

Jackie reached in and took her hand like he was taking her out to the dance floor and removed the rings. I walked out because of the smell, and I heard the rings fall into his pocket, one by one, that *chunk* sound as unmistakable as the sound of cars hitting each other—a sound you never forget once you hear it and it sickens your gut. And then I heard another sound. It was them pearls, pinking the floor like hail. Jackie had cut the necklace with that knife. To get the pearls off her neck of course. He couldn't have uncurled it. My mind went chasing after the picture of Jackie pulling her forward so the pearls wouldn't fall down by her feet, maybe trying to wrestle that heavy rope over her crown, the head lolling back and forth, maybe her mouth coming open. I turned around and run the best I could. I didn't give a goddamn. I limped until my leg was on fire, but I kept on limping and hopping until I was at the pharmacy on Halsted Street. I ordered a vanilla Coke and drank it all in one slug, standing up. Then I didn't know where the hell to go. I just stood there. When Jackie picked me up there later, he didn't speak of it. I didn't either.

We never did.

A week later, Auntie Maggie was wearing one of those short coats with a fox collar. Unkie had a double-breasted suit. He got embarrassed when I saw him wearing it, when I was out delivering flowers for Buffo's. Jackie bought all kinds of flowers and a golden crucifix for Patricia Finnian, and one night I saw him with her in the Studebaker, her long white arm around him, Jackie just looking straight ahead, although Patricia was easy three years older. He gave new card tables to the sick home, where the simple kids lived. He spent the money fast. I don't know who he sold the stuff to. Not Jaworsky's or anybody who knew our family, or we would have heard.

The "desecration" of the tomb was on page one of the *Chicago American*. The queen was named Magda, like my aunt. By then, Jackie was already gone, to basic.

He came home after Christmas.

I took good care of the car. Jackie said I could use it anytime, but I only ever used it on Sundays to drive Nora Finnian around for an hour. And I backed it out into the driveway to wash and wax it. The others came over to look. Pat and Tommy Carney and Louie and Herman Kozyk, even though Herman was already married. It was that good a car. I almost felt like it was mine.

My dad had up and decided I was going to go to college. So I was working at a bank, as a teller, a job he got for me from Mr. Cohacki, who built the apartments where the old Wonderland Ballroom and Hotel stood. I had to wear the same two outfits all week, so Jackie's sister Karin hid some scraps from her sewing class in high school and made me a red shirt and a blue collar to vary things. She give it to me the week before Jackie come home from Fort Leonard Wood, Missouri. Unkie and Auntie were going to have a party before he was sent out (to the eastern front because he could speak German, Hungarian, and a little Russian and Polish, he was that smart). So I had myself barbered up, a real good shave and a three-dollar haircut.

When I walked in, my mom was having coffee with Auntie Magda.

She dropped her cup and screamed, and my mother looked like she was going to slap me.

Auntie ran upstairs.

"What the hell?" I said, forgetting I just cursed in front of my own mother.

"Are you a fool I raised?" she screamed at me. "You get your hair cut before your cousin is sent to war?" She spat on the ground three times like Nana did if anyone sat at the corner of the table or a bird crashed into the window. "Don't you know this is a worse omen than you could make up if you tried a million times?" She told me to go back to the barber and get the clippings and burn them, and I said I would, but Jesus Christ, who would do that? I sat on the stoop until I saw Jackie come around the corner of Sheffield Avenue carrying his duffle. Man, he looked a foot taller. He looked like a grown man, instead of only seventeen. I felt like I was his baby brother.

"They work you hard," he said, rolling up his sleeve to show me his upper arm that looked like it had an apple under the skin. Then he kissed me on both cheeks.

"Will you bring Nora tonight?" he asked me, because he knew from the letters I was seeing Nora, and then Auntie Maggie came running, giving me a look like I made the milk sour.

Reb Jaworsky got drunk that night and toasted Jackie and the other boys for fighting like the Maccabees to save his people and all good people; and the whole neighborhood went in and out the doors until my mother just wadded up the newspapers she always laid down to keep the linoleum clean and sat down on the piano stool. She played old songs like Chopin and waltzes, and new songs about the girls who waited for boys who never come home or boys who did. Nora came when she got off work at the store where she sold perfume.

It happened then. Not long after she got there.

Sure, we had some wine to drink. Jackie said he was used to wine by then. The army gave you beer for free. But I wasn't drunk. Though Nora was an Irish girl, Jackie gave her our blessing, a kiss on each cheek. "You be good to my brother until I come home," he said. He nodded at Joanie, who was wearing high heels, though she was only in the sixth grade. "Little Joanie," he said.

"You're that handsome in your uniform," said Nora. I was jealous.

Nora had black hair cut real short the way girls were starting to do then, and the kind of eyes some Irish have, like a pond turned over after a storm. Angry at me because I was stuck on an Irish, my mother still melted when she saw those eyes. Joanie has them, too.

Nora is Sister Mary Dominic now, a Benedictine that's cloistered. She could be Sister Eleanor Finnian these days if she wanted, but she does not want to. She can only see her sisters and her mother and father twice a year through the bars. She went in the convent when she was eighteen, that same spring. But then, she was just a beautiful girl, who loved a laugh and a dance—a girl among five sisters, whose father thought she'd never find a husband, there being so many Finnian girls. She never said a strange word to me before that night or since then. Just, when we went to her veiling ceremony, years later, with all Nora's family, and saw her married to Christ in her beautiful bridal dress, she looked straight at me, not at her sister. But that one look felt as though she'd grabbed the flesh under my chin between forefinger and thumb and squeezed.

I knew she remembered the night at the party.

She remembered that something had happened. It scared her, like a tap inside her ribs that wasn't her own heart. That's what she was telling me at her veiling, not one word said.

And while I'm pretty sure Nora didn't know what come out of her mouth, she'd seen my face and Jackie's and what we did afterward. That moment must have slithered over her, the way static electricity will run up your arm just before a storm. For what she said, it wasn't in Nora's voice. Nora's voice was light as a laugh, tilted up with a bit of a flirt or a tease. That voice was slow and dead, and it come like in a trance or what have you, from somewhere else, long ago.

I know as sure as I'm sitting here that was why she took holy orders. Her mom was probably glad of it—raising a nun being almost as good as raising a priest, though not quite. But Nora would have a pack of kids now and a man of her own if it hadn't been for that moment at the party. She wasn't no pale, praying kneeler, Nora, but a girl born for mischief. Kathleen was more religious, even Joanie, my wife. Something happened that she couldn't name, no more than we could. And if she knows the half of it, like I do, she must wake up in her iron bed at night all ice and sweat like me, and she must beg the merciful Lord for his protection. I think of her alone there, and I pray she don't know all I know. I hope it's just a sense she has, like a child's memory of a grandparent who died generations ago. It wasn't a thing Nora deserved. Or anyone. She was a good girl.

It started when Jackie fished in his pocket and took out a tiny cross, one he'd carved on a base of apple wood. Like I said, he'd been using the Barlow knife for more and more intricate carvings, even before he went into the service; and he went on doing it at night in the barracks to pass the time. He had pockets full of whittlings—tigers and linked chains, little trees, a cup and teapot he'd sent Auntie Maggie, and little cowboys on horses for the little kids on the block. It was natural to him, being an artist, kind of, like he was. He did it as quick as you or me would deal out a hand of cards. That he fetched out a cross instead of a flower or a star for Nora was a coincidence. As far as we knew, Nora soon would be as wild as Patricia. At least that was what I was hoping. I was hoping I'd get me more than a kiss one time—a feel at least. Maybe Jackie hoped so, too. Girls then had a soft spot for boys headed for what might be a young death. Still, a cross was what it was, with clefts and flourishes and even a small blunt image of the body of Christ.

Jackie gave Nora the cross. She reached for it eagerly, but then she closed both her soft white hands tight. She looked down at them. Her nails were dug into her palms, like claws.

And that voice-that-was-not-Nora said, "The man who owned the knife was not dead. He died of thirst. It took three days for him to die." Jackie jumped and the little carved cross fell between them to the carpet. "The bone in that knife's handle belongs to the earth. It is a wolf's bone. Zora's."

Not meaning to frighten Nora, I half yelled at her, "What? Zora or Nora?"

I was hoping that what she'd said was just her own name. I knew it hadn't been. What I was thinking about, of course, was of the old goddess of midnight and dawn, the dark woman Zoraya, that Nana and Grandma Sala told us about when we were babies.

Nora misunderstood me. There was laughter and talk overlapping itself all over.

"Who's Zola?" She laughed. "Is that your talk for Nora?"

She took a cold beer out of the pail of ice—glancing at her parents first to make sure they didn't see—and bent down to pick up the cross. "This is a beautiful small thing you've made. Thank you, Jack." She leaned forward as if to give him a hug around the neck, as thanks, the way a girl will. But Jackie's face was white and moist as new bread. He stiffened and pulled back from Nora and said not a word. For just a second, he and Nora looked like their eyes were bound together on a wire. The sweet, familiar grin melted from Nora's face. A blush spread over her neck like someone had spilt a pot of pink woman's face paint. She took hold of the hem of her dress and spun off in that dancing way she had, making sure we saw the turn of her fine legs in their cotton hose. "See you later, boys," she called back to us.

"You heard it, too," Jackie said to me then, quiet, so no one under all the gabble could hear him but me. He took the knife out of his pocket and told me to take it. I wouldn't. I held up both hands like a baby that's been burned. He said Go, Jan, give it to the Field Museum for nothing. I said I would tell Papa to give it to the Field Museum, and for him to just put it down. We knew Papa wouldn't. Neither one of us knew if the knife was cursed before Jackie used it to break into the tomb—cursed by our soldier ancestor who stole it off a dying boy—or only afterward. But we could tell the curse had jumped from the knife into Jackie, no matter how many crosses he whittled. We could tell it was so strong that it spread to Nora for a minute. Damned if we knew why. Maybe it was layers of sin, old and new, none of them really Jackie's fault, waiting for the knife to come out of the box and spring on him, making him different, little by little, taking pieces of him that were good and turning them wrong.

Quickly, I told my cousin, "That's all there is to it. It was just a strange thing and they happen."

"It doesn't matter," Jackie said finally, after he'd gone over to the table and gulped down two fingers of whiskey. "There's nothing can be done."

He ran his hand along his short hair and squeezed his forehead. Then he pulled Patricia Finnian out onto the floor and danced with her, their hips together like snakes wound around each other. The two of them took off in the car, not coming back until everyone was gone. If I hadn't been awake still, I wouldn't have heard them. I don't think it was the first time Patricia had been out until dawn; but Auntie Maggie was murderous the next morning, slamming Jackie's coffee down in front of him like she meant it to slop over and burn him. Jackie made plain he wasn't his mama's little boy no more, and just asked for the sugar. If he could fight a war, he could damn well spend the night with a woman.

That night, in honor of the feast day after Christmas, we put our feet together on an axe under the table, the tradition for luck. Uncle Gaston and Uncle Josef were home. And they toasted Jackie and me.

"To the pair of Jacks," Uncle Josef said, and glanced at our friend Reb Jaworsky, who came to dinner though our old strange ways didn't mean a thing to him or his wife or their three kids, any more than their feasts did to us. Uncle Josef added, "And to the man with the axe. The king of diamonds." Mr. Jaworsky blushed. I guess it was in bad taste to mention having money. It was good of Reb Jaworsky to come. He was a white Jew; and we cared how bad it was for them over there. His children were still small, too young for soldiers. He was too old. But he had a brother in Poland still.

I drove Jackie to the train station in his car. He was wearing his green uniform then, and used the sleeve to rub a speck off the black hood. I handed him his big bag and told him not to be no hero.

"Not me, brother Jan," he said. "I'll be back for sweet Patricia one fine day." But when I went to hug him, he pulled away.

"Be good," he said, and swung up on the steps. It was wrong. It was all wrong, us parting from each other that way. But maybe Jackie didn't want whatever it was to jump to me.

I married pretty young.

Joanie was only seventeen, but our girls took their time coming. We did a lot of dancing and strolling to the movies before we was ever parents—when so many of them we'd grown up with already were.

I went to the place where Jackie is buried almost on a whim, like a jet-setter. I was a father two times already. I should have been too busy to take time away from Joanie and my girls, not to mention my job as the owner of Nickolai and Nickolai Plumbing and Heating. It was Joanie told me to go ahead and take the trip—that Sam, my helper, could manage without me for a week. She knew that something worked on my mind about Jackie, and from her mother, she heard tales of how close we were. We could afford it, and she had not the slightest wish to go along. To her, Eastern Europe was still stained dark with blood. When Joanie travels, she wants to go to California or Florida. She didn't want to go to where our families came from then or now.

"You've been good to me always, Jan," she said seriously. "You never took a drink or raised your voice to me and the children. If you need to do this, you should." The dreams had started by then—long before we were married. Maybe Joanie thought the trip would lay them to rest.

After the plane landed, I rented a junk of a car and drove with maps from the Triple A up narrow roads between forested hills. The place was easy enough to find, from the letters sent me by Jackie's best friend in the war, a boy named Anton—that told me the story of the way they'd got lost from their unit in the night, *like we were drinking swallows of fog with every breath.*

The mountains they finally fetched up against were the Carpathians. The woods were dark and snow-heavy still in March. They found a clearing, and Jackie took out his knife and stripped some logs high up a dead tree, small to burn good. He sat sharpening a twig into an arrow point in case they saw a rabbit. There was no food in their packs but biscuits days old; and although their coats and hats were good, their boots were shot.

They couldn't even hear the gunshot they were so lost.

Finally, they laid down evergreen boughs and huddled next to the fire in their coats.

It was long after midnight when Anton woke to hear Jackie talking. Anton opened his eyes.

The woman was standing right in the snow, wearing a long white dress, her short dark hair uncovered. She was holding out her hand. She wore no coat and she didn't shiver.

"It wasn't me," Jackie pleaded. "It was my grandfather, no, it was my great-grandfather took it from the man. And when I took those rings, I was just a kid, a fool kid. Lots have done worse." The woman just shook her head and held out her hand. Jackie finally dropped the Barlow knife into her palm.

The knife went right through and clinked on a rock.

Anton wrote to me that he tried to put himself back to sleep again. He threw himself down and closed his eyes. And he laid with his face in the snow until his skin burned and didn't move. He licked the snow if he felt thirst. The hours crawled past. He pulled his itching green greatcoat over his head, and God save him, even when he heard Jackie cry out, he didn't move. He was like us—his own grandmother brought him up on tales of the *Wili* and the *Wampyr.* No coat on the beautiful dark-haired girl, he thought, as the wind scored his naked hands. No coat and her arms were bare. A madwoman, he thought, from the hospital that was one of their coordinates on the map they had. And he thought, this poor land, tossed back and forth between bully countries like a child's beanbag. But all the time, even under the greatcoat, he could sense the woman beside him, soundless and patient. Finally, she said, "You will live long enough to see many children, Ee-van." Anton was sure he heard it. He asked who was Evon. He wrote me that in the first letter. And it wasn't until years later, after we had exchanged eight, ten letters, that I told him that Ivan was my own given name.

By the time I was in my early middle years, they could copy even an old picture in a few hours at the drugstore. I had them copy a picture of me and Nora Finnian, that night at that party. I wrapped one copy, the larger one, in office paper and sent it to Anton. I knew he would say that the woman in the white dress was Nora, and he wrote back special delivery and said it was.

And then I never heard from him again. The letters I sent came back unopened; but no postman had written on them, in big letters, NO SUCH PARTY.

All I have to say is one thing more. I wish I could set it down better. I can't explain.

Anton found Jackie in the morning dead. You knew that. The knife lay beside his head, and Anton picked it up and used it to strip a little birch sapling for a cross and lash it with the supple bark. He buried Jackie under rocks, said the rosary, then threw the Barlow knife and heard it hit the face of the cliff. He ran. German patrols fanned out looking for stragglers never even saw him when he ran right past them. It was like he was made of the fog himself. He ran until his leather boots turned to strips, then barefoot, until he came to a farmer's barn. The farmer made off like he didn't know Anton was there but left food for him in the manger every night.

There was not a mark or a drop of blood on Jackie, Anton wrote, in the last letter.

There was only this, a huge nail, driven through his hand. The wound had not bled. It was the long nails Gypsy roofers use, them they call tinkers. Out there in the wilderness where there wasn't a village or a farm about, there was this nail, like one of those nails so long they could not get an ironmonger in Jerusalem to make one to use to crucify our Lord, and so they had to go outside the city until they found a Gypsy woman, who made the nails all unknowing, like Jackie made those flowers.

I never went to college.

I worked with Dad. When Dad got older, I kept the company and he did the books. The name is the same on the truck, though it's only me and Sam and my nephew, Karin's boy Brian Olsky. No more Nickolai boys. I thought I would have sons. And then I had only daughters, five daughters, just like Mr. Finnian did. I keep it the same, though. All my daughters had sons. I have seven grandsons. My daughter Polly went to college for a teacher, but she wants to take over my business, call it Nickolai and Daughter. I don't think she will, though I would like a family business.

She's not afraid of anything.

I am.

In that mountain field, I looked the better part of a long summer day and the following morning for the Barlow knife. I knew it was the right place because of Anton's photos he took when he went back once himself, of this clumber of rocks that looked just like a rowboat and the little birch whip Anton planted over Jackie. It had grown into a tree with fretful arms.

But I never found it.

The nail, I found. What, twenty-five years had passed. It should have been deep under a foot of dirt, what with winter snows and summer mudslides. But it was there, waiting for me. And though I missed Jackie every day, I knew that if I picked it up, all Jackie knew in the shadow of that mountain would fly up into me. I left the nail lie.

Many years later, one of the girls was talking about this band called that: Nine Inch Nails. Sharper than I meant, I asked her did she know what that name meant. One day, in the car, their song come on. Polly turned it up loud. It sounded like someone kicking a pipe organ to death.

I never told a living soul. Only Mama. She tried to make light, but her mouth squirmed helplessly on its own. She made the sign of the cross, the Orthodox cross—head, two hearts, stomach.

It was just chance he got the knife and me the bayonet. Papa didn't favor either of us boys. What if Jackie got what was meant for me? Wasn't that nail there—unmarked, uncovered, plain as a judgment? Left alone, all us Nickolais, we live long lives. Polly may call me "Gramps," but I could have twenty more years. What if your fate got switched with someone so like you in every way it could fool God himself—God or whatever else there is that waits? What if that fate is there still, and knows my given name? It's like Jackie said. There's nothing can be done.

About "Two of a Kind"

I Sing Bradbury Everlasting

When I was a very young woman, and Ray Bradbury was already a senior citizen, I was trying to impress a guy I liked by reading a story to his little daughter. The story was called "I Sing the Body Electric!" If you happened to see a charming 1982 TV production that starred Edward Hermann, you might know it as *The Electric Grandmother*.

The story was more than I bargained for.

Like every child in school, I'd read *Dandelion Wine* and the short novel *The Halloween Tree.*

But returning to Ray Bradbury as an adult, I found myself unable to get through "I Sing the Body Electric" in one sitting. And it was not because the little girl, who was about six, was bored. She wasn't.

It was I.

I wasn't bored.

I was overcome—first by the writing and then by emotion I couldn't suppress with my newfound adult authority. I sat in the rocking chair and sobbed, as I did the first time that I read that Charlotte was not only a true friend, but a good writer.

I felt the way you feel when you find something long gone and dear, something lost for so long you've forced yourself to forget how wonderful it was, so you didn't yearn for it.

I had forgotten just how good Ray Bradbury was. I had forgotten how subtle and deceptive were his stories, like Betty Smith's *A Tree Grows in Brooklyn* and Harper Lee's *To Kill a Mockingbird,* riven with the kind of fierce mysteries that adults like to pretend don't exist.

If you don't know it, "I Sing the Body Electric!" is the story of a widowed father who takes his children to a factory to assemble a robot nanny for them, a perfect grandmother. And as for perfection, it was, and is, simply one of the most perfectly pitched and moving stories I've ever read. Eventually, as children will (witness *Toy Story* 3), the little ones outgrow their need for the granny who can spin kite string from her fingertips. But when they are old, their father gone and their own children adults, and have become frail, those same children return to find their electric grandmother as loving and spry as ever.

Later the same week, I read again to the little girl. The story was *The Homecoming,* the tale of the Halloween-night party that annually reunites an extended family composed of pre-*Twilight* vampires, werewolves, and shape-changers of all descriptions, much to the excitement and grief of Timothy, the youngest child, who is disabled, a mutant. Timothy has the misfortune of having been born human.

At the end of the story, Timothy's mother (the original Morticia Addams) comforts him. Should he die, she promises, all of them will visit him every year on the Homecoming, and tuck him in, all the closer.

If I'd been moved before, now I was undone. Ray Bradbury's writing is sentimental in the sense that Steinbeck's is, but it's never syrupy. It's simply the iteration of honest human emotions we can neither outrun or deny.

My relationship with that little girl's dad was not destined to last. He must have thought I was a sissy. Oh, well.

I soon wrote to Ray Bradbury.

This was so long ago that, in the newsroom where I worked, I still had a typewriter next to my computer (which was the size of a commercial oven). What I wrote, I can't recall. I only know I went on and on. I'm sure I said that I hoped perhaps one day I could write something with such strange inventive terror and tenderness.

You must imagine the face of the clerk in the big newsroom who, a few weeks later, brought me an envelope drawn all over with dragons and witches, and castles shadowed by dark wings, and shuddering, beckoning trees, and bats with the eyes of shiny dimes.

It was addressed only "TO JACQUELYN MITCHARD, A VERY GOOD WRITER INDEED."

Again, I burst into tears.

That was the beginning of a correspondence and a friendship that has lasted thirty years, and quite a number of letters, and several dinners together. Once, when the great man was in a city nearby (as an expert on vampires, he was addressing a national convention of dentists), I arrived laden with books, one to be signed for each of my (then) six children.

"I know who you are!" he said with a tolerant laugh, and we talked about many things—my hope that *The Homecoming* would one day be a film and how Mr. Bradbury's growing up in the era that Ronald Reagan was growing up in Dixon, Illinois, was very good preparation for writing *The Martian Chronicles.*

That was the thing of it, Mr. Bradbury said.

The reason that Rod Serling and some few others succeeded with a very specific kind of science fiction and horror (and this is also true for other heirs, notably Stephen King) was that they saw the manifest and immense oddities in daily life. And they asked, Why not? Who would not want a grandmother who never tired of playing and never left you alone, whose feelings could never be crushed—even when you didn't need her? Who would not grieve for a child born into a family of bloody immortals, whose fate was mortality? What kind of human being would want an alien species' child, born of Venus, as a pet? (We have the answer to that in the stories of people who buy and try to raise chimpanzees, who, as surely as we, are people—although not human people.)

Ray Bradbury taught me that the secret of writing was the secret of life. Look closely. Be generous. Be honest with genuine emotion. Remember the details. Observe the impossible through the filter of the possible. Show but don't manipulate.

Now Mr. Bradbury is ninety-two.

Not long ago I read "I Sing the Body Electric!" to my son Will, a second-grader and the seventh of my nine children.

The story is not cloying. It was not then. It has not aged. It had not then. It is as subtly humorous and precise as it ever was, and as heartbreaking.

"Wouldn't it be nice if we could put you away until we were old grandpas?" Will asked, with the icy candor of childhood.

"It sure would," I said. "But maybe it would be better to put Daddy's mother away."

I'm not bad with icy candor myself.

But it would. It would all be good. Ray Bradbury's worlds are fierce and sometimes violent, but they are never vile. Whatever events befall the characters, they do so within the gentle protectorate of a man who, as a writer, valued human dignity and warned of human foibles and believed that humor must inform both.

When I was nearly forty, more than fifteen years after that first note, I sent Mr. Bradbury a copy of my first novel. I did not expect him to write back. He had been ill, I'd heard, and had only recently gotten better. However, a week later, I received a note written in his own hand. It read, *Well. I was correct. Wasn't I?*

As it seemed to me then, and later, and now, I suppose he was and is right—in most ways.

When I sat down to write my first tale of terror, "Two of a Kind" (presented here, for your approval), I followed the example of Ray Bradbury on the deepest level, perhaps without really realizing how much I was thinking of him.

Some of the strangest details of the story of the Nickolai family came from my own colorful tree. My grandmother really did have twin cousins who married brothers; and the boy who robbed the tomb of the Gypsy queen lived to regret it. Other events in the story were borrowed from the lives of others, including the five Irish sisters, four of whom entered the convent (although none was a teleporting vampire).

I kept things humble. A rusty knife. A lame leg. A plumber, like my father, in business with his brother-in-law, like my father. A two-flat in a neighborhood whose sounds and smells and sights I know as well as my prayers.

Perhaps as a result, I love this story. I all but admire it, almost as though someone else's hand inspired and guided it.

Maybe someone else's hand did guide it.

Ray Bradbury has many children, and many heirs.

—Jacquelyn Mitchard

FAT MAN AND LITTLE BOY

Gary A. Braunbeck

Setting down the bulky square insulated bag, the little boy used his key to unlock the back door, looking around to make sure no one had followed him, and let himself into the house—more specifically, the kitchen. He pulled plates and glasses from the cupboards, removed knives, forks, and spoons from the cutlery drawer, hauled four large bottles of soda pop (still unopened) from the colossal refrigerator and two sizeable trays from the counter, which he immediately positioned on the rolling metal serving cart. It usually took him fifteen minutes to get everything ready; today it took less than ten. He was nervous and a bit frightened. He was afraid this might be his last time visiting this house.

Positioning everything on the trays so the cart was not off balance, he rolled through the kitchen doorway, took a left, and made his way into the fat man's enormous living room.

"Well, hello there, boy," said the fat man from his bed, which was really *four*, all king-sized, all pushed together to make a bed the size of two parked flatbed trucks. The fat man's upper body was held up by about a thousand pillows because if he were ever to lie all the way down, he would not be able to breathe. He always had trouble breathing, so he kept a tall oxygen tank next to the bed.

"Hello, sir," replied the little boy, rolling the cart up to the side of the fat man's bed, careful not to knock over the oxygen tank. "I got the pizzas like you wanted. Double cheese and pepperoni and hamburger and onions and green peppers on all four of them." He twisted off the cap on the first two-liter bottle of soda pop and poured glasses for himself and the fat man.

"Did anybody follow you here?"

The little boy shook his head and prepared the fat man's first tray. "I don't think so. I took a bunch of shortcuts. I got lots of them all over." He reached into his pocket. "I got your change."

"You keep it."

"But it's almost *twenty dollars*!"

"We'll call it hazard pay and let my accountants throw hissy fits over it."

"Thank you. Now I'm *really* glad I took all those shortcuts."

The fat man smiled. "I knew you were a wise one, my boy. Don't ever listen to those cretins who make fun of you, be it at home or at school." He accepted the first glass of pop, remembering at the last second to remove his oxygen mask before taking the first gulp. "Ahhh, refreshing." He watched as the little boy prepared the first tray for this feast. "Hell of a world out there now, isn't it? Hell of a world. All of those beautiful people, hale and hearty and happy, and all of them so much the very *right* size. Wasn't enough that all of the movies and television shows and commercial and magazines showed only people with perfectly aligned white teeth whose bodies were so flawless it was almost stupid, nosiree. They had to go and—bear in mind, boy, this was long before you were born, so I'm guessing you've never heard of this—they had to go and pass laws saying that individuals like myself, that is, persons of the 'larger-than-legal' body size, we beached whales, we human obesedons, we well-padded folk who are resplendent in our Tubby-the-Tuba-like corpulescence—and if that's not an actual word, it damn well ought to be, don't you think?—they passed laws stating in murky yet curiously adjective-heavy legalese that we of the you-should-pardon-the-expression jiggly ginormous girth guild were not allowed to leave our homes until such time that our bodies were of a more, oh, how did they phrase it? Ah, yes, I have it now, 'aesthetically agreeable appearance.' Foolhardy flibbertigibbets, the lot of them. It's enough to make a man lose his appetite." He winked. "Just not *this* one."

The little boy smiled as he finished preparing the first tray. The fat man had a wonderful way of talking. It always made the little boy smile. When he went home after these visits, he often wrote down many of the things—the "pearls of wide-load wisdom" as the fat man called them—that his large friend imparted. The fat man talked to him like he was a real person, not some child who everyone made fun of and spoke to in that awful little-baby voice. He liked that. He liked that right down to the ground.

"Well, don't just stand there gawking," said the fat man. "My God, Fedor Jeftichew—better known as Jo-Jo the Dog-Faced Boy—looked more with-it than you do at this moment. Now, sit down, pile high your plate, for you are still a growing boy, and let us begin our magnificent banquet."

It was always something to watch the fat man eat a meal. Every slice of pizza, every forkful of roasted vegetables, every hunk of garlic bread, spoonful of pudding, and delicate triangle of baklava was scrutinized with the intensity of a jeweler examining a fine and rare stone. Sometimes the fat man would even pause after his assessments to say something like, "The crunch of pizza crust sounds like the crackle of distant lightning in the middle of a summer's night, when you were still young enough to dream that Martian spaceships were hiding up there," or "There's nothing, *nothing*, I say, like the smell of steam from a hunk of warm, fresh-baked bread when you first tear it in half; it's the gentle comfort of picturing Grandma in the kitchen baking through the night because you're visiting and she has no one to bake for since Grandpa passed away," or "The sensation when you first take a cold drink is like feeling this glorious bird made of ice spreading its wings in your chest, giving you the power of flight with every chill so you can soar up above and leave all the cruelty of man," and "It should be a sin for a person to gobble down a truly excellent cheeseburger; it doesn't matter if you're eating at a restaurant or backyard cookout, somebody bygod took the time to cook it with their own hands, and their labors should be appreciated, even if they never know how much you admire their skill with a grill and spatula."

And it wasn't only the fat man's audio narrations, it was also the *sounds* he made while eating; it was almost like music: the wet smacking noises made by his large lips accompanied by the timpani sounds of silverware; the basso profundo of his occasional belches; the long notes of a melancholy oboe whenever his stomach rumbled; and the final, triumphant glissandos of a pianist at the finale of a symphony as the fat man put down his napkin, eased back, and released a pleasant sigh.

This meal was no different, except today the fat man seemed to glow from within with each bite taken, each morsel savored, each crumb licked from his fingertips. The little boy thought he'd never seen a happier person, until, just for a moment, the fat man paused near the end of the feast and seemed to be staring at something really depressing a hundred yards away.

"I must say, boy, this was without a doubt the finest last meal a man could ask for, and a man could expect no finer a companion with whom to share it than you."

"Last meal?" said the little boy, feeling his stomach tighten and something grip his throat from the inside.

"I'm afraid so. Time to sleep the big sleep, go toes-up, get the oxygen monkey off my back, heed Nature's signal of retreat, buy the farm and turn in the warranty card and dance the meat-freeze mambo. Would you be so kind as to hand me that black case on the nightstand?"

The little boy did so, asking, "What's in there?"

"As far as anyone will know or care, it's my diabetes medication."

"But it . . . it isn't, is it?"

The fat man grinned. "See? You just keep proving that I was correct in my conclusions about you. A fine, smart boy you are. And so kind, so brave, the way you know all those shortcuts to get here and not have them spot you and follow along. Were they ever to enter this house and behold that I have become the size of a small planet, they would realize that I've not made effort one toward becoming more aesthetically agreeable and place me under arrest. And don't think for a moment that you would escape severe punishment, dear boy, though I imagine nowhere near the level of that which would be dropped on my head like a curse from heaven. Undoubtedly arrangements would be made to knock down a wall or two so a crane could be more easily employed to lift me away and then deposit me in the bed of a tractor trailer. I refuse to chance that sort of public humiliation, being airlifted like some Vietnamese elephant so they can haul me to one of their 'readjustment facilities,' where I would subsequently be put down like some stray dog. None of that for me, thank you very much." He opened the case and removed the first of three hypodermics. "If that must be my fate, then I will exit stage left under my own direction."

After injecting the contents of the first syringe into his system, the fat man looked at his last-dinner companion and friend and said, "May I be permitted to say that it has been a pleasure and a great honor to have you as companion, bagman, and best friend?"

"Really?" said the little boy. "I'm your best friend?"

"As best as they come," replied the fat man, sinking the plunger of the second syringe. "And I shall miss you until time and space are no more."

"I'm gonna miss you, too. You're the only friend I've ever had."

The fat man's eyes were starting to glaze over. "Dear me, that pusher fellow wasn't having me on when he said this was the strongest stuff available." He held the final syringe in his hand. "Listen to me. After I fall asleep, do not tell anyone for at least a day. Promise me?"

"I promise."

"And I believe you. I want you to have enough time . . . enough . . . time . . ."

"For what?" said the little boy, his voice cracking like the weak ugly crybaby everybody said he was. "Time for what?"

The fat man grasped a thin, long, silver chain that hung around his neck and gave it a firm tug, pulling it free. A single key dangled at the end. He handed it to the little boy. "Time for you to take anything and everything you want from this house. Books, movies, the stereo, anything. And after you do that, you take this key and go to the bank. I've already made arrangements. A man will take you to my security deposit box. Use this key to open it."

"What's in there?"

"Three things—oh, speaking of three . . ." He emptied the

last syringe. His entire body shuddered, and kept on shuddering. He reached out and took both of the little boy's hands in one of his. "You'll find three things: an envelope containing money, a lot of money—it's been so long I don't recall the exact amount, but, trust me, it's quite a lot, and it's all yours. And you will find the two things I've treasured for all of my life: an ancient book with my grandmother's handwritten recipes and poems, her lovely, funny, sad, lonely poems; and a slightly torn black-and-white photo of a little boy not unlike yourself, standing with his beaming parents before he leaves for his first day of first grade. He looks happy and strong and ready to take on the world, because, you see, his body is aesthetically agreeable, and all of his dreams and goals are waiting for him to catch up to them. He's ready to take on the world, to have a life chock-full of adventures. He's ready to wake up every day laughing and fall asleep singing, never stopping, never sad, growing up running at full speed so he can chase the horizon like a joyous fool and drink down the sky from a golden chalice. Nowhere in his eyes do you see any hint of evil glands that will later slow him and then stop him altogether. I want you to have it. Put it in a nice frame, not ostentatious, and hang it high on a bright wall where everyone can see his face and hear the morning song and the evening laughter. Will you do this for me?"

The little boy couldn't speak, so he nodded.

"Of course you will. I had no doubt." His grasp weakened, his hand slipping quietly down to his side. "Falling asleep now." His head tilted to one side, but then his eyes snapped open. "One last thing," he whispered. "Always remember that no one will dare mock you if you know how to throw your weight around. Ha! I knew I had one more in me." And with that, he fell asleep, humming a song the little boy did not recognize.

After a few minutes, the little boy wiped his eyes and blew

his nose, lifted himself on the bed just high enough to kiss the fat man's cheek, and quietly left. But not before grabbing the remaining slices of the last pizza.

The fat man would have hated to see any food go to waste.

About "Fat Man and Little Boy"

I have been a reader of the Great Man all of my life. He's never failed to amaze, move, or pointedly disturb me. He taught me the grace of metaphor and the importance of never standing at arm's length from your own heart. I hope my contribution here evokes the wonder of false mummies, heartbroken sea-beasts, and those who make tragic discoveries long after midnight.

—Gary A. Braunbeck

THE TATTOO

Bonnie Jo Campbell

At the county fair, MacGregor bought a long strip of tickets from a man with one arm, and he and Silvie Ross climbed aboard the Tilt-A-Whirl and then the Zipper, the Starship 2000 and then the double Ferris wheel. They swooped, circled, and spun so wildly that they all but set themselves free from gravity. As they perched momentarily at the top of the Ferris wheel, MacGregor kissed both of Silvie's flushed cheeks, then her lips. Beyond her pretty bare shoulder he saw the whole world stretching out, full of possibility. Then the huge contraption heaved them toward the earth, and MacGregor, caught up in the excitement of falling, shouted, "Marry me!" He didn't even consider that they'd only been dating a few months or that he had no ring to offer her. Apparently Silvie didn't think of these things either, because at the bottom, she said yes. The embrace that ensued on the way back up nearly knocked off MacGregor's glasses.

As they reached the top again, MacGregor glimpsed his home to the east, a quarter mile from the fairgrounds, the house he'd just inherited from his parents, may they rest in peace. He held

Silvie close and pointed out the visible bit of gray-green roof not shaded by the big sycamore tree; they couldn't see the white clapboards or the dark-green trim, but recognizing that familiar place just now, just after the woman he loved had agreed to be his wife, brought tears to his eyes. His parents had lived in that house until seven months earlier, when they were killed in a car crash in Nevada, their first vacation since visiting the Wisconsin Dells on their honeymoon. MacGregor had never meant to be president of MacGregor Ball Bearing Inc., where he had worked every position from delivery boy to engineer, but he knew that fifty-three employees, including Silvie, the head of accounting, were depending on him to keep the company going.

MacGregor and Silvie returned to the ground and took their time moving along the midway, seeing each other in a new way as they strolled through the balmy evening, holding hands so as not to lose each other in the throng of teenagers and families. They stopped at the shooting gallery, and MacGregor went first. He picked up the BB gun and aimed. The tin bird cutouts seemed to slip around even while he had them in his sights. Then it was Silvie's turn. When she aimed, MacGregor marveled at her solid stance, her heavy mane of nearly black hair, and her slim figure that felt strong and sweet in his arms. Her first, second, and third shots hit home, and she chose a polka-dot snake and wrapped it around her neck.

"I'll put this behind the door to stop drafts in winter," she said.

She was the practical one between the two of them. People said MacGregor was a daydreamer, not suited to run a company, but with Silvie at his side, he thought he just might be able to do it.

At the coin toss, it cost MacGregor four dollars to win a shell-shaped ashtray.

"I can help you quit smoking, you know," Silvie said, dropping the ashtray into her purse. "And if you do, it'll take down the company's insurance rates." She had wanted him to quit smoking since he'd met her, but it meant something different to him now that they were going to be married. For the first time, he felt as though he could really kick the habit.

They entered a tent with a sign advertising WORLD OF NATURAL WONDERS in which they saw a tiny pony, too small to be ridden even by a child. While they stood there a young carnival worker came in and put a striped kitten on the pony's rump, and the kitten lay down and curled up sweetly there. There was a goat with five legs, a calf with two heads, and a pig so fat it couldn't stand, but MacGregor felt uneasy looking at the animals' deformities and their drooping eyes. Just past the mirror maze they found another tent with a sign whose peeling paint read THE ILLUMINATED WOMAN.

"I'm not sure," MacGregor said when Silvie pulled him into the line. He felt shy at the notion of ogling a tattooed lady in front of his bride-to-be.

"Oh, don't be a prude," Silvie said. Silvie, his future wife! Her face was incandescent in the fading light. He wrapped his arms around her and lifted her off the ground. He'd long known her mind to be sharp as an axe—though she was only thirty, just three years older than him, his father had made her head of the accounting department—but until they'd started dating, he hadn't known how kind she was, and how much fun. His mother used to accuse him of living with his head in the clouds, but this was the closest he'd ever come to feeling that buoyant.

He doled out a few more tickets, and they entered the twelve-by-twenty-foot tent. MacGregor expected to see a big woman posing in a bathing suit, her skin covered entirely with tattoos, but the woman seemed of average height and size, and she wore glasses. It was hard to tell her shape precisely, because she was sitting on a cushioned stool facing away from them. She seemed young, or certainly no older than MacGregor. She was paying no attention to the half dozen carnival patrons in the tent, who were mumbling and pointing at her, but was instead engaged in writing something in a notebook. Her hair was pulled into a sensible bun, and she wore a backless black evening gown that revealed the brilliant colors stretching from her tailbone up to her hairline. MacGregor noticed that the images on her skin appeared to be moving.

"They must be playing a film on her back!" Silvie said, moving closer to the burgundy velvet rope, of the type found at old-fashioned movie houses. It was the most elegant piece of equipment at the fair, MacGregor thought, but it kept him eight feet away when he wanted to move in and get a closer look. The sign dangling by a gold chain warned that patrons stepping over or under the rope would be *violated.* He stood behind the woman and waved his hand around, trying to locate the beam of light from the projector he thought must be directed at her.

Playing across the young woman's back was a scene of a man and a boy paddling a canoe on a pristine river. Aspens quaked in a light breeze, and weeping willow tendrils dragged in the water. MacGregor leaned over the rope and saw fish moving beneath the surface, dozens of speckled trout and whiskered catfish. It'd been years since he'd been fishing or canoeing, though he and his father had gone most weekends in the summer when he was a boy. His father had loved being outdoors, and it pained him whenever they found trash caught in a snag or saw the remnants of a dirty campsite on a sandbar. Now, in the scene on the young woman's back, a blue-eyed dark-haired boy in the front seat turned, and MacGregor started at the sight of the familiar face. Could it be him? Could that man in the back of the canoe with the round face and salt-and-pepper hair be his father? Oh, how he missed his father! Was that his mother, waving from the riverbank? Was there some alternate universe in which his parents were still alive to advise him?

Silvie elbowed him and pointed out a pair of mallards landing on the river, and MacGregor shook away the crazy idea that his own life would intersect with a carnival illusion. In a matter of months, the momentum of his decisions would carry him down a road he'd never anticipated traveling. He was the president of his father's company! About to marry a bright, beautiful, accomplished woman! When he was the age of that boy in the canoe, he'd dreamt of being an astronaut, of exploring other planets and maybe even alternate universes. But it had been a foolish desire, considering how poor his vision had been since third grade; astronauts, like all pilots, needed excellent eyesight.

"This is just marvelous!" Silvie said, her face aglow.

MacGregor loved seeing Silvie enthralled—so often he feared he was boring her with his melancholy talk about his parents and his musing about the properties of ball bearings. Just today as they'd driven to the fair, he'd been explaining to Silvie how radically they could reduce friction and extend equipment life through the use of enhanced surface finishes and special coatings.

"Look, it's changing," Silvie said. The young woman's back seemed to waver, and then they could make out an old-fashioned steam train coming around a curve. It passed through a stand of woods, beyond which a herd of deer grazed on the side of a hill.

As the train chugged over a river, MacGregor pointed to the tattooed woman's shoulder blade, upon which a couple sat eating drumsticks and potato salad.

"Maybe that's you and me," MacGregor said.

"We look very happy and handsome," Silvie said jokingly.

MacGregor could tell from the way that she put her hand on his arm and sighed that she was ready to leave the tent. But he wanted to stay in order to understand how the pictures were forming and reforming. To him it didn't seem like a movie. For starters, the movement was slow, and the scenes were perfect in every detail, and when the scene had changed, it hadn't done so abruptly. For a moment it had seemed that each cell on the surface of the woman's skin contained both the previous image of the river and the new image of the train, before becoming fully the train and its landscape. MacGregor couldn't help thinking the scene was moving by some power of the young woman's body. As he watched, the man and woman on the picnic blanket moved away from each other. Their faces had gone serious. The man's eyebrows were drawn down, and the woman seemed to be saying something angrily. What might they be arguing about? He took Silvie's hand and pulled it to his heart. What could they possibly argue about in such a beautifully illustrated world?

As MacGregor and Silvie watched the scenes move across her back, the tattooed woman remained engaged by whatever she was writing. MacGregor tried repeatedly to get a glimpse of her notebook, but each time he adjusted his position to see over her shoulder or past her arm, she would shift slightly (deliberately?) and block his view. He was moving along the velvet rope, his eyes on her curved profile, when, without warning, tears began streaming down her cheeks. The hand holding the pen continued to move across the paper as she quietly cried.

MacGregor stepped back a few feet from the rope.

"Poor girl," he said to Silvie. "It must be exhausting to be in a sideshow."

"Well, at least she's got a job," Silvie said. "I worked with girls like this in Scouts."

"Girls like what?"

"Girls without a solid upbringing," Silvie whispered. "A job helps them make sense of their lives, helps ground them."

MacGregor nodded. After being a Girl Scout herself for years, Silvie had volunteered as a troop leader, and she now sat on the local board of directors. She was a woman who cared about the people around her as much as she cared about the figures in the red and black columns at MacGregor Ball Bearing Inc.

"Let's go look in the 4-H animal barns," Silvie said, and moved toward the exit. "I love seeing which chickens and rabbits won the blue ribbons."

MacGregor looked over his shoulder at the Illuminated Woman one last time and saw the father and son in the canoe again, except that now the canoe was plunging over a waterfall, and the fiberglass canoe was crashing onto the rocks. Half of the canoe bobbed in the frothy water where the limp bodies of the father and son floated. MacGregor didn't turn away until Silvie took his hand and led him out of the tent.

That night, MacGregor lay alone in his bed, unable to sleep after the excitement of the day. He had tried to persuade Silvie to stay with him, but she'd wanted to go home and call her mother to tell her the good news. When MacGregor closed his eyes, he saw a brief image of Silvie's face, but then that image wavered and he saw again the colorful visions on the Illuminated Woman's back, the water flowing more dramatically, more realistically than real water had ever flowed. The sun shone on the river to make it sparkle, to reveal the gleaming fishes below, and the man and boy in the canoe sparkled too as they paddled. He saw once again their broken bodies at the bottom of the falls and felt again the sorrow he had experienced that afternoon, but he had never been afraid of sadness in a story. The last image, the ruined canoe bobbing alongside those bodies, made him think and worry and reflect. He didn't know why the story of the canoe trip had been interrupted by the story of the train, unless someone from the train was going to see the tragic scene and make a wise observation.

He wondered what stories would play across his body if he had such a tattoo. Maybe the images would play out the history of ball bearings, culminating in his future successful development of new hybrid ceramic ball bearings that operated so smoothly they would last a thousand years without lubrication or replacement. Maybe an image would appear of his crowning achievement: a machine the size of a three-story building that purified polluted air using almost no energy—he and his father had invented the bubbling, humming antipollution machine during one of their jaunts on the river. He imagined cars that flew along the ground and then rose up into the sky effortlessly. He imagined a rocket ship taking off, its destination another galaxy. Then he saw Silvie shimmering in her wedding dress. He saw his mother's wedding ring gleaming on her finger. He hoped he and Silvie would be as happy as his parents had been, growing closer and more affectionate over the years. He wanted Silvie to gaze upon him with pure delight, as his mother had gazed upon his father, as his father had gazed upon his mother in return.

The following afternoon, Silvie was tied up with an audit and had to stay late at work. MacGregor kissed her goodbye and started to go home but then decided to return to the fair. He walked along the midway with his hands in his pockets. He bought a short string of tickets and handed them over at the entrance to the tent of the Illuminated Woman. There was no one else inside. He approached her with his eyes focused on the grass so as not to get distracted.

"How are you doing that?" he asked from behind the velvet

rope, but he got no response. "Pssst. Hey, miss? Please. Is there anything you can tell me?"

"Why are you interrupting me?" the young woman said, and her simple clear voice charmed MacGregor. She spoke with an unfamiliar accent, and he wondered where she was from. This afternoon she was reading a big book called *Greek Mythology*.

"How are you making your tattoo move?" he asked. "What's the trick?"

"Can't you see I'm working?" She barely glanced at him before shaking her head and going back to her reading. MacGregor saw that there was a light shining on the pages of the book. He realized that the light was coming from a tiny bulb she wore on her necklace. He admired it because he liked to read in bed, and something like that would come in handy. Silvie read too, but only for fifteen minutes each night, which was exactly how long it took her to read a chapter of one of her romance novels.

"Do you spend all day in this tent?"

"My aunt and I trade off. Not that it's any of your business."

"Don't you get bored?"

"How could I be bored?" She nodded toward a stack of books and a smaller stack of spiral notebooks on the table next to her. MacGregor kept looking at her, and she finally put down her book, turned to him, and pushed her glasses up along the bridge of her nose. "What do you want?"

"A tattoo like yours. Just a small one." He saw that her glasses were as thick as his own. His mother had told him he'd ruined his vision by reading in the dark.

"Do you want to be in a sideshow?" she asked, narrowing her eyes.

"Heck, no. I'm a company president."

"You're too young to be any kind of president." She glanced over at the entrance, as if to assure herself that nobody else was looking in.

He blushed. "I know. My father died, and I inherited the company. I shouldn't admit it, but it doesn't really play to my strengths." It felt strange to say it out loud. "But I'm trying, because I know he'd want me to."

"What about what *you* want?" she asked. "What would you be doing, you know, if you could do anything you wanted?"

"I'd be in space. On my way to Mars."

"You'd better write to your senator, then. The human space program is in the toilet." She softened her words with a smile, and he saw she had a blemish, maybe a pimple, on her chin. She unpinned her hair, which was almost as dark as Silvie's but uneven, with stringy bangs. She combed her fingers through it, pulled it up again, and repinned it with her barrette. After all that, it looked the same as before.

"I have written my senator," he said. "And my congressman. And the president."

She continued to smile at him. "Your shirt is buttoned up wrong," she said.

"Oh." He unbuttoned and rebuttoned.

"Usually when men undress in my tent, I call security."

"Oh." MacGregor realized he should have turned away from her.

"So you think you want a tattoo like mine," the young woman said. "Well, you'll have to talk to Madame Needles in the fortune-telling tent. She's my mom. Tell her you're a company president. But don't let her see your socks, because they don't match."

"Oh. Okay."

"But don't say I didn't warn you. Madame Needles takes things very seriously. She won't even pay me unless I take all my vitamins every day. She's obsessed with vitamins, which means I get to burp up fish oil for the first two hours of every shift."

MacGregor thanked her, and the young woman went back to reading, and finally MacGregor let himself look at her tattoo. Today she was wearing a purple evening gown, and on her skin there appeared a woman with snakes for hair, and MacGregor watched, mesmerized, as they twisted out from her scalp. One of the snakes lunged out suddenly and snapped at him, and he jumped back with a yelp.

A big man came into the tent and told MacGregor his time was up.

"We don't allow screamers in here," the big man said.

When MacGregor didn't move away from the velvet rope quickly enough, the man grabbed him by the arm and pulled him out of the tent. As the man dragged him along, MacGregor saw that he had a tattoo on his biceps and that the tattoo was an image of the man himself. In the image, the man was flexing his biceps. MacGregor was pretty sure those tiny biceps also featured an even tinier image of the man, and so on.

"Did Madame Needles give you that tattoo?" MacGregor asked.

"Get lost."

MacGregor found the tent with the sign MADAME NEEDLES: TAROT, FORTUNES, AND BODY ART, and when he stepped inside, he found a small, plump woman whose skin shone with a strange golden hue. Her hair too, which at first had seemed gray, was gold. Or maybe it was the angle of the sun as it pitched toward the horizon that made it seem so.

He introduced himself and said that the Illuminated Woman had sent him.

"And what can I do for you?" Madame Needles asked, a bright curiosity in her eyes. MacGregor didn't believe in future telling, but he felt a bit disappointed that she didn't already know. He explained that he wanted a tattoo.

"I'm looking for a husband for my daughter, Mr. McGregor," she said. She grinned and her teeth were pure shining gold. "And for that reason I'll give you a beautiful tattoo. You are the first man she's ever sent to me."

"Well, I, ah, I want the tattoo. Very much," MacGregor said. "But I'm already engaged to be married."

"I don't see a ring." She sounded like her daughter, but it wasn't a strange accent; it was more that both women made each sentence seem like the line of a song they happened to be singing.

"But men don't usually wear engagement rings," he said. Or did Madame Needles somehow know that he hadn't bought Silvie a ring yet? "And it's true. We'll be married next May. She's a wonderful woman, my fiancée."

"You seem very single to me, Mr. MacGregor, and May is nine months away."

"Your daughter seems nice. I'm sure she could date if she wanted to."

"Nice? Ha!" The woman stood and shook her head. "She's an impossible child! She's twenty-five and she just reads and writes all day." Madame Needles's scowl marred her exotic demeanor.

"She's mesmerizing," MacGregor said. He hadn't found anything pitiable about her. "Girls don't have to get married these days if they don't want to."

"If you have ideas about despoiling my daughter out of wedlock, forget it."

"Oh, no, nothing like that," he said. It was just that she seemed content with her reading and writing, although MacGregor did wonder what she'd been crying about the previous day. Had she known how the story was going to end, that the father and son would go over the falls and drown? Did she make the story end that way?

"Soon she'll be an old maid," Madame Needles said, "and I'll never have any grandchildren. I'll die miserable and alone in the poorhouse while she's writing her magnum opus. Better if she were like her aunt. I tattooed my sister, and those tattoos sit still and behave. None of her colors creep around and excite the marks—I mean customers."

"I want a tattoo that moves."

"You want. You want. Everybody wants." She gave him a sidelong glance. "But how badly do you want it?"

"I want it very much," he said. "Please. Can you really do it?"

She shrugged her golden shoulders. "I'll do what I do, but there's no telling how it'll turn out. The rest is up to you." She opened the drawer in her desk and took out several sheets of paper. "First, I'll need you to sign some forms."

There was a liability release in case he got blood poisoning from the needles and a nondisclosure form, saying he would not to give away Madame Needles's tattooing techniques, and it contained a noncompete clause forbidding him from joining a sideshow. He read through the forms and reached for the pen in his pocket, but Madame stopped him with a hand on his wrist. She lifted his hand and pricked his finger with a needle and then smeared his blood across each of the signature lines in turn.

She named the fee, and MacGregor fought to keep from gasping. It was ten times the outrageous amount he'd anticipated, but he paid it. He described the tattoo he wanted, the size of a playing card, of a red bird perched on a branch above a blue stream, against the golden sun. It was an image he'd seen in dreams.

She pulled a wooden bowl off the table and shoved it into his hands. "This is going to hurt," she said. "You can bite down on the edge of the bowl." She slipped a black satin sleep mask over his eyes and had him lie back in the chair. When the first needle penetrated the center of his chest, he howled. It sank deeper, seemed to enter his heart.

He felt Madame Needles pull back and heard the rustle of the tent flap.

"Does the screamer need an escort off the premises?"

MacGregor recognized the voice. It was the man with the tattoo on his biceps.

"I'll let you know," Madame Needles said. She leaned in close to MacGregor's ear. "Do you want this badly enough?"

MacGregor took a breath. He recalled watching the girl's tattoo, feeling it move his senses, his thoughts, and his emotions. He remembered how it had thrilled Silvie. But it was more than that. He didn't just want the tattoo; he needed it. There was something primal bubbling inside him that needed a way out, and he was sure this was the way, through his skin. He bit down again on the edge of the bowl, nodded for Madame to continue. As she drove the needles in again and again, the pain became surreal, moving beyond any pain he'd ever known. He squeezed his eyes shut, but his tears seeped out anyway and soaked the mask over his eyes. His teeth cut into the rim of the wooden bowl. He did not open his eyes until she was finished. He thought that about a half hour had passed, but when he walked shakily to the door of the tent to look out, the sky was dark, and even the midway lights and music were off for the night. The rattle of cicadas was almost deafening.

MacGregor kept the tattoo a secret until the following weekend, when he and Silvie took a three-day vacation to Sanibel Island in Florida. Their suite overlooked the Gulf of Mexico, and on their first day there they saw pileated woodpeckers, roseate spoonbills, and alligators from their balcony. When Silvie picked up her novel that night in bed, MacGregor took off his shirt, pulled the gauze from the tattoo, and sat before her.

"You got a tattoo!" she said, her expression one of mild alarm. She reached up and touched it. MacGregor had avoided looking at the tattoo himself, even when he cleaned it and applied new bandages. He had wanted to share the experience of first seeing it with Silvie. As he had hoped, it began to move under her fingers, at first slowly. The wind rustled the bird's feathers; the wings opened and closed. They watched as the bird on his breastbone lifted and flew through air. It soared above a boat, which sailed from a port into a blue-green ocean. Waves gently slapped the sides of the boat. MacGregor saw upside down what Silvie saw and marveled at how the tattoo swelled and changed to show every detail.

"It's real," she said. Her smile showed pure delight. "It's marvelous!"

He nodded, but Silvie was less happy a while later when a storm blew in, and the boat capsized, and all the tiny people were pitched into the merciless, shark-filled sea.

"Sorry," MacGregor said, and Silvie opened her book and read a chapter.

The following night MacGregor posed in front of the mirror, and together they watched a silver airplane take off and soar out of the atmosphere. It made its way around the moon. MacGregor allowed himself to feel a little proud. Madame Needles had seemed unsure whether the tattoo would move the way he wanted it to, but it was working. The ship soared with the sun glinting off its wings until it exploded without warning. A dozen bodies were strewn across space.

"I don't like this story," Silvie said, and turned away.

MacGregor did not want to stop watching. He wanted to see how the story really ended, what might give meaning to the tragic demise of the astronauts who had died during their mission. The tattoo seemed to have doubled in area since the story began, and MacGregor wondered if the Illuminated Woman had started out with a small tattoo as well. While Silvie got ready for bed, MacGregor watched the last remaining astronaut plunge toward Earth. When he hit the atmosphere, he became a bright stream of light, a falling star.

Across his skin, MacGregor felt the movement of the explosion and of the man's falling, but that wasn't the extent of it. The pictures showing on his chest were like the mushrooms growing atop the soil, connected by tendrils to the greater body under the surface. If this were a projection of images, they came from inside, not out.

"I know you wonder why I read romance novels," Silvie said, turning to him later in bed. "You think they're written for foolish girls."

"No," he said, though he did wonder. He had tried to read one of her novels, but he'd fallen asleep in the middle of the first chapter.

"It's because all day long I have to make critical decisions. There's money, livelihoods, resources at stake. I act with confidence, but I can only hope my decisions are the right ones. When I come home, I don't want to worry. I want to know that everything will turn out well and that everyone will be happy and that justice will be served."

"Thank you, Silvie," MacGregor said. "Now I do understand."

She needed life outside of work to be worry-free, and he would make it that way for her as best he could. She already did so much for him. When he was at a business meeting or a cocktail party and veered off onto the wrong track, Silvie would guide him back. He wanted to do the same for her.

One Saturday morning in March, MacGregor woke breathless from a dream of flight, still feeling the joyful energy of soaring above his house, moving at the speed of cars over the street below. He listened to the purr of Silvie's snoring. He smelled her perfume from the day before and slowly turned his head on the pillow to gaze at her smooth face in the gray predawn light. She stayed over every Friday night, and in two months she would be there beside him every night, forever. Beyond her, on the nightstand, lay her current novel, silhouetted against the window. The pages were fluffed out prettily, suggesting that her book was part of her decorating scheme, which included the handsome off-white window dressings, the ribbed bedspread, and the new, slightly luminescent paint on the walls. She said remodeling made the room belong to them. This had been his parents' bedroom, and MacGregor didn't care what it looked like. He had grown up an only child, and the most important thing to him was having another soul lying beside him, sharing his life. He would go along with any remodeling Silvie wanted.

MacGregor's chest prickled. Silvie had recently suggested he keep the tattoo covered all the time. She had walked in on him watching a story at work more than once, and she was concerned about the hold the tattoo had on him, how it was distracting him from more important things. He couldn't argue with the truth of the matter, that the work of being president was tiresome to him, and he had taken to hiding out in his bathroom to revive himself. He had managed to resist looking in the mirror for more than a week now, until this morning, when a vision of flying without aid of any machine had invaded his dreams. If he hadn't felt the urgent prickling, he would have remained in bed, absorbing the pleasures of lying with Silvie, would have wrapped an arm around her and pulled her close. Instead, he slipped out of bed, tiptoed to the bathroom, closed the door, and turned on the light. Silvie had helped him to quit smoking, but giving up cigarettes had been easy compared with resisting his compulsion to look at the tattoo. He turned the lock on the door and stuffed a bit of tissue into the oversized keyhole. His heart was pounding as he looked around the small tiled room, at the modest claw-footed tub, at the old-fashioned light fixture covered with a frosted seashell glass shade. The old bathroom mirror had a funhouse quality; he and Silvie had stood beside each other in front of it and laughed at their distorted reflections.

MacGregor pressed his ear against the painted wood of the

door. Silvie's snore was one of his favorite household sounds, along with the toaster popping up and the dryer spinning. In the world outside, he loved the sounds of jets and rockets taking off, though he'd only heard the latter on television. MacGregor unbuttoned his pajama shirt. He slid his arms from the sleeves, and when he looked in the mirror, the color in the playing-card-sized tattoo dazzled him. He took a deep breath and let the tattoo expand and rush to fill the smooth skin of his chest. The first mysterious effect of the tattooing process had been that he had lost the modest amount of hair he'd had there, and it had never grown back. He took a deep breath and inhaled the colors, which smelled of air so rich and oxygenated that it filled not only his lungs but his whole being. When he exhaled, all the stress of the week fell away at once, and the picture of the bird and the branch and the stream and the sun began to change.

A rocket sat on a launchpad surrounded by complicated machines. The machines were operated by white-coated scientists whose faces glowed with intelligence and focus. MacGregor took another deep breath, and the men and women began to move, to tap their fingers on their whisper-thin handheld computers, to point out and discuss objects of interest around them, to compare calculations. As MacGregor's focus returned to the rocket ship, he saw it increase in proportion to the scene, and the scientists disappeared from view. Somehow, as MacGregor's heart pumped blood out through his arteries and back through his veins, the point of view moved so he could see inside the capsule atop the boosters, where two women and three men in silver suits were making final preparations and buckling themselves into their seats. To MacGregor they seemed perfect human specimens, strong-bodied and healthy, and their eyes showed a love of adventure. Or was there a shadow of something sinister crossing one man's face? Did the fifth astronaut have an ungenerous spirit, a tendency toward cruelty or sullenness? Was his desire for space less pure than the others'? MacGregor's concern faded as he felt the collective excitement of the other astronauts. He also felt their fear and sadness and understood that they were leaving behind their loved ones in order to journey into the unknown.

One of the men in the capsule resembled MacGregor, with blue eyes and thick eyebrows and dark, unruly hair. So much so that MacGregor was almost sure it *was* him. Neither of the women resembled Silvie, however. He knew Silvie wouldn't venture into space, not even with him at her side, reassuring her. She didn't like not knowing what was coming next. She was most content when she was following her routine of work and relaxation, having coffee on the patio in the morning or taking a brisk walk in the early evening. She was continually opening windows to let in breezes and wouldn't like the cramped quarters of the space capsule, in which everything was designed for efficiency and maximum function.

MacGregor, too, would miss many things about Earth, especially the familiar objects from his house and his desk at work, the way his tools felt in his hands, but he knew that for him the memories of the objects could suffice in their absence. MacGregor would miss Silvie most of all, but he could take comfort in the memories of her that he would carry into space. Behind and beyond the rocket, there stretched the vision of MacGregor's own planet's beauty: a glittering silver desert and purple mountains. Beyond that, somehow, defying the laws of perspective, he could see the vast and shining ocean. From a high cliff, a giant bird launched itself, flew across the water on golden wings, and on the bird's back was a young woman. Her arms were wrapped around the creature's neck. Her hair whipped around in the wind, and she was laughing. At first he thought it was Silvie, hoped it was Silvie, but when she shook her head to get her hair out of her eyes, he saw that she was wearing glasses and that they were held fast to her head with an elastic strap, like the one he'd worn as a kid. MacGregor laughed with delight, realizing as he did so that he hadn't felt delighted in quite a while. He fell backward against the door, and it rattled.

"Gerald?" Silvie called from the bedroom, and MacGregor's heart seized.

"I'll be right out," he said just loudly enough to be heard, trying to not interrupt the flow of the story. The golden bird vanished behind a hill.

"I'm worried about you, Gerald. Please come out and talk to me," Silvie said. She jiggled the doorknob, and the tissue fell out of the keyhole and onto the floor.

"Just a minute," he whispered. When he was experiencing a story in this way, he knew how life could be extraordinary, how the simple four-chambered human heart and the primitive human brain could begin to understand the universe. And he thought that if Silvie would watch the story unfold with him—if she could shake her fears about how it might end—she would feel inspired as well. The rocket blasted off with a flame more brilliant than a lightning strike. MacGregor gripped the sink as the rocket tore free of the earth with a violence that seemed more than the rocket or the planet, or he himself, could endure—his heart felt nearly wrenched from his chest, and he was out of breath by the time the rocket was airborne. As he watched in the mirror, he could see magnificent Earth from space, its blue oceans and green lands still beautiful despite the pollution and all the other human folly that threatened to destroy it. As the planet shrank to the size of a marble, then a pale blue dot, the scene darkened, and then the rocket was swimming far from home, through the sea of stars. MacGregor kept hold of the sink to steady himself against the joyful energy of barreling through space.

"Are you looking at that tattoo?" Silvie asked. He could tell from her voice that her face was pressed up against the other side of the door.

Silvie had done so much for him. She had carried him through the grief of losing his parents. She had supported him as president of MacGregor Ball Bearing Inc., though she was better suited to run the company than he was. It was her ability to manage money, employees, and schedules that had allowed him to be anything more than an engineer.

"We need to get you some help, Gerald," Silvie said thoughtfully.

MacGregor tore his eyes away from the mirror. He looked down at the tiny hexagonal tiles that made up the old floor, the same cool tile his bare feet had known when he was a kid. There was a slight rise near the radiator, where the floor had buckled, reminding him of a shoulder blade. As he studied the tiles, he began to see a vision move across the floor. The picture was not as vivid or colorful as his tattoo, but it played out in shadows that brought him feelings from a long time ago. Some boys filled a bottle with dry ice, shook it up, and shot a cork across a pond. They sent a model rocket two hundred feet into the air in the field behind his house. MacGregor both saw and felt himself riding his bike along the sidewalk and then gathering speed on the downslope, and though the adult MacGregor knew the poor boy was headed for a crash, he grinned at the wind in his face. MacGregor still felt like that kid, twenty-one years later.

"I saw a giant bird flying over the ocean, Silvie," MacGregor said as he stepped into the bedroom. "Big enough that a girl was riding on its back."

"Oh, Gerald," Silvie said tiredly, "we both know what's going to happen." She was sitting on the bed with her back to him, and the bed was already made up. She wore the pearl-colored bathrobe she kept at his house.

"What do you mean?" he asked.

"The rocket always crashes. The volcano always explodes and kills the villagers. I don't want to see a girl plunge into the icy depths."

"This is a new story. Things might be different."

"Gerald, we've been through this. The lions in the veldt tear apart the sweet little gazelle. Cold, empty space swallows the astronauts. Somebody is going to shoot that big bird out of the air. I've lived with your stories for more than six months, and my hope has run out."

"The rocket doesn't always crash," MacGregor insisted. "And the gazelle is the lions' natural prey—that can't be helped."

"If the rocket doesn't crash, if the astronauts land safely, then in the next story they go on to kill the peaceful inhabitants of the new planet with their human stupidity."

"Oh, honey," MacGregor said. "So what if some of the stories don't exactly end happily? I just wish we could watch together, to experience the adventures together, the good and the bad."

The sun was rising outside their window, and Silvie's shiny bathrobe exploded with color. Shapes began to form across her shoulders, and MacGregor began to see a vision of himself and Silvie in the future. Her hair was white, and his was gray, and they were holding hands in the garden in spring. He didn't understand how this was happening, how the stories were stretching beyond his own body, appearing all around him. In the vision, MacGregor clung with his free hand to a walker. White-haired Silvie lifted both hands to her head, groaned, and then collapsed to the flagstone path to lie among the tulips and daffodils.

Silvie gave no indication that she was seeing the images on her robe.

"I need my stories to be happily ever after," she said. She

picked up the novel from her nightstand and held it in MacGregor's direction until her bookmark fell out. He saw on the cover a muscular, shirtless man with long hair and a woman with soulful eyes and even longer hair. "Why can't you create a happily ever after for me?" she asked, tears glistening in her eyes.

"But the stories exist on their own, Silvie. They come to me just as they are." He felt as though he were mainly a conduit for the stories, but maybe he was, somehow, creating them. Maybe his very nature was creating them. And maybe there would be a way to control them by force of will, but that wasn't what he wanted.

"Gerald, I don't think I can't live with you this way."

"What can I do, Silvie?"

"I've been thinking about it," she said, and stared out the window. "And I don't think I can marry you unless you have the tattoo removed."

MacGregor's heart thudded and slowed. He stumbled into the bathroom and looked in the mirror, and there he saw the color drained from his skin, saw the brilliant visions replaced by a web of scar tissue, the explosion of life replaced by an expanse of angry flesh that pinched and stretched like the residue of a life-threatening burn. He felt physically ill. He bent at the waist, crossed his arms over his chest. He knew what Silvie didn't know, that the tattoo was more than ink on skin. The tattoo could not be removed without gouging out his heart.

He hadn't realized he was holding his breath, but when he breathed again, the sick feeling went away. His skin tingled as the spaceship hurtled through space, and he uncrossed his arms and saw the stars again. Inside the capsule, the five astronauts floated weightlessly and joked with one another. One woman was eating dried cherries, and she tossed one toward the open mouth of one of the men, but the cherry flew in impossibly slow motion, and the woman and the man both laughed and discussed their pea-plant experiment until the fruit finally reached the man, and he bit it out of the air. As a child, MacGregor had tried to eat like an astronaut—powdered drinks and vacuum-sealed protein bars. Now he tasted the sweet sourness of that dried cherry!

When MacGregor returned to the bedroom, he found Silvie dressed and packing her overnight bag with the few things she kept at his house.

"No, Silvie. I love you. You're the most important person in my life."

"I love you, too, Gerald. It's your choice." She finally looked at him.

"See, Silvie, the rocket landed safely on a new planet," he said, and pointed to his chest. "It's Mars. Look, four of the astronauts are getting out. Everything's going to be okay this time."

"They all have guns," Silvie said anxiously.

"For protection, or in case of wild animals. Silvie, look at the planet. The sky is red! Can you smell it? The dust smells of flowers and vanilla. Everyone is safe." To his joy, he found he really could smell the dust. He felt the hot breeze on his skin.

"They're not safe, Gerald. They're probably bringing germs that will infect everyone on the new planet. Or else they'll try to take away the Martian riches, and a war will break out. I've seen these stories too many times. I can't take any more."

"But look. The astronauts have met a Martian family, a couple and two children. They're all conversing. Everything is friendly. You can tell by their hand gestures." MacGregor noted the hands of the Martians, their fingers long and elegant compared with the stubby mitts of the Earthlings. The sky behind them glowed the rich orange-red of campfire coals. MacGregor imagined the Martians and Earthlings sitting around a fire, and soon enough they were indeed sitting around a fire, conversing telepathically, cooking Martian fish and giant mushrooms they grew in their basements.

"What about that fifth astronaut lurking in the background?" Silvie said.

"He stayed at the rocket."

"He's right there now, drinking whiskey from a bottle. I can hear him cursing."

"No," MacGregor said, but he knew she was right. The man seemed unlike the others. He was suspicious and angry. And now he was drunk and armed.

"Somebody's going to die," Silvie said. She looked away from him and stuffed her slippers and bathrobe into her bag. "Eventually somebody's going to die. Don't deny it."

"Eventually we all die, honey."

"Well, I can't face it."

"Just look at the light reflecting off the Martian canals as evening falls. It reminds me of your eyes, Silvie." He closed his eyes to imagine the story more vividly, and he heard the door shut. He wanted to run after her, but he needed to see the story through. As Silvie said, most of the stories ended with trouble, just as marriages ended in death or divorce. He thought he might work at keeping a story alive longer, putting off disaster, just as he might convince Silvie to give him one more chance. It occurred to him that he should run after her and beg for another chance. And yet, readers and watchers and listeners needed a story to end sometime.

MacGregor and Silvie's separation was as amicable as MacGregor could have hoped. He arranged an emergency meeting of the board of directors, and they agreed with him that Silvie should become acting president, while MacGregor would retain his majority stake in the company but return to being an engineer. He felt relieved to move his things from his father's office back to his old desk in the fabrication shop. At the beginning of August, Silvie drove to his house in a new electric car she'd bought, in order to pick up some winter clothes she'd stored in his attic. She stepped out into the gravel driveway, wearing a trim-fitting pants suit in charcoal gray. She wore high-heeled shoes that barely covered her pretty toes. Her heels sank through the gravel and into the earth.

"I'm sorry things didn't work out for us," Silvie said. "I guess we're another one of your tragic stories."

MacGregor put the last box of clothes into the trunk of her car and invited her to stay and have some coffee. When she declined, he took off his glasses and cleaned them on his shirt. When he put them back on, Silvie was shaking her head at him and smiling as she might at a child. When she backed into the street, MacGregor walked out to the end of his driveway to watch the silver electric car, as sleek as a rocket ship, head down the road, and that's when he saw the billboard for the county fair, August 4–9. He was surprised to realize that the fair was opening that day. His skin began to tingle, and his heart began to flutter crazily. Was it possible that the Illuminated Woman would be there? He'd seen her in his stories and dreams, but he hadn't considered seeking her out. He could hope that Madame Needles had failed in the last year to find her daughter a husband. Of course she had failed, for the girl knew her own mind! MacGregor wanted to see her, to lose himself in her brilliant visions, to listen to her voice sing, to look into the eyes behind her dark-rimmed glasses. He had been ashamed to think of her this way when he was engaged to Silvie, but now there was nothing to keep him from visiting her and trying to know her better. And maybe now that he had his own stories, she might want to see him, too.

About "The Tattoo"

My idea in writing "The Tattoo" was to get up close and personal with an illustrated man. For a long time I'd suspected that such ink was not just skin deep, and now I've confirmed it. Writing this piece gave me a chance to study the ways stories move across a person's body. Ray Bradbury is one of America's most important philosophers, and he's inspired me since I was a kid. What a great honor it is to be part of this anthology. I thank Heidi Bell for helping me with this story.

—Bonnie Jo Campbell

BACKWARD IN SEVILLE

Audrey Niffenegger

Helene stood at the front railing on the upper deck in the dark, watching as the ship maneuvered at a funny angle too close to a low stone bridge. A few people stood near her, all watching quietly as the crew worked on the deck below them. The band was playing Ellington at the other end of the ship; couples would be dancing neatly, persistently. In the cabins below, most of the passengers were asleep.

Helene's father, Lewis, had been sleeping when she left their cabin, his face collapsed without the dentures, his mouth open, snoring. In sleep he frightened her. *Let him wake up tomorrow,* she prayed every night, though she was not religious. *Don't take him from me yet.*

The *Persephone* wasn't very large for a cruise ship. There were 300 passengers and 150 crew members. Helene had never been on a cruise before and had braced herself for bingo, seasickness, and enforced camaraderie, though her father kept assuring her it wasn't that kind of cruise. "It's low-key, mostly excursions to churches and lectures on Matisse. You've never been to Rome or Barcelona; you'll love it. The Mediterranean is very calm in

June. Don't worry so much, Sweet Pea." She had nodded and smiled. Of course she would love it; he wanted her to love it.

The ship moved backward and then sideways, away from the port and the bridge. They were in a canal; they had been docked in Seville for two days. In Seville, Helene had gone on an excursion to a convent, a very sad convent run by an order called the Poor Clares. All the nuns were from Africa and had been cloistered until recently, but then the Poor Clares had become too poor and now they sold baked goods and let tourists come inside for a few euros each. Helene felt bad for them. She thought of the Sistine Chapel and St. Peter's, which had been her first excursion. "You'd think they could redistribute the wealth a little," she said to her father when she got back to the ship. "I don't imagine nuns are too high on the food chain," he replied. Storks were nesting in the chimneys of the convent. They made Helene want to cry.

The canal was narrow and the *Persephone* had to back her way out of it. Seville was serene and yellow under the artificial lights strung along the canal. The ship moved slowly. Seville receded. Helene tried to remember where they were headed . . . Lisbon. Then home. They would fly to London and then back to Chicago.

Lewis had been tired before they began the trip. At the airport he'd said, "Just a minute, Helene," and stood gasping, leaning on his cane in the middle of the security line as she realized that he should have had a wheelchair, her heart sinking as she remembered that he always refused to use a wheelchair. She screwed up her courage and asked him anyway and was surprised when he nodded, still breathing heavily, eyes closed. A wheelchair arrived and Lewis sank into it and folded his arms across his chest, his cane sticking out like a shepherd's crook. Helene didn't travel much, but Lewis always had; it was all familiar to him, but she felt nervous as the attendant pushed Lewis along and eventually deposited them at the gate. She watched her father sit, chin sunk into chest, and she finally admitted to herself that he was terribly old. *When did this happen? He was always fine, and now . . .*

Her mother had died in February. It was her mother's place Helene occupied here on the ship. She slept in the narrow bed her mother should have slept in, ate the bland food her mother would have eaten. Lewis accepted Nora's absence with grace; he might say, "Your mother would have liked that," or "Your mother always did this," but he never made Helene feel that he would have preferred his wife's company to hers. When Helene was small she had stolen her mother's lipstick and gone down to breakfast with scarlet lips. Her parents had smiled at each other and pretended not to notice as she left lip prints on her juice glass. It was like that. Helene was forty-five years old, by far the youngest passenger on the ship.

The other passengers at the rail were all in pairs. They were white-haired and bent but exceedingly compatible, each husband inclining toward his wife when she spoke quietly into his ear, all of them dressed for dinner with care, all leaning on the rail for support with a glass of wine or a cocktail clutched in one hand. Helene thought of Evan. *Is that what we would have looked like in forty years?* She had met Evan when she was twenty-eight and he was thirty-six. He'd always seemed on the verge of marrying her; she'd been patient. When he broke up with her fourteen years later and married a girl half her age, she understood that she'd been gullible and that he was a jerk, but oh well, and so she had lapsed into a quiet permanent rage.

It would be nice to have a drink, but lethargy kept her at the railing. The canal unspooled backward around the ship. It gave Helene the feeling that time was reversing, that things might be undone. *Daddy wouldn't be old, Mom wouldn't have died, Evan would come back and we'd have kids, it would all be different,*

I would change everything. I would change. Trees and houses came from behind her; little boats began to appear in the water as the canal widened. Soon they would turn the ship and sail forward. Everything flowed away into the distance and the darkness.

One of the women at the rail dropped her cane, and her husband bent painfully and retrieved it for her. *How he cares for her,* Helene thought. *No one takes care of me; it's always me taking care of somebody.* When she was a child she had been very timid, scared of strangers, thunder, the poodle next door, escalators, anything new or loud, anything that moved, pretty much. Her mother had kept her close, kissed her on the tip of her ear, whispered encouragement. Her father had brought her funny presents—a tiny silk umbrella from Paris, a tin of green tea from Kyoto. "It's okay, Sweet Pea, I've got your back. Now go get 'em."

I wasted my life.

She imagined the Poor Clares, tucked into their neat beds in their cloister, secure in the night, in belief. How good it must be to believe. Lewis and Nora were indifferent to religion. When Helene was nine she had asked about God. Lewis had taken her to synagogue and Nora had taken her to church, once each, and they had asked very carefully if she wanted to go back and she'd said no thank you, sensing their lack of enthusiasm. Now Helene wondered what her father believed, now when he was so close to death, when death had already claimed her mother. *He was never afraid.* He'd watched the couples dancing tonight with a smile. "Want to?" he asked his daughter. "Your heart," Helene replied. "Not me, you—you should dance. Go on." She shook her head and continued to sit by him.

Helene looked over the railing. The water was down there somewhere, she could hear it churning. The first day they were on the ship there had been a muster of all the passengers. They had been instructed in how to use their life jackets and where to gather if the alarm sounded. They had been told never to even think of diving off the ship; it was a long way down, you could break your neck, you could drown. Sharks could eat you. You might never be found.

I wish I could give the rest of it to him, Helene thought. *Daddy would know what to do with another half a life. To me it's just a burden.* Helene closed her eyes and tried to pray. She opened her eyes and felt foolish.

The canal was wide enough now, and the ship began to turn. The world revolved around Helene and she saw the way ahead; they were about to pass under an enormous bridge. She tilted her head back to see the silhouette of the underside of the bridge, menacing and close in the dark. She felt dizzy. She looked down and saw her hands on the railing, hands suddenly unfamiliar, knobby-knuckled and spotted.

Oh! she thought. *Is it really that easy?* She put her hands to her soft, wrinkled face, looked down at her now-loose clothing. Her heart pounded; her vision blurred. Aches and pains beset her. The sounds of the world were suddenly muted. The ship sailed on as before.

Helene began to creep along the railing, back to the cabin, joyously certain of what she would find there.

About "Backward in Seville"

In June 2011 I accompanied a friend on a Mediterranean cruise. The ship was small (for a cruise ship), and most of the other passengers were older British people, many of them regulars who came every year and knew one another. My friend had been on many such cruises. She had taken them with her husband, and after he died she had been accompanied by various friends. We sat with different people at meals, and when our dining companions discovered I was a writer they always asked, "Are you going to write about this cruise?" "No, no," I said. "I'm just here to hang out with my friend."

Before I got onto the ship I had already decided to write in response to Ray Bradbury's "The Playground," which has always seemed to me equally horrifying and touching, a perfect evocation of the terrors of parenting and childhood. So as I wandered the ship's decks watching the other passengers, I was thinking about impossible gifts, and it was a very small mental flip to imagine a grown child trading places with her elderly parent, instead of a parent taking the place of his child.

So I did end up writing about the cruise after all, and if any of my fellow passengers read this, I hope you will pardon my impudence. It was too perfect to resist.

—Audrey Niffenegger

EARTH (A GIFT SHOP)

Charles Yu

Come to Earth! Yes, that Earth. A lot of people think we're closed during construction, but we are not! We're still open for business.

Admittedly, it's a little confusing.

First, we were Earth: The Planet. Then life formed, and that was a great and good time.

And then, for a little while, we were Earth: A Bunch of Civilizations!

Until the fossil fuels ran out and all of the nation-states collapsed and a lucky few escaped Earth and went out in search of new worlds to colonize.

Then, for what seemed like forever, we were Earth: Not Much Going On Here Anymore.

And that lasted for a long time. Followed by another pretty long time. Which was then followed by a really long time.

Then, after a while, humans, having semi-successfully established colonies on other planets, started to come back to Earth on vacation. Parents brought their kids, teachers brought their classes on field trips, retirees came in groups of twenty or thirty. They wanted to see where their ancestors had come from. But there was nothing here. Kids and parents and teachers left, disappointed. *That's it?* they would say, or some would even say, *It was okay I guess, but I thought there would be more*.

So, being an enterprising species and all, some of us got together and reinvented ourselves as Earth: The Museum, which we thought was a great idea.

We pooled our resources and assembled what we could find. To be sure, there was not a whole lot of good stuff left after the collapse of Earth: A Bunch of Civilizations! One of us had a recording of Maria Callas singing the Violetta aria in *La Traviata*. We all thought it sounded very pretty, so we had that playing in a room in the museum. And I think maybe we had a television playing episodes of *The Tonight Show Starring Johnny Carson*. The main attraction of the museum was the painting we had by some guy of some flowers. No one could remember the name of the guy or the painting, or even the flowers, but we were all pretty sure it was an important painting at some point in the history of paintings and also the history of people, so we put that in the biggest room in the center of everything.

But parents and teachers, being humans (and especially being descendants of the same humans who messed everything up in the first place) thought the whole museum was quite boring, or even *very* boring, and they would say as much, even while we were still within earshot, and we could hear them saying that to each other, about how bored they were. That hurt to hear, but more than that what was hurtful was that no one was coming to Earth anymore, now that it was a small and somewhat eclectic museum. And who could blame them? After the collapse of civilization, school just has never been the same. By the time kids are done with their five years of mandatory schooling, they are eight or even nine years old and more than ready to join the leisure force as full-time professional consumers. Humans who went elsewhere have carried on that tradition from their days on Earth. They are ready to have their credit accounts opened, for their spending to be tracked, to get started in their lifelong loyalty rewards programs. Especially those humans who are rich enough to be tourists coming back here to Earth.

Eventually one of us realized that the most popular part of the museum was the escalator ride. Although you would think interstellar travel would have sort of raised the bar on what was needed to impress people, there was just something about moving diagonally that seemed to amuse the tourists, both kids and adults, and then one of us finally woke up and said, well, why not give them what they want?

So we did some research, in the few books we had left, and on the computer, and the research confirmed our hypothesis: Humans love rides.

So Earth: The Museum was shuttered for several years while we reinvented ourselves and developed merchandise and attractions, all of the things we were naturally good at, and after another good long while, we finally were able to reopen as Earth: The Theme Park and Gift Shop, which did okay but it was not too long before we realized the theme park part of it was expensive to operate and kind of a hassle, really, as our engineering was not so good and we kept making people sick or, in a few cases, really misjudging g-forces, and word got out among the travel agencies that Earth: The Theme Park and Gift Shop was not so fun and actually quite dangerous, so we really had no choice but to drop the theme park part and that is how we became Earth: The Gift Shop.

Which was all anyone ever wanted anyway. To get a souvenir to take home.

We do have some great souvenirs.

Our top-selling items for the month of October:

1. *History: The Poster!* A 36" x 24" color poster showing all of the major phases of human history. From the Age Before Tools, through the short-lived but exciting Age of Tools, to the (yawn) Age of Learning, and into our current age, the Age After the Age of Learning.

2. *War: The Soundtrack.* A three-minute musical interpretation of the experience of war, with solos for guitar and drums. Comes in an instrumental version (for karaoke lovers).

3. *Art: The Poster!* Beautiful painting of a nature scene. Very realistic-looking, almost like a photograph. Twenty percent off if purchased with History: The Poster!

4. *God, the Oneness: A Mystical 3-D Journey.* 22-minute DVD. Never-before-seen footage. Comes with special glasses for viewing.

5. *Science: The Video Game.* All the science you ever need to bother with! Almost nothing to learn. So easy you really don't have to pay attention. For ages three to ninety-three.

6. *Summer in a Bottle.* Sure, no one can go outside on Earth anymore because it's 170 degrees Fahrenheit, but who needs outside when they have laboratory-synthesized Summer in a Bottle? Now comes in two odors: "Mist of Nostalgia" or "Lemony Fresh."

7. *Happiness: A Skin Lotion.* At last you can be content and moisturized, at the same time. From the makers of Adventure: A Body Spray.

Other strong sellers for the month include Psychologically Comforting Teddy Bear and Shakespeare: The Fortune Cookie. All of the items above also come in ring tones, T-shirts, cups, and key chains.

And coming for the holidays, get ready for the latest installment of Earth's greatest artistic work of the last century: *Hero*

Story: A Hero's Redemption (and Sweet Revenge), a computer-generated script based on all the key points of the archetypal story arc that we humans are.

Which brings us back to our original point. What was our original point? Oh yeah, Earth: The Gift Shop is still here. Not just here, but doing great! Okay, maybe not great, but okay, we're okay. We would be better if you came by and shopped here. Which is why we sent you this audio catalog, which we hope you are reading (otherwise we are talking to ourselves). Earth: The Gift Shop: The Brochure. Some people have said the name, Earth: The Gift Shop, is a bit confusing because it makes it seem like this is the official gift shop of some other attraction here on Earth, when really the attraction is the gift shop itself. So we are considering changing our name to Earth (A Gift Shop), which sounds less official but is probably more accurate. Although if we are going down that road, it should be pointed out that the most accurate name would be Earth = A Gift Shop, or even Earth = Merchandise, since basically, if we are being honest with ourselves, we are a theme park without the park part, which is to say we are basically just a theme, whatever that means, although Earth, an Empty Theme Park would be an even worse name than Earth = A Gift Shop, so for now we're just going to stick with what we've got, until something better comes along.

So, again, we say: Come to Earth! We get millions of visitors a year, from near and far. Some of you come by accident. No shame in that! We don't care if you are just stopping to refuel, or if you lost your way, or even if you just want to rest for a moment and eat a sandwich and drink a cold bottle of beer. We still have beer! Of course, we prefer if you come here intentionally. Many of you do. Many of you read about this place in a guidebook, and some of you even go out of your way and take a detour from your travels to swing by the gift shop. Maybe you are coming because you just want to look, or to say you were here. Maybe you are coming to have a story to tell when you get back. Maybe you just want to be able to say: I went home. Even if it isn't home, was never your home, is not anyone's home anymore, maybe you just want to say, I touched the ground there, breathed the air, looked at the moon the way people must have done nine or ten or a hundred thousand years ago. So you can say to your friends, if only for a moment or two: I was a human on Earth. Even if all I did was shop there.

About "Earth (A Gift Shop)"

The Ray Bradbury story that inspired me was "There Will Come Soft Rains," which is about a fully automated house that is still running all of its domestic routines after its human inhabitants have all perished. I was drawn to the idea of telling a story about people through their technology. We can imagine the morning rush of the family who lived in this house: up out of bed, into the shower, down the stairs for toast and oatmeal, coffee for the parents, out the door to face the day at school and work. Our technology will outlive us (unless, of course, we all become cyborgs, in which case I suppose we will become our technology), and future archaeologists will write research papers on their discoveries of the cultural artifacts we are leaving behind.

In my story, I wanted to imagine what it would be like to look at our artifacts now, as outsiders, in a kind of real-time archaeology, or self-anthropology. The artifacts I invent are a bit exaggerated, but not much. Shopping at a mall or theme park these days, I am amazed at how skilled we are at "productizing" things, and I imagine what these packaged cultural products will look like to people a few hundred years from now. In trying to come up with somewhat silly ideas for products, it struck me (not for the first time) how prescient Mr. Bradbury was, how amazing it is that he came up with the "parlor walls" of *Fahrenheit 451* almost sixty years ago(!), and now we can go to the local big-box retailer and buy a high-definition 52-inch flat-screen parlor wall for five or six hundred dollars.

—Charles Yu

HAYLEIGH'S DAD

Julia Keller

Hayleigh and Sharon were forbidden to play in the basement. Hayleigh's dad, Ed Westin, had been uncharacteristically severe on that point. "Never, never, *never,*" he said, inserting a sudden dark barb of seriousness into his otherwise mild voice, to indicate that he meant business, "play in the basement, girls. Got it?" He could be a teaser, a clown; he was definitely one of those "fun dads" whom Sharon deeply, silently admired—her own father, Larry Leinart, being a sour, dreary, disapproving man who seemed to nurse a secret grudge throughout his day, touching it constantly with his thoughts the way you bump a sore finger against everything you reach for—but on the subject of the basement, Hayleigh's dad was not fun at all. He was firm. Borderline scary.

"Are we totally clear on that, kids?"

They nodded. Not in unison: Hayleigh nodded first, because this was, after all, her house and her dad, and then Sharon joined in.

"So we're clear," Ed Westin reconfirmed. His face was blank. No smile crossed it, which was unusual; he had a permanent wrinkle on each side of his mouth, just from smiling so much. At this moment Hayleigh's dad reminded Sharon of her own father—hard and mean—although Sharon could tell that Mr. Westin's mood was prompted by concern for their safety, so she forgave him. And anyway, most of the time Hayleigh's dad was *nothing* like her dad, in all kinds of ways. Ed Westin was short and kind of pudgy. The girls had discussed this clinically, neutrally, not cruelly. Larry Leinart was tall and slender, with a narrow waist and wide shoulders. His dark suits fit him perfectly, like animal skin.

In a way, Sharon had often thought, it was the reverse of how things ought to be. Ed Westin was the one you'd think would be sleek and solid, because he worked outside with his hands. He was an electrician for Cozad Brothers Construction. Larry Leinart sat behind a desk all day; he was a lawyer with a big law firm downtown. However, as Sharon had been quick to point out to Hayleigh, her father didn't handle interesting cases involving murders or kidnappings. Instead he focused on things such as corporate mergers and property transfers. No wonder he was so glum all the time. His work was boring and he had to dress up for it. Suit, tie, stiff white shirt, loafers. Whereas Hayleigh's dad got to wear jeans and a flannel shirt and boots and a baseball cap.

Sharon and Hayleigh had both turned eight years old that fall. They had not been best friends very long. Friendship was a serious thing, with clear, grimly implacable rules. Everybody had one and *only one* best friend, and that person had to be chosen as your companion *every single time*, on the playground at recess, or eating lunch in the cafeteria, or whatever.

Sharon had always wanted to be friends with Hayleigh Westin, but until recently, it just hadn't been possible. Hayleigh's original best friend was a thin, quiet girl named Samantha Bollinger, and Sharon's original best friend was actually a boy: Greg Pugh. Normally the gender rule for best friends was absolute—girls with girls, boys with boys—but Greg's family had lived next door to Sharon's family since before either Sharon or Greg was born, and he and Sharon had been playing together since they were toddlers, so they got a pass. They were best friends through the first and second grades and the first part of the third.

Then Samantha Bollinger's parents split up and she and her mother left town. It was very sudden, and to Sharon's delight, it left Hayleigh without a best friend. Sharon was happy to fill the void. Greg Pugh was on his own now.

A few times that fall, when Hayleigh and Sharon were bored, they would ride their bikes slowly past Samantha's old house—it was two streets over from Hayleigh's house—and let their eyes slide over in that direction. Samantha's dad still lived there, all by himself. If he happened to be getting into his car at the time and spotted them, he would glare. Once, he started to raise his fist, as if he wanted to shout something, but then seemed to get hold of himself. He lowered his fist. He was a mean dad, Sharon instantly realized, not a fun dad.

Samantha's house didn't look the same anymore. No bike lay on its side on the front lawn, its tires still spinning because it had been flung away moments ago by Samantha when she raced inside for a juice box. The curtains in the window of what had been Samantha's bedroom weren't pink anymore. Her dad must've changed the curtains. The house seemed to breathe sour air in and out too slowly, like an old person with respiratory problems.

Samantha had been a runner, the best runner in school, with long legs that moved with such natural grace that she didn't even seem to be trying; it looked as if running was a normal state for her, like walking is for other people. Yet once Samantha was gone, she was gone, almost as if she'd been running somewhere at dusk one evening and had just kept right on going, her long, thin body merging with the purplish pink twilight, folding herself into it, like somebody leaving the stage of the school auditorium and slipping between the heavy pleats of the curtain, and after a slight stir in the fabric—*poof*, that's it. Gone.

Sharon was not a good runner. She was chunky. Borderline fat. Increasingly, that had begun to irritate her father—he had started commenting on her food intake, turning the family dinner table into a very tense place—but Sharon's size didn't seem to bother Hayleigh at all. Sharon, in fact, was the opposite of Samantha Bollinger in lots of ways. Samantha was quiet, and Sharon was talkative. Samantha had been a "poor-to-average" student—that was a phrase Sharon had overheard when two teachers were chatting about Samantha one day, and she loved its suggestion of shabbiness, of hopeless mediocrity—while Sharon excelled in her classes. Sharon was "bright," a word that several of her teachers had used when referring to her. She liked English and math and science. She was fascinated by rockets and space travel. Also atomic energy.

Maybe, Sharon thought, Hayleigh appreciated the contrast. Maybe she'd been secretly tired of Samantha Bollinger and her perfect stride and the way she'd sit in class, the knees of her long legs bumping up against the bottom of the desk, her face glazed with incomprehension, not even bothering to *pretend* she understood what the teacher was saying. Sharon always pretended, even if she was lost. She wasn't lost often, but when it happened, she still leaned forward, still looked bright and earnest and eager. Her theory was that if you looked like you got it, sooner or later, you'd get it.

When Sharon told Hayleigh's dad about that theory, Ed Westin had laughed and said, "Fake it till you make it, sweetie, fake it till you make it!" He seemed proud of her, as if for the moment she was actually his daughter, his flesh and blood, which gave Sharon a funny little flutter in her stomach. It wasn't a bad feeling at all. She worried at first about the disloyalty to her own family, but then she just let go and enjoyed the feeling. It was like riding your bike barefoot on a summer day: You knew you weren't supposed to do it, because it was dangerous—if you caught a toe in the spokes, there'd be a bloody mess—but it felt so good and so free that you did it anyway.

Hayleigh's dad had to leave. He was supposed to stay there Saturday morning while Sharon and Hayleigh played—that was the deal, that was the arrangement, that was what Sharon had told her mom before she left her house—*Hayleigh's dad is gonna be there the whole time, geez, it's fine*—but now he had to go.

Sharon could tell he didn't want to, but he had no choice.

He had called his boss to check on a job. That's when he got the bad news. It was about the wiring. Somebody else had done something wrong, another electrician had "screwed up royally," according to what Hayleigh's dad was saying into his cell phone. His voice was crisp and businesslike, even though he had just described himself to his boss as "really, *really* pissed off." Hayleigh and Sharon listened avidly to his end of the call.

"Okay," Hayleigh's dad was saying. He was pacing, holding the cell with one hand, scratching the back of his head with the other. "Okay. Okay, Roy. Yeah. I think I can get it done. But you tell everybody else to back off, okay? Don't mess with it. I'm on my way."

He flipped his cell shut and looked down at Hayleigh and Sharon. They were stretched out on the floor of the living room. They were just hanging out, which was typical for a Saturday.

Hayleigh had assured Sharon—so that Sharon in turn could assure her mom—that her dad would stick around, would keep an eye on them. It was silly, really; they were plenty old enough to stay by themselves. And sometimes, for short periods of time, they were allowed to. When Hayleigh came over to her house, for instance, Sharon's mom would sometimes leave for a little while to pick up stuff at the dry cleaners, and that was okay. Sharon wasn't sure the Westins ever left stuff at the dry cleaners, the way the Leinarts did every single week, because, Sharon knew, her dad's shirts and suits had to be dry-cleaned perfectly and he could be "a real prick about it," which was the phrase Sharon had heard her mom use once, when she didn't know Sharon was listening.

"It's just for a little while," Hayleigh's dad was saying to them. "An hour, maybe. Hour and a half, tops. We've got this big project out by the mall—you've seen it, right? The office park? Well, some friggin' idiot put the breakers in wrong, and the whole thing's arcing and sparking."

Sharon was impressed. Her father would never have said "friggin'" in front of her. Nor would he expose the sort of passion that Ed Westin was showing. Ed Westin cared about his job, about things being done the right way. Sharon could tell. He had once worked for NASA, Hayleigh had told Sharon, and she said it casually, but they both knew how cool that was. He'd been in the U.S. Navy at the time, and he and his crew had been called in to do some electrical work on one of the space shuttles. He didn't talk about it, but when Sharon looked at his hands, she could imagine it: Hayleigh's dad, twisting wires, checking connections, then nodding at somebody and giving the thumbs-up sign. He made sure everything would work perfectly in outer space.

"So it won't take me very long," he said. "I'll be back before you know it. Way before lunchtime. I promise."

He was looming over them, frowning, like he wasn't quite sure. Hayleigh and Sharon were lying on their stomachs on the living room carpet, their chins propped up on their palms. They'd been watching TV—it was a rerun of *Buffy the Vampire Slayer*, which Sharon was not allowed to watch at home, a fact that added a special bit of deliciousness to the show—when Hayleigh's dad came into the room, talking on his cell. Hayleigh had politely turned down the volume on the set during her father's call.

"You girls'll be okay, right?" he said. He looked dubious. Sharon could see how torn he was, torn between two kinds of duty.

"Sure, Dad," Hayleigh said. She didn't elaborate, didn't ridicule his concerns. Sharon took note: Hayleigh didn't overplay her hand. Too much reassurance was always a red flag for a parent. Hayleigh, Sharon had to concede, was pretty smart. Not book-smart—that was Sharon's specialty—but smart when it came to dealing with parents.

"Okay," he said.

Then came the warning. "But no playing in the basement, you two," Hayleigh's dad added. "Absolutely, positively not. Okay?"

Bored nods from both of them. Hayleigh didn't even take her eyes from the TV screen, which Sharon thought was another nice touch. On the screen, Buffy had just karate-kicked a bad vampire.

"Never, never, *never* play in the basement. Got it?" Hayleigh's dad went on. "Are we clear on that, girls?"

Sharon nodded again, but Hayleigh—unexpectedly clever Hayleigh!—looked up at her father as if she'd forgotten he was even there, so absorbed was she in the plot of the *Buffy* episode. They were so wrapped up in the drama that, chances were, Hayleigh's dad would leave and return without either girl having moved an inch from her spot right here on the living room floor. Frankly, Hayleigh's expression implied, there was zero chance that they would even *think* about the basement, much less venture down there. They were far too preoccupied to remember that the basement even *existed*.

The girls continued to stare at the TV screen while Hayleigh's dad foraged for his truck keys and his dark blue windbreaker and his red baseball cap with COZAD BROS woven in cursive white letters across the crown. As he pulled open the front door, still looking a bit worried, he said, "See you later, girls. If you need me, I've got my cell," and they grunted back at him, which, here in Hayleigh's house, constituted an acceptable reply but in her own house, Sharon knew, would not have been tolerated. And then he was gone.

At first they didn't move. They watched the TV screen, their chins still perched in their palms. Then each girl's eyes slid over to meet her friend's eyes. They heard the truck starting up in the driveway, the dull, dusty roar. The roar slacked off as Hayleigh's dad backed his truck out of the driveway.

The noise diminished again and then disappeared completely. They were alone. Unsupervised.

They didn't say a word, but each girl knew exactly what the other one was going to do, as surely as if it had been planned, plotted, carefully choreographed days ago.

It was a race to see which girl could scramble to her feet faster—although it really wasn't much of a race at all, because Sharon was slow and clumsy on account of her weight, so Hayleigh won easily—and then to see who could be the first to make it to the kitchen in order to lunge for the black knob on the white basement door.

Hayleigh got there first, but before she could turn the knob, Sharon had arrived, too, right beside her, and she put her hand on top of Hayleigh's hand. So, in effect, they opened it together.

And likewise, once they'd opened the door and bolted across the threshold, and even though Sharon was large, they were able to head down the stairs side by side, breaking the rule at exactly the same moment, so that it could never be said that one girl was more responsible, that one girl was more to blame for what happened than the other girl. You could not say that.

* * *

Which one of them turned on the light over the basement stairs?

Sharon couldn't remember whose fingers had actually scrabbled at the wall switch just inside the basement door, dousing the staircase with light. It didn't matter. All she knew was that they were hurrying down those stairs, elbows bumping, feet shuffling in that tumbling rhythm induced by a succession of downward steps, and there was an overhead light to show them the way, to keep them from tripping. They were giggling, too, but the giggles popped up in between their panting breaths, so the giggles sounded like hiccoughs. The steps creaked a little bit, especially right at the top.

Why were they rushing? Sharon wasn't sure. Hayleigh's dad would be gone for at least an hour. It took about twenty minutes to drive out to the mall; it might take even longer on a Saturday, when the traffic stacked up because everybody was crazy to get to The Limited and Forever 21 and Sears. Even if Hayleigh's dad finished his job right away, which wasn't likely, given the seriousness of his voice when he talked to his boss—it seemed, Sharon thought, like a big, complex task, a real mess—they'd still have way over an hour to explore.

So why did they fly down the basement stairs, bumping and laughing?

She didn't know. Hayleigh probably didn't know either, Sharon guessed. Hayleigh had only been down here a few times herself, she'd told Sharon, even though she lived here; this was her dad's special place.

It just seemed natural for them to go down the steps quickly, headlong, not tentatively. Maybe it was because, if they chickened out on the way, their scrambling momentum would carry them forward. Somehow they both had known, without talking about it, that the moment Hayleigh's dad told them not to go down into the basement—"Never, never, *never*"—they'd come here. Right away. When you're best friends with someone, Sharon reflected, that's what happens: You start to know what the other person is thinking. It's automatic.

They reached the bottom of the staircase. And then Sharon understood. She immediately realized why Hayleigh's dad had declared the basement off-limits. This was Ed Westin's workshop, and it was gorgeous. The kind of space you don't want a couple of kids messing up.

It was the coolest workshop Sharon had ever seen. Everything gleamed. There were high wooden workbenches along three walls. Rising from the backs of the benches were square sheets of dark brown particleboard perforated by dozens of small, elegant holes. Tiny silver hooks jutted from the holes. From the hooks dangled a stunning variety of tools—hammers, chisels, drills, clamps, levels—in graduated sizes. It was all neatly organized.

Sharon didn't know the names of a lot of the tools. She knew hammers, of course, and screwdrivers and drills, things like that, but some of the more specialized tools looked complicated. They looked densely compacted with a single-minded purpose. You could, Sharon thought with deep satisfaction, build anything down here. Anything you wanted to build.

A cabinet, a bookcase, a table, a boat. Anything.

Even a rocket.

"It's the tools," Hayleigh said. "That's why he doesn't like us coming down here. Messing with his stuff."

Sharon did not require the explanation. She'd never have even *touched* anything in this room. It was all too beautiful. Too perfect. She wouldn't consider putting a finger on one of the workbenches, because the wood had been stained a deep honey color, shiny and rich, a color that looked as if a dozen years of sunlight had been trapped in the lacquer. She'd never pick up one of the drills. She had too much respect for Hayleigh's dad to do that.

"It's *amazing*," Sharon said.

"Yeah."

They were still standing at the bottom of the stairs. They hadn't moved forward since arriving there, arms hanging at their sides, heads turning.

Sharon wasn't sure how she knew, but she did: Hayleigh's dad was building something very special in this basement. That was why he didn't want people coming down here. Sure, he was worried about them possibly bothering his tools—but there was more to it than that.

A *lot* more.

The realization gave Sharon a tingling sensation in the tips of her fingers and her toes. She knew what Hayleigh's dad was building down here.

She couldn't tell Hayleigh that she'd figured it out. Because the thing was, Hayleigh might not know herself yet, and it would be embarrassing for Hayleigh if Sharon—who wasn't even related—knew before his own daughter knew. Sharon loved puzzles; she loved thinking hard about something until the answer came to her, clearly and vividly. She was good at doing that. Good at crossword puzzles, and sudoku and Scrabble and chess. Anything that required furious concentration, with some imagination sprinkled in, too. Hayleigh seemed to appreciate Sharon's mind—she didn't resent it, she wasn't the least bit jealous of it—which made Sharon wonder why Hayleigh had wasted all that time with Samantha Bollinger, who, after all, wasn't very bright. Borderline stupid.

"Your dad worked for the space shuttle, right?" Sharon said. She knew the answer, of course, because they'd discussed it many times, but she wanted to lead Hayleigh toward the truth about her dad's project. Hayleigh would think she'd gotten there all by herself, and would be proud and pleased with herself. Sharon would never reveal that she'd helped her solve it, helped her with a series of hints. It would be enough for Sharon to know, deep in her heart, that she had made her friend feel smart.

"Yeah," Hayleigh said. She shrugged. "When he was in the navy."

"So he likes space stuff, right?"

"Yeah, I guess."

"I bet he could build anything." Sharon swept her chubby arm around the room, indicating the vast bounty of tools. "With all this stuff, I mean. I bet he could build whatever he wanted to."

"Yeah. So." Another shrug.

Hayleigh started to walk toward one of the benches. Sharon pinched a piece of Hayleigh's T-shirt when her friend went by; the fabric stretched out behind her as she kept on going.

"Wait," Sharon said. "You can't touch anything. Your dad'll know we were here."

"Let go." Hayleigh pulled her T-shirt out of Sharon's grasp. Then she shrugged. Sharon had once counted how many times Hayleigh shrugged in the course of just one hour: The astonishing total was seventeen.

"I'm not gonna *do* anything," Hayleigh went on. "I'm just looking around."

"Well, be careful."

Sharon wished Hayleigh would pay attention and concentrate. She was close. So close. Close to figuring out what Sharon had figured out about what Hayleigh's dad was building down here.

As she watched Hayleigh touch the tools, one by one, just a brief tap with two fingers and then on to the next tool, all around the room, Sharon let a picture of her own father rise up in her mind. Dressed in a suit and tie, he was holding a slim black leather briefcase, frowning. You could not fit *any* of these tools in that stupid briefcase, Sharon thought. Not a single one. Her father didn't know how to build anything. He always called people to do work on their house: plumbers, carpenters, electricians. He'd called somebody to put a brick patio in the back. And if something broke—the stove or the refrigerator, the TV—he called somebody to handle that, too. Her father was always mad about something. Something was always "the height of absurdity." That was the phrase he used. Her dad didn't like things that were illogical or pointless or wasteful. He didn't like half-finished projects or unmade beds or dirty dishes left in the sink. Or fat daughters.

But Hayleigh's dad was different. He smiled a lot more than Sharon's dad did, and made jokes, and teased her and Hayleigh—but that wasn't the *most* different thing about him, Sharon now understood.

When they had first reached the bottom of the basement staircase, Sharon noticed it in the corner. That was her first clue. A piece of gray metal, shiny, cupped like a giant palm, running from the floor to the ceiling, resembling the side of an airplane *or* . . .

A rocket.

That was it. That was the secret.

Hayleigh's dad, Sharon realized, was building a rocket in this basement. He couldn't discuss it, because it was probably illegal. You were probably supposed to get a government permit or something. But Hayleigh's dad was not the kind of person who filled out forms and waited around for government permits—unlike her own dad, Sharon thought, who always did things the right way, followed all the rules, just so he could complain when things didn't work out *after I did everything they told me to do*, he'd say bitterly—no, Hayleigh's dad wasn't like that. He was a rebel. He'd do it his own way. If he got into trouble—well, fine. He'd accept the consequences. Pay the price.

Sharon didn't know how she knew, but she knew. It was a

rocket. Hayleigh's dad had the skills, and he had the tools, and naturally he didn't want kids fooling around with his stuff. He was building a rocket down here, and one night, one night very soon, Sharon quickly theorized, he would move it outside, maybe load it into the back of his truck and take it out to the park—*no*, Sharon scolded herself, *not the park, that's a dumb idea, way too public*—take it out to the country, out to a big field with no houses in sight. There he'd kneel down and set up his rocket and light the fuse and run away and then squat down behind a tree, a finger stuck in each ear, and watch as the rocket rose with a great *whoooooosh* into the night sky, shedding sparks and smoke and one long, trailing, beautiful yellow-blue flame, as vivid and pure as the respect Sharon felt for Hayleigh's dad, respect for his dream, and for the fact that he had worked so hard to make it come true. Respect and awe.

Had Hayleigh figured it out yet? Sharon couldn't tell. Her friend was still strolling around the basement, grazing the tools with her fingertips, and Sharon began to get an odd sense that Hayleigh had been in this basement more often than she'd said she had. She seemed way too familiar with the layout, Sharon noticed. When she touched a tool, it wasn't with any degree of surprise at how it felt; she'd sneaked down here many times, Sharon suspected. It made her think slightly less of her friend.

Surely, though, if Hayleigh came down here with any regularity, then she'd figured it out by now. She must know her dad is building a rocket, Sharon thought. And maybe she'd told Samantha Bollinger.

Sharon felt a flicker of jealousy. She decided that she had to ask Hayleigh about it.

"Did you ever," Sharon said, "bring Samantha down here?" She had tried to sound casual, but her voice betrayed her. It was shaky, too high-pitched. There was also a hint of belligerence in it.

"Huh?"

"Before she moved away, I mean," Sharon said. "Did you and Samantha ever come down here, too?"

Hayleigh shrugged. She'd positioned her palm along the front of one of the tall workbenches. She followed the smooth beveled edge all the way to the end of it. Then she looked back at Sharon. Her eyes were blank.

"Samantha," Hayleigh said, "didn't move away."

"What?"

"Samantha disappeared. They never found her. She rode off on her bike one day, and she never came home. She'd told her mom she was coming over here, but that wasn't true. We never saw her." Hayleigh's voice was flat. Calmly informational. "It drove her mom crazy and she killed herself. Remember? She locked herself in that garage and turned on the car engine, and that's how she died. Don't you remember that, Sharon? I don't know why you always want to go past their house. Just her dad lives there now, all by himself. He's gotten sort of crazy. Crazy from being so sad. And from thinking all these weird things about me and my dad."

It was true. Sharon had to admit it. She had blocked out the real story of Samantha Bollinger, told herself another story she liked better, changed Samantha's fate, so that it suited what Sharon wanted to feel.

"Anyway," Sharon said. "You get it now, right? You've figured out what your dad does down here, right?"

"Yeah," Hayleigh said. She shrugged. "I guess I'm sorta surprised that you figured it out, though. So soon, I mean."

So soon? Sharon wanted to laugh. *I'm smart,* she thought. *I may be fat and ugly, but I'm smart, okay? I'm a smart girl.*

That's what her father had said to her once: *At least you've got brains.* She could fill in the first part of the sentence, the part he didn't say but clearly meant: *You may be fat but at least you've got brains.*

"Your dad's building a rocket down here," Sharon said, blurting it out. She wanted to giggle, too, just from how thrilling it all was. *A rocket! Think of it!*

"But listen," Sharon added quickly. "I can keep a secret. Really. I won't tell anybody."

Hayleigh looked at her.

There was a noise at the top of the basement stairs. The board creaked sharply when the weight hit it, the concentrated mass of a booted foot. *Hayleigh's dad can fix that* was the thought, lightning-quick, that came to Sharon. *He can fix that squeak. Bet it's already on his to-do list.* She didn't take her eyes away from Hayleigh's eyes. The next noise was a heavy clumping transit down the stairs. With an extraordinarily fluid motion Hayleigh's dad hooked his hand around Sharon's neck, while with his other hand he covered her mouth, cutting off her scream.

He was dragging her toward the shiny metal in the corner, pulling her by her neck as if she were a large, lumpy sack, her fat legs useless and churning, and Sharon had a realization—extra-bright, extra-sharp, an explosion of insight illuminating her mind's sky—that he had only pretended to be talking to his boss, that there hadn't been any emergency at any job site. Then Sharon had another vision, just as bright, just as sharp, a vision of flying over rooftops and passing over her very own house, and down below were her mom and her dad and her sisters, Elizabeth and Meagan, and her dog, Oliver, and her chemistry set, the beakers and flasks lined up in a tidy row across the top of her bookshelf, just the way she'd left them. She imagined the sound of Hayleigh's voice on the phone, earnest and concerned: *I don't know Mrs. Leinart she left my house a while ago to walk home and she didn't say she was stopping anywhere I don't know we'll call if we hear from her oh yes.*

Then Sharon heard the shriek of the metal as it scraped against the basement floor, she saw the shiny flap of that metal as Hayleigh wrenched it back with experienced fingers, and she smelled a dirty, earthen smell, dark and wet and cold and final. Something pushed hard at her back and something smashed against the side of her head and Sharon was falling, falling bluntly and heavily, like a rocket from the sky.

About "Hayleigh's Dad"

With Ray Bradbury, I ate dessert first. That is, as a kid with an insatiable literary sweet tooth, I devoured the science-fiction stories and the thrilling tales, inhaling them with awe and gusto the same way I gorged on Tootsie Rolls and Caravelle candy bars, reveling in *The Martian Chronicles* and *The Illustrated Man.* Later, as an adult, I came to the main course: the novels and the essays—and those same short stories upon which I had feasted as a child. Now, however, I could appreciate the artistic rigor that had gone into making them seem so effortlessly tossed off. They read like facts of nature, not like written works, which is the surest proof of Ray Bradbury's phenomenal, cloud-topping imagination: His stories feel inevitable.

The direct inspiration for "Hayleigh's Dad" is "The Whole Town's Sleeping," a diabolically creepy Bradbury story whose ending left me limp with exhaustion and buzzing with fear. Never before or since has a story taken hold of me in quite that way. As I read it the first time, it gripped my arm and carried me along, trusting and compliant—and then, at the end, it yanked the solid earth right out from under me and tossed me into darkness. I flailed. I gasped. And subsequently wondered what clever alien species had, under cover of night, delivered this bespectacled wizard to our unsuspecting world, this "Ray

Bradbury," this genial genius, this possessor of magical powers and inimitable narrative derring-do.

Discovering Ray's book of essays *Zen in the Art of Writing* was a major turning point in my literary ambitions. He gave me permission to dream, to be bold, to take off the training wheels and snip the line tethering me to convention and propriety. "For the first thing a writer should be," he declared, "is excited. He should be a thing of fevers and enthusiasms," whose words "slammed the page like a lightning bolt." My fingertips still sizzle when I recall this passage.

To those aliens who gave us Ray Bradbury—what other plausible origin could there be for this brilliant, dazzling craftsman and poet, except one involving extraterrestrial intervention?—we ought to say thanks, and to make it very, very clear that they can't have him back.

—Julia Keller

WHO KNOCKS?

Dave Eggers

When I was a kid in the suburbs of Chicago, during the summer we'd go to Quetico Provincial Park up on the border of Minnesota and Canada. "Provincial" implies that the place was small, but Quetico was, and still is, a million-acre nature preserve—so big you could go days and days without seeing another soul.

We would go on camping trips up there—weeks of canoeing and portaging, spotting bears and moose and deer, sleeping under star-soaked skies. The park was isolated and so pristine that you could actually drink the water straight from the lakes. You'd stick your paddle in, tilt the wide part to the clouds, and let the water run into your mouth.

I miss Quetico, but I won't be going back anytime soon. Not after what happened to a girl named Frances Brandywine.

This was a few years ago. Frances was seventeen at the time, black-haired and with a reckless nature, determined always to leave the well-trod path, to break new ground and be alone.

Frances was up in Quetico with her family, in a remote part of the park, camped on the shore of one of the deeper lakes—a lonely body of dark water carved millions of years ago by a passing glacier.

One night, after her family went to bed, Frances took the rowboat out, planning to find a quiet spot in the middle of the lake, lie on the bench of the boat, look up at the sky, and maybe write in her journal.

So she left the shore and rowed for about twenty minutes, and when she was satisfied that she was over the lake's deepest spot, she lay down and looked up at the night sky. The stars were very bright, the aurora borealis shimmering like a neon lasso. She was feeling very peaceful.

Then she heard something strange. It was like a knock. *Clop clop.*

She sat up, guessing that the boat had drifted to shore and run aground. But she looked around the boat, and she was still a half mile from shore. She leaned over the side, to see if she'd hit anything. But she saw nothing. No log, no rocks.

She lay back down, telling herself that it could have been any number of things—a fish, a turtle, a stick that had drifted under the boat.

She relaxed again, and soon fell into a contented reverie. She had just closed her eyes when she heard another knock. This time it was louder, a crisp *clok clok clok*. Like the sound of someone knocking hard on a wooden door. Except this knocking was coming from the bottom of the boat.

Now she was scared. She leaned over the side again. It had to be an animal. But what kind of animal would knock like that, three short, loud knocks in rapid succession?

Her mouth went dry. She held on to each side of the boat, and now she could only wait to see if it happened again. The silence stretched out. A few minutes passed, and just as she began to think she'd imagined it all, the knocks came again. But this time louder. *Bam bam bam!*

She had to leave. She lunged for the oars, got them into place, and began rowing. The water was very calm, so she should have made quick progress. But after rowing feverishly for minutes she looked around and realized, with cold dread, that she wasn't moving at all. Something was keeping her exactly where she was.

Her mind clawed through options. She thought about leaving the boat, swimming to shore. But she knew the water was so cold that she'd freeze before getting far. And besides, whatever was knocking on the bottom of the boat *was in that water.*

Again she tried rowing. She rowed and rowed, on the verge of tears, but she went nowhere.

She stopped. She was exhausted. Her heavy breathing filled the air. She cried. She sobbed. But soon she calmed herself, and the boat was silent again. For ten minutes, then twenty. Again she tricked herself into thinking she'd imagined it all.

But just like before, just when she was beginning to get a grip on herself, the knocking came again, this time as loud as a bass drum. *Boom boom boom!* The floorboards of the boat shook with each strike.

Now she made a bad decision. She decided to lower one of the oars into the black water, trying to feel if there was some land-mass, even some *creature* she could touch. As soon as the oar had broken the water's surface, though, she felt a strong, silent tug at the other end and the oar was pulled under.

She screamed and jumped back. Now she had no options. All she could do was sit, and hope, and wait. Wait for the morning to come. Wait for whatever was going to happen to happen.

The knocking went on through the night. Sometimes it was sudden and loud: *bam bam bam!* And sometimes quieter: *tap tap tap*. Every so often it was almost musical: *knock knock kno-ahk*.

She passed the time writing in her notebook, recording each sound, each strike. And it's only because of this notebook that we know what happened that night. Frances can't tell us. She was never seen again.

The boat was found on shore the next day, empty but for the journal. On those pages were her frantic jottings, all written in her distinctive hand.

All but the last page. When it was found, that page was still wet, and on it were four words, looking as if they'd been written quickly, with a muddy finger, perhaps in justification. They said: "I *did* knock first."

About "Who Knocks?"

I was introduced to Ray Bradbury in grade school, when we read "A Sound of Thunder," and the experience was powerful, knowing that he'd grown up in Waukegan, a few towns away from where I was raised. And every year or so thereafter, we were assigned one or another Bradbury text, and always I was floored by his boundless imagination. I have to admit, though, that I hadn't read him in many years until a few years ago, when I picked up an old edition of an anthology edited by Alfred Hitchcock called *Stories Not for the Nervous*. In it was a Bradbury story about time travel, crime, marriage, and film, all set in the 1930s in Mexico—a lot to cover in a ten-page story. But Bradbury pulled it off, brilliantly, and my respect for his body of work—the breadth and scope of which is stunning—was renewed.

—Dave Eggers

RESERVATION 2020

Bayo Ojikutu

Daily, Joseph descended the stairwell, then walked along the ground-floor path aside his housing unit. He'd slip coins into a red machine at corridor's end to buy a can of Coca-Cola—and so he'd continue to believe that the old America was nearby. No matter the ninnies' chants, nor what he did not see along the way to that symbol of vending democracy. No flags whipped in mountain wind, nor stone totem temples to founders and settlers, nor upright souls traipsing along paved gold—yet Coca-Cola remained the Chief Bottler of Empire, never to slough off into the abyss. Joseph tasted the nectar slowly, let bubbles sting along his lip and throat, and felt the bite at what remained of his kidneys, and he knew. That pang, according to the fathers who'd settled their compound, was the magic elixir of treasure snatched up from dirt, hands raking through the bounty, suicide left as the aftertaste of plunder, masked by syrup and sugar and coca dope. The soul that sipped, for spare silver coin—that soul swallowed all that was to be had from the living earth, God bless it.

Now when those options were taken, and the compound's admin replaced Coke machines with a new set of off-brand selections for sale—or perhaps Royal Crown blue (did RC exist still? Perhaps in the Old World?)—while still demanding the same coin for the purchase, then he would listen to the rabble-rousing youths who blocked the square's streets each rush hour. And he might accept then that all that was good in the life of liberty was kept from them.

"They caught Chevy yet?"

There was nothing to be had in pretending the question went unheard. "Not that I know."

"Haven't heard from him yourself neither?" Joseph looked at the peach-skinned bit of androgyny perched beneath his elbow as he lowered the Coke can. Hair whipped all about the youth's shoulders; earrings poked both earlobes; another joined his nostrils together while dirty silver jutted from his upper bicuspid; eyeliner decorated the blink in doughy eyes. He carried a maroon-and-pink-checkered skateboard beneath his stubby left arm. Hadn't the settlers come to their compound to eradicate, or at least escape, such living confusion among the young? Joseph brought the beverage back to his mouth.

"Truthfully," the boyish teen purred. "You can trust me. I'm not with them."

"Mmmh, 'them.' Surely." Joseph stepped away as he mocked, although he recognized the teen as one of his son's young clamoring followers from the neighboring downstairs units.

"For sure," the boy begged. "I heard them chanting Chevy's name today in the square, after school. On my way—"

"Yeah? You made it to school today dressed like that?"

"Of course, sir, I did." He hopped and pumped a fist as if protesting in the center himself. "*Chevy! Chevy! Viva Chevy! Viva la libertad!* All afternoon, just like that."

Carbonation bit Joseph's innards as it passed along, and the soda shivered his empty gut. "In Foreigner, hey? That's how they said it in the square? What does that mean, even?" He crinkled the Coke can's rim, his taste finished.

The boy dropped his skateboard to the white stone path and scooted at Joseph's side as they headed from the machine, west toward the center square. "Not sure," he said. Lying, most likely, Joseph guessed. "Sounds like 'life and liberty.' For your son. Like he's a hero—"

"But you're not with them?" He did not intend for the boy to answer.

"I'm not with them who's lying about Chevy, trying to mark us with criminal insult on the fortieth anniversary. Not them, sir. I'm with the people."

"Demo," Joseph said, repeating the strange word Chevy had used for the rabble-rousers of his class before leaving the compound's walls.

"Yes, sir," the boy agreed, two words blown in skateboard wind. "Demo crazy. That's us."

Joseph squinted to read the sideways words scribbled along the black cotton of the boy's T-shirt, neck to hem, as he rolled along: IN THIS DARK PIT, ALONE, YOU ARE LOST. BUT HERE, I CAN SEE. TAKE MY HAND. FOLLOW ME.

The wording recalled lines from one of the rhymeless poems Joseph had found on Chevy's computer after the boy left to live with his mother. Joseph wondered who was behind printing and selling T-shirts of the boy's scribble. He could fathom neither the culprit nor the youth whose skateboard cut through an alley angling toward Reagan Square. He heard no more chanting from the core of the compound either—if it had ever been more than a figment of the skateboarder's imagination. There was only an echo of the translations of *freedom* and *love* and *life*. He wondered whether the skateboarder repeated the words while scooting off, singing another protest chant. Had he ever even mentioned love? The father tossed his Coke can into a recycling bin at alley's edge.

His street-cleaning team perched at curbside, behind their electric municipal truck and its twelve-foot trailer, hiding themselves and their equipment from the rush-hour pedestrians in the square.

"You're doing late shift, Joe." Ali wielded no more authority within the compound's officialdom than the others, yet he spoke louder than the center-square din, in the tenor of something more than a question: between a suggestion and a rough bit of advice for the most senior crew member. He continued, "Tonight's your turn, all yours."

Joseph glanced toward his chest, and his hand idly brushed the red-and-blue municipal badge stitched high on his work suit. "It's Tuesday. I was just out here Sunday night."

"So what?" Ali barked.

Sensing his compromised position, Joseph gazed at the white stone beneath them as he responded. "There's still four of us."

Marta and Harold interrupted their fiddle with the cumbersome water sprays and concrete blasters leaned between the corner and their electric truck. They watched Joseph in the corners of opposing eyes. "Can't hold any of us accountable for this," said Harold.

"But you," Marta blurted in Joseph's direction, "that's something else. Can blame you and yours all day, hey?"

Joseph swallowed the first response to his mind. His eyes trailed along the sidewalk. The others did not continue their argument—Marta and Harold pushed the oblong cleaning machines along a ramp and into the municipal truck's trailer, and

Ali peeked around the cabin, watching as the rush-hour pedestrians faded, solemnly replaced by battalions of university youths, toting signs scrawled with demands that dripped blood—calling for recognized "dreams" and "hopes" and "changes" and "acts," lest they begin "tearing down these walls" in their left fists, while their rights tossed cigarette butts off into the cracks and corners of the compound's main square.

"Yeah," Ali said over his shoulder. "You're cleaning this mess, Joe. It's on you."

"By myself? Not if we're going by a fair rotation."

"Fair?" Ali growled. "Who promised—"

"We agreed, when we started working Reagan."

"That was back before . . . ," Marta blurted again. Harold's and Ali's unblinking stares stopped her.

Joseph walked the ramp's incline, dragging a machine cord at his front. When he reached the trailer, he looked out on the center's western arc of buildings. Glimmering steel temples of outgoing capital & commerce, energy & oversight, responsible for looming over the dwelling's entirety and employing some 80 percent of the compound's quarter million residents in one way or another. A bank of digital-projector screens reached from the pinnacle of each skyscraper, featuring permed and tanned bobble-head voices humming updates as to the happenings in the Old World beyond compound walls. Joseph turned to the Rocky Mountain sky above, then to the square's crawling matinee and its repeated script. The day, time, and temperature according to the International Mercantile Bank Tower ticker blinked first and last against his eyelids as Marta and Harold jumped down from the trailer, escaping the father of the one whom the IM ticker had called an "anarchist" just two days prior.

2-July—60, 5:13P, 68 degrees-

He looked down at his coworkers. "I was out here Sunday—

gets so quiet after eleven—begs you to think about things. Used to be when we were kids, remember, we all still carried the Old World's ways on our shoulders. Still used the words we know better than to speak. My father hated the man in the unit next to ours, only because he was a foreigner, and that guy, I think his name was Arturo—Pops called him *el chico próximo*—his family hated us because they blamed bitter blackness for all that had gone wrong back in the Old World, said we'd ruined it for those who appreciated life bottom-up."

"That's what we used to say about *los negros*, too," Marta recalled, glancing shiftily at Ali and Joseph. "Bitter. Not me, mind you, my family said so. No slight intended."

"Slight?" Ali bristled. "Slight at what? Why're you looking at me for? I look like *los negros* to you? You blind or something?"

Ali raised a hand to his eyes, turned the limb palm to back in careful assessment. His coworkers took him in, too, from the flared beige jumpsuit bottoms tucked into rugged work boots to the nest of wiry black wool combed skyward atop his head.

"What do *los negros* supposed to look like?" redheaded Harold asked between clearing his throat. "I don't remember."

"Who remembers?" Joseph agreed. He rubbed callous hands together hungrily, then cupped the dome of his bald head as he recalled his point. "That's what I was thinking about here the other night, too. You take away everything they said was true in the Old World: God and tongues and skin, and who you're fucking. The only thing left to make sense of up and down is generations. Between us and our children."

The protest sounded three blocks west of the electric truck, a murmur to the workers. "And our fathers, too. Maybe they knew nothing for no *n* words." Harold looked toward the center square, or at Ali, as he spoke. "But they sure'd still call you 'boy' and get away with it."

"What're you talking about?" Ali spit and sneered, yet never glanced toward the trailer. "Did you say 'age' or 'Aids'? Jeez . . . do you hear them out there? What kind of way to commemorate is this? What has it come to? You're cleaning up for sure, Joe."

"Who would've thunk it could've been your own child? Writing such vicious muck. Your son?" Marta spoke into her chest, and Joseph was the only one of the team to hear her. "Shame, you never imagine such a thing."

"No shame to it. They know no better. The boy is nineteen, by God. Barely started university. Never had anything like a chance," Joseph heard himself defending. Ali lifted the truck's steel ramp from First Street. Marta looked up from herself as the metal jammed against narrow storage slits, and Joseph leapt down to street level. "Isn't any such thing as 'Post-Age,' is there? Can't even pretend it—what would it look like? Our years is the only difference we have."

"What do they want?" Ali's tantrum continued. "To go back out there? What do they know?"

The echo of bobble-head words streamed along the ticker between street cleaners and protesters: *Compound Police Still Seek Terrorist in Plot to Detonate Explosives Along High-Speed Muni-Train Route as Reagan Square Disturbance Heightens.*

The nearest flank of protesters read the ticker, too, and they cheered. Joseph heard some small portion of the crowd chant his son's name with clear and vigorous tongues above the murmur, just as the skateboarding boy had claimed.

He climbed into the municipal truck's passenger seat, wondering at the connection the screens drew between plot and disturbance. He saw Chevy behind his eyelids, and he asked the specter: If a bunch of learn-ed university students went about rejecting all else the compound has told them, why were the very same ninnies so willing to cheer its most ridiculous link about you?

Ali cleared his throat behind the electric truck's steering wheel, and Joseph caught the fake street-cleaning supervisor staring past Marta and Harold, watching him in the cab's side-view mirror. He nodded.

"All right," he said, and pointed to his municipal badge. "I'll clock in to clean Reagan tonight."

"Alone?"

Joseph nodded his acceptance again. The electric municipal truck veered to U-turn away from the compound protest. He told himself that he would decide whether some difference existed between anarchy and terror once midnight quiet fell over Reagan Square.

Their family had been among the compound's first settlers. Joseph was five when they'd come, and he remembered only dim blinks, a few clipped and fading blurbs from the Old World. The tales of substance he'd passed on to his only son regarding the place of his birth were those given him by his elders.

They'd spoken of the end of water back home—decrepit fronts, shores, lines, and beaches where most of them had lived. They described the Old World as no different from those new compounds, except for the girded walls towering from the compound's limits. Borders obstructing the horde's glimpse into the world before them; blocking old privileged lenses, too, from gazing into lives led by those freed behind steel.

Otherwise, the Fed had promised Joseph's elders—and they'd passed word on to the children—that the developments were but redesigned inner cities. A series of "Just Compounds," they'd called the dwellings, concentrated east to west along the U.S. mountain and river chains, walled-off replicas with the red lining and crumbled rust of the belted Mid-Atlantic Mecca scoured clean. Leaving the neon, blinking amenities of civilization at the ready access of the poorest qualified souls who agreed to migrate.

Not until Joseph approached his teenage years did the few wayward teachers begin telling him and his first-generation peers unfiltered tales of nighttime torture in the Old World's facilities, incarcerated dark men screaming at blue eclipse, pain often wrought by their own possessed hands. How the mystery of eleven shackled and mutilated brown youths washed up on waterfront sands on one bloody night spurred protests first, and then the Riots of 2015. "Willful Fury," the teachers had called the events. No one established responsibility for what appeared mass imprisonment and murder, but it did not much matter. The appearance of the brutalized corpses afforded teeming hordes ninety summer days to set fire to the last remains of those wards and woods dark souls had called their corners of the American cities. Their flames burned even blight to embers, smoldering with a bitter black smoke that would have consumed the old cities whole had the Great Society not foreseen those urban margins emblazoned fifty years earlier and girded their towers accordingly.

That was what the young protesters called what they were doing in Reagan Square: commemorating the compounds' history, demanding the realization of dreams and unfulfilled promises that reached back to settlement. As back in the summer of Joseph's own birth in July 2015, just as mass rage engulfed the city and the birth of a child convinced Joseph's parents that they could no longer cotton to the way of things in their Detroit home, America had conceived of a solution to the peculiar problem to which its people clung in their struggle for exceptional identification. Recompense had through separation, by choice: reconciliation effected behind steel that was imported from China.

"Joseph Charles?"

The Federals were not foolish enough to remove the cities' colored populations all alone: too much Old World history in such a policy. The initial calls for migration included all those with cumulative credit scores below 650, recovering drug addicts and alcoholics, the aged and infirm, dwellers with histories of eviction, foreclosure, or personal bankruptcy, alien immigrants, sex offenders, social workers, and evangelical preachers. Before the academic mavens and identity warriors could claim such stipulations as mere code for the Old World's dark, disenfranchised hordes, the Federals invited willing citizens, too—those looking for a "reboot on living circumstance"—to join the compounds as volunteer "mentor settlers."

"Mr. Charlie . . ."

Joseph angled the power hose high to blast the protest graffiti loose from tile siding. Chemically treated water sprayed his goggles and gloves as he yanked the hose free from the eighth rung of his strapped security ladder. The tile siding chipped slightly around the defacing—yet the spiraling blue symbols remained in splayed place. Joseph recalled how shiny the compound's structures had seemed on the surface, not so long before. Back when he was a child certainly, but even later, when young Chevy was still a wide-smiling toddler with brown pupils glimmering wonder.

Joseph knew that he wouldn't be spraying the dawdle of adolescent rage till half past eleven every other night if the administration still forced the feral youths of his son's lot to read old America's founding constitution. If they knew the compact the people had originally made with their history (with its drafters and amenders, its appendices and its funny 60 percent math), knew that the free mass had been bound to an agreement with their appointed rulers for their own good, then they could appreciate the audacious hope afforded by their lives in the compound. Appreciate compound life as superior to any clamoring alternatives. Yet once their madness was let loose without history's insight, it was amok, emboldening juveniles to mime tales of theatrical rebellion in a walled-off square. Rattling cages for old freedoms and emptied democracy in a rebellion spent up by bankrupted history—especially given that such insanity was all that the people were brought there, all that they'd come there to conquer.

"You are Joseph Charles, father of the one whom they call Ché, no?" The woman's face hovered before each of the flat screens high above Joseph's work ladder. Taut gray skin pulled into creases between her eyes and the corners of her lips, then stretched along her throat where her neck and skull met. White-blond hair hung warrior short, chopped just beneath earlobes, behind insistent chlorine-pool eyes.

Governor Westgrove cleared her narrow throat and pursed lips, waiting for the center square's cleaning man to pause spraying the commodities building and stand at something like attention upon his municipal ladder. Her voice trembled staccato, the angels and judges of her stern tribe forever beaming down from black mountain sky over Joseph and the square, in plasma hologram.

"Chevrolet," Joseph said, correcting the five faces. "My son is Chevrolet Charles. After the car brand, from the Old World. Not Ché, no; we call him Chevy for short."

"Have you seen the young man?" The sound of the woman's voice was not as curt as her glare led him to expect. Joseph heard something like an apology in her tone, or so he convinced himself in the moment. If not an apology, then at least unexpected compassion.

"No, not at all," Joseph answered quickly, hoping not to

betray anything in the way of emotion himself. "Not he, not his mother."

"But you do know where they are?"

Joseph straightened himself up on the ladder and looked directly into the third hologram to his right. "Detroit, I suppose," he said, before blinking away her eyewitness gaze.

The lines along the right side of Westgrove's face lifted upward. "This is important, Joseph, critical for all of us. We may need Chevy here."

"He won't come back. The boy earned his pass from the last administration. With his mother."

"Just in case. Good to know where to find him, if he is needed." Westgrove straightened the pearls at her exposed neck. "It is an important thing you can do for us, Joseph. I have children of my own, two girls—may I call you Joe?"

The street cleaner looked away from the middle hologram before answering. "It's fine."

"Joe, I know how difficult it is to raise them; all we can do is hope that they choose the proper paths in this life. Even when we have circumscribed—uhm, circled—contained—"

"I get you."

"—their paths. We do what we can, as long as we can. And then, when they go too far, we try to rein them back in as best as possible. It ain't pretty. Order and authority. That's what the Old World lost before we left it, brother—the settlers faced similar circumstances back with the violence of the gangs destroying their cities."

"No need to convince me." Joseph latched the cleaning hose to his ladder and descended backward along the rungs, peeking over his shoulder at the damp sidewalk stone. Westgrove had pronounced *violence* as if it were a musical instrument, stringing dated and elegant melody through tightly wound lips.

"I blame it on his mother. Always was an ingrate radical—got worse as the years went on. Thought the opposite would be. Don't most calm down as the years pass? Well, hers went the other way. How could the boy not show effects?"

Westgrove's right hand reached toward Joseph, as if she intended to take hold of his shaved dome and bring him to her comforting, translucent bosom. "It is difficult. But we march forward. Know that this path is superior to the other. The walls keep us safe."

"Forty-foot steel walls all around." Joseph heard the agitation in his words, even as he could not place its source. "Safe from what?"

Westgrove's eyes wagged and her tongue clicked softly along ivory upper dentures. "Your son was a brilliant student, something like a *wunderkind* from what I hear. He earned his pass. But therein lies the problem: They go beyond the walls, and you can't tell what notions infest their minds."

"It was the mother," Joseph insisted.

"Who knows beyond the walls?" the governor repeated. "He hasn't gone too far just yet; he has time to reboot. We believe that he can be brought back home."

"If you want him to come back here to the compound, told you, he won't. Or are you asking that I lead you people to him? Which is it?"

"I was speaking of home in the figurative sense, Joe—I'm sorry. If you can point us to your son, I believe we can help him. We can rectify this." Westgrove's hologram stiffened and her arms disappeared from the projection. "You've heard all about this terrorist threatening to attack our compound. Plotting against our people: innocents, children, for some shrill, nonsense cause."

"Chevy has nothing to do with that," Joseph said, careful to balance his tone. "I don't care what these ninnies chant in the square. All the boy did is put some words on a screen. Not his fault where anybody else took it. Blame the mother for that, too. Always posed herself as some kind of artist."

"We're not looking to indict your son necessarily, Joe. We know what he's capable of." The pause between the governor's words were clips of hurried breath. "We think we know what he was intending in his messages. Correction is all that we're after. Correction and rectification."

Joseph laughed and shrugged at once. "Before last week, I hadn't heard that word *terrorist* since I was a boy. Since my father—"

"You will lead us to him, then?" Westgrove's withered hand reached toward her projector's power button. "Think of this administration as extended family, and connecting us to your son as our collective intervention."

"Everything ends in *-tion*, *-ive*, or *-ist* to you. Words mean more when they're longer? Is that a rule, Governor?" He chuckled at the pallid gray woman. "So, we're family: I should call you Big Mother Governor?"

" Sister, just sister, Joe, my brother. History is behind us. This is for the best."

Westgrove's faces disappeared from Reagan Square's skyline, and the center returned to its soft silver nighttime haze. Joseph climbed the municipal safety ladder, stopping at the fifth of two dozen rungs, just high enough to take hold of the water hose, and he looked up at the blue graffiti marking the commodities building. From that height, the circles appeared drawn in letters that spoke through fresh cracks in the building edifice. Each spiral painted in turning phrases, repeating their vandalism on the skyscraper's alley side—REVOLUTION TURNS, BACK TO THE BEGINNING, THE ONLY WAY, SANS CHANGE, VIVA CHEVY—flushing into empty tile before repeating from the first.

About "Reservation 2020"

"Reservation 2020" wells up from themes treated in Ray Bradbury's longer works, *Fahrenheit 451* and *Something Wicked This Way Comes* in particular. I read *Fahrenheit* as using its futuristic landscape to comment on profound social change observed in the America (United States) in which Bradbury crafted the novel—change wrought by post–World War II technological advancement, the altered political climate partially born from that advance, and the presumptuous winds of progress blowing all about the author's hinterland home. While *Fahrenheit* looks forward in time with wary eyes, *Something Wicked* looks back to childhood through a nostalgic lens cast upon an idyllic place no longer to be, both within the context of that novel and within the author's own living narrative: Bradbury's prose had taken up Green Town before *Something Wicked,* and he would come back to that place of lost innocence again. On each fictive visit, the plates beneath the village's reality had shifted.

Essential to Ray Bradbury's fiction are his love for the beauty of words and his recognition of history's prevailing sway. The horror at the core of *Fahrenheit 451* seems to me the human tragedy had when words bound by historic context smolder in readerless ruins at a bonfire set by those appointed to safeguard social progress. How could Bradbury the writer not ponder the coming of such a future as he beheld the beginning and end of all-out wars, the expediting of life all about him, and the arrival of the graphic babble-box screen in just about every living room in every village strewn across the landscape that he called home?

Today Ray Bradbury seems a prophet, foretelling a time in which the narrative of change is told not in books but in clipped tweets, ticker tapes, and graffiti blurbs, reiterated ad nauseam by plasma-screen heads spouting words ripped of meaning. At his finest, the author uses poignant language and foreboding setting to warn of this carnival lurking at the edge of town.

—Bayo Ojikutu

TWO HOUSES

Kelly Link

Soft music woke the sleepers in the spaceship *The House of Secrets*. They opened their eyes to soft pink light, crept like vampires from their narrow beds. They gathered in the antechamber. Outside the world was night, the dawn a hundred years away.

The sleepers floated gracelessly in the recycled air, bumped softly against one another. They clasped hands, as if to reassure one another that they were real, then pushed off again. Their heads were heavy with dreams. There were three of them, two women and one man.

There was the ship as well. Her name was Maureen. She was monitoring the risen sleepers, their heart rates, the dilation of their pupils, each flare of their nostrils.

"Maureen, you goddess! Bread, fresh from the oven! Sourdough!" Gwenda said. "Oh, and old books. A library? It was in a library that I decided I would go to space one day. I was twelve."

They inhaled. Stretched, then slowly somersaulted.

"Something brackish," said Sullivan. "A tidal smell. Mangrove roots washed by the sea. I spent a summer in a place like that. Arrived with one girl and left with her sister."

"Oranges, now. A whole grove of orange trees, all warm from the sun, and someone's just picked one. I can smell the peel, coming away." That was Mei. "Oh, and coffee! With cinnamon in it!"

"Maureen?" said Gwenda. "Who else is awake?"

There were twelve aboard *The House of Secrets*. Ten women and one man, and the ship, Maureen. It was a bit like a girls' summer camp, Gwenda had said, early on. Aune said, Or an asylum.

They were fourteen years into their mission. They had longer still to go.

"Portia is awake, and Aune, and Sisi," Maureen said. "For two months now. Aune and Portia will go back to sleep in a day or two. Sisi has agreed to stay awake awhile yet. She wants to see Gwenda. They're all in the Great Room. They're throwing a surprise party for you."

There was always a surprise party. Sullivan said, "I'll go and put my best surprised face on."

They threw off sleep. Each rose or sank toward the curved bulkhead, opened cunning drawers and disappeared into them to make their toilets, to be poked and prodded and examined and massaged. The smell of cinnamon went away. The pink light grew brighter.

Long-limbed Sisi poked her head into the antechamber and waited until Gwenda swung out of a drawer. "Has Maureen told you?" Sisi said.

"Told what?" Gwenda said. Her hair and her eyebrows had grown back in her sleep.

"Never mind," Sisi said. She looked older; thinner. "Dinner first, then all the gossip."

Gwenda wriggled through the air toward her, leaned her face against Sisi's neck. "Howdy, stranger." She'd checked the ship log while making her toilet. The date was March 12, 2073. It had been two years since she'd last been awake with her good friend Sisi.

"Is that a new tattoo?" Sisi said.

It was an old joke between them.

Head to toes Gwenda was covered in the most extraordinary pictures. A sunflower, a phoenix, a star map, and a whole pack of wolves running across the ice. There was a man holding a baby, a young girl with red hair on a playground rocket, the Statue of Liberty and the state flag of Illinois, passages from the Book of Revelations, and a hundred other things as well. There was the ship *The House of Secrets* on the back of one hand, and its sister, *The House of Mystery*, on the other. You only told them apart by the legend scrolled beneath each tattoo.

You didn't get to take much with you when you went into space. Maureen could upload all of your music, all of your books and movies, letters and videos and photographs of your family, but how real was any of that? What of it had any weight? What could you hold in your hand? Sisi had a tarot deck. Her mother had given it to her. Sullivan had a copy of *Moby-Dick*, and Portia had a four-carat diamond in a platinum setting. Mei had her knitting needles.

Gwenda had her tattoos. She'd left everything else behind.

There was the Control Room. There were the Berths, and the Antechamber. There was the Engine Room, and the Long Gallery, where Maureen grew their food, maintained their stores, and cooked for them. The Great Room was neither, strictly speaking, Great nor a Room, but with the considerable talents of Maureen at their disposal, it was a place where anything that could be imagined could be seen, felt, heard, savored.

The sleepers staggered under the onslaught.

"Dear God," Mei said. "You've outdone yourself."

"We each picked a theme! Maureen, too!" Portia said, shouting to be heard above the music. "You have to guess!"

"Easy," Sullivan said. White petals eddied around them, chased by well-groomed dogs. "Westminster dog show, cherry blossom season, and, um, that's Shakespeare over there, right? Little pointy beard?"

"Perhaps you noticed the strobe lights," Gwenda said. "And the terrible music, the kind of music only Aune could love. A Finnish disco. Is that everything?"

Portia said, "Except Sully didn't say which year, for the dog show."

"Oh, come on," Sullivan said.

"Fine," Portia said. "2009. Clussex 3-D Grinchy Glee wins. The Sussex spaniel."

There was dancing, and lots of yelling, barking, and declaiming of poetry. Sisi and Sullivan and Gwenda danced, the way you could dance only in low gravity, while Mei swam over to talk with Shakespeare. It was a pretty good party. Then dinner was ready, and Maureen sent away the Finnish dance music, the dogs, the cherry blossoms. You could hear Shakespeare say to Mei, "I always dreamed of being an astronaut." And then he vanished.

Once there had been two ships. It was considered cost-effective, in the Third Age of Space Travel, to build more than one ship at a time, to send companion ships out on their long voyages. Redundancy enhances resilience, or so the theory goes. Sister ships *Light House* and *Leap Year* had left Earth on a summer day in the year 2059. Only some tech, some comic-book fan, had given them nicknames for reasons of his own: *The House of Secrets* and *The House of Mystery*.

The House of Secrets had lost contact with her sister five years earlier. Space was full of mysteries. Space was full of secrets. Gwenda still dreamed, sometimes, about the twelve women aboard *The House of Mystery*.

Dinner was Beef Wellington (fake) with asparagus and new potatoes (both real) and sourdough rolls (realish). The chickens were laying again, and so there was chocolate soufflé for dessert. Maureen increased gravity, because it was a special occasion and in any case, even fake Beef Wellington requires suitable gravity. Mei threw rolls across the table at Gwenda. "What?" she said. "It's so nice to watch things *fall*."

Aune supplied bulbs of something alcoholic. No one asked what it was. Aune worked with eukaryotes and Archaea. "Because," she said, "it is not just a party, Sullivan, Mei, Gwenda. It's Portia's birthday party."

"Here's to me," Portia said.

"To Portia," Aune said.

"To Proxima Centauri," Sullivan said.

"To Maureen," Sisi said. "And old friends." She squeezed Gwenda's hand.

"To *The House of Secrets*," Mei said.

"To *The House of Secrets* and *The House of Mystery*," Gwenda said. They all turned and looked at her. Sisi squeezed her hand again. And they all drank.

"But we didn't get you anything, Portia," Sullivan said.

Portia said, "I'll take a foot rub. Or wait, I know. You can all tell me stories."

"We ought to be going over the log," Aune said.

"The log can lie there!" Portia said. "Damn the log. It's my birthday party." There was something shrill about her voice.

"The log can wait," Mei said. "Let's sit here a while longer, and talk about nothing."

"There's just one thing," Sisi said. "We ought to tell them the one thing."

"You'll ruin my party," Portia said sulkily.

"What is it?" Gwenda asked Sisi.

"It's nothing," Sisi said. "It's nothing at all. It was only the mind playing tricks. You know what it's like."

"Maureen?" Sullivan said. "What are they talking about, please?"

"Approximately thirty-one hours ago Sisi was in the Control Room. She asked me to bring up our immediate course. I did so. Several minutes later, I observed that her heart rate had gone up. She said something I couldn't understand, and then she said, 'You see it, too, Maureen? You see it?' I asked Sisi to describe what she was seeing. Sisi said, '*The House of Mystery*. Over to starboard. It was there. Then it was gone.' I told Sisi that I had not seen it. We called up the charts, but there was nothing recorded there. I broadcast on all channels, but no one answered. No one has seen *The House of Mystery* in the intervening time."

"Sisi?" Gwenda said.

"It was there," Sisi said. "Swear to God, I saw it. Whole and bright and shining. So near I could almost touch it. Like looking in a mirror."

They all began to talk at once.

"Do you think—"

"Just a trick of the imagination—"

"It might have been, but it disappeared like that." Sullivan snapped his fingers. "Why couldn't it come back again the same way?"

"No!" Portia said. She slammed her hand down on the table. "It's my birthday! I don't want to talk about this, to rehash this all again. What happened to poor old *Mystery*? Where do you think they went? Do you think somebody, *something*, did it? Will they do it to us too? Did it fall into some kind of cosmic pothole or stumble over some galactic anomaly? Did it travel back in time? Get eaten by a monster? Could it happen to us? Don't you remember? We talked and talked and talked, and it didn't make any difference!"

"I remember," Sisi said. "I'm sorry, Portia. I wish I hadn't seen it." There were tears in her eyes. It was Gwenda's turn to squeeze her hand.

"Had you been drinking?" Sullivan said. "One of Aune's concoctions? Maureen, what did you find in Sisi's blood?"

"Nothing that shouldn't have been there," Maureen said.

"I wasn't high, and I hadn't had anything to drink," Sisi said.

"But we haven't stopped drinking since," Aune said. She tossed back another bulb. "Cheers."

Mei said, "I don't want to talk about it either."

"That's settled," Portia said. "Bring up the lights again, Maureen, please. Make it something cozy. Something cheerful. How about a nice old English country house, roaring fireplace, suits of armor, tapestries, big picture windows full of green fields, bluebells, sheep, detectives in deerstalkers, hounds, moors, Cathy scratching at the windows. You know. That sort of thing. I turned twenty-eight today, and tomorrow or sometime soon I'm going to go back to sleep again and sleep for another year or until Maureen decides to decant me. So tonight I want to get drunk and gossip. I want someone to rub my feet, and I want everyone to tell a story we haven't heard before. I want to have a good time."

The walls extruded furnishings, two panting greyhounds. They sat in a Great Hall instead of the Great Room. The floor beneath them was flagstones, a fire crackled in a fireplace big enough to roast an ox, and through the mullioned windows a gardener and his boy were cutting roses.

"Less gravity, Maureen," Portia said. "I always wanted to float around like a ghost in an old English manor."

"I like you, my girl," Aune said. "But you are a strange one."

"Funny old Aune," Portia said. "Funny old all of us." She somersaulted in the suddenly buoyant air. Her seaweedy hair seethed around her face in the way that Gwenda hated.

"Let's each pick one of Gwenda's tattoos," Sisi said. "And make up a story about it."

"Dibs on the phoenix," Sullivan said. "You can never go wrong with a phoenix."

"No," Portia said. "Let's tell ghost stories. Aune, you start. Maureen, you can do the special effects."

"I don't know any ghost stories," Aune said slowly. "I know stories about trolls. No. Wait. I have one ghost story. It was a story that my grandmother told about the farm in Pirkanmaa where she grew up."

The gardeners and the rosebushes disappeared. Now, through the windows, you could see a farm, and rocky fields beyond it. In the distance, the land sloped up and became coniferous trees.

"Yes," Aune said. "Like that. I visited once when I was just a girl. The farm was in ruins then. Now the world has changed again. The forest will have swallowed it up." She paused for a moment, so that they all could imagine it. "My grandmother was a girl of eight or nine. She went to school for part of the year. The rest of the year she and her brothers and sisters did the work of the farm. My grandmother's work was to take the cows to one particular meadow, where the pasturage was supposed to be better. The cows were very big and she was very small, but they knew to come when she called them! What she would think of me now, of this path we are on! In the evening she brought the herd home again. The cattle path went along a ridge. On one side there was a meadow that her family did not use even though the grass looked very fine to my grandmother. There was a brook down in the meadow, and an old tree, a grand old man. There was a rock under the tree, a great slab that looked something like a table."

Outside the windows now were a tree in a meadow, and a brook running along, and a rock that you could imagine would make a fine picnic table.

"My grandmother didn't like that meadow. Sometimes when she looked down she saw people sitting all around the table that the rock made. They were eating and drinking. They wore old-fashioned clothing, the kind her own grandmother would have worn. She knew that they had been dead a very long time."

"Ugh," Mei said. "Look!"

"Yes," Aune said in her calm, uninflected voice. "Like that. One day my grandmother—her name was Aune, too, I should have said that first, I suppose—one day Aune was leading her cows home along the ridge and she looked down into the meadow. She saw the people eating and drinking at their table. And while she was looking down, they turned and looked at her. They began to wave at her, to beckon that she should come down and sit with them and eat and drink. But instead she turned away and went home and told her mother what had happened. And after that, her older brother, who was a very unimaginative boy, had the job of taking the cattle to the far pasture."

The people at the table were waving at Gwenda and Mei and Portia and the rest of them now. "Ooh," Portia said. "That was a good one. Creepy! Maureen, didn't you think so?"

"It was a good story," Maureen said. "I liked the cows."

"So not the point, Maureen," Portia said. "Anyway."

"I have a story," Sullivan said. "In the broad outlines it's a bit like Aune's story."

"You could change it up a bit," Portia said. "I wouldn't mind."

"I'll just tell it the way I heard it," Sullivan said. "It's Kentucky, not Finland, and there aren't any cows. That is, there were cows, because it's another farm, but not in the story. It's a story that my grandfather told me."

The gardeners were outside the windows again. There was beginning to be something ghostly about them, Gwenda thought. You knew that they would just come and go, always doing the same things. Maybe it was the effect of sitting inside such a very Great Hall, surrounded by so many tapestries. Maybe this was what it was like to be rich and looked after by so many servants, all of them practically invisible—just like Maureen, really—for all the notice you had to take of them. They might as well have been ghosts. Or was that what the servants thought about the people they looked after? Capricious, powerful without ever really setting foot on the ground, nothing you could look at for any length of time without drawing malicious attention?

What an odd string of thoughts. She was fairly sure that while she had been alive on Earth nothing like this had ever been in her head. Out here, suspended between one place and another, of course you went a little crazy. It was almost luxurious, how crazy you were allowed to be.

She and Sisi lay cushioned on the air, arms wrapped around each other's waists so as not to go flying away. If something disastrous were to happen now, if a meteor were to crash through a bulkhead, or if a fire broke out in the Long Gallery, and they all went flying into space, would she and Sisi manage to hold on to each other? It almost made her happy, thinking of it. She smiled at Sisi and Sisi smiled back.

Sullivan had the most wonderful voice for telling stories. He was describing the part of Kentucky where his family still lived. They went hunting the wild pigs that lived in the forest. Went to church on Sundays. There was a tornado.

Rain beat at the windows. You could smell the ozone beading on the glass. Trees thrashed and groaned.

After the tornado passed through, men came to Sullivan's grandfather's house. They were forming a search party to go and look for a girl who had gone missing. Sullivan's grandfather went with them. The hunting trails were all gone. Parts of the forest had been flattened. Sullivan's grandfather was part of the group that found the girl at last. She was still alive when they found her, but a tree had fallen across her body and cut her almost in half. She was pulling herself along by her fingers.

"After that," Sullivan said, "my grandfather wouldn't hunt in that part of the forest. He said that he knew what it was to hear a ghost walk, but he'd never heard one crawl before."

"Ugh," Sisi said. "Horrible!"

"Look!" Portia said. Outside the window something was dragging itself along the floor of the forest. "Shut it off, Maureen! Shut it off! Shut it off!"

The gardeners again, with their terrible shears.

"No more old-people ghost stories," Portia said. "Okay?"

Sullivan pushed himself up off the flagstones, up toward the whitewashed ceiling. He did the breaststroke, then dove back down toward the rest of them.

"Sometimes you can be a real brat, Portia," he said.

"I know," Portia said. "God, I'm sorry. I guess you spooked me. So it must have been a good ghost story, right?"

"Right," Sullivan said, mollified. "I guess it was."

"That poor girl," Aune said. "To relive that moment over and over again. Who would want that, to be a ghost?"

"Maybe you don't have a choice?" Gwenda said. "Or maybe it isn't always bad? Maybe there are happy, well-adjusted ghosts?"

"I never saw the point of ghosts," Sullivan said. "I mean, they're supposed to haunt you as a warning, right? So what's the warning in that story I told you? Don't get caught in the forest during a tornado? Don't get cut in half and die horribly?"

"I thought it was more like they were a recording," Gwenda said. "Like maybe they aren't there at all. It's just the recording of what they did, what happened to them."

Sisi said, "But Aune's ghosts—the other Aune—they looked at her. They wanted her to come down and eat with them. So what was she supposed to eat? Ghost food? Would it have been real food?"

"Maybe it's genetic," Mei said. "So if being a ghost runs on your father's side of the family, and on your mother's side of the family too, then there's a greater risk for you. Like heart disease."

"That would mean Aune and I might be in trouble," Sullivan said.

"Not me," Sisi said comfortably. "I've never seen a ghost." She thought for a minute. "Unless I did. You know. *The House of Mystery*. No. It wasn't a ghost. How could a whole ship be a ghost?"

"Maureen?" Gwenda said. "Do you know any ghost stories?"

Maureen said, "I have all of the stories of Edith Wharton and M. R. James and many others in my library. Would you like to hear one?"

"No, thank you," Portia said. "Have you ever seen a ghost, Maureen?"

"How would I know if I had seen a ghost?" Maureen asked.

"One more story," Portia said. "And then Sullivan will give me a foot rub, and then we can all take a nap before breakfast. Mei, you must know a ghost story. No old people though. I want a sexy ghost story."

"God, no," Mei said. "No sexy ghosts for me. Thank God."

"I have a story," Sisi said. "It isn't mine, of course. Like I said, I've never seen a ghost."

"Go on," Portia said. "Tell your ghost story."

"Not my ghost story," Sisi said. "And not really a ghost story. I'm not really sure what it was. It was the story of a man that I dated for a few months."

"A boyfriend story!" Sullivan said. "I love your boyfriend stories, Sisi! Which one?"

We could go all the way to Proxima Centauri and back and

Sisi still wouldn't have run out of stories about her boyfriends, Gwenda thought. And in the meantime all they are to us are ghost stories, and all we'll ever be to them is the same. Stories to tell their grandchildren.

"I don't think I've told any of you about him," Sisi said. "This was during the period when they weren't putting up any ships. Remember? They kept sending us out to do fund-raising? I was supposed to be some kind of Ambassadress for Space. They sent me to parties with lots of rich people. I was supposed to be slinky and seductive and also noble and representative of everything that made it worth going to space for. It wasn't easy, but I did a good enough job that eventually they sent me over to meet a bunch of investors and big shots in London. I met all sorts of guys, but the only one I clicked with was this one English dude, Liam.

"Okay. Here's where it gets complicated for a bit. Liam's mother was English. She came from this super-wealthy family, and by the time she was a teenager, she was a total wreck. Into booze, hard drugs, recreational Satanism, you name it. Got kicked out of school after school after school, and after that she got kicked out of all of the best rehab programs too. In the end, her family kicked her out. Gave her money to go away. After that, she ended up in prison for a couple of years, had a baby—that was Liam. Bounced around Europe for a while, then when Liam was about seven or eight, she found God and got herself cleaned up. By this point her father and mother were both dead. One of the superbugs. Her brother had inherited everything. She went back to the ancestral pile—imagine a place like this, okay?—and threw herself on her brother's mercy. Are you with me so far?"

"So it's a real old-fashioned English ghost story?" Portia said.

"You have no idea," Sisi said. "You have no idea. So her brother was kind of a jerk. And let me emphasize, once again, this was a rich family, like you have no idea. The mother and the father and brother fancied themselves as serious art collectors. Contemporary stuff. Video installations, performance art, stuff that was really far out. They commissioned this one artist, an American, to come and do a site-specific installation. That's what Liam called it. It was supposed to be a commentary on the American way of life, the postcolonial relationship between England and the U.S., something like that. And what it was, was he bought a ranch house out in a suburb in Arizona, the same state, by the way, where you can still go and see the London Bridge. He bought the house, and the furniture in it, and even the cans of soup in the cupboards. And he had the house dismantled with all of the pieces numbered, and plenty of photographs so that he knew exactly where everything went, and it all got shipped over to London, and then he built it all again on the family's estate. And simultaneously, several hundred yards away, he had a second house built from scratch. And this second house was an exact replica of the original house, from the foundation to the pictures on the wall to where each can of soup went on its shelf in the cupboard."

"Why would anybody ever bother to do that?" Mei said.

"Don't ask me," Sisi said. "If I had that much money, I'd spend it on booze and nice dresses for me and all of my friends."

"Hear, hear," Gwenda said. They all raised their bulbs and drank.

"This stuff is ferocious, Aune," Sisi said. "I think it's changing my mitochondria."

"Quite possibly," Aune said. "Cheers."

"Anyway, this double installation was the toast of the art world for a season. Then the superbug took out the mom and dad, and a couple of years after that, Liam's mother came home. And her brother said to her, I don't want you living in the family home with me. But I'll let you live on the estate. I'll even give you a job with the housekeeping staff. And in exchange you'll live in my installation. Which was, apparently, something that the artist had really wanted to make part of the project, to find a family to come and live in it.

"This jerk brother said, 'You and my nephew can come and live in my installation. I'll even let you pick which house.'

"Liam's mother went away and prayed about it. Then she came back and moved into one of the houses."

"How did she decide which one she wanted to live in?" Sullivan said.

"That's a great question," Sisi said. "I have no idea. Maybe God told her? Look, what I was interested in at the time was Liam. I know why he liked me. Here I was, about as exotic as it gets, this South African girl with an Afro and cowboy boots and an American passport, talking about how I was going to get into a rocket and go up in space, just as soon as I could. What man doesn't like a girl who doesn't plan to stick around?

"What I don't know is why I liked him so much. The thing is, he wasn't really a good-looking guy. He wasn't bad-looking either, okay? He wasn't tall, or short either. He had okay hair. He was in okay shape. But there was something about him, you just knew he was going to get you into trouble. The good kind of trouble. When I met him, his mother was dead. His uncle was dead too. They weren't a very lucky family. They had money instead of luck, or it seemed that way to me. The brother had never married, and he'd left Liam everything.

"When we hooked up, I thought Liam was probably a stockbroker. Something like that. He said he was going to take me up to his country house, and when we got there, it was like this." Sisi gestured around. "Like a palace. Nice, right?

"And then he said we were going to go for a walk around the estate. And that sounded superromantic. And then he took me to this weather-beaten, paint-peeled house that looked like every ranch house I'd ever seen in a gone-to-seed neighborhood in the Southwest, y'all. This house was all by itself on a green English hill. It looked seriously wrong. Maybe it had looked a bit more solid before the other one had burned down, or at least more intentionally weird, the way an art installation should, but anyway. Actually, I don't think so."

"Wait," Mei said. "The other house had burned down?"

"I'll get to that in a minute," Sisi said. "So there we are in front of this horrible house, and Liam picked me up and carried me across the threshold like we were newlyweds. He dropped me on this scratchy tan plaid couch and said, 'I was hoping you would spend the night with me.' We'd known each other for four days. I said, 'You mean back at that gorgeous house? Or you mean here?' He said, 'I mean here.'

"I said to him, 'You're going to have to explain.' And so he did, and now we're back at the part where Liam and his mother moved into the installation."

"This story isn't like the other stories," Maureen said.

"You know, I've never told this story before," Sisi said. "The rest of it, I'm not even sure that I know how to tell it."

"Liam and his mother moved into the installation," Portia prompted.

"Yeah. Liam's mummy picked a ranch house, and they moved in. Liam's just a baby, practically. And there are all these weird rules, like they aren't allowed to eat any of the food on the shelves in the cupboard. Because that's part of the installation. Instead Liam's mummy is allowed to have a mini-fridge in the closet in her bedroom. Oh, and there are clothes in the closets in the bedrooms. And there's a TV, but it's an old one and the artist has got it set up so that it only plays shows that were current in the early nineties in the U.S., which was the last time that this house was occupied.

"And there are weird stains on the carpets in some of the

rooms. Big brown stains, the kind that fade but don't ever come out.

"But Liam doesn't care so much about that. He gets to pick his own bedroom, which is clearly meant for a boy maybe a year or two older than Liam is. There's a model train set on the floor, which Liam can play with, as long as he's careful. And there are comic books, good ones, that Liam hasn't read before. There are cowboys on the sheets. There's a stain here, in the corner, under the window.

"And he's allowed to go into the other bedrooms, as long as he doesn't mess anything up. There's a pink bedroom, with two beds in it. Lots of boring girls' clothes, and a diary, which Liam doesn't see any point in reading. There's a room for an older boy, too, with posters of actresses that Liam doesn't recognize, and lots of American sports stuff. Football, but not the right kind.

"Liam's mother sleeps in the pink bedroom. You would expect her to take the master bedroom here, but she doesn't like the bed. She says it isn't comfortable. Anyway, there's a stain on it that goes right through the comforter, through the sheets. It's as if the stain came up *through* the mattress."

"I think I'm beginning to see the shape of this story," Gwenda says.

"You bet," Sisi says. "But remember, there are two houses. Liam's mummy is responsible for looking after both of them for part of the day. The rest of the day she spends volunteering at the church down in the village. Liam goes to the village school. For the first two weeks, the other boys beat him up, and then they lose interest and after that everyone leaves him alone. In the afternoons he comes back and plays in his two houses. Sometimes he falls asleep in one house, watching TV, and when he wakes up he isn't sure where he is. Sometimes his uncle comes by to invite him to go for a walk on the estate, or to go fishing. He likes his uncle. Sometimes they walk up to the manor house and play billiards. His uncle arranges for him to have riding lessons, and that's the best thing in the world. He gets to pretend that he's a cowboy.

"Sometimes he plays cops and robbers. He used to know some pretty bad guys, back before his mother got religion, and Liam isn't exactly sure which he is yet, a good guy or a bad guy. He has a complicated relationship with his mother. Life is better than it used to be, but religion takes up about the same amount of space as the drugs did. It doesn't leave much room for Liam.

"Anyway, there are some cop shows on the TV. After a few months he's seen them all at least once. There's one called *CSI*, and it's all about fingerprints and murder and blood. And Liam starts to get an idea about the stain in his bedroom, and the stain in the master bedroom, and the other stains, the ones in the living room, on the plaid sofa and over behind the La-Z-Boy that you mostly don't notice at first, because it's hidden. There's one stain up on the wallpaper in the living room, and after a while it starts to look a lot like a handprint.

"So Liam starts to wonder if something bad happened in his house. He's older now, maybe ten or eleven. He wants to know why are there two houses, exactly the same, next door to each other? How could there have been a murder—okay, a series of murders, where everything happened exactly the same way twice? He doesn't want to ask his mother, because lately when he tries to talk to her, all she does is quote Bible verses at him. He doesn't want to ask his uncle about it either, because the older Liam gets, the more he can see that even when his uncle is being super nice, he's still kind of a jerk.

"The kids in the school who beat Liam up remind him a little of his uncle. His uncle has shown him some of the other pieces in his art collection, and he's told Liam that he envies him, getting to be a part of an actual installation. Liam knows his house came from America. He knows the name of the artist who designed the installation. So that's enough to go online and find out what's going on, which is that, sure enough, the original house, the one the artist bought and brought over, is a murder house. Some high school kid went nuts and killed his whole family with a hammer in the middle of the night. And this artist, his idea was based on what rich Americans used to do at the turn of the last century, which was buy up some impoverished U.K. family's castle and have it brought over stone by stone to be rebuilt in Texas, or upstate Pennsylvania, or wherever. And if there was some history, if there was supposed to be a ghost, they paid even more money.

"So that was idea number one, to reverse all of that. But then he had an even bigger idea, idea number two, which was, What's a haunted house? How can you buy one? If you transport it all the way across the Atlantic Ocean, does the ghost (or ghosts, in this case) come with it, if you put it back together again exactly the way it was? And if you can put a haunted house back together again, piece by piece by piece, then why can't you build your own from scratch, with the right ingredients? And idea number three, forget the ghosts: Can the real live people who go and walk around in one house or the other, or even better, the ones who live in a house without knowing which house is which, will the experience be any different for them? Will they still be haunted?"

"You are blowing my mind," Portia said. "No, really. I don't know if I like this story."

"I'm with Portia," Aune said. "It isn't a good story. Not for us, not here."

"Let her finish it," Sullivan said. "It's going to be worse if she doesn't finish it. Which house were they living in?"

"Does it really matter which house they were living in?" Sisi said. "I mean, Liam spent time in both of the houses. He said he never knew which was which. The artist was the only one who had that piece of information. He even used blood to re-create the stains. Cow blood, I think. So I guess this is another story with cows in it, Maureen.

"I'll tell the rest of the story as quick as I can. So by the time Liam brought me to see his ancestral home, one of the installation houses had burned down. Liam's mother did it in a fit of religious mania. Liam was kind of vague about why. I got the feeling it had to do with his teenage years. They went on living there, you see. Liam got older, and I'm guessing his mother caught him fooling around with a girl or something, in the house that they didn't live in. By this point she had become convinced that one of the houses was occupied by unquiet spirits, but she couldn't make up her mind which. And in any case, it didn't do much good. If there were ghosts in the other house, they just moved in next door once it burned down. I mean, why not? Everything was already set up exactly the way that they liked it."

"Wait, so there were ghosts?" Gwenda said.

"Liam said there were. He said he never saw them, but later on, when he lived in other places, he realized that there must have been ghosts. In both places. Both houses. Other places just felt empty to him. He said to think of it like maybe there was this kid who grew up in the middle of an eternal party, or a bar fight, one that went on for years, or somewhere where the TV was always on. And then you leave the party, or you get thrown out of the bar, and all of a sudden you realize you're all alone. Like, you just can't get to sleep without that TV on. You don't sleep as well. He said he was always on high alert when he was away from the murder house, because something was missing and he couldn't figure out what. I think that's what I picked up on. That extra vibration, that twitchy radar."

"That's sick," Sullivan said.

"Yeah," Sisi said. "That relationship was over real quick. So that's my ghost story."

Mei said, "How long were you in the house?"

"I don't know, about two hours? He'd brought a picnic dinner. Lobster and champagne and the works. We sat and ate at the kitchen table while he told me about his rotten childhood. Then he gave me the whole tour. Showed me the stains and all, like they were holy relics. I kept looking out the window and seeing the sun get lower and lower. I didn't want to be in that house after it got dark."

"So you think you could describe one of the rooms, the living room, maybe, to Maureen? So she could re-create it?"

"I could try," Sisi said. "Seems like a bad idea, though."

"I guess I'm just wondering about how that artist made a haunted house," Mei said. "If we could do the same here. We're so far away from home, you know? Do ghosts travel this far? I mean, say we find some nice planet. If the conditions are suitable, and we grow some trees and some cows, do we get the table with the ghosts sitting around it? Are they here now?"

Maureen said, "It would be an interesting experiment."

The Great Room began to change around them. The couch came first.

"Maureen!" Gwenda said. "Don't you dare!"

Portia said, "But we don't need to run that experiment. I mean, isn't it already running?" She appealed to the others, to Sullivan, to Aune. "You know. I mean, you know what I mean?"

"What?" Gwenda said. "What are you trying to say?" Sisi reached for her hand, but Gwenda pushed away from her. She wriggled away like a fish, her arms extended to catch the wall.

On the one hand, *The House of Secrets* and on the other, *The House of Mystery*.

About "Two Houses"

When I was ten or so, I was a student at Westminster Christian Academy in Miami, Florida. There was a school library, and I remember discovering *The Illustrated Man* there, on a spinning rack. I'd read fantasy novels before—Tolkien, C. S. Lewis, Le Guin—and I'd read the fairy tales of Hans Christian Andersen and the Brothers Grimm. But I'd never read stories like this before. They took place in a world that I recognized. The characters' lives were familiar to me. But the things that happened to them were marvelous, terrifying, haunting. Those stories have lived inside my head ever since. They're part of my DNA. I love Ray Bradbury's stories, his language, his ideas, his characters—the married couple who run away from the war, the murderous baby, the lodger with the mysterious insides. I love his astronauts, and the mortal boy born into an immortal family. I love his witches, his Martians, his psychologists, and all of his characters who make regrettable bargains.

It was hard to start writing a story for this anthology, because once I started to revisit some of my favorite Bradbury stories, I wanted to keep on reading. I don't have much to say about "Two Houses." One of the ghost stories was told to me by the writer Christopher Rowe. The other was lent to me by the writer Gwenda Bond. Thanks to both of them, and of course, and always, to Ray Bradbury.

—Kelly Link

WEARINESS

Harlan Ellison®

Very near the final thaw of the Universe, the last of them left behind, the last three of the most perfect beings who had ever existed, stood waiting for the transitional moment. The neap tide of all time. The eternal helix sang its silent song in stone; and the glow of What Was to Come had bruised itself to a ripe plumness.

The ostren fanned itself. Melancholia had shortened it; one

entire set of faculties could do nothing but sigh. And it had grown uncommonly warm for her, in sight of the end.

The velv could not contain his trepidation, peering out around the perplexing curvature of space.

But the tismess, that being who had summoned the helix, knew boldness was required, here and now at the final moments. And it stood boldly forth, waiting for the inevitable. All three—there were no others—were at the terminus of uncountable multiple trillions of aeons, and weary.

Heaviness hung, a dire swaddling.

"What is there to fear?" the tismess said, rather more nastily than it had intended. *Reify,* it had thought, urgently.

Heaviness hung, undiminished.

"What is there to fear?" Again, trying to flense the tone of nastiness, chagrined at its incivility, the velv whimpered and stared at the great helix, receptors clouding as the brightness fattened. The point of alarm had been reached and abandoned long since. "I am the last," it said.

"As is each of us," thought the ostren. "We are, each of us, you and you each, we are, each of us, the end of the line. Out of time, all time, the last. But why are you frightened?"

"Because . . . it is the end. The question at last answered. There will be no more. No more I, no more you, no more of any living species. Does that not terrify you?"

"Yes," thought the ostren. "Yes. Yes, it does."

The tismess was silent.

And the great helix solidified, its colors steadied, and the last three stared as only they were able, looking into the future, for the past and present were now gone, looking to see what would overwhelm them as they were vaporized, gone like their kind, gone forever, not even motes, not even memories. And they saw, the three last, absolutely perfect beings; they saw what was to come.

"Oh, how good," whispered the velv, her tissues roiling most golden. "How wonderful. And I'm not afraid . . . not now."

The ostren made the sound that very little children had once made when they had truly learned where the puppy farm is. But there was no fear, either, in the ostren.

For the tismess, as it was all coming to an end, suddenly there was what there was to be seen.

What was on the other side.

Before him, immediately before him, was the darkness. Heavy, breathing yet silent, it seemed to go on forever. But that *was* the other side. And beyond that darkness was something: something he could *call* the "other side." Could he see it, could he even imagine it, there had to *be* another side beyond this side. He reveled in the moment of knowledge that all there had ever been would go on, would start anew perhaps, would roll on through the final night, no matter how long. There *was* an "other side."

But of course, in truth, what he was seeing was only another aspect of the only darkness—and not even darkness; nothing.

What he was seeing was every thought he had ever had, every song he had ever sung, everyone he had ever known, every moment of his trillion aeons never knowing he had nowhere else to go, all and everything of memory; where he had stood, what he had done and what had been done around him, what there was and what there could ever have been.

In that instant, he saw backward into memory, backward into the night that had preceded the first thought.

Far away, a galaxy became as dust and vanished, leaving no print, no recollection, no residue. Then, one by one, in correct stately procession, the solitary stars went blind.

The question was answered: *Sat çi sat bene.*

"A painting is a sum of destructions."
—Pablo Picasso (1881–1973)

About "Weariness"

Running the unacceptable risk of writing an afterword oh by the way "note" a thousand times longer than the story itself, I sit down to explicate the "Bradbury connection" to this, perhaps my last-published story. Like Ray, I am now old, and there is an infinitude more to recollect and savor of links between Bradbury and Ellison. Truly, it should suffice for even the most marrow-sucking obsessive fan that Ray and I have known each other close on forever.

Ray contends that in very short order he and I will be sitting down together cutting up touches with Dickens and Dorothy Parker, shuckin' 'n' jivin' with Aesop and Melville.

Uh . . . well, okay, Ray, if you say so.

(I am rather less condolent with that Hereafter stuff than is Ray. As has averred Nat Hentoff, I come from, and remain as one with, a grand and glorious tradition of stiff-necked Jewish atheists. Ray and I have a long-standing wager on this one, which of us is on the money and which is betting on a lame pony. Sadly, the winner will never collect.)

La dee dah. Back where we began. Too many words, yet I'll attempt that undanceable rigadoon.

These days of the electronic babble, every doofus with some handheld device calls every other male he knows *brother.*

"Hey, Bro! Whussup, Bro? Howzit goin', Bro?"

Strangers: brother. Casual acquaintances: brother. Same-skin-color supermarket bagger: brother. Other-skin-colored guy who tipped you when you parked his Beamer: brother. Much like the oafishly careless, empty, and repetitious whomping of the once-specific, cherished, and singular word *awesome,* the sacred word *BROTHER* has become, in inept mouths, a dull and wearisome trope. (*Awesome* is the word one uses for Eleanor Roosevelt, Mount Kilimanjaro, and pitching a no-hit no-run ball game. Not available for the crappy cheese quesadilla you had this afternoon, or for anybody who Dances with the Stars. With or without a wooden leg.) Same goes for yo *bruth*-thuh.

I had only one sib, my late sister. The men of my lifelong existence whom I would countenance as my brother are less than the number of dactyls on my left hand, and they know who they are.

Apparently, Ray Bradbury and I are *brothers.*

Not in some absurd catchall absurdity of vacuous gibber, but actually and really, "we are brothers."

Whence cometh this assertion?

From Ray Bradbury. That's whence.

"You know, Harlan," he said to me, leaning in and grinning that Midwestern just-fell-off-the-turnip-truck grin, "we are brothers, y'know. You and I, together."

I grinned back at him with *my* hayseed Midwestern mien, onaccounta we are both paid liars, one from Waukegan and one from Cleveland, and I played his straight man by responding, "How's that, Ray?"

(The players freeze in situ as the Bloviating Narrator fills in the background data, thus slowing the movie and thus shamefacedly doing the necessary bricklaying.)

The table across which Ray was leaning was in a booth at

one of my and Ray's all-time favorite restaurants, the Pacific Dining Car in downtown Los Angeles. The night was in 1965. Our dining companions had both gone off to the toilets. That is to say, *she* had gone off to one; her husband had gone off to another. Her name was Leigh Bracket; his name was Edmond Hamilton. The queen of fantasy writing. Great movies based on Hammett and Chandler. A legend in this life. The Eric John Stark stories. A kind and imperially gracious woman. One of the best people ever known to me. Ed looked like something out of *American Gothic*. They called him Galaxy Smasher—the true creator of the space opera. Dozens and dozens of stories all the way back to the advent of Gernsbach: The Star Kings series. All those great comic books, and the Captain Future pulp novelettes. Droll, cosmically smart, one helluva plotter, and kind to tots like me and Ray. They were the Strophe and Antistrophe of our literary infancy.

So, they're gone, Bradbury and I are alone, grinnin' & schmoozin', and he proceeds to explain to me that he and I are *brothers*. Not my word, *his* word. (Not to make this too clear, but I have a chasmlike abomination of bloviating sf fans who, upon the death of someone they once met in an elevator, begin to leak like WikiAnything, just to buy themselves the face time at a memorial. "Oh, yes, I knew Isaac as if he were my brother . . ." "Oh, lawdy, I pluckt up rootabuggas with Cliff Simak in de fields . . ." "Yes, Octavia Butler and I were ever so close . . .") This unlikely story I tell actually happened. Go ask Bradbury if you think I'm fudging it. But better hurry . . .

Anyhow, I says back to him, "How's that, Ray?"

And he says back to me, "Them."

And I says to him, "Ed and Leigh?"

And he says back to me, "Our father and mother. They raised us." I have no memory of the rest of the actual verbiage.

Well, Sir, wasn't that a keen moment!

You see, I was working at Paramount at the time, on one or another of the crippled creations Rouse and Greene had hired me to do for vast sums of money (I was in my "hot 15" at the time). And Leigh, whom I'd known since my teens in Ohio, was writing a dog for Howard Hawks called *Red Line 7000,* starring James Caan (who, coincidentally, played the role of Harlan Ellison in an *Alfred Hitchcock Hour* based on my *Memos from Purgatory* only a year or so earlier). Also at Paramount.

Our offices were near to hand.

Ray doesn't drive. I drive. Every time we both got booked into the same lecture gig at some jerkwater literary potlatch, I drove. Bradbury lectured.

Me, he lectured. (Our politics are about as close as our faiths.)

So, I was always the wheelman on the caper.

Leigh didn't have (what she used to call, to mock James M. Cain) a "short" that night, and I can't remember what Ed's story was. But I wound up doing the driving down to the Pacific Dining Car, and we left straight from the studio. Ray must've come by cab; he met us at the Bronson Gate, and I did my thing downtown for a good big T-bone dinner. Also Bermuda onion, Rondo Hatton's jaw-sized tomatoes with Roquefort dressing, and Zucchini Florentine. Ray drank; I never touch the stuff. We had an absolutely nova-squooshing dinner.

Thus, before I run on at greater length, the answer to the question "Can you reminisce a bit about your Ray Bradbury connection?" is frozen in Ray's asserveration: We're brothers.

He said so.

But, not to make a big foofaraw of it, Ray has trouble remembering who I am, and who Harlan Ellison is. And then he'll remember, howl "Live Forever!" or some such impossibility at me, and recall me as "Ah, yes, the Terrible-Tempered Mr. Bang." And I'll smile wanly, and scream back at him, "*Nothing* lives forever, Ray, you crazy old coot! Not the Great Pyramid of Giza, not the polar ice caps, not a single blade of green grass, you nut-bag!"

And that is the link between us, the "connection." Nobody ever writ it large on the northern massif of Mount Shazam . . . you gotta *agree* with your brother.

You just got to love him.

—Harlan Ellison

CONTRIBUTORS

Neil Gaiman was the first author to win the Newbery Medal and the Carnegie Medal for the same book with *The Graveyard Book* (2008). He wrote *The Sandman*, now available in collected graphic novel form, and such books as the Hugo- and Nebula-winning *American Gods*. He dedicated his last short-story collection, *Fragile Things*, to Ray Bradbury and Harlan Ellison. He has three children and two dogs, and his wife has a ukulele.

Margaret Atwood is a poet and novelist (*The Handmaid's Tale, Oryx and Crake, The Year of the Flood*); her latest book is *In Other Worlds: SF and the Human Imagination* (Doubleday, 2011).

Jay Bonansinga's debut novel, *The Black Mariah*, was a finalist for a Bram Stoker Award, and film rights sold to George Romero. The *Chicago Tribune* calls Bonansinga "one of the most imaginative writers of thrillers." His novels include *Perfect Victim, Shattered, Twisted*, and *Frozen*. His nonfiction *Sinking of the Eastland* was a *Chicago Reader* "Critics Choice Book" as well as the recipient of a Superior Achievement Award from the Illinois State Historical Society. The *New York Times* bestseller *The Walking Dead: Rise of the Governor* (St. Martin's), coauthored with *The Walking Dead* TV and comics creator Robert Kirkman, is his latest novel.

Sam Weller is the authorized biographer of Ray Bradbury and the author of the bestselling *Bradbury Chronicles: The Life of Ray Bradbury* and *Listen to the Echoes: The Ray Bradbury Interviews*. He is a two-time Bram Stoker Award finalist. Weller has written for the *Paris Review*, National Public Radio's *All Things Considered*, and many other publications. His short stories have appeared in numerous anthologies, journals, and magazines. Follow him on Twitter @Sam__Weller.

David Morrell is the award-winning author of *First Blood*, the novel in which Rambo was created. His many *New York Times* bestsellers include the classic espionage novel *The Brotherhood of the Rose*, which was adapted into an NBC miniseries that premiered after a Super Bowl. An Edgar, Anthony, and Macavity nominee, Morrell is a three-time recipient of the Horror Writers Association Bram Stoker Award and was named a ThrillerMaster by International Thriller Writers. His fiction has been translated into twenty-six languages.

Thomas F. Monteleone has published more than ninety short stories and twenty novels, including the *New York Times* bestseller *Blood of the Lamb*, which was also a *New York Times* Notable Book, and the bestselling *Complete Idiot's Guide to Novel Writing*. Monteleone's TV credits include *Tales from the Darkside* and PBS Television's *American Playhouse*. He is the founder of the twice-annual Borderlands Press Writers Boot Camp for novelists and short-story writers.

Lee Martin is the author of the novels *The Bright Forever*, a finalist for the 2006 Pulitzer Prize in fiction; *Break the Skin*, *River of Heaven*, and *Quakertown*. He has also published two memoirs, *From Our House* and *Turning Bones*, and a short-story collection, *The Least You Need to Know.* He teaches in the MFA program at Ohio State University.

Joe Hill is the author of two *New York Times* bestselling novels, *Heart-Shaped Box* and *Horns*, and a prizewinning collection of stories, *20th Century Ghosts.* He also scripts the Eisner Award–winning ongoing comic *Locke & Key.* Once upon a time, he earned a fellowship in Ray Bradbury's name. You can follow him on Twitter @joe_hill.

Dan Chaon is the author of *Fitting Ends* and *Among the Missing*, a finalist for the National Book Award, which was also listed as one of the Ten Best Books of the year by the American Library Association, the *Chicago Tribune*, the *Boston Globe*, and *Entertainment Weekly*, and cited as a *New York Times* Notable Book. Chaon's fiction has appeared in numerous journals and anthologies and won both Pushcart and O. Henry awards. His short story "The Bees" appears in *All American Horror of the 21st Century: The First Decade. Stay Awake* (Ballantine) is his newest collection. Chaon teaches at Oberlin College.

John McNally is the author of three novels: *After the Workshop, The Book of Ralph*, and *America's Report Card*, and two story collections, *Troublemakers* (winner of the John Simmons Short Fiction Award and the Nebraska Book Award) and *Ghosts of Chicago.* He is also the author of two nonfiction books: *The Creative Writer's Survival Guide: Advice from an Unrepentant Novelist* and the forthcoming *Vivid and Continuous: Essays and Exercises for Fiction Writing,* both published by the University of Iowa Press. McNally is an associate professor of English at Wake Forest University.

Joe Meno is a fiction writer and playwright who lives in Chicago. A winner of the Nelson Algren Literary Award and a Pushcart Prize and a finalist for the Story Prize, he is the bestselling author of five novels and two short-story collections including *The Great Perhaps*, *The Boy Detective Fails*, and *Hairstyles of the Damned*. He is a professor in the fiction writing department at Columbia College Chicago. His nonfiction has appeared in the *New York Times* and *Chicago* magazine.

Robert McCammon is the award-winning author of seventeen novels, including *Boy's Life*, *Swan Song*, and *Mister Slaughter*. He has been a lifelong fan of Ray Bradbury's work.

Ramsey Campbell is "Britain's most respected living horror writer" (*Oxford Companion to English Literature*). His novels, including *The Doll Who Ate His Mother*, *Incarnate*, *The Hungry Moon*, and *The House on Nazareth Hill*, and short stories have earned him more awards—World Fantasy Awards, British Fantasy Awards, Bram Stoker Awards, and the International Horror Society's Living Legend and Horror Writers Association Lifetime Achievement Award—than any other writer in the genre.

Mort Castle published his first novel in 1967; since then, there have been more than five hundred publications of short stories, articles, comic books, poems, et cetera, and fifteen books with his name as writer or editor, including the "bible for aspiring horror writers" *On Writing Horror* (Writer's Digest Books) and *The Strangers*, a novel that, in translation, made the Polish edition of *Newsweek*'s Top Ten Horror-Thriller Books of 2008 list. He is a seven-time Bram Stoker Award nominee and a two-time winner of the Black Quill Award (for editing). Castle and Jane, his wife of forty-one years, live in Crete, Illinois, a town noted for its bubbling fountain and the bandstand in the park. Castle is ranked as the best five-string banjo player in his height, weight, and age group.

Alice Hoffman is the author of many bestselling novels including *Practical Magic*, *The Red Garden*, and *The Dovekeepers*. She is currently a visiting scholar at Brandeis University.

John Maclay is the author of more than one hundred published horror and fantasy short stories, many of which have appeared in mass-market anthologies alongside stories by Ray Bradbury, Isaac Asimov, Clive Barker, and Stephen King. His most recent collections are *A Little Red Book of Vampire Stories*, *Dreadful Delineations*, and *Divagations*. At Maclay & Associates, 1984–1995, he was publisher of the Masques anthology series and other books in the fantasy and horror field.

Jacquelyn Mitchard, longtime journalist and essayist, is the author of twenty-one books of fiction, including five *New York Times* bestsellers. Nearly five million copies of her books are in print, in twenty-six languages. Her first novel, *The Deep End of the Ocean*, was the inaugural selection of the Oprah Winfrey Book Club. She served on the 2004 fiction jury for the National Book Award and is the first Faculty Fellow at Southern New Hampshire University. She lives in Massachusetts with her husband and nine children.

Gary A. Braunbeck's work has garnered six Bram Stoker Awards, an International Horror Guild Award, and a World Fantasy Award nomination. And, he says, that is the "end of anything remotely interesting about him."

Bonnie Jo Campbell is the author of *Once Upon a River*, *Q Road*, *Women & Other Animals*, and *American Salvage*, and a finalist for both the 2009 National Book Award finalist and the National Book Critics Circle Award. She is a 2011 Guggenheim Fellow. She lives in Kalamazoo, Michigan, with her husband and her donkeys, Jack and Don Quixote.

Audrey Niffenegger is the author of *The Time Traveler's Wife,* *New York Times* bestseller, British Book Award winner, and basis for a film, as well as *Her Fearful Symmetry, The Night Bookmobile,* and numerous hand-printed and hand-bound books. She is at work on a new novel, *The Chinchilla Girl in Exile.*

Charles Yu was named one of the National Book Foundation's "5 Under 35" for his debut short-story collection, *Third Class Superhero.* His first novel, *How to Live Safely in a Science Fictional Universe,* was a *New York Times* Notable Book and named a Best Book of the Year by *Time* magazine. Yu's writing has appeared in numerous publications, including *Harvard Review,* the *Gettysburg Review,* the *Mid-American Review,* the *New York Times,* *Playboy,* and the *Oxford American.* He lives in Los Angeles with his wife, Michelle, and their two children.

Julia Keller, winner of the Pulitzer Prize, is the author of the young adult novel *Back Home* and the nonfiction book *Mr. Gatling's Terrible Marvel: The Gun That Changed Everything and the Misunderstood Genius Who Invented It.* She was a Nieman Fellow at Harvard University and has taught at Princeton University, the University of Notre Dame, and the University of Chicago. Her mystery novel, *A Killing in the Hills,* will be published by St. Martin's in 2012.

Dave Eggers is the author of many novels and works of nonfiction, including *Zeitoun* and *What Is the What.* He is the editor of *McSweeney's.*

Bayo Ojikutu is an award-winning novelist—*47th Street Black* and *Free Burning*—and Pushcart Prize–nominated short-story writer. His work has appeared in various magazines and journals. Ojikutu, his wife, and his son currently reside in the Chicago metropolitan area.

Kelly Link is the author of three short-story collections. With her husband, Gavin J. Grant, she runs Small Beer Press and edits the occasional anthology as well as the zine *Lady Churchill's Rosebud Wristlet.* They live with their daughter, Ursula, in Northampton, Massachusetts.

Harlan Ellison® has been called "one of the great living American short story writers" by the *Washington Post*; the *Los Angeles Times* said, "It's long past time for Harlan Ellison to be awarded the title: '20th Century Lewis Carroll.'" In a career spanning more than forty years, he has written seventy-five books and more than seventeen hundred stories, essays, articles, and newspaper columns, two dozen teleplays, and a dozen motion pictures. He has won more awards than "any other living fantasist," including the Hugo eight times, the Nebula three times, the Bram Stoker six times (including the Lifetime Achievement Award in 1996), the Edgar Award of the Mystery Writers of America twice, the Georges Méliès fantasy film award twice, two Audie Awards (for the best in audio recordings), and the Silver Pen for Journalism, the latter awarded by PEN, the international writers' union. A documentary on Ellison, *Dreams with Sharp Teeth*, was released on DVD in 2009.

CREDITS

version of Dave Eggers's story appeared on the National Public Radio program *This American Life* in 2011.)

READ MORE BY
RAY BRADBURY
FROM HARPERCOLLINS PUBLISHERS

NOVELS

THE MARTIAN CHRONICLES
ISBN 978-0-207993-0 (paperback)
The masterfully imagined chronicles of Earth's settlement of the fourth planet from the sun.

DANDELION WINE
ISBN 978-0-380-97726-0 (hardcover)
A deeply personal, well-loved fictional recollection of the sacred rituals of boyhood.

SOMETHING WICKED THIS WAY COMES
ISBN 978-0-380-97727-7 (hardcover)
A masterpiece of dark fantasy from one of the most beloved authors of all time.

DEATH IS A LONELY BUSINESS
ISBN 978-0-380-78965-8 (paperback)
A stylish noir tale of murder and mayhem set in 1950s Venice, CA.

A GRAVEYARD FOR LUNATICS
Another Tale of Two Cities
ISBN 978-0-380-81200-4 (paperback)
A young scriptwriter spends a mysterious, magical Halloween in a Hollywood graveyard.

GREEN SHADOWS, WHITE WHALE
A Novel of Ray Bradbury's Adventures Making *Moby Dick* with John Huston in Ireland
ISBN 978-0-380-78966-5 (paperback)
Bradbury's tale of writing the screen adaptation of Melville's *Moby-Dick.*

FAREWELL SUMMER
A Novel
ISBN 978-0-06-113154-7 (hardcover)
Fifty years in the making, the sequel to Bradbury's beloved classic *Dandelion Wine.*

STORY COLLECTIONS, ESSAYS, AND MORE

SHADOW SHOW Edited by Sam Weller and Mort Castle, with an Introduction by Ray Bradbury
All-New Stories in Celebration of Ray Bradbury
ISBN 978-0-06-212268-1 (paperback)
An anthology of short fiction by 27 authors, each of whom was inspired by the legendary work of Ray Bradbury, including Neil Gaiman, Margaret Atwood, and more.

THE BRADBURY CHRONICLES By Sam Weller

The Life of Ray Bradbury

ISBN 978-0-06-054584-0 (paperback)

The first fully authorized biography of Ray Bradbury . . . "This is my life! It's as if somehow Sam Weller slipped into my skin and my head and my heart—it's all here." —Ray Bradbury

BRADBURY SPEAKS

Too Soon from the Cave, Too Far from the Stars

ISBN 978-0-06-058569-3 (paperback)

A collection of essays offering commentary on Bradbury's greatest influences.

THE ILLUSTRATED MAN

ISBN 978-0-06-207997-8 (paperback)

Eighteen startling visions of humankind's destiny in one phantasmagoric slideshow.

THE GOLDEN APPLES OF THE SUN

And Other Stories

ISBN 978-0-380-73039-1 (paperback)

Thirty-two of Bradbury's most famous tales—prime examples of the poignant poetry of the human soul.

I SING THE BODY ELECTRIC!

And Other Stories

ISBN 978-0-380-78962-7 (paperback)

Twenty-eight classic Bradbury stories and one luscious poem.

BRADBURY STORIES

100 of His Most Celebrated Tales

ISBN 978-0-06-054488-1 (paperback)

Treasures from a lifetime of words and ideas—tales that amaze and enthrall.

THE CAT'S PAJAMAS

Stories

ISBN 978-0-06-077733-3 (paperback)

A walk through the six-decade career of this "latter-day O. Henry" (*Booklist*).

WE'LL ALWAYS HAVE PARIS

Stories

ISBN 978-0-06-167014-5 (paperback)

A treasure trove of Bradbury gems—eerie and strange, nostalgic and bittersweet, searching and speculative.

A PLEASURE TO BURN

Fahrenheit 451 Stories

ISBN 978-0-06-207102-6 (paperback)

A collection of sixteen vintage stories and novellas that informed *Fahrenheit 451*.